No Other Choice

Sophie closed her eyes as the talon carved into her flesh, hating that she had no choice. His nail bit deeply, more deeply than any natural nail could have done.

It wasn't the pain that persuaded her. It was the fact that there'd be no chance of escape if she couldn't fly. She had to escape. She had to survive.

Whatever the price.

She begged the Great Wyvern to forgive her weakness.

"Her name is Sara Keegan," she said in a quiet rush, knowing she might be condemning the woman to death.

In the same moment that Sophie uttered the mortal woman's name, the name of the *Pyr* who would mate with Sara became clear. Sophie blinked as she felt a whisper of hope.

"And the *Pyr* who will feel the firestorm?" Boris demanded.

"You cannot ask me that. It is forbidden."

"I have just asked you."

"You said one name."

"I lied," Boris said easily. "It's a bad habit of mine. Tell me who he is."

"I don't know." The Wyvern gritted her teeth, not wanting to tell these villains more.

"Liar! Cut her again."

The talon of her tormentor cut so deeply that Sophie cried out in pain. They would cripple her without a moment's regret, and abandon her in this endless desert. She'd die, and where would the *Pyr* be then? Without a prophet as they entered the greatest battle of all time. She owed her kind better than that.

"It is the Smith," she confessed, hating the choice she had to make. She felt their shock and awe.

"His name. Confirm his name."

The talon touched her flesh. "Quinn Tyrrell. You knew that already."

KISS OF FIRE

A DRAGONFIRE NOVEL

DEBORAH COOKE

A SIGNET ECLIPSE BOOK

SIGNET ECLIPSE
Published by New American Library, a division of
Penguin Group (USA) Inc., 375 Hudson Street,
New York, New York 10014, USA
Penguin Group (Canada), 90 Eglinton Avenue East, Suite 700, Toronto,
Ontario M4P 2Y3, Canada (a division of Pearson Penguin Canada Inc.)
Penguin Books Ltd., 80 Strand, London WC2R 0RL, England
Penguin Ireland, 25 St. Stephen's Green, Dublin 2,
Ireland (a division of Penguin Books Ltd.)
Penguin Group (Australia), 250 Camberwell Road, Camberwell, Victoria 3124,
Australia (a division of Pearson Australia Group Pty. Ltd.)
Penguin Books India Pvt. Ltd., 11 Community Centre, Panchsheel Park,
New Delhi - 110 017, India
Penguin Group (NZ), 67 Apollo Drive, Rosedale, North Shore 0632,
New Zealand (a division of Pearson New Zealand Ltd.)
Penguin Books (South Africa) (Pty.) Ltd., 24 Sturdee Avenue,
Rosebank, Johannesburg 2196, South Africa

Penguin Books Ltd., Registered Offices:
80 Strand, London WC2R 0RL, England

First published by Signet Eclipse, an imprint of New American Library,
a division of Penguin Group (USA) Inc.

First Printing, February 2008
10 9 8 7 6 5 4 3 2

For Kon, as always

ACKNOWLEDGMENTS

Creating a new world means questions and decisions, and I'm grateful to all of these people for their help and enthusiasm. Thanks to the many patient librarians who helped me research dragon lore. Thanks to Kristen Schubach, who helped with the graphics on my Web site. Thanks to Diana Troldahl for checking details in Michigan for me. Thanks to Pam Trader for answering my many computer-related questions and for planning yarn missions with me. Thanks to Ingrid Caris for listening. Thanks to Jennifer Taylor for explaining astrological influences so well and loading me up with reference materials. Thanks to my editor, Kara Cesare, for her enthusiasm and for pushing me further into the *Pyr* world. Thanks to my agent, Dominick Abel, for doing what he does so very well. Finally, thanks to my husband, Kon, who knows quite a bit about making sparks fly.

Prologue

March 3, 2007

The reckoning had begun.

All around the world, gazes turned skyward for the total lunar eclipse. Not everyone realized that it was the first eclipse of a new cycle, that it was the beginning of an age of reconciliation.

There were thirteen who knew.

No sooner had the shadow of the earth passed over the full moon than the first six met in the quiet reaches of southern Libya. The moon glowed red and unnatural, as unnatural as many might have found the sight of the dragons spiraling down from the darkened sky. The members of the high circle gathered silently, as was prearranged, honoring custom. They landed unobserved beneath the path of the eclipse.

There was no need for conversation: the process of ordination had taught them their responsibilities, though none had known whether they would be summoned until now. Dread and anticipation mingled in one of the eldest, Donovan, as he watched his fellows arrive. He didn't like foretold events, didn't like the sense they always gave him that there was more controlling his future than his own will. Heat rose from the sand underfoot and the sky appeared to be stained with blood.

Erik arrived last, his onyx and pewter figure casting an eerie shadow as he wheeled with confidence out of the sky. He moved as if the black velvet sack he carried weighed nothing. Donovan knew that sack's contents and the burden Erik carried.

The blessing was murmured in old-speak by all of them, even skeptical Donovan. The bag's cord was loosed to reveal the treasure of their kind, still nestled in the shadowed interior. The Dragon's Egg was as dark as night, as fathomless as obsidian, and the surface of the stone gleamed as if wet.

The sight of it gave Donovan the creeps.

"It's not working," Niall said.

"Nonsense. It must taste the moon's light." Erik was impatient with doubt and skepticism. "Give it room." The others withdrew slightly and Donovan restrained the urge to destroy the sacred relic. It was older than any of them, mysterious and potent, and to his thinking, it brought more trouble than it solved.

Erik spun the Dragon's Egg three times, requested an augury of the Great Wyvern, and released it. The stone spun like a top across the scorching sand. When it came to a halt, the six clustered closer, as close as Erik would permit.

For a long moment, only the reflection of the moon's red glow was visible in the orb. The eclipse was already progressing—if Erik felt the press of time passing, he gave no outward sign. Their leader was as cool and composed as always, as confident as Donovan had always known him to be.

Donovan was inclined to prod the stone. If he kicked it

hard enough, it might shatter. Before he could move, though, the orb sparkled, as if lit from the inside. Lines of gold appeared in the darkness, running across and around its surface.

"First it traces the planet," Rafferty said, for those who had not witnessed the marvel before. The outline of continents appeared, as if drawn in gold by a frantic mapsmith.

"North America," said Donovan, recognizing the shape of the continent displayed on the top. He sighed. "It figures. Why can't we ever be dispatched to Italy, where the women are gorgeous, or some South Seas island, where they're naked?"

"Silence!" Erik commanded. Rafferty chuckled darkly until the leader silenced him with a look.

Nothing happened after the continents were drawn. The shadow of the earth moved relentlessly across the full moon. Sloane stirred restlessly until Erik held up a hand.

Finer hairlines, straight lines of force, appeared on the Dragon's Egg. The ley lines could have been lines of longitude and latitude, because they triangulated a precise location. What they really marked were lines of energy, earth energy, energy that might as well have been Roman roads for the readiness with which Donovan and his kind could follow them.

The lines targeted the nexus where the next firestorm would begin. The ley lines glowed briefly as they made a conjunction; the six leaned closer, anxious to read the location before the gleaming lines faded to darkness.

"Ann Arbor," Erik murmured, his old-speak echoing with authority in the thoughts of his fellows. "I will go."

"I will be your second, if you wish it," Donovan said, speaking out of some impulse he could not name.

"You will all second me," Erik declared. "It is time." A frisson of alarm passed through the group. Donovan exchanged a glance with Rafferty, knowing that the old prophecy must be correct for Erik to make such a demand.

The final battle had come.

And the world would never be the same.

Further south, in the Kalahari Desert, the other seven gathered in a dark parody of the high circle. They also appeared in the sky when the eclipse was complete, although not all of them flew under their own power. The last of their number was a terrified captive, harnessed and shackled, who fought and bit to no avail.

They were six powerful males, all in their dragon form, and they easily held the lone female down in the hot sand. She was afraid when she saw them all together, afraid of their intent.

She knew the role she had to play, but she was too old to easily trust in destiny. She had grown skeptical and timid.

The odds of victory were long—perhaps too long.

All the same, she tried to trust the truth she had been shown.

"What do you want from me?" she demanded.

"A prophecy, of course," declared the dragon who had his claw upon her neck. He might have been made of turquoise and hammered silver, and he was larger and more brutal than any *Pyr* she had ever known. He dug his talons deeper into her neck and when she caught her breath in pain, he chuckled.

"A name," clarified the leader, a magnificent ruby red dragon with trailing plumes. "All I want is a name."

"Your name is Boris," she said, and he laughed. It was an unpleasant sound.

He leaned closer, his breath hot and dry, his eyes glinting with malice. His scales were brilliant and looked to be edged in brass; she knew he was old to have taken that metallic sheen. "I want the name of the human who will feel this firestorm."

"I can't tell you that."

"Of course you can." His smile was reptilian. "You are the Wyvern, keeper of prophecies. You know such things."

"I am untrained. I cannot predict—"

"Cut her wings." His terse command cut short her protest. She watched, incredulous, as a topaz yellow dragon moved to do Boris's bidding. The one who held her neck indicated a tender spot, scratching it so that she flinched; then the yellow one took pleasure in showing her his sharpened talon. It was long and black and had an edge that looked wickedly sharp, especially against the pale delicacy of her own skin.

Sophie choked on her shock. "But it is forbidden to injure the Wyvern!"

"We do not play by the old rules," Boris said in old-speak, his tone contemptuous. "Times demand that useless formalities be abandoned."

Sophie knew she would never erase the echo of his hatred from her thoughts. "But . . ."

The topaz dragon slid his sharp talon across the tendon at the root of her wings and giggled. Sophie felt the pain of the cut, could not mistake the warm trickle of her own blood across her flesh.

"Hers is red," exclaimed the topaz dragon.

"You'll have to make her bleed more to be sure," insisted her turquoise captor. "Go on. Cut deeper."

Sophie closed her eyes as the talon carved into her flesh, hating that she had no choice. His nail bit deeply, more deeply than any natural nail could have done.

It wasn't the pain that persuaded her. It was the fact that there'd be no chance of escape if she couldn't fly. She had to escape. She had to survive.

Whatever the price.

She begged the Great Wyvern to forgive her weakness.

"Her name is Sara Keegan," she said in a quiet rush, knowing she might be condemning the woman to death.

In the same moment that Sophie uttered the mortal woman's name, the name of the *Pyr* who would mate with Sara became clear. Sophie blinked as she felt a whisper of hope.

"And the *Pyr* who will feel the firestorm?" Boris demanded.

"You cannot ask me that. It is forbidden."

"I have just asked you."

"You said one name."

"I lied," Boris said easily. "It's a bad habit of mine. Tell me who he is."

"I don't know." The Wyvern gritted her teeth, not wanting to tell these villains more.

"Liar! Cut her again."

The talon of her tormentor cut so deeply that Sophie cried out in pain. They would cripple her without a moment's regret and abandon her in this endless desert. She'd die, and where would the *Pyr* be then? Without a prophet as they entered the greatest battle of all time. She owed her kind better than that.

"It is the Smith," she confessed, hating the choice she had to make. She felt their shock and awe.

"His name. Confirm his name."

The talon touched her flesh. "Quinn Tyrrell. You knew that already."

"I thought he was dead," Boris mused, sparing a cold glance to a golden dragon who had thus far been silent.

"I never believed he was," said that dragon, with a defensiveness to his tone. This one, too, was old, and his scales gleamed with the mysterious lights shared by tigers' eye stones.

"He lives because you failed," Boris said coldly. "Here is your chance to finish what you began, Ambrose. Try not to make a mess of it this time."

The golden dragon inclined his head as if submissive, but Sophie saw the flash of fire in his gaze. She would never turn her back on him if she had the choice.

Boris looked back to the Wyvern, and she dreaded what he might say. "You can keep her until the next eclipse in August, Everett," he told her captor, and that dragon laughed. Sophie's blood ran cold. "Don't wound her. Not yet." Boris tickled her chin with his talon, as if she were a favored pet, and she yearned to bite him. "She has shown some talent for usefulness."

That wasn't all of it, though. Boris leaned closer, his breath as hot as a desert wind. Sophie closed her eyes but she couldn't evade his voice. "I would not recommend you giving Everett any trouble. He tends to be somewhat volatile and forgets his own strength."

Everett chuckled and poked his talon into her wound. The Wyvern knew it was no accident.

She was glad her eyes were closed. Let Boris think her weak. What these *Slayers* did was wrong and they would be exterminated. Little did they realize that their wickedness gave her strength. Justice would prevail, evil would be vanquished, and the true *Pyr* would triumph.

She was the Wyvern.

She would ensure that they paid for their crimes.

Somehow.

The eclipse could not be fully viewed in Traverse City, but its pull could be felt all the same.

Quinn was ready.

He fired his forge in anticipation. It was unlikely he would have company with the snow piled outside, but he took precautions anyway. He locked the doors of his studio and covered the windows, ensuring that no one could witness his secret. It was no accident that he had kept it so well for so long. It took diligence to work iron, diligence to hold a secret, diligence to train to meet one's destiny.

Quinn didn't have to see the progression of the eclipse to feel when it was complete. He knew, right to his marrow, when it was time. He took a deep breath and shifted to his dragon form, memories crowding into his thoughts.

It was the first time in centuries that he had permitted his body to do what it did best; he realized only as he changed how much he had missed the transformation. The sense of power was magnificent, heady, and addictive. He felt joyous and strong and powerful.

And this time he was. The past had forged him into what he was. He was tempered and strong and ready to claim his mate. It was time for the Smith to ensure his own succession.

Quinn breathed fire into the forge, sending its flames higher and hotter than coal and coke could have made them. The heat would have driven him away in human form, even with his protective gear, but his dragon form welcomed the fire.

With his talons, he removed the mermaid door knocker from the fire where she waited. She was red-hot, gleaming and glowing, on the verge of turning into liquid. He finished the end of her tail with sure strokes. He had known when the iron took this feminine shape beneath his hand that his turn had come; he had known that he could finish the work only in dragon form.

His firestorm was coming.

The others, good and bad, would follow the beacon of its heat.

This time, he would triumph.

This time, he would protect what was his to defend.

He exhaled mightily, sending sparks dancing throughout his workshop, infusing the hot iron with his desire. The mermaid glittered as if she were made of fire, caught in a magical wind of Quinn's making. She looked to be filled with sparks, but in truth, she was filled with the power of his will.

He was the Smith.

His talisman was struck.

Let them try to stop his firestorm.

Chapter 1

Ann Arbor
The following July

Sara was tired and hungry and hot by the time she left the New Age bookstore that had been her aunt Magda's pride and joy. It was late and it wasn't the first time she'd thought that taking over the business might not have been such a good idea.

That wasn't just because the stock was weird.

She'd made a lot of changes in six months and it was only natural that she'd remember the good bits of her past life when her present life challenged her. She yawned as she locked the door of the shop, tucking her reading choice for the night under her arm. She felt the emptiness of Nickels Arcade behind her and reminded herself that she'd left the big city behind.

Sara glanced down the silent pedestrian passageway and wished that she had her aunt's psychic gene.

Some things didn't change—she still walked as briskly as a city girl. She was still organized and efficient, still an ace accountant, still had a plan of attack for every obstacle in her path.

Including Magda's records, which seemed to have been kept in Sanskrit.

Sara would conquer them, one line item at a time.

She got only halfway to the State Street exit before something fell to the sidewalk behind her. It rattled, then rolled, the sound of metal on stone echoing in the arcade.

Sara had a bad feeling, but she looked over her shoulder anyway.

Whatever had fallen glittered. It was right on the threshold of her shop, and it hadn't been there a minute before. It was small and round and it winked, as if calling her back to pick it up.

As if.

Sara spun to continue and stopped cold.

A man stood in the exit. He was right in the middle of the center arch, the streetlights behind turning him into a menacing silhouette. He hadn't been there before and Sara guessed the coin had been thrown to distract her.

"I do love predictable women," he said, and laughed. It wasn't a friendly laugh. He pulled a balaclava over his face before stepping out of the shadows.

Sara quickly considered her options. There was an exit at the other end of the arcade. It was darker on Maynard Street and less busy, but given the alternative, Sara could live with that.

She pivoted and ran.

She heard the man coming after her. His steps were longer than hers; she heard him gain on her with every step, and her heart thundered with fear. She remembered every track meet she'd ever competed in and pushed herself to go faster.

This was a race that she had to win.

Sara ran as if her life depended on it. Quite possibly it did. With every step, she was more certain she was going to make Maynard. She was half a dozen steps from the doors. She was reaching for the handle . . . she brushed it with her fingertips. . . .

He seized her shoulder, hauling her to a stop.

Sara screamed.

The man flung her against the display window of the last shop with terrifying force. She fell against the glass and wished it had broken. The alarm might have summoned help. She came up fighting, swinging her book at her assailant's head while she had the chance.

She missed, but only because he ducked.

He snarled and caught her wrist in his hand. He twisted it quickly behind her back and the book fell from her grasp. He slammed Sara's chest against the window so hard that it vibrated. It *still* didn't break. Sara clenched her teeth in pain. She blinked back tears, realizing that he didn't care whether he hurt her.

Bad news there.

Sara wasn't going to whimper, even if she was terrified. She opened her eyes to find dozens of empty ring boxes displayed in the jeweler's window in front of her. The reflection of her attacker's silhouette loomed over her, dark and menacing.

She wished he weren't wearing the balaclava. She wanted to give the police a good description.

Assuming she got out of this alive. She didn't need Magda's tarot cards to have a very bad feeling about her own future.

"I don't have much cash," Sara said, surprised to hear herself sound so calm and collected. "But you can have what there is." She held out her purse with her free hand.

He seized it without releasing her. Sara had a heartbeat to

hope before he flung her purse across the arcade. Its contents scattered noisily.

"Money isn't what I want," he whispered. Sara saw the flash of his teeth as his hands closed around her throat from behind. "I hope you've said your prayers, Sara."

He knew her name. Sara had time to be stunned before he squeezed.

Then she couldn't take a breath. She panicked as his fingers tightened relentlessly around her neck.

He was going to kill her, right there.

Sara struggled. She scratched and bit and tore at his hands, but his grip didn't waver.

She let herself shiver and go limp, hoping he'd think she was weakening. He chuckled just a little, but it was enough to show that he had let down his guard.

With her last bit of energy, Sara drove her heel up hard, aiming for his crotch. At the very least, she might cramp his style.

She missed.

She saw his fist coming in time to duck. He still caught her shoulder, the force sending her tumbling to the pavement. He was stronger—or angrier—than she'd realized. The skin tore on Sara's knees and her dress rose up to her thighs as she tumbled. She tried to roll to her feet, but he landed heavily on her back. He pinned her down with his weight, his knee on the back of her waist, and locked his hands around her throat again.

"Feisty," he whispered in her ear. Sara shuddered. "I like my women with some fire in them." He seemed to find this funny. He tightened his grip and Sara immediately felt faint.

She couldn't move because of his weight on her back. She struggled and tried to scream, but only managed a gurgling noise. She fought for her own survival, even knowing the odds were long. Her vision began to get dark around the edges and she fought harder.

She was losing.

Then Sara heard a hiss and saw a flash of light. Maybe this was what dying was like. The bookstore was loaded with books that talked about going toward the light.

Funny, but she'd thought it was supposed to be a white light. This one was orange, like firelight.

Then the weight on her back was gone and Sara was lying alone on the pavement, gulping at air. She felt weak and dizzy. She scrambled away from her attacker, instinctively putting distance between them, then flinched at the crackle of flames.

She looked for the fire and knew that she was hallucinating.

There wasn't a fire in the arcade.

There was a dragon.

Sara blinked and looked again, but it couldn't have been anything else. It was a dragon, just as they were drawn in children's books, but alive. Here. Sara couldn't make sense of what was illogical and impossible. She stared as the fabled beast reared up on his hinds, his leathery wings spanning the width of the arcade. He was silver and blue, gleaming in the night like a jeweled brooch.

But much, much bigger.

He was furious. Sara could tell by the way his tail swung, by the way his eyes glittered, by the smoke coming out of his nostrils.

Sara backed away. Her attacker was lying on the other side of the arcade, as if he'd been snatched up and flung aside. There was a trickle of blood beneath him.

He moved when the dragon exhaled fire and the flames licked his boots. The man leapt to his feet. He took one look at the dragon—as if he couldn't believe his eyes, either—then ran. The dragon leapt in pursuit, sending a furious bellow of fire after him. The floor of the arcade shook with each bound the dragon took and Sara thought that the glass in the shop windows really would break.

Her attacker just ran.

There was smoke in the arcade after his footsteps faded from earshot. Sara swallowed when the dragon turned his attention on her. He moved slowly, deliberately, and she couldn't swallow the lump of terror in her throat. She backed away but found the glass of a shop window behind her.

She wasn't sure her situation had improved.

Sara heard a low growl in the dragon's throat, almost like a purr, and wondered what he had planned for her. She looked left and right, but knew she had no chance of outrunning this creature. She glanced up, thought she saw the silhouettes of other dragons through the glass roof of the arcade, and decided she was losing her mind.

That was the only rational explanation for seeing dragons.

The dragon eased closer, his movements surprisingly graceful for his size. This time he made no noise as he moved, and she could faintly hear traffic in the distance. His scales seemed to be made of metal and gleamed with each step he took. She could see his strength. His eyes were bright and when she looked into their fathomless blue, Sara's heart fluttered. He leaned closer and seemed to smile at what he saw.

Her.

Lunch.

Sara closed her eyes, said a prayer, and feared the worst. It didn't come.

"Are you all right?" A man's voice persuaded Sara to open her eyes again. It was a wonderful voice, as rich as bittersweet chocolate, low and persuasive and masculine. Maybe she was dreaming.

Maybe she didn't want to wake up.

"Hello?" he said again. Sara opened one eye with caution.

A man crouched beside her, looking concerned. He was a few feet away, as if uncertain whether to approach or touch her.

There was no sign of a dragon, or of a murderer wearing a balaclava. Sara checked.

Twice.

She and the man with the great voice were alone in the arcade. He hadn't been there before, even though Sara was sure she'd closed her eyes only for a heartbeat.

Had she passed out? She tried to swallow and knew she hadn't imagined that the attacker had tried to choke her. Her throat was aching and she'd probably have a major bruise. Trauma could make people lose track of time, couldn't it?

"Where did he go?" she asked, surprised that her voice was so husky.

"The guy with the balaclava?" At her nod, the man indicated the State Street exit. "He took off. Are you all right?"

Maybe she had blacked out and imagined the dragon.

Instead of the more likely case of a passerby intervening.

This passerby.

Sara looked at the man in front of her. He wore jeans and a black T-shirt and laced black boots that might have been military issue. His hair was dark and wavy, his muscled build impressive.

His voice made her want to shiver, but in a good way.

"I think so," she admitted, and saw the brief flash of his smile.

"Good." He seemed relieved, which was nice. He was handsome in a rugged way, and Sara decided it would be a bad plan to ask him whether he'd seen any dragons around.

It was bad enough to be wondering about her sanity herself.

He watched her, and the intensity of his gaze made Sara feel all hot and tingly. It was almost as if he were memorizing her features. Or fascinated by her. He was six or seven feet away, but she could see that his eyes were a brilliant blue.

Just like the dragon's had been. Her delusion was starting to make a bit of sense. Kooky sense, but that was better than no sense at all.

Maybe she needed to stop reading the stock in Magda's store.

Sara was keenly aware of the torn flesh on her knee, her loosened ponytail, her slipped bra strap.

Her gender.

As opposed to his gender.

"What happened? Do you know that guy?"

Sara sat up and smoothed her skirt, feeling disheveled. "No. He just jumped me." Sara's hand rose to her throat. "I think he was trying to kill me."

"I'm glad he didn't succeed." He offered her a hand to get up, and Sara couldn't see a reason to decline any offer of help. His hand was warm and she could have sworn that a spark danced between their fingertips.

But that was impossible.

As impossible as a dragon saving her from a thug, then disappearing as if he'd never been. Maybe she needed to get something to eat. She'd worked through dinner, after all.

He stepped away from her, as if sensing her uncertainty. "Why don't you pick up your things? I'll keep an eye out."

"Thanks." Sara couldn't understand her strange sense that she was safe. She certainly didn't trust it. She forced herself to think the worst.

She didn't know this guy, either.

They could have been working together.

She folded her arms around herself and tried to sound collected, even if she couldn't look it. "What do you want?"

He smiled, ever so slightly. The smile claimed his lips slowly, as if he had all night to smile, and that slow motion made Sara feel warmer than she had all day.

Which was saying something, given the current heat wave and the unreliability of the air-conditioning unit in the bookstore.

"I'd just like to see you safely on your way."

"In return for?"

"Knowing that you're safe."

"That sounds very chivalrous."

His eyes twinkled. "Who says chivalry is dead?"

"Well, I have, once or twice." Sara felt she had to admit it.

"Maybe I shouldn't have stopped then," he said, but she knew he was teasing.

Sara couldn't help but smile. "Maybe I had it wrong."

"Maybe." He smiled, as if he found her fascinating and attractive.

Given her current state, that was almost as nutty as her thinking she was seeing dragons. It was time to go home, get something to eat, and get some sleep.

Sara picked up her scattered belongings. She ensured that she faced him every time she bent down, telling herself it was only sensible to be skeptical. He didn't seem to mind. She jammed everything back into her purse, not caring that it was in a jumble. She'd sort it out after she had a locked door between herself and the world.

Meanwhile, her savior waited patiently. Sara had a weird sense that he would wait for as long as she chose to take. He was very still, but watchful, and it was easy to feel safe in his presence. Sara closed her purse, then picked up her book. He seemed intrigued by her, in a way that was both sexy and disconcerting. In another time and place, she'd have been flattered.

Right now, she wanted to be home. "Okay. That's everything."

He tilted his head to read the title of her book. "*Guardian Angels Among Us*?"

Sara felt herself blush. "Who knew that there really were any?"

His smile made her feel warm. "An angel is one thing I'm not."

Sara watched him, struck by his choice of words. "That sounds as if there's more to you than meets the eye."

He held her gaze for a moment, as if deciding what to say, then changed the subject instead. "Which way is most convenient for you?"

They were closer to Maynard, but Sara didn't like how dark and quiet it tended to be. She wasn't going to jump from the frying pan to the fire. "State Street," she said, gesturing to the other, more distant, exit.

He indicated for her to precede him, a gentlemanly gesture that might have been intended to put her at ease.

Instead, it made Sara nervous. She didn't like her pervasive sense that she was safe.

It was illogical, after all, to trust a stranger.

Even if she sensed that she should.

Sara walked to the end of the arcade as fast as she could, feeling his presence behind her. Her own footsteps echoed, the heels of her sandals clicking so loudly that she couldn't hear his steps at all. She was hot and tingly, as if sparks were dancing over her flesh, and she was pretty sure it wasn't just adrenaline.

Would he want something from her? Her name? Her number? A champion's kiss?

Sara stepped out of the arcade and took a deep breath

in relief. The streetlights gleamed brightly. There were students in the Diag and a few more on the street. The all-night coffee shop was busy and two couples were coming out of the Mexican restaurant at the end of the block. The organizers for the art show were chatting as they chalked booth lines on the sidewalk and road in preparation for the show the next day. One glanced up and smiled at her.

It was like another world. It was hot enough for the sidewalk to melt, because evening hadn't brought much relief from the heat wave. But still, this was all familiar.

And safe.

Sara was safe. Her knees weakened.

She turned to thank her savior for intervening, but there was no sign of him.

Where could he have gone so quickly? Sara looked down the street. She peered into the arcade. She even looked up into the glass ceiling covering the arcade.

He was gone. He might have vanished into thin air.

But he had been there. He had helped her. Sara knew she hadn't been hallucinating.

Well, except for the dragon bit. There was a bit of blood on the floor of the arcade, which convinced her that she hadn't completely lost her mind.

That was when Sara realized that the golden glimmer that had been in front of her shop was gone, too.

Had she imagined that? Or had it rolled out of sight?

Sara wasn't going back to check.

It was time to go home. She gripped her book and her purse, stepped out to the curb, and hailed a cab.

One thing was for sure: herbal tea wasn't going to settle her nerves on this night. She'd pour herself a single malt Scotch, from the bottle she'd gotten from her parents' home.

She'd salute the man who had helped her and the one who had taught her not to give up without a fight.

Then she'd savor every drop.

Even if she choked on it.

If nothing else, the Scotch would help her sleep.

Quinn was too old to believe in coincidence.

It wasn't an accident that he had met his destined mate right when someone had tried to kill her. He had no doubt that the assailant was a *Slayer*, and not a random thug.

His mate needed his protection.

Since she didn't yet know that they were destined lovers, he didn't want to frighten her. He would protect her without her being aware of what he did.

Quinn followed the cab that she had taken, moving like a shadow on the side streets. He didn't have to keep her in sight, not now that he had caught her scent. He was aware of her presence, as long as she was within his proximity. He let his intuition guide him and caught up when she was stepping out of the taxi on a quiet street in the west end.

He lingered in the shadows of a hedge, remaining so still that he didn't attract mortal attention. She looked tired and a little jangled, and he wished he could have anticipated the attack before it happened.

She had fought back, though. He liked that tenacity.

She might need it before the firestorm had passed.

She pushed a hand through her long fair hair when the cab pulled away, and only seemed to realize then that her hair was loose over her shoulders. It gleamed like spun gold. She pulled it into a ponytail and twisted it back, then rummaged in her purse for a way to fasten it. Then she jingled her keys as she walked toward an exterior staircase on a neat little Cape Cod house.

Evidently she lived on the upper floor. Quinn watched

her climb the stairs, seeing exhaustion in her every move. He waited until she was inside her apartment, certain that she would lock the door against intruders.

Maybe she would lean against it and sigh with relief. She wasn't, however, as safe as she might think she was.

Quinn would fix that.

He waited to ensure that she wouldn't see him. She opened her windows a small increment to let in some air and turned on a couple of fans. He watched through the kitchen window as she got a soda from the fridge. She rolled the cold can across her forehead, and the sight of her pleasure made Quinn smile. When she dropped the blinds low and disappeared from view, Quinn heard water running. She was in the shower. Knowing she wouldn't see him, he circled the house silently.

He liked the strong aura that the house had. If he'd had to pick a house for her to sleep in, this would have been the one. It sang to him of the psychic gift his mate was prophesied to possess. Her foresight would protect her, but Quinn would give her even more insurance. With a *Slayer* hunting her, she needed a better protection than mere locks could provide.

The sky was clear and he couldn't sense any other *Pyr* in his vicinity—that didn't mean there weren't any, though. Quinn wasn't the only one who could disguise his presence, especially in human form.

He pulled the coin from his pocket, the one he had picked up from the arcade. It was gold and he shook his head at the fleur-de-lis that was embossed on it. On the other side was John the Baptist in his hair shirt. It was a florin, a medieval coin from the Italian city of Florence, and Quinn remembered the first time he had ever seen one.

He wondered whether the *Slayer* meant to challenge him

personally, or just to make it clear that he knew Quinn's firestorm involved this woman.

It didn't matter. Yet.

He'd diffuse the challenge and prove he was the Smith. Quinn closed his hand over the coin and breathed into his fist. He listened to the rhythm of the metal and shaped his song to persuade it to his will. Three times he exhaled into his hand, willing the coin to become his own.

When he opened his hand, the coin had changed. A mermaid adorned one face of it and a hammer the other. Quinn smiled at the appropriate combination. Sometimes the metal knew the truth better than he did.

Then he flicked the coin skyward, demanding that it find its place. He saw its gleam as it landed on the chimney, spun, and settled. It would warn any attacker who approached from above that this territory was claimed and defended. Quinn knew without seeing the coin that the hammer side was up. His mate's home was an extension of Quinn's lair.

But he could protect it even more.

Quinn circled the house, keeping his distance as he identified all of the exits and entrances. He strolled through the side streets, keeping the house in view, memorizing its openings.

Its weak points.

Then he began to exhale his smoke, weaving it and guiding it to enclose the apartment in a protective cocoon. Once the building had been encircled three times, Quinn walked back downtown. He kept the vision of the apartment clear in his thoughts and focused on weaving an unbroken wreath of smoke.

Only another *Pyr* or a *Slayer* would be able to see the smoke. It would be a sign of his mate's presence and his own, but the time for secrecy was past. She had been targeted. Somehow the *Slayers* knew more about her than Quinn did.

The source of their information was irrelevant; all he cared about was preventing a repeat of the past.

He owed Elizabeth's memory at least that much.

Chapter 2

"*Help me, please!*"

The woman's cry instantly brought Sara awake. It was so loud, as if it echoed inside her head, and so filled with pain that she couldn't ignore it. She leapt out of bed and went to the window.

It was sunny and bright, even this early in the morning, and the neighbor who loved to garden had her sprinklers on. Birds chattered as they flew through the water, but the grass was turning brown despite Mrs. Shaunessy's efforts. The heat was already shimmering above the road and there was so little breeze that the trees were barely moving.

Sara scanned the street, but couldn't see anyone who might have been calling for help. Nigel Shaunessy, as rumpled and amiable as always, ambled out to move the sprinkler. The woman across the street was on the porch with her toddler, looking as sleepy as the child was active.

But someone had called for help.

Sara went into the kitchen and opened the blinds, because that window looked out the other way. The house she had inherited from her aunt was a sweet little house on a corner. There was a bit more traffic on the other street, and a man standing on the opposite sidewalk.

He was looking directly at her.

That had to be her imagination.

Was it Sara's imagination that he looked to be about the same size and build as the guy who had attacked her the night before?

She closed the blind with a snap. Her hands shook as she made a pot of coffee and told herself that she was silly. She'd known it would be different living in a small town. She'd known the pace would be slower and she'd expected to miss the good bits of her high pressure job.

She didn't miss airports; she did miss travel to different places, on the company's expense account.

She didn't miss working all night, several nights in a row, fighting to make the numbers crunch in a better way for a proposal; she did miss the triumph of being part of the team that made the deal come together.

She didn't miss high blood pressure, indigestion from eating the wrong food at the wrong time, stress, loneliness, or the sense of having no real home or roots.

She had to admit that she missed the sense of being a part of something bigger.

She hadn't expected being alone to feel so lonely.

Was she so lonely that she was making things up, to make her life sound more dramatic and interesting than it was? Sara had never craved drama particularly and she thought she was too practical for that kind of thing.

She went back to the window and flipped up the blind. The opposite sidewalk was empty and she wondered whether she had imagined the guy standing there.

Just the way she'd imagined someone calling for help.

And a dragon coming to her rescue the night before. Uh huh.

It was just a plain old Wednesday morning, and the sooner she got her thoughts collected and headed to the store, the sooner she'd get the store computerized. Sara poured herself a cup of coffee and felt more human after the first sip. She made herself a proper breakfast, because Magda's books would wait, and felt better again.

As well as more logical. Clearly, she was under stress and her mind was working overtime. She might not have her aunt's psychic abilities, but she certainly had plenty of imagination. It made perfect sense that she would have a nightmare after her scare of the night before, even more sense that she'd see threats where there weren't any. She carried her coffee into the bathroom and stopped cold when she saw her reflection.

The bruises on her neck clearly showed the mark of the man's fingers. He had wrapped his hands around her neck to squeeze the life out of her.

And he had called her by name. The hair rose on the back of Sara's neck.

Or had she imagined that, too? Sara decided that she must have. After all, it wasn't logical for her to have a stalker. She wasn't rich or gorgeous or sexy. Accountants, no matter how ace they were, didn't have those sorts of problems. Women in their thirties who ran New Age bookstores, reduced, reused and recycled, and lived quiet sensible lives didn't have stalkers.

Movie stars did. Heiresses. Maybe porn stars.

Sara spied the empty glass by her bed and guessed the likely reason for her nightmare and her paranoia. Having a shot before bed might have worked for her father, but it clearly wasn't the solution for her. She took her father's beloved single malt and poured it down the drain.

She topped up her coffee and treated herself to a piece of her European chocolate stash from the fridge.

Better to stick with what she knew.

Quinn liked doing outdoor art shows; the look of busy booths in the sunshine, the rumble of happy crowds, the sound of street musicians and the smell from food vendors brought back a thousand memories of a thousand times and places.

At this particular show, though, Quinn was restless.

The sight of his mate had haunted him all night long. He could still see her, fallen and lifeless as her attacker tried to squeeze the life out of her. Even the memory made his heart jump and his guts clench. He should have been there sooner.

He'd been late, one more time.

But there was more to his mate than met the eye: she'd picked herself up and carried on. She was slender and small and full of unexpected passion. She was a fighter, and Quinn liked that.

He could still feel the heat of the spark that had lit between their fingers.

The thrill of the firestorm, though, was tainted by the threat against her. She had been targeted because of him, after all, and Quinn couldn't forget that, much less how familiar it was.

He could sense her presence in his vicinity, but as soon as she had come downtown in the morning, he'd lost her in the hustle and bustle. The show was too crowded and her scent was too new to him for him to accurately target her position.

She was tantalizingly close, but he didn't know where.

He didn't have to like that.

To the casual observer, Quinn might have seemed to be a man at ease, even if, in reality, he was anything but. He sat at the back of his booth in an old lawn chair, his straw fedora pulled low over his eyes. A passing shopper might assume he was dozing in the humid heat of July, but Quinn seldom truly slept and he wasn't going to do so now.

He'd never liked waiting.

It was late morning when Quinn felt a prickle of awareness that meant the presence of another of his kind. He deliberately held his casual pose when a man stopped and glanced into the booth.

It was another *Pyr.*

There was nothing remarkable about the man, nothing that would hint of his abilities. He was tall and his hair was jet-black with a touch of silver at the temples. He wore jeans and a black leather jacket, despite the heat.

Their gazes met. An electric shock jolted through Quinn. It was an unmistakable sensation, one that Quinn recognized even though he hadn't felt it in centuries. It wasn't the same man who had attacked Quinn's mate the night before—this man was taller and leaner. He also moved differently. He was lithe and possessed a sinewy strength, while the attacker had had a stockier build.

That didn't prove his innocence. Anyone could have accomplices. Quinn studied him through narrowed eyes, memorizing his features.

Two *Pyr* in his presence in rapid succession meant that Quinn's firestorm *had* drawn interest from his fellows.

He would have preferred to have been wrong about that.

The stranger glanced at the sign hanging at the front of Quinn's booth and smiled as he read it. He moved slowly into the booth, making every appearance of browsing Quinn's wares. Quinn simply waited: he wasn't going to make this easy.

"You should breed," the stranger said.

Quinn was startled. It had been centuries since he had heard old-speak, the guttural communication favored by his

kind. Old-speak was brief and deep and ancient. Its low fre-
quency sounded like a faint rumble to perceptive mortal
ears, but was clear to the keen senses of the *Pyr*.

"Why?" he responded in kind, his lips barely moving.

The stranger picked up a door knocker in the shape of a
fist, as if considering a purchase. "We are too few."

Quinn didn't see this as his problem to resolve, although
it was interesting to have the argument made so soon after
his encountering his destined mate. Again, he doubted that
it was a coincidence. "You breed, then."

The stranger glared at Quinn, his eyes a blaze of green.
"We are too few. Better we all breed."

Quinn owed this stranger no answers. He sighed, as if
weary. "But, so few princesses."

The stranger smiled again. "Fewer virgins, perhaps."
Their gazes met and held, some camaraderie flickering to
life between them.

Quinn didn't trust it. He didn't trust any *Pyr* and he didn't
want to make any friendly connections. He glanced over the
crowd that filled the street. One woman paused before
Quinn's booth and returned his glance with a boldness that
made him smile.

"Perhaps," he conceded.

The stranger snorted, his cutting glance toward the
woman making her move on. He surveyed the street in his
turn. "No shortage of damsels in distress," he mused.

Quinn's eyes narrowed.

The stranger took a step back and stared pointedly into
the throngs of people. The street was packed with bodies in
the sunshine. Quinn saw the crowd part, seemingly of its
own volition.

But the break was too neat and too many people moved
in unison.

It wasn't an accident.

Especially since directly in Quinn's line of sight was his destined mate. She looked more tidy and composed, her hair twisted up and her linen shirtdress neatly pressed. She had a bright scarf knotted around her neck, but Quinn didn't need to see the bruise to know that it was his mate.

Or that the other *Pyr* knew it, too.

Quinn sat straighter, unable to hide that he was impressed.

"Tasty," the stranger said with another appreciative survey of Quinn's woman. He put the door knocker back in place on the display, glanced at Quinn, and smiled a knowing smile. "Breed. While you can," he counseled, then left.

"Hey!" Quinn called audibly, but the stranger didn't look back. Quinn got up to follow, but his visitor had disappeared into the milling crowd.

As surely as if he had never been.

Which was saying something, given Quinn's keen eyesight.

Quinn stood at the entry to his booth and pushed up the rim of his straw fedora, looking for a hint of the stranger's passage even as he knew he wouldn't find one. The other *Pyr* was old and skilled; he had powers Quinn hadn't even known were possible and he was more aware of the location of Quinn's mate than Quinn was.

This didn't look good.

Sara blinked.

It was the strangest thing. She'd gone out for a coffee, as morning business was slow in the shop, and had been pushing her way through the throngs of shoppers. The art fair had drawn a lot of tourists, and South State was jammed. It was hard to get angry at people having a good time, but still she felt guilty to have left the shop closed for so long.

She'd just started to despair of getting back to work soon,

when the crowd had parted, all at once. A passage had opened, the way the Red Sea had divided before Charlton Heston.

Right across the street, she could see a booth. There was a man shopping in the booth, but that wasn't what caught her eye.

It was the man lounging in the lawn chair at the back of it. She felt the same heady tingle of his gaze upon her as she had felt the night before. Her feet seemed to root to the spot.

It was her guardian angel.

Sara couldn't help but stare. She told herself that she was confirming her suspicion that he was who she thought he was, but she knew it was a lie. She was just looking.

Or maybe she was ogling. He looked every bit as good as she remembered, even in daylight, and her pulse responded to the sight of him in exactly the same way it had the night before.

She should thank him.

If it was someone else, it would be better for her to not make an idiot of herself. Confirming his identity was a perfect rationalization for standing and staring, although it wasn't the real reason Sara did so.

It was as if she couldn't *not* stare.

The potential customer left abruptly and her defender stood up, coming to the front of the booth. He pushed back his hat and stared after the departing man with a frown, as if offended by something he'd said.

Sara didn't much care. Her heart was galloping as soon as she could see his face fully. He was wearing jeans and a dark T-shirt as well as those black boots, but he'd thrown a Hawaiian shirt over the T-shirt. He wore a straw fedora with a striped band, which was just as incongruous as the vivid print shirt.

Sara smiled despite herself. Anyone should be able to see

that this man was a fighter, not a whimsical, possibly harm-less, artist in a giddy shirt.

As if he had heard her thoughts, he looked directly at her. She was shocked that he had no doubt of her presence, much less of her exact location.

Her mouth went dry as they stared at each other; then she saw him begin to smile.

It was that slow smile. It made her think of chocolate melting, oh so slowly. That must have been why she salivated.

Her knees went weak and that made her feel stupid. It wasn't as if she'd never been attracted to a man before. Sara wasn't about to pretend she hadn't seen him and she wasn't going to be rude. She owed him a thank-you, and this was the time to deliver it.

In the sunshine.

In the middle of a crowd.

Sara took a deep breath, sipped her latte as if she had all the time in the world, and crossed the street.

That slow smile broadened, making her pulse leap; then he retreated into the shadows of his booth. He returned to his chair, watching her all the while. He seemed to understand that she was uncertain of him, and she liked that he gave her a bit of space. She could see in the daylight that he was tanned, and the tan made his eyes look more vibrantly blue. She wasn't imagining the very real male appreciation in her gaze, nor was she imagining how feminine his glances made her feel.

Sara had never felt so aware of her body in her life. She was glad that she had chosen the red sundress this morning. It was a good color for her, and the way the hem fluttered around her ankles always made her feel elegant.

To think she'd chosen it just to hide the nasty scab on her knee. She'd knotted a scarf around her neck to hide the massive bruise that had appeared there, and hoped she didn't look like a victim of domestic abuse. Her hair was neatly pulled up into a ponytail, bouncing the way she liked it. She wore only her mother's amber pendant and her watch, and had a different purse on her shoulder. She felt neat and clean, exactly as she had not felt in meeting him the night before, and that fed her confidence.

His eyes gleamed with humor as she paused to read the sign over the booth. Her heart stopped, then skipped.

"Here Be Dragons?" she said, certain it had to be a coincidence.

Didn't it?

"Who else should guard the treasure?" he asked. He stretched out his long legs and crossed his ankles, as if to reassure her that he meant to stay put in his chair, and thus offered her no threat.

Sara chose to be reassured. She stepped farther into the booth, knowing she was holding her cup of coffee a little too tightly. "I wanted to thank you."

He inclined his head slightly. "It was nothing."

"Not to me."

He smiled then and nodded agreement. "Fair enough."

Sara didn't know what she expected of him, but it wasn't indifference. "No, really, thank you. I don't know what he would have done. . . ."

He interrupted her crisply. "You must have more imagination than that."

Sara swallowed and it hurt, as much of a reminder as she needed of her attacker's intent. "All right. I do know what he would have done, and that's why I'm thanking you."

"I was in the right place at the right time." He didn't seem to realize that he had even made a decision to help her, or that many people would have chosen not to get involved.

Sara decided not to enlighten him. It might help another woman on another day.

She smiled. "Well, thank you. I really appreciated it."

"You're welcome." His eyes were so blue. He didn't blink; he didn't stare; he just held her gaze captive. It was as if time slowed in his booth. Sara felt her mouth go dry. Goose bumps rose on her flesh and her skin tingled.

"Did you sleep well?"

"With the help of a Scotch," she admitted, then blushed. "My father's solution for stress. It's not usually one for me."

"It's not a bad one." He shrugged. "Maybe that was my problem. I should have had a drink."

"You didn't sleep well?"

"No. Not at all." He spoke firmly, his gaze clinging to hers. The heat grew between them, and Sara told herself not to read anything into his emphatic answer.

He couldn't care about what happened to her. After all, she didn't know him. She didn't even know his name.

She turned away from him abruptly and found business cards displayed on the table before her. The holder was iron, and wound around the stack of cards like a grapevine.

"Quinn Tyrrell?" Sara read, hearing the question in her voice.

He inclined his head slightly. "That's me."

Quinn. What an unusual name. Sara wanted to say it out loud one more time. *Quinn*. Instead, she considered the work displayed for sale. "Is this your work, then?"

"Yes."

"You're a blacksmith?" She felt stupid when she asked the question, as the answer was obvious.

Quinn didn't mock her, though. "Yes, I am."

It wasn't a very common profession and Sara couldn't help but look his way again. She noted the muscles in his shoulders and guessed how he had developed them. She had a sense of his strength, even when he was still. She thought that he was in his midthirties, maybe just a bit older than she was.

He was watching her intently and she felt herself blush, so she turned back to his wares.

"You?" he asked, the word a low rumble that gave Sara shivers.

"I'm an accountant." It sounded boring, so she kept talking. "I used to call myself an ace accountant, but now that I gave up the glory work, I'm just a plain old CPA."

"I doubt you could ever be a plain or old anything."

Sara found herself blushing furiously and looked away from his appreciative gaze to his work. "I didn't think there were any blacksmiths anymore."

"There are a few."

"Is it a hobby or a livelihood?"

"It's what I do," he said and she liked how direct he was. "I also do some sculpture, but historical reproduction work is the bulk of my work." He shrugged. "My shop is filled with custom railings, fences, and gates."

"And iron."

Quinn smiled. "Wrought iron when I can salvage it."

"I thought all of this was wrought iron."

He shook his head. "No. Wrought iron is an alloy that was popular in the eighteenth and nineteenth centuries. It's not in large-scale production anymore."

"So you salvage it?" Sara liked the idea of that.

Quinn nodded. "Sometimes I can buy it from buildings that are being demolished or renovated." He smiled, as if amused by himself, and Sara was enchanted. "I have a bit of a stash."

"A bit?"

"A barnful," he admitted.

"But why? Is there something special about it?"

"Just the way it works." Quinn unfolded himself then and came to stand beside her, moving with athletic ease that did crazy things to her pulse. Sara sizzled with him so close. He was so tall and broad: although she wasn't tall, she felt even more feminine and petite than she usually did. She could smell the sunblock lotion he'd used, and the scent of coconut milk was oddly reassuring.

Maybe that was what was making her dizzy.

Or maybe it was the heat, which seemed to have suddenly intensified.

"See this?" He handed her a door handle from the table. The handle was substantial, and the two ends—where the handle would be fastened to the door—were shaped as leaves. "This is made from mild steel." He picked up another one that wasn't much different—beyond the leaves having more detail and there being a vinelike quality to the handle itself—and offered it to Sara. She put down her coffee to take it in her other hand. "And this is wrought iron."

They were both heavy and made with a skill she appreciated. "They feel the same."

"But they didn't work the same." He tapped the wrought-iron one. "I made this one first, then worked to replicate it in the mild steel. See how much more I could add to the leaves?"

Sara nodded, then turned the two in her hands. "They aren't priced the same."

Quinn shook his head. "Mild steel is cheaper. The wrought iron is more of a boutique item."

Sara watched him, liking that he was less taciturn when he talked about his work. She wanted to hear his voice and she wanted to know what he cared about, so she prompted him to say more. "What's the difference then, after you've made them? They look so similar."

"They won't age the same. The wrought iron has a grain, like wood, and that will become more evident if it corrodes."

"Is that what I see in the handle?"

"Yes. A lot of people who are doing historic reproduction work prefer it, if they can get it."

Sara could see that he was passionate about his work and she liked that. There was something appealing about people who were good at what they did and proud of their skill.

She put down the two door knockers and took another sip of her coffee. Quinn had door knockers and drawer pulls, as well as birdbaths with gleaming bowls of hammered steel supported by black twining vines. All of his designs were drawn from nature, based on keen observation. She liked the birdbaths in particular, as well as the scaled fish that leapt from a copper bowl with a small fountain, the pump hidden behind a stone. There was a binder on one table, filled with photographs of larger work.

"I never would have thought being a blacksmith would be a good way to make a living," she mused, before realizing that he might find her question too bold. She smiled in apology. "Sorry. I've been accused before of thinking too much about the money."

Quinn's smile was warm, evidence that he wasn't offended. "There's nothing wrong with being practical. It's not a way to get rich, but I have simple needs."

Sara was feeling one very basic need, one that should be simple but had been complicated in her own life. *Quinn.* His name seemed to whisper in her thoughts. She wanted to ask him a thousand nosy questions but didn't dare.

He gestured to the scarf knotted around her neck and anger flashed in his eyes. "Is that from last night?" he asked, and she knew he could see the edges of the bruise. It must be getting darker—just her luck.

"You're not supposed to see the bruise with the scarf."

Quinn's lips set and even after he averted his gaze, Sara could still feel his anger. It had been a long time since anyone had been enraged on her behalf.

Quinn took a breath, then glanced back at her, his gaze simmering. "Just pull it up a bit on this side," he counseled softly, then tugged the silk for her before she could do it. His fingertips brushed against her throat, his skin so warm where it brushed hers that she felt something inside her melt.

But it was his deep voice that made her sizzle.

Or maybe it was the heat. Sara looked away from him, feeling a lot more innocent than she was. She took a nervous gulp of her coffee and her hand fell on a door knocker.

It was shaped like a mermaid, one whose tail knocked against the back of the knocker. The tail struck on a small scallop shell that seemed to float on the waves that shaped the back of the knocker. Sara picked it up and examined the work, liking the mermaid's sinuous tail. The mermaid's hair flowed around her like a cloud and the pose seemed both happy and provocative. There was something about the mermaid's shape that tempted Sara to curl her fingers around it.

Or stroke it.

"She's wrought iron," Quinn said. "I could never have gotten that detail in her tail otherwise."

"She's beautiful."

"Thank you." He was watching her closely, as if she fascinated him. Sara felt her color rise, but tried to act as if she was unaware of him.

In reality, she was more aware of Quinn than she'd ever been of any man.

Maybe she needed to get out more.

Maybe she should go out with Quinn.

It was a ridiculously appealing idea, considering that she knew just about nothing about him.

What better way to find out more?

Sara checked the price on the knocker, then found herself turning to Quinn. "I'd like to take this. For my shop."

"You have a shop?" He seemed surprised.

"A bookstore. In the arcade there. I was just locking up last night when, when . . ."

He glanced down at the door knocker with a slight frown. "You don't need to buy something from me. It's enough that you're safe." He gave her a piercing glance.

"But I like it and I need a door knocker." She half suspected that those weren't the only reasons she was doing this. She knew that every day, when she unlocked the door of the shop, she would see that iron mermaid and think of Quinn.

Maybe the mermaid would watch over her instead of him.

She almost rolled her eyes at that uncharacteristic thought. Maybe she should get her nose out of the stock in her bookstore.

She held out the mermaid again, and this time, he accepted it from her. Sara watched Quinn's hands—long-fingered and strong, tanned, his nails cut blunt—as he examined the mermaid himself. He smiled that slow smile again, the one that was having a serious impact on her pulse, and slanted a glance at her. He had dark lashes, thick ones, that framed the blue of his eyes perfectly.

"Good pick. I like this one, too," he said to her surprise. "There's something special about her." He ran his finger down the length of the mermaid in admiration.

A bead of sweat slid down Sara's spine at exactly the same time. Sara shivered, imagining that strong finger sliding down her own length. His touch would be resolute but gentle; she was strangely sure of it. She could almost feel his caress, as if his finger were sliding over her skin instead of the little iron mermaid.

"She seemed to shape herself," Quinn mused, "and the result was so perfect that I knew she had it right." He brushed his thumb across her tail. "Maybe she'll watch out for you instead of me."

Sara stared at him, surprised that he would echo her own whimsical thought. He smiled a little and she tried to think of something clever to say.

No luck.

He turned then, and wrapped the mermaid in yellow and orange tissue with surprising care. Sara tried to catch her breath and regain her composure while his attention was diverted. She didn't have a lot of luck with that, either. She felt hot, hotter than she knew she should have been.

Maybe it was the weather. She wasn't used to humidity like this.

Maybe it was the stillness of the air under his booth canopy, or the sunlight beaming through the canvas.

Maybe it was Quinn. She fought the urge to fan herself. He placed the mermaid in a sturdy bag made of kraft paper, then tucked a small plastic bag with four screws into the side. He added one of his business cards.

Sara gave him her credit card and their fingers brushed in the transaction. Was it her imagination or did that spark light between their fingers again? She almost jumped, but had no real desire to pull away.

Again, Quinn granted her that leisurely smile. He paused to look at her card and she assumed he was checking the company. But no. He slid his thumb over the raised letters of her name as if caressing them, and again, Sara had the urge to shiver in the sultry heat. Her mouth went dry.

"Sara," he said and the sound of her own name warmed Sara to her toes. His next words were murmured so low that they seemed to resonate in Sara's bones. "Did you know that your name means 'princess'?"

"Is that funny?"

He looked up, his gaze shimmering, and the breath left her lungs completely. She was snared, caught in a timeless moment. She couldn't do anything but look back at him, couldn't do anything other than stare into the blue heat of his eyes.

"No," he murmured and she felt the word as much as she heard it. "It's just perfect."

Sara blushed. She was hot, on fire from her hair to her toes, burning and yearning in a way that couldn't be natural yet felt exactly right.

Just perfect, in fact.

She couldn't look away from Quinn, couldn't control the desire that pushed everything else from her thoughts. She wanted to know how he felt against her, wanted to know how he would kiss and how he would caress. She wanted to feel his hands on her, wanted him to do more things slowly than just smile.

She thought about dipping him in chocolate and licking it all off. It was a wicked and playful thought, one that practical Sara Keegan shouldn't have had, but she couldn't push it out of her mind once she had it.

The chocolate would melt in this heat.

And she wouldn't care. She'd just smear it further.

It was official then: she was losing her mind. Sara tore her gaze away from his before she said something she'd regret, sipped her coffee, and nearly choked on it.

"Do you need help installing the knocker?" Quinn asked.

"No, I can do it myself, thanks," Sara said quickly, then could have kicked herself for ensuring that she wouldn't see him again. "Actually, I have tools in the shop but if you had time to hang it during the show, that would be nice."

Quinn's obvious pleasure made her warm all over again.

"I will. I'd like to see her in her proper place. It's easier to let the special ones go if I know where they are."

"I can understand that. It must be hard to part with your work, especially as she's so lovely."

He shook his head slightly. "She's perfect. Just perfect." He smiled, that languorous smile that brought the simmer in Sara to a raging boil. A twinkle lit in his eyes. "Maybe she shaped herself just for you."

That was an idea Sara was accustomed to finding in the stock of Magda's shop, but not one she was used to finding so appealing.

"The Scrying Glass. It's just down there. I'll see you whenever you have time," Sara said all in a rush, wishing she could have thought of something witty.

Quinn nodded agreement, then greeted another shopper entering his booth. Sara ducked out of the stall, her grip tight on the bag that contained her door knocker. It seemed that there was more air outside the booth and she took a shaking breath.

Nothing like a hot latte to make you sweat.

That wasn't it and Sara knew it. She looked back once and blushed to find his gaze lingering on her, even as he talked to another customer.

Quinn. She didn't know five things about him, but she was going to see him again and that was enough to make her wildly happy.

Maybe it was just the spontaneity. Sara had spent the last decade planning every detail of her life, and it hadn't gotten her anywhere. She decided as she walked back to the shop that she would go with the flow, and just see where things went with Quinn.

Being in his company was already pretty interesting.

Chapter 3

Sara removed the BACK IN FIVE MINUTES sign on the inside of the door of The Scrying Glass. She unpacked the mermaid and laid the knocker on the counter, liking the shape of it even more than she had in Quinn's booth. She couldn't help but slide her fingers over its smooth, curved surface. She caught her breath, remembering the way Quinn had touched it and how she had almost felt his hand on her own back.

Sara forced herself to think about more practical things than how a particular blacksmith would look naked.

Or chocolate-dipped.

Instead, she turned her attention back to Magda's books for the shop. They might as well have needed a secret decoder ring, for all the sense they made, but Sara was determined to translate them and get the data entered into the new software she'd bought for the store. It was time that The Scrying Glass entered the twentieth century, especially as that century was over. Magda's tendency to scribble her records and receipts on napkins or stray pieces of paper didn't make Sara's job any easier, nor did the shoe box filing system of choice.

She wasn't an ace accountant for nothing, though, and she had a vested interest in making the shop run more efficiently. It was hers now, after all, and would be her primary source of income. She'd saved a lot of money from her high-flying days in information technology, but nothing lasted forever.

Especially money.

The Scrying Glass looked as if it had been open since the dawn of time. It had always reminded Sara of used bookstores she'd visited in England, where you never quite knew what you'd find, and where your discovery could sometimes surprise even the proprietor. It was eccentric and intriguing and disorganized and full of character—just like Aunt Magda had been.

Sara had spent summers with her aunt Magda for as long as she could remember and the bookstore had been a central feature in those visits. Sara had done pretty much every job in the bookstore in those years. She'd sorted and shelved stock. She'd moved sections of books. She'd run the cash and gone to the bank. She'd unpacked boxes of new shiny books. That had always been Magda's favorite job and Sara still felt as if her aunt was looking over her shoulder each time she cracked open a shipment.

And they had read. There had been no rules at Aunt Magda's about what was suitable reading for a young girl, and Sara had spent summers reading voraciously. Summers in Ann Arbor were the one fixture of her childhood, given how often she and her parents had moved. Her aunt's house, with the mismatched teacups and batiks over the windows, the strange little collections of stones and shells, and the incense holders of every variety had been both exotic and the closest thing Sara had had to a permanent home.

The Scrying Glass hadn't really changed in thirty years.

The bookshelves were old wood, polished to a golden patina. The walls had been painted a rich burgundy at some distant point in time. The floors were laid with black-and-white checkerboard tiles, which looked to be stone, and there was a heavy crown molding around the perimeter of the shop at the ceiling. The windows were leaded glass and there was the most wonderful brass sign hanging over the door in the arcade.

When Magda had died in May, so close to so many other challenges, Sara had found that she couldn't sell the shop. Instead, she'd followed her heart and quit her job, moved into the apartment on the second floor of Magda's house, rented the main house, and become a bookshop owner. It had seemed like exactly the right thing to do.

Sara wasn't crazy about the shop's New Age specialty, but changing it would mean sacrificing that wonderful sign. There was also a good bit of established traffic, given how long Magda had owned the store. Sara was determined to serve her aunt's memory and was struggling to learn more about the stock.

She also wanted to make the shop her own. Sara tried to be proactive in making the world a better place—her bookstore now had the food bank donation box and the women's shelter donation box to show for it. She'd already added some used books to the store's selection, books she found at yard sales and thrift shops, and had a couple of regular browsers in that section who disliked the idea of books in landfill sites as much as she did.

The cash desk was beside the door of The Scrying Glass, a heavy oak counter with a beveled pane of glass set into its top. The new computerized cash register looked out of place, but Sara wasn't going to do everything by hand just for appearances. Magda couldn't have had a clue about the shop's finances, unless her tarot cards had kept her informed, and Sara had no idea how her aunt had done the taxes.

She'd get to that, once she had something resembling accounting books.

Sara pulled out the current bane of her existence, the inventory, and tried to make sense of the dates and titles on page three. Maybe she needed the eponymous scrying glass to figure them out. Maybe it was a good thing she'd gotten an extra large latte. She would get all of this sorted out and entered into her computer, even if it killed her.

Or drove her insane.

She wished that either scenario seemed a bit less likely than they often did.

The shop was muggy, but Sara wasn't ready to go another round with the temperamental air-conditioning unit just yet. She'd delayed using it for as long as possible, trying to save electricity, but with the duration of this heat wave, the shop had slowly filled with hot air. When a customer had left, complaining of the heat, Sara had surrendered and turned on the air-conditioning unit.

It hadn't worked.

Not until the fix-it guy had come from Malone's Appliance Repair and then it had worked perfectly. It must have started just as he started to walk down the arcade. It had run so flawlessly during his service call that he'd obviously thought Sara was nuts for calling for service. Sara didn't think he'd gotten back to his truck before the unit had died again.

They'd done this four times and she was tired of the game.

She opened the shoe box and grabbed a fistful of paper shards. Maybe she'd call Malone's later.

*   *   *

Sara didn't know how much time had passed when the brass bell over the door jingled.

"Good afternoon," she said as a man stepped into the shop.

"Good afternoon." He smiled in return and glanced about himself. His black hair was touched with a distinguished bit of silver at his temples. He wore jeans and boots, and a leather jacket that must have been hot in this weather. "What a unique shop." His accent was faintly British.

"Thank you. We specialize in New Age books, the occult, mythology, and fantasy fiction." Sara was always surprised to hear herself talking as if there were more people involved in running the bookstore. The word *we* just popped out of her mouth all the time. Maybe it was because the shop felt so strongly imbued with Magda's presence. Either way, she didn't feel alone here. "Can I help you find anything specific?"

"I'll just browse," he said. "It looks as if I'll easily find something of interest."

"Well, don't be afraid to ask." Frowning slightly in concentration, Sara returned to the inventory as the man moved between the bookshelves.

There was something familiar about him, but Sara couldn't place him. She must have seen him somewhere. . . .

But she couldn't put her finger on where or when.

Maybe she was wrong.

Just like the total value on the store inventory seemed to be wrong. She was sure there wasn't another shoe box anywhere. Sara pulled out a calculator and started to crunch the numbers for the umpteenth time.

"Where would I find books on mythology?" the man asked, peeking out from behind a shelf.

Sara pointed. "Back corner, about eye level on the right."

"Thank you."

He disappeared again. Sara looked back down to her records and something flashed in her peripheral vision.

It was the mermaid.

Sara glanced at the door knocker, then stared in wonder. The mermaid was gleaming like a coal left in the fire. She remained black, but her edges—the lip of her scales, the tips of her tail fins, the ends of her swirling hair—were orange.

As if she'd been touched by fire.

Or even made of fire.

But the door knocker wasn't painted. It had been all black when she bought it.

How strange. Sara reached to pick it up for a closer look.

"Ouch!" She dropped the mermaid when it burned her fingers. The glass top on the cash desk rattled when the wrought iron hit it.

How could the mermaid be hot to the touch? The color seemed to ebb and flow, and Sara had the strange sense that the door knocker was acting like a beacon.

The air-conditioning unit chose that moment to sputter and hum to life.

Sara was an analytical person and not one easily spooked. Door knockers did not broadcast messages. All the same, there was no obvious reason for the mermaid to be hot. It wasn't in the sun; it wasn't in a reflection; it wasn't on a hot surface.

But it *was* hot, all the same. She touched it with a cautious fingertip, just to be sure, and winced as her finger was singed.

"This is exactly what I was looking for," the man said suddenly, interrupting her thoughts. He was right in front of Sara and had approached the counter without her hearing him.

She ignored the door knocker and smiled at him. "I'm glad to hear it."

He put three books down on the counter. The bottom one was a large coffee-table book, slick with illustrations; the one on top of it was an older, leather-bound book that Sara hadn't seen before; and the third volume was a children's book.

"How interesting." Sara touched the cover on the leather-bound one. "I didn't even realize this book was here."

"You do have quite a good selection."

Sara turned the book in her hands. *"The Habits and Habitats of Dragons: a Compleat Guide for Slayers."* She smiled. "It sounds like a whimsical volume, the treatise of one of those Victorian hobbyist scholars."

Her customer didn't smile. In fact, he bristled. "I assure you that Sigmund Guthrie was quite serious about his so-called hobby."

The slight emphasis he put on the last word and his scathing tone made Sara glance up. "Slaying dragons?"

"Exactly," her customer said solemnly. "I've been looking for this volume for a long time." He stared at Sara as if she should find this particularly meaningful, but she didn't.

Her mother had always said that it took all kinds of people to make a world. If this man wanted to believe that there were dragons to slay, and wanted to buy a book about that very activity, Sara would be glad to take his $189.99 plus tax.

That didn't mean that he was right.

She'd been meeting a lot of people with unusual perspectives in The Scrying Glass. The sooner she got used to it, the better.

She flicked the cover open again to confirm the price. "There must be other people looking for this one, as well."

"That wouldn't surprise me. It's rare." His smile turned rueful. "At least, I've had a difficult time finding a copy."

Sara didn't want to ask whether he shared the author's hobby and was looking for tips.

She decided to change the subject. "The inventory number indicates it was bought for the store three years ago. Have you been in before?"

"No, I'm from Chicago. I came for other business and just stumbled across your store." His smile broadened. "It's true that we find what we seek in the most unlikely of places." He said this with an odd emphasis, as if it should also mean something to her.

As if it were a code phrase.

Sara looked at him then, really looked at him. There was something strange about him and it wasn't just his decision to wear a leather jacket when the sidewalks were melting. His voice was melodic. When she met his gaze, it looked almost as if there were green flames flickering in the depths of his eyes.

Then she blinked and he was looking back at her, his eyes as normal as could be.

Flames in people's eyes and door knockers that heated by themselves. Dragons and stalkers and women screaming for help who didn't really exist. Maybe Sara *was* losing it.

The coffee-table book was *Dragons Through Time, in Illustration and Story.* The cover showed an orange dragon breathing fire at a mounted knight, presumably Saint George, who seemed very small in comparison. The children's book was called *The Dragon Next Door.*

"I sense a theme," she said lightly.

The man shrugged. "Yes." He tilted his head as if listening to something, but Sara couldn't hear anything. Whatever he thought he heard, it prompted him to nod slightly, as if in approval.

Sara focused on the mundane. She rang the books into the cash register and totaled it up. "It's $278.65 altogether."

Her customer looked at her with obvious surprise. "Oh, the books aren't for me."

Sara had been putting the books into a bag, but stopped. "Did you want them gift wrapped?"

"I don't think that's necessary." When she hesitated, he leaned closer. "You see, I chose them for you."

Sara blinked. "For me?"

"Yes, of course."

"Perhaps you don't realize that I own this bookstore?"

"That makes perfect sense, given that you are the Seer."

"I beg your pardon?"

"It is prophesied that the Seer and the Smith will be the first partners of the new age." He reached across the counter and tapped the books. "The sooner you inform yourself, the better."

Sara knew then where she had seen him before. "You were in Quinn's booth this morning." He had been arguing with Quinn, if Sara guessed it right.

"That's less important than the books." Her noncustomer gestured to the books. "You need to read these, particularly Guthrie's volume, as soon as possible."

"I'm reading a sample of all of the stock. . . ."

"No." He leaned across the counter and spoke with sudden intensity. That flame was back in his eyes. "You must read Guthrie's book immediately, in order to defend yourself. It's a matter of life and death."

"Life and death?" Sara echoed. She had an urge to do what he wanted her to do, even though it made little sense.

His gaze fell to the scarf knotted around her neck. "Surely I don't have to tell you that the *Slayer*s will murder you to keep the prophecy from coming true?"

Sara took a step back. "Who are you?"

"I am Erik Sorensson, leader of the *Pyr*. I will do all I can to help you, but you must also help yourself. You are the

Seer. Much relies upon you. Inform yourself now, while you can."

Before Sara could process all of that information, he pivoted and marched out of her store. Sara was surprised how quickly he disappeared—he turned toward Maynard Street, but by the time she got to the door of the shop, he was gone.

Much the way Quinn had quickly disappeared the night before. Her hand rose to her throat, which still ached from her attacker's fingers. Someone *had* tried to murder her. Had it been this Erik Sorensson? Sara didn't think so. He seemed slimmer and taller, and also intent on helping her. So, how had he known about the attack?

Her gaze returned to the books he had gathered. She was surprised to see the mermaid door knocker still glowing on the counter.

She was even more surprised when Quinn burst into her shop right behind her. It was probably a bad sign that she was so glad to see him that her pulse skipped and her knees turned to butter.

His eyes were snapping and his manner was intense.

"Are you all right?" he demanded.

Before she could answer, much less ask the reason for his concern, she saw his gaze flick to the door knocker. It was fading to black, as if Sara had imagined its being red and hot, as if it were reassured that Quinn had arrived.

It *had* sent a message.

To Quinn.

The air conditioner whirred to a higher setting even though no one had touched the thermostat.

Sara might have concluded that all of the above was impossible, except what happened next was even more impossible. Quinn came farther into her shop and caught his breath in surprise. He seemed to shimmer in the oddest way, as if his edges were glowing.

Exactly as the mermaid had glowed. His eyes blazed and he became larger.

Much larger.

Just as Sara thought things couldn't get odder, Quinn became a massive blue and silver dragon.

It was the same dragon that had saved Sara from her assailant the night before. She blinked and gaped at him, but he lashed his tail and looked straight back at her.

With eyes of blazing blue.

The scariest part was that things were starting to make sense.

Quinn was caught off guard by the scent of another *Pyr* in Sara's shop. He'd expected some threat when the mermaid had summoned him, and had hurried to get to Sara. The throngs of people had conspired against him and he had been afraid he'd arrive too late.

Again.

But Sara was fine, if surprised to see him. Quinn was composing a plausible explanation for his sudden appearance when he stepped right into the scent of another *Pyr*.

In close proximity to his destined mate.

Who had already survived an attempt on her life.

Quinn had no chance to stop his body's reaction. He had shifted in a heartbeat and he was shocked by his own body's determination to defend what was his own. Usually it took a few moments for him to shift: apparently the presence of his mate changed the time line.

He'd have to remember that.

Sara retreated behind the cash desk to watch him. Her expression was wary and he could almost feel her pulse leaping, but at least she hadn't fainted in terror.

He verified that the other *Pyr* was indeed gone from the shop, not just hiding in a back corner. Then he exhaled, composed his thoughts, and changed back to his human form.

Sara watched him, her eyes wide.

"You want to run for the door?" he asked, trying to lighten the moment.

"You did that last night," she said, pointing at him. "I did see a dragon and it was you. It really happened and I'm not losing my mind."

Quinn nodded and held his ground, letting her set the pace of their discussion.

She sat down hard, then gestured to the door knocker. "And it called you, by heating up when that guy came into the shop."

The air-conditioning unit was blasting out frigid air, but this wasn't the time to suggest to Sara that she conserve electricity.

Quinn nodded agreement again. "What guy?"

Sara took a steadying breath and looked around her shop as if seeking something that made sense. She took a couple of breaths before she answered and Quinn was impressed by her resilience.

"It was the same guy who was in your booth this morning. The one with the leather jacket." She gave Quinn a hard glance. "He said he was the leader of the *Pyr*. He said some prophecy foretells the mating of the Smith and the Seer and that I should read these books—especially this one—before someone kills me. Does that mean anything to you?"

It was all happening too fast. Quinn folded his arms across his chest and leaned against the door frame. He'd keep his distance for the moment.

"Leader?" he mused, a bit surprised by this news. Quinn had his doubts about the practicalities of formal organization among shape shifters. "If nothing else, it means that my suspicions were right."

Sara braced her hands on the counter and exhaled. "Okay." She ran a hand over her forehead, brushing aside a couple of strands of hair. "Maybe we could start off simple. How did you make the mermaid call you?"

Quinn winced. "Well, that's hard to explain."

Sara's smile was impish. "That's a cheating answer. I thought I was asking the easy question."

Quinn smiled back at her in relief. "It's not simple. In fact, it's impossible to explain. It's something I learned to do by following my instincts, and I'm not sure how I'll teach anyone else to do it."

"Why would you have to?"

"Because it's my responsibility to pass my skills to another."

"Like an apprentice?"

"Yes," Quinn agreed, thinking it a bit soon to talk about hereditary powers of the son he and Sara hadn't conceived yet. She seemed to be waiting for more, so he continued. "You see, the art of the smith has been considered mystical for a long time, maybe because things are transformed in the forge."

"Metal is reshaped," Sara agreed.

"Sometimes other attributes change as well as shape. Steel becomes stronger. So, maybe it makes sense that people believed there was magic involved in transforming iron into weapons with gleaming blades, and that smiths had mystical powers."

Sara flicked a glance at the door knocker.

Quinn kept talking. It seemed to be his best chance. "The idea is old, and goes back at least to the Greeks. Hephaestus was the smith of the Greek gods. He was supposed to have been lame, but he must have had either charm or magic on his side."

"How so?"

"He was married to Aphrodite."

Sara blushed. "The goddess of love. Even I remember that."

"The goddess of love and beauty." Quinn paused. "I've heard that magical power was given to smiths by the goddess, in return for faithful worship of the eternal feminine, and that Amazons deliberately lamed smiths because they were so useful. There's an old link between smiths and strong women."

Sara's cheeks were red, but she held his gaze. "If you believe that sort of thing."

"Don't you?" Quinn glanced pointedly around him. She had to believe in the mystical to run a shop like this.

But Sara laughed lightly. "Don't be fooled by appearances. I'm Sara Keegan, ace accountant, and The Scrying Glass, well, it's come along a bit early to be my midlife crisis, but maybe it still counts."

"I don't understand."

Sara's tone became more definite. "I believe in math. I believe in charts and ledgers and books that balance and spreadsheets that tally. I believe in the right answer at the right time."

Quinn had a heartbeat to realize that his mate was the least likely person on the planet to believe in what he was before Sara spared a glance to the store. "My aunt Magda, though, believed in everything else."

Quinn was relieved by this. Psychic abilities ran in families, particularly in the female line. Maybe Sara didn't know what she could do.

"When Aunt Magda died and left me everything, I had the crazy thought that I could ditch my frequent flier cards and have a quiet life instead. It was just a whim, but it sounded too good to ignore." She shrugged. "I decided to make a change and here I am."

"So what makes you a great accountant?"

Sara laughed. Her eyes sparkled and he knew she had loved her job. "I was on the deal team for an information technology company. We did outsourcing deals and I was Ms. Math. There were seven of us and we convened in various locations every week to work out proposals. It was my job to make the numbers work, so that we made money and the client got the pricing they needed to save money. It was fascinating and challenging and some of the best work I've ever done." She spun a pencil. "We were the rainmakers, the dream team who brought home the deals to support the company's growth. It was good work and it paid really well."

"But you gave it up."

Sara frowned. "We traveled all the time. Out Sunday, home late Friday night. I can tell you the layout and the shortcuts between gates in every major airport hub in the continental U.S. I had a wad of frequent flier cards and hotel favored-guest cards, but no time to take vacation and use any of them." She spared him a glance. "I don't know why I'm telling you all of this."

Quinn smiled. "Because I'm a good listener?" He arched a brow. "Because it was tangible and real?" She sobered at that. Quinn shrugged. "Or maybe because you already know something pretty personal about me."

"I didn't imagine it, did I?"

"Do accountants hallucinate?"

She laughed and shook her head, then tapped her pencil on the counter. She was self-conscious now, but Quinn wanted to know more.

"Why did you give it up?"

Sara sighed. "My mother had always wanted to go to Machu Picchu but they never had the money. When my father retired from the service this year, I gave them the trip with my points. I was supposed to go with them, but at the last minute, a new deal opportunity came up and I went to Des Moines with the deal team instead." She swallowed, her brows tightening as she watched the pencil spin.

"What happened?"

"They were killed on that trip." Sara blinked back tears and straightened. "That made everything seem so pointless, the money and the fancy restaurants and the high-power toys. Then Magda died and my coworker Brian had his marriage go south and my boyfriend bailed and you know, I'd just had it."

"Fair enough."

"You think so? Most of my friends thought I was crazy." She looked at him, her gaze clear. He admired her strength, not only in making a major change in her life but recovering from such a loss.

"Sometimes it takes a lot to challenge our idea of how our lives should be."

She poked at a shoe box on the counter. "To finally audit the books, you mean?"

"Something like that." Quinn smiled. "No other family?"

She shook her head.

"Then we have something else in common, besides preferring a simple life," he said lightly. "We're both alone."

Sara looked up and her gaze locked with his. It was warm in the shop and got warmer as Quinn stared back at her. The sounds of activity in the arcade sounded distant and irrelevant.

The woman before him was the focus of his attention. As their gazes held, Quinn felt their breathing match rhythms. He was aware of the beat of her heart, thanks to his keen senses, and he heard his own pulse synchronize with hers.

The firestorm was as magical and potent as he'd believed.

Quinn could smell the heat on Sara's skin, the mingling of her perfume and her own scent, and it fed the heat simmering in his own veins. She licked her lips and inhaled slowly, a move that made her breasts rise and Quinn's desire burn.

She was his mate, his destiny, his prize.

His princess.

The weight of Sara's ponytail fell over her shoulder, making him want to push it back from her neck. Her hair was brushed to a smooth gleam of burnished gold, no less attractive than it had been all disheveled the night before. Her skin was tanned to honey and looked so soft and precious that he wanted to brush his fingertips across her.

Right under her ear. He'd kiss her there and find out if she was as delicate as she looked.

Or maybe as strong as she appeared. He wanted to unknot that scarf and caress her neck, smoothing away the bruise there.

And then, he'd kiss the rest of her.

Slowly.

Thoroughly.

Sara caught her breath and looked down at the books on the counter, her cheeks still flushed. Quinn wondered whether she had heard his thoughts or simply sensed them. "Do you know this prophecy about smiths and seers?"

"Nobody says it's true."

"What do you mean?"

"That I'm skeptical about some things, too."

She looked up in surprise and Quinn shrugged. "I believe in the fire and the forge. I believe in what I see and what I feel. I believe in the firestorm; I believe in duty and loyalty. Prophecies are another thing altogether."

Sara seemed to find this persuasive. "Sounds like we have even more things in common," she said quietly, then tore her gaze away. "So, what's the prophecy?"

"The union of one Smith and one Seer is supposed to

herald a big change for the *Pyr*," Quinn corrected softly. "If you believe that sort of thing."

"The *Pyr* being . . . ?"

"What I am." He didn't blink when she glanced at him. Quinn decided to say it aloud. "Dragon shape shifters."

Sara thought about this, which was better than her running, screaming, or tossing him out. "*Pyr* as in *pyromaniac*?"

Quinn smiled in his surprise. "Not the good guys, anyway. *Pyr* is the Greek word for fire or heat. We control the elements, including fire, hence the name. As in *pyrotechnics*."

"Pyrex," Sara said thoughtfully. "Because the glass is resistant to heat."

"Pyre, because it burns."

Her eyes sparkled suddenly and Quinn was intrigued by the unexpected glimpse of humor. The green in her hazel eyes was more predominant when she laughed. "Pyramid power?" she asked, her tone playful.

Quinn laughed. "Different section of your bookstore." He shook a finger at her when her smile broadened. "And no Pyrrhic victories, please."

"Oh, anything but that," she agreed with mock horror.

Quinn glanced around the store. "You know, the answer to every question you have about me is probably in here."

"I haven't read all the stock yet." Sara's lips twisted. "And I don't believe a lot of what I have read. My aunt Magda, who started this shop, *she* was psychic. Also a bit of a flake, but a loveable one."

Sara sighed and smiled, running her fingertips across the counter. She frowned slightly, and Quinn was touched that she couldn't hide her affection for her aunt so easily. They must have been close. Quinn remained silent, knowing how such a loss could hurt.

"I don't know anything about this stuff," Sara said after a moment. "And what I read, well, let's say that I'm skeptical. And what you just did, well—" She met his gaze, a wary twinkle in her own. "I'm long past thinking that there are perfect men out there, but what you can do is really odd."

She hadn't seen anything yet.

But she was open to him.

Quinn walked toward Sara and felt the heat increase between them. Her eyes widened slightly and he knew she felt the firestorm, too.

There was a trickle of perspiration on her neck and several tendrils of hair clung damply to her skin. Her lips parted when there was only the counter between them, and she looked both soft and welcoming. In this light, he could see that the hazel of her eyes was composed of a thousand shades of green and gold and brown, and that the gold was becoming dominant. He could also see the faint freckles on her nose and scattered across her chest. He wanted her, and knew he would have wanted her even without destiny on his side.

She was his destined mate.

They would be stronger together than apart, transformed by the firestorm the way that the forge transformed iron into steel.

But first he had to win her trust.

And with Sara, Quinn guessed that the truth would be the key.

"This is the firestorm." Quinn held up his hand, his palm toward her, his fingers splayed. She raised her own hand, understanding his expectation so intuitively that he knew she was wrong about her psychic abilities. She slowly touched her hand to his, matching her fingertips to his own, and he liked that she wasn't fearful. She was a warrior princess, exactly the kind of mate he would have chosen for himself.

Destiny had gotten it in one.

Their hands were an inch apart when sparks flew. He saw Sara gasp when the fire leapt back and forth between their hands; then he caught her hand within his own.

He locked their fingers together as his blood simmered from the contact. When he felt her trembling, he put her hand upon his chest, trapping her hand against the thunder of his heart. Her eyes widened as she stared at him, but she didn't pull away.

"You can't evade the firestorm, Sara," he said with quiet force. "And neither can I."

Sara felt as if the world had stopped.

And then erupted into flames. She stared into the endless blue of Quinn's eyes, feeling his heartbeat beneath her hand. She was hot, hotter than she could ever remember being, but it felt exactly right.

The warmth between them made her want to curl up against Quinn, step into his arms, draw close to his fire. It made her want to go with him. Anywhere. Everywhere. Maybe it was what made her intuitively trust him, the way she didn't usually trust people she'd just met. It made her want to learn everything he knew. There was a shimmer under her skin and a sizzle in her veins.

Logically, she was sure it had to be plain old lust she was feeling, and that would be trouble enough. But she had a sense that Quinn was another order of magnitude of trouble.

Sara was thinking she was past due for this kind of trouble. Magda had told her a thousand times that she worked too hard to enjoy life's pleasures. Her mother's last words to Sara had been that Sara had to stop working and start living.

Maybe it was time Sara balanced her deficit.

With Quinn. The air-conditioning unit whirred with sudden vigor.

The breath of glacial air seemed to clarify Sara's thoughts. Quinn was a dragon shape shifter who made sparks dance between their hands.

Maybe she should start off a little slower. Keep it simple.

Date a normal man, for example. She pulled her hand from Quinn's grip and took a step back.

There was a mighty rattle from overhead, a wheeze from something mechanical, and then the air conditioner died. The shop seemed suddenly very silent as the pair of them looked up.

"What was that?" Quinn asked.

Sara glared at the ceiling. "That stupid air-conditioning unit has broken again." She shook a finger at him. "Now, this *is* irrational. I'll call Malone's, and as soon as the repairman crosses that threshold, I guarantee that thing will start up again. It'll purr as contentedly as a kitten the whole time he's here and he won't be able to find anything wrong with it. That's happened four times already this week."

"Maybe there isn't anything wrong with it."

"Did that sound to you as if there was nothing wrong with it?"

Quinn leaned against the counter. "Maybe it didn't like you pulling away from me."

Sara laughed even though Quinn was serious. "Right. Next you'll be telling me that Magda is haunting the place."

"Does she?"

"Of course not! There's no such thing as ghosts."

He smiled ever so slightly, as if she was the whimsical one. "Are you sure?"

"Yes," Sara said firmly.

"Then how do you explain your air conditioner?"

"Maybe I just need a better repairman. There has to be a broken part or some rational reason why it breaks down."

Quinn looked up, apparently thoughtful. Sara took

advantage of the moment to study him. Maybe it said something about her lack of a social life that she thought he was the sexiest man she'd ever seen, even knowing what she knew.

Or maybe that said more about just how sexy Quinn was.

He looked at her so suddenly that he caught her staring, and Sara flushed. "You have to know that seers inherit their gift," he said. The air conditioner sputtered to life, prompting him to smile the slow smile that melted Sara's bones.

And her reservations.

Maybe he had magical powers of another kind.

"That was a coincidence," she said, hating that her tone lacked conviction. "I'm no seer."

Quinn arched a dark brow. He picked up the mermaid, which was obviously cold again, and turned it over. "Where do you keep those tools? I'll hang the door knocker while I'm here."

"There's a toolbox in the back closet, over there." When Quinn would have turned away, Sara reached out and touched his hand. She was still startled by the spark, but liked that he paused at her touch. "What's this prophecy, Quinn?"

He hesitated for a moment, then seemed to recite something he'd memorized a long time before.

> *When the Dragon's Tail demands its price,*
> *And the moon is devoured once, not twice,*
> *Seer and Smith will again unite.*
> *Water and air, with fire and earth*
> *This sacred union will give birth*
> *To the Pyr's sole chance to save the Earth.*

Quinn held Sara's gaze for a telling moment as she struggled to make sense of his words, then tossed the mermaid in his hand and turned away to fetch the tools.

She was going to have Quinn's child?

And their baby would save the planet?

Unfortunately, it wasn't the first odd thing Sara had heard that day. She swallowed and felt pain in her neck, a reminder that someone had wanted to kill her.

And Erik had warned her as much. She blinked and looked down at the books that the leader of the *Pyr* had chosen for her.

Quinn returned with a drill and an extension cord, as well as a screwdriver. He moved with the athletic grace Sara already associated with him, as if he were totally in touch with the realities of the world. She cleared her throat slightly and he glanced up. "I didn't imagine the dragon bit, did I?"

Quinn shook his head. "Sorry. No."

"Do you do that often?"

"Not as much as I once did." He paused, then seemed to decide to say more. "It's not always under my control."

"Sometimes it just happens?"

"No, it's predictable." He opened the door and positioned the knocker. He glanced at Sara and she nodded approval of the location. "Lunar eclipses bring it on, so I keep an astronomical calendar. Even if I can't see the eclipse, I feel its effects."

"I didn't think there was a lunar eclipse today."

"There wasn't." Quinn looked grim. "You have to understand that it's a fighting form, triggered by the need to protect something or someone."

"Like someone you like?" Sara asked, the words sounding silly as soon as she uttered them.

"A treasure." Quinn fired a hot glance her way. "Like my destined mate."

She stared at him in astonishment, but he gave no signs of being crazy or having meant to say something else.

His destined mate.

A prophesied child.

"You could, you know, just tell me that you practiced magical tricks," Sara said, trying to return to a semblance of normal conversation.

"But that would be a lie," Quinn said flatly. His eyes blazed. "I'm not going to lie to you about what I am, Sara. It's a bad precedent."

She had to agree with that. "Maybe I didn't see what I thought I saw." As she spoke, Sara realized how much she wanted this to be true. Quinn was the most attractive man she'd met in a long time and it would have been nice to have everything be uncomplicated between them. She was ready to fall in love, ready to make a lifetime commitment, ready maybe even to find her future with a man like Quinn.

She'd really prefer that the man in question not be nuts. Or weird. Or a stalker.

She was fussy like that.

"Then let's review," Quinn said softly. He put his left hand on the cash desk. He glanced around them but the bookstore was empty. He closed his eyes briefly and straightened slightly. He seemed to become radiant before Sara's own eyes. He took a deep breath and opened his eyes.

They glittered like blue ice.

She sat back in alarm, then looked down at his hand. The nail on his thumb had changed to a long talon. He let her look at it, turning his hand so she could see the talon from all angles.

It looked awfully real. Sara had to be sure.

She reached across the cash desk and grasped his thumb. Quinn seemed startled; he caught his breath but he didn't pull away. He was warm, as usual, and she felt a pulse of heat at their point of contact. His skin seemed to be getting warmer where she touched him, and sparks danced from that point of contact.

She looked at Quinn and he smiled. He seemed content to let her examine his talon with her touch. Sara fingered its sharpness and felt the length of its point.

It was real and it was part of him.

"Change it back," she challenged, knowing there could be no trick while his hand was within hers.

"Are you sure?"

Sara nodded. "I want to feel it, to know that it's not an illusion."

Quinn nodded agreement.

She held Quinn's gaze and his thumb, sensing that he was mustering his strength for something. His eyes narrowed, he exhaled, and Sara felt the nail change shape beneath her grip. His eyes glittered for a moment, then returned to normal.

Sara lifted her hand from his, and his thumb nail was just as it should be. "How did you do that?"

"I decided to." He shrugged, as if shaking something off, then pushed a hand through his hair.

"It's not logical," Sara protested. She was fascinated despite herself. She supposed she should have been afraid, but she was intrigued. Quinn seemed exotic and mysterious, but honest all the same. Sara felt even more attracted to him than she had before.

Maybe she was the one who was nuts.

Magda had often said that it was good for a person to believe ten impossible things before breakfast. It was only just past lunch, so Sara was running late, but she had to think that this day was setting some kind of record on her Impossible Things Scale.

It said something that reading Sigmund Guthrie's book about slaying dragons was the most reasonable choice of what to do next.

Chapter 4

Sara was with him until he mentioned destined mates. Quinn saw the change in her expression, saw skepticism replace any desire to believe. It was further than he'd expected to get on his first try, although, as always, he would have liked to have achieved more.

How could he protect her unless she accepted their linked future? Quinn bit back his frustration and focused on hanging the door knocker, giving her a bit of time to come to terms with all he'd said.

A bit of time was pretty much all they had.

"Did the guy who claimed to be leader of the *Pyr* say what his name was?" he asked as he marked the position for the door knocker.

"Erik Sorensson," Sara replied. "Why?

Quinn turned to stare at her. "Are you sure?"

"Yes. Do you know him?"

"Yes." Quinn drilled a hole for the screw, his annoyance rising. It figured. Erik Sorensson. There was no shaking that guy and no matter how much he took from Quinn, he always turned up looking for more.

"What did he look like?"

"I thought you knew him."

"We've only met in dragon form."

Sara blinked, but didn't question that further. "Tall, slim, and trim. Good-looking. Black hair with gray at the temples. Black leather jacket, despite the weather. A bit intense, really." Sara frowned. "I think he was in your booth this morning."

Quinn's blood ran cold. It was no wonder he hadn't recognized Erik, as they hadn't ever met in human form—and the times their paths had crossed hadn't endured long enough for Quinn to have a good sample of Erik's scent.

Until today.

Was Erik leading the true *Pyr*, or the *Slayers*? Quinn was inclined to believe the latter, given his own experiences with Erik. He had a very bad feeling about Erik speaking to Sara, but didn't want to frighten her further.

Quinn secured the mermaid to the door, then glanced up to find Sara immersed in one of the books Erik had chosen for her. What exactly had the so-called leader of the *Pyr* suggested that she read? Quinn put the tools away and cleaned up the bit of sawdust, and Sara kept reading.

"Is his recommended read any good?" he asked.

Sara glanced up and shrugged. "I don't like it much."

"Why not?"

"It's nasty." She flipped to the front cover, then back. "This Sigmund Guthrie guy was obsessed with killing dragons and making sure they stayed dead. There are all these rituals and mystical mumbo jumbo." She smiled and wrinkled her nose in a way that made her look young and cute. "I'd think that dead was dead, but that shows what I know."

"There's probably some key truth buried in the mumbo jumbo. It's an old way of ensuring that ways of power stay secret."

"Really?" She considered this and surveyed the shelves. "I read one book that talked about healers disguising the one active ingredient in their potions by including lots of other stuff."

"Eye of newt and toe of frog."

"Or is it hair of dog?"

"It might not matter, if that's the disguise." Quinn was relieved when she smiled.

"It makes sense in a way. Like protecting your technical secrets to keep anyone else from profiting from them." She glanced at the cover of the book again, then drummed her fingers on it. "Why do you think he wanted me to read this?"

Quinn leaned on the door frame. He had an idea but he didn't like it much. "Well, according to the prophecy, you're supposed to be the Seer."

Sara laughed. Quinn was entranced by the sight. Her eyes sparkled, like sunlight on the surface of the sea, and kept dancing when she sobered. "I am *so* not a seer. It was a family joke that I was the only one who didn't have an intuitive bone in my body."

"Yet here you are."

She ran her hands across the counter. "I used to spend summers with my aunt Magda here, and help in the shop. She was so different from the rest of my family that it was like visiting another planet."

"How so?"

"She consulted her tarot cards about everything. I mean, *everything*. She shopped at thrift stores, which meant she had the oddest wardrobe ever. And whenever I thought she was just weird, she'd look at me and tell me exactly what I was thinking."

"Because she could read your thoughts."

Sara shook her head. "No. She was just a good judge of character."

"Aren't they two sides of the same coin?"

She was startled by that idea. "That sounds like something my mother would have said. Magda was actually my maternal grandmother's sister."

"Is it true that psychic abilities are often inherited, on the female side?"

Sara smiled. "I've heard that before, too. My mother used to read tea leaves, actually. She said it helped her make new friends when we moved, and we moved a lot."

"Was she ever right?"

"Yes. Usually." Sara blinked and hesitated. "She said she was just a good judge of character."

Quinn laughed.

"It doesn't matter," Sara protested, that smile playing with her lips. "I'm the practical one. I'm the one who adds it all up at the end of the day. That's what I do. I don't know why I'm even giving this nonsense any credence. It's crazy."

Quinn could sense that he was losing her again.

He could only think of one way to show her that this—and he—was real.

Sara inhaled sharply. "I should call Malone's about that air conditioner," she said quickly. "It's really hot in here."

"It's not the air conditioner, Sara. It's the firestorm." Quinn knew immediately that he'd said too much.

"No," she said with a firm shake of her head. "No. This is nuts. There is no firestorm. There is no prophecy and if there is, it's about somebody other than me. I've got an inventory to reconcile and a bookstore to run and you've got an art show to do." She lifted her chin and glared at him with defiance that only made him want to protect her.

The scarf around her neck and the bruise it hid were all too potent a reminder of the price he'd pay if he failed.

He'd paid it before, thanks to Erik Sorensson. The situation took on more urgency for him.

"You have to come with me," Quinn said with resolve.

"Excuse me?"

"We have to stay together. It will be safer for you."

Sara lifted one brow, her tone making her skepticism clear. "Because you're the Smith and I'm the Seer?"

"You don't have to believe it, Sara, to recognize that someone tried to kill you last night."

She swallowed and looked down. "It could have been an attempted mugging."

"Did he take your purse?"

She swallowed and frowned. "I won't stay late, if that makes you feel better."

"The only thing that will make me feel better is if you come with me, right now." Quinn leaned forward for emphasis when her lips set. "It's not safe for you to be alone, not now that they know where you are."

"I thought your door knocker was your sentinel."

"I didn't get here fast enough." Quinn disliked the reminder but he wouldn't shirk the truth. "Anything could have happened to you in that time. If Erik had intended to hurt you, it would have been over by the time I got here." He knew his voice was rising and he didn't care. "That's not good enough."

Sara folded her arms across her chest and leaned back. "I thought you could sense when I'm in trouble? Like you did last night?"

Her doubt irritated Quinn, because he was having doubts himself about his ability to protect her. "They know where you are, Sara, and they're determined to stop the firestorm. . . ."

"Why? What does the firestorm mean?"

Quinn gritted his teeth, not having wanted the conversation to go in this direction just yet. "It's a mating sign," he admitted, knowing he sounded annoyed because he was.

"A mating sign?" Sara's eyes widened. "The other dragon shape shifters want to keep you from having sex?"

Quinn wasn't sure that telling Sara more was going to make this any better. He didn't have the chance, anyway. Sara crossed the store with decisive steps. He'd hit a nerve and he wasn't sure what it was.

"You're getting a bit ahead of things, don't you think?" she said when she turned. "We've only just met, so maybe you don't realize that I'm not the kind of woman who goes for quickies or one nighters."

"Sara, it isn't about—"

"No, it never is, is it? It's always about forever and ever, until it's done and then the man of the hour has somewhere else to be. I've read that book and seen that movie, thanks just the same." Her expression turned hard. "It wasn't compelling enough to be worth buying tickets again."

Quinn knew that look. It was the look of a woman who had been wounded in relationships before but still believed in love.

"Forget the mating sign and the prophecy, then," he argued. "You have to admit that someone tried to hurt you and might try again. Let me ensure your safety, at least."

"No. I can take care of myself." Sara hauled open the door and gestured to the arcade. "Thanks for hanging the door knocker, Quinn. Maybe I'll see you around."

Quinn tried one last time. He had to—it wasn't just a matter of life and death; it was a matter of his mate's life and death. He paused beside her on the threshold. "Sara, it's not what you think. Protecting you is my responsibility. . . ."

Her gaze was hard. "I've done just fine protecting myself for thirty-four years, Quinn, thanks. I find it's easier to just rely on myself than to count on someone who might not hang around."

"You haven't protected yourself against *Slayers*, Sara.

You don't know what you're up against. You *can't* know what you're up against, and you haven't got the tools to fight back."

"But there were no *Slayer*s in my life until you turned up and I'm not convinced there are any now. One nasty attempted mugging doesn't make a whole team of bad guys. Have a good day, Quinn."

"Sara! I'm not leaving you alone!" Quinn held his ground, knowing that she couldn't physically toss him out of the shop. He'd change shape if he had to. He'd do whatever was necessary to ensure that she was safe.

Then Sara looked him straight in the eye and said the only thing that could have changed his mind. "I don't want you to stay."

Quinn knew then that if he won this battle, he'd lose the war.

"You're wrong," he said softly. "It's risky."

"I'll take my chances," she said, without a hint of hesitation.

On some level, he admired her bravery. On another, he hoped it wouldn't cost them everything. He only left her then because he had one weapon in his arsenal that she didn't know about.

"Fair enough." Quinn stepped through over the threshold. "Will you do me a favor?"

"What?"

"Lock the door."

She smiled. "That's not very good for business."

"But better for your health."

She shrugged, but he liked that she was considering his suggestion. Maybe she wasn't as confident as she wanted him to believe. He knew how much it hurt to trust someone and then be let down by that person, and he couldn't blame her for wanting to avoid that.

They'd only just met, after all. He needed time to win her trust.

Quinn could only hope that he had that time. He paused and leaned closer to her, lowering his voice. "I'm going only because you want me to," he said. "You understand that, don't you?"

"And you don't like it. I get that, too." Sara didn't look as if she found his protectiveness offensive.

Quinn could understand the desire to fend for oneself. After all, he was the one who preferred to be self-reliant. It would have been nice not to have had this particular trait in common with his mate, but Quinn could understand it.

He spared a glance up and down the arcade, well aware that Sara was watching him. People wandered its length, considering the merchandise in the shop windows and appearing harmless. He couldn't smell any other *Pyr*. He met Sara's gaze, not troubling to hide his concern. "You know where to find me."

"Will you hear me if I scream?" she said, teasing him slightly.

"I'll hear you *decide* to scream," he said with conviction and saw her surprise. "I just hope that's good enough."

She didn't flinch, though, and didn't recant. Sara just nodded, then shut the door firmly. Quinn smiled in relief when he heard her turn the lock. She flipped the sign to read OUT FOR LUNCH, then pulled down the blinds.

It was a start. Quinn summoned his will and breathed a trail of smoke. He couldn't protect Sara's person with his smoke but he could mark a location as being his territory. Her shop would be his territory, just as her home was.

That would protect Sara, so long as she remained within the store. He walked back to his booth, focusing his effort on his task. Quinn breathed smoke and wove a protective cocoon around The Scrying Glass, hoping that what he could do would be enough.

He had his doubts.

Sara leaned against the locked door of The Scrying Glass and heaved a sigh. She didn't like Sigmund Guthrie's book and didn't want to read any more of it, despite Erik's advice. It was a vicious and bloodthirsty volume, the author a bit too interested in carnage and cruelty to make it an enjoyable read.

Sara felt a headache dawning and wondered whether low blood sugar was the real culprit. Maybe she had been hallucinating when Quinn turned into a dragon.

And when the mermaid gleamed.

And when his nail changed to a talon.

Or maybe it was all true.

There was something a bit too appealing about the idea of a mating sign with Quinn Tyrrell. He was incredibly sexy and she liked being in his company. She liked his sense of humor and how easy it was to talk to him. He made her feel feminine and precious, which wasn't all bad.

But casual sex was not her thing, even dressed up with talk of destiny. Sara had made the mistake of confusing the patter with the truth once before and she wasn't going to do that again. And counting on other people, well, that always led to a letdown. She could count on other team members professionally, but emotional reliance was another thing altogether.

She had only to look at the last year of her life to see the truth of that. It would have been easier to face her parents' accidental death followed by that of Aunt Magda if Tom hadn't chosen to bolt from her life at the same time.

The only good thing was that she hadn't married him. The break had been quick and clean: he'd been there one

Sunday when she flew out and vanished from her apartment and her life as surely as if she'd never known him by the time she returned on the subsequent Friday.

If wanting more from a man than one night of sex made her an idealist and a romantic, well, Sara could live with that. She wanted a long-term partnership, a commitment that continued after a weekend of sex, and she wanted it enough to wait for it.

She would not think about Quinn and chocolate.

Not now.

Besides, she couldn't be Quinn's destined mate since she wasn't a seer. That was that, and it was nonnegotiable, even if it did leave her feeling a bit down.

What she needed on a more immediate basis was lunch. Sara headed to the back room and the small fridge where she'd put her sandwich earlier that morning. At least the fridge was still working—the shop was as hot as a furnace.

Again. Four service calls and four miraculous self-cures. Sara knew the repairman had just parked his truck on Maynard Street when the unit recovered.

Even though that made no damn sense.

But then, nothing else did on this day.

Once in the back room, Sara glared at the control for the air-conditioning unit.

This had no discernible effect on its operation.

The unit itself was on the roof of the building. There was a control in the back of the shop, with a thermostat, and a fan housed in the ceiling. There must have been ductwork above the plaster, because there were several vents in the ceiling of the shop. Sara thought they looked ugly in the beautiful plaster, but she'd finally appreciated them when the weather turned hot.

At least when the air conditioner had worked. There was also a hot air intake at the back of one side wall, which was no less ugly, but it was less visible due to the shelves of books.

The repair guy from Malone's had put a sticker with their phone number on the thermostat. As if Sara would call them again, when they hadn't been able to fix the unit before.

The strange thing was that this back room was much colder than the shop. Sara assumed that was because it was farther from the windows and door that would be letting the heat in, but she shivered all the same.

She poked at the thermostat, having no idea what she was doing but needing to do *something*. She set the temperature lower, hoping the unit would begin a cycle.

It sputtered, momentarily inspired, and fell silent again.

Sara pushed the needle below fifty degrees in her frustration. There was a brief rumble overhead, then nothing.

"Stupid thing," she muttered. "It's not that cold even in this room." She shoved the indicator down to thirty degrees.

The fan whirred for a moment, then something rattled all the way across the ceiling of the shop, as if a bolt were being tossed across the length of the ductwork. It pinged on the far side and the fan slowed to silence.

"I'm not calling for service again!" Sara told the thermostat and gave it a smack with her hand. Of all the irrational things that had happened, this was the worst. An air-conditioning unit was mechanical, a machine, that should work or not work according to perfect logic.

Sara thought about a sexy man who remained sexy even when he changed into dragon and back, the chance that she had a stalker who wanted to kill her, the fact that everyone she'd loved was dead, how hungry and hot she was, and smacked the control again in frustration.

The thermostat cover popped off.

It fell to the floor and Sara swore. She used every one of

the words she'd learned as an army brat, stringing them all together into one long cuss.

It was a very satisfying monologue.

And it changed nothing.

So, she scrambled after the thermostat cover, which had disappeared under an ancient chair of Magda's. It was the one Sara had been meaning to donate to Goodwill to make more space, but she hadn't yet figured out how to get it there without a car. She stretched to reach underneath it and her fingers brushed against an army of dust bunnies as well as the thermostat cover.

They also touched velvet.

Velvet?

Sara got down on her hands and knees to peer under the chair. There was a little bit of velvet tumbled against the wall, as if it had fallen from the chair.

Well, that wasn't implausible. There was so much stuff stacked in this tiny room that anything could fall and not be found again. And she'd even ditched a bunch of it. Sara reached in and grabbed both the thermostat cover and the velvet.

It proved to be a small drawstring bag, of the softest and reddest velvet Sara had ever seen. It was heavier than she'd expected and Sara opened the drawstring.

There was a deck of dog-eared tarot cards inside.

Sara stood up in a hurry. Were these Magda's cards? She'd been wondering what had happened to them, but had assumed she'd inadvertently pitched them in her cleaning of house and shop.

Had Magda ensured that Sara got these?

The air conditioner whirred to life, as if agreeing with that whimsical thought.

Again.

"Don't mess with my mind like that," Sara said crossly and the unit fell silent again.

Coincidence. Sara was sure of it. There must be faulty wiring at root and the last thing she needed was a fire. She clicked the cover back onto the thermostat, then opened the electrical box. She flicked the circuit breaker for the air conditioner, cutting the power to it until she got it serviced again.

She returned to the cash desk, only realizing when she got there that she still held the velvet bag of tarot cards. She looked around, checking for witnesses, then surrendered to impulse.

What was the worst thing that could happen?

Sara drew a card.

It was called "The Lovers" and it was faceup in Sara's hand.

She had a pretty good idea that she knew what that meant, but she grabbed a book on tarot cards from the appropriate section and looked it up, just to be sure.

"A destined lover appears in your life," she read. She ate her sandwich without tasting it, maybe because she was thinking more about chocolate than tuna salad. *"A romantic relationship comes to physical union."* She closed the book and stared at the cards. "That was a fluke," she told them and drew another.

It was the same card, in the same orientation.

After she drew the card six times, Sara had an idea. Maybe it was a whole deck of the same card. She flipped the deck over and spread it across the counter. She checked it carefully, but there was only one card called "The Lovers."

She took a deep breath, shuffled, and drew another card.

"The Lovers."

"All right!" she said to the store. "All right, Magda. I give up! What if I admit that there's something to all of this weird stuff?"

The air conditioner whirred to life and ran with quiet efficiency.

But that was impossible! Sara ran to the back room and confirmed that there was no electricity running to the unit. The circuit breaker was just as she had left it, but the unit was running more smoothly than it ever had.

So, it was an air-conditioning unit that didn't actually need electricity. On this particular day, that actually seemed reasonable.

Plus, it was as green a solution to summer heat as Sara could imagine. If she could somehow distribute ghosts to every household in America, so that appliances ran without requiring electricity or creating emissions, she could save the planet for everyone.

Now she did sound crazy.

Sara leaned her forehead against the wall. "If you can fix it so I don't get an electrical bill for this, that would really convince me," she whispered.

The air conditioner kicked up to a higher power.

Sara remembered that she had turned the thermostat really low. She adjusted it to a moderate temperature and the unit purred happily.

Just when it seemed that things couldn't get weirder, the book fell.

Sara pivoted slowly, the hair rising on the back of her neck. There was no one in the shop but her. She knew it. She'd locked the door.

But there was a book on the floor in the aisle that led from the cash desk to the back room. It was bound in red linen.

Sara left the back room with a certain caution. She looked into the back corners of the store, then down the adjacent aisles. "Hello?" she called, feeling stupid when no one answered her.

She was alone. Of course. She eased toward the book, looked down at it for a minute, and then realized what had happened.

Someone had just left it on the edge of the shelf. Gravity had won. There was nothing spooky about that. She picked up the book and put it back into the gap at eye level where it must have been.

Then she returned to the front to eat her lunch.

She only made it to the end of the aisle before a book fell behind her again. Sara glanced back, her heart skipping a beat when she saw that it was the same book.

Impossible was starting to sound like a relative term.

She strode down the aisle, picked up the book, and shoved it back on the shelf. This time, she stayed and waited. She had just long enough to feel dumb before the book started to move toward her.

It was as if a finger was pushing it off the shelf.

An invisible finger.

The book was apparently shoved the last increment and Sara jumped back as it fell to the floor in front of her. She peered into the gap but there was no one there.

The hair on her neck stood up and saluted.

"Aunt Magda? Are you messing with my mind?"

Was it Sara's imagination that the air conditioner began to run even more smoothly?

She picked up the book and looked at the spine. She hadn't gotten to this section in her reading yet.

Awakening the Psychic Within.

Sara laughed. She knew when to take a hint.

Quinn marched back to his booth. Prepared to brood, he threw himself into his lawn chair. He thanked the volunteer, who scurried away from his dark mood with obvious relief. Maybe Sara hadn't run when he'd shifted shape, but things couldn't be said to be going well. He had to respect her choice, but he didn't have to like it.

He had three days left in Ann Arbor.

He didn't want to think about how long it would take the *Slayers* to make another attempt on Sara's life.

But he didn't want her to think she had a stalker named Quinn Tyrrell, either. He buttressed the protective smoke that he had exhaled to surround her store and worked on the cocoon around her house for good measure. Maybe he could ensure that he was with her when she moved between the two locations.

A guy could only hope.

"It's enough to make a *Pyr* yearn for the good old days," a voice murmured in old-speak.

Ambrose?

Quinn blinked in shock. No, it couldn't be Ambrose. Ambrose was dead. It would be too good to be true to have Ambrose beside him again, offering him advice and knowledge, but Erik had killed him. Ambrose was dead, and Quinn regretted that fact for the umpteenth time.

The old-speak had to be coming from Erik. Only a *Slayer* would mess with another *Pyr*'s mind like this. Quinn should have anticipated the game.

The voice continued, low and persuasive. "Ah yes, there was a time when a princess could be captured and seduced at leisure, well away from the assistance of well-intentioned, if somewhat misguided, suitors."

The voice could have been Quinn's own thoughts. It was in his head, but not from his head. The old-speak was heavily threaded with guile. There was an intruder, thinking in Quinn's head, meshing his ideas with Quinn's own. The voice sounded like Ambrose, who had been dead a good seven centuries. Quinn felt a reluctant surge of admiration.

Erik was good.

Quinn couldn't detect any recent sign of Erik's scent and doubted that the other *Pyr* was close by. There was no one else who looked *Pyr*, although it was difficult to tell with human forms. No one was even looking directly at him.

The mermaid, he knew, was stone cold, so Sara wasn't in danger.

Quinn decided to lure the speaker. He might learn something. He sent out the whisper of old-speak, broadcasting it since he didn't know the location of the other *Pyr*.

"These days, any given princess would just call the cops on her cell if she was abducted," Quinn said. "And authorities are unlikely to have a sense of humor about dragons in their precinct."

He heard an exhalation of surprised laughter, one that he was quite sure came on a puff of smoke.

He looked, but couldn't see it.

"How right you are," the voice acknowledged. "Women, although delightful, can be so troublesome." The voice became fainter, although whether that was due to distance or the speaker weakening, Quinn couldn't be sure. "Unpredictable."

He spoke again, hoping to lure the speaker closer. "That's not part of their charm?"

The chuckle sounded like the tumbling of old rubble. "Oh, I take great delight in Sara's choices, I assure you." Quinn's heart clenched at the other *Pyr*'s ready use of his mate's name. "Which of us, do you think, is watching her more closely?" There was another throaty laugh, and then silence.

It was more than silence: it was the absence of another being.

The other *Pyr* was gone.

Although he'd left Quinn with plenty to think about.

Quinn didn't doubt that Erik had planned it that way.

It was close to her usual closing time when Sara got to the end of the book on psychic powers. She glanced at her watch and decided to leave the store early to avoid a repeat of events of the night before. She wanted to push her way through a crowded arcade instead.

The book was interesting, as it suggested that everyone was psychic on some level: the trick was opening one's mind to perceive what was already there. Many people used tools, like crystal balls, more to focus their thoughts and impressions than as instruments per se.

Sara's gaze fell on Magda's tarot cards. They were as good a focus as anything. She shuffled the deck and chose a card, flipping it over and placing it on the counter.

"The High Priestess."

And it was upside down.

Sara pulled out her reference book and smiled when she read that the card concerned matters of intuition. She already knew that cards that were inverted were interpreted as being negative versions.

So, this could be about her denying her own intuition.

But Sara had had that message a couple of times already and although she was still skeptical, she thought the cards could have coughed up something a little more compelling. On a whim, she stared at the card, trying the meditation technique mentioned in the book she'd just read.

It was a pretty card, with a woman sitting like a queen on a throne, a heart at her feet and a scepter in her hand. Even upside down, it was attractive. Sara focused her attention on the card and felt everything around her slip away. The hum of the air-conditioning unit faded to nothing. The sound of footsteps and voices in the arcade slipped into a fog. The colors of the books and posters surrounding her disappeared from view. Even the oak edge of the countertop seemed to dissolve beneath her fingers.

There was only the card. The colors of the woman's garments seemed to become more vivid. Sara was certain that the background had changed: she didn't remember the woman being seated in a dark cave. She'd been sure there were fields and sunshine on the card. The woman pictured on it smiled back at Sara.

But upside down, that smile was sad.

And Sara hadn't noticed the shackle on the woman's ankle.

The woman's mouth seemed to move, as if she were speaking to Sara. Sara leaned closer and heard her scream.

Don't hurt me!

It was the voice Sara had heard in her dream that morning, but even more anguished than it had been. The woman's pain was almost tangible and the sound of her fear made Sara's stomach knot. She touched the edges of the card, wanting to help but not knowing how.

It is forbidden to injure the Wyvern!

Sara heard a shackle rattle, as if the woman fought to free herself. She heard something else, a dark chuckle, the sound of a man who liked to hurt women.

NO!

The woman's voice rose to a scream that curdled Sara's blood, then faded to nothing.

Sara picked up the card, but it was the same as it had been in the first place. A woman sat on a throne and smiled. She wore no shackle. She sat in the sunshine surrounded by fields. Sara turned the card over, wondering whether she'd imagined the woman's cry for help.

But she felt shivery and frightened, as if she'd witnessed

a crime and done nothing to prevent it. A shadow seemed to pass over her and she shuddered. She blinked and looked around. It no longer seemed so smart to be alone in the shop, no matter what time it was. She gathered her things, shoved the tarot cards into her purse, and opened the door of the shop.

There was a gold coin on the threshold, one that hadn't been there earlier.

Sara thought of the coin that had been tossed to distract her the night before. She looked up and down the arcade, but saw only tourists and shoppers. That didn't make her feel any less nervous. She snatched up the coin, locked the door behind herself, and ran toward the State Street exit.

Quinn's booth was there. Quinn would know what to do.

Sara didn't see the man step out of the shadows at the other end of the arcade and leisurely stroll after her. She would have been frightened if she had noticed him, for his silhouette would have been familiar to her.

A gold coin wasn't the only thing she'd seen the night before.

Chapter 5

Quinn was restless all afternoon. He was terse with potential customers, although he still did a good bit of business. Maybe people expected artists to be preoccupied and cranky. His thoughts were on Sara, part of him wanting to sit vigil outside of her shop and the other part of him knowing that would end his courtship of her before it started.

He paced.

He reviewed the old-speak that sounded like Ambrose and didn't like it one bit.

He reviewed his memories of Erik's treachery and liked those even less.

Finally, he packed up his booth impatiently. The show didn't end until eight that night, but Quinn couldn't stand around any longer. He couldn't even trust his instincts, as his desire to go to Sara became stronger with every passing moment.

Was something wrong?

Or did he just dislike his own inactivity?

Probably he was remembering his failures of the past.

He dismantled his awning with practiced ease and was putting the last piece into his trailer when he caught a whiff of something. He pivoted to find Sara heading directly for him, her quick movements telling him that something *was* wrong. She was visibly upset and looked on the verge of tears.

Quinn already knew that wasn't like Sara.

He abandoned the awning pieces and met her across the street. He caught her elbows in his hands and looked into her eyes when he felt her trembling. "What's wrong? What happened?"

And why hadn't he sensed it sooner?

She leaned into his embrace just a little, just enough to tell him that she had been coming to him. "It sounds crazy."

Quinn smiled. "It probably won't to me."

She glanced up and smiled tentatively. "Maybe not. Do you know who the Wyvern is?"

Quinn thought he had been prepared for anything but Sara's question surprised him all the same. "The Wyvern? Of course." He shook his head and clarified. "I know the concept of the Wyvern, but I don't know who she is or where she is. Why? What do you know about her?"

"I heard her." Sara licked her lips. "I was trying to meditate and I pulled a tarot card and I heard the Wyvern scream for help."

"How did you know it was the Wyvern?"

"It was a woman." Sara closed her eyes and frowned, then swallowed. She was visibly troubled. "Someone was hurting her, Quinn, and she said that it was forbidden to injure the Wyvern." She opened her eyes and looked up at him. "I don't think whoever was hurting her listened."

Quinn was troubled. He didn't doubt that Sara believed she had truly heard the Wyvern's call for help. He was skeptical, though.

Did Erik know about this?

Or was he responsible for it?

Sara shuddered, then lifted her chin. "I heard her this morning, too. Who is the Wyvern and how can we help her?"

"Let me think for a minute." Quinn slipped an arm around Sara's shoulders and led her to his booth. She sat in his lawn chair as he packed up the last of the awning. Her gaze flicked over his black pickup truck and silver trailer, then watched him. She looked smaller, if determined, and he didn't care for the change.

"Have you eaten?" When she shrugged indifference, Quinn led her from his booth. "First things first," he said and she smiled.

They walked across the Diag, their fingers interlaced, to a stall selling falafels. At her nod of agreement, Quinn bought several and they claimed a bench in the shade to eat.

"The Wyvern is unique among us. The *Pyr* are all male," he began to explain. "And the gene passes in families. My father was the Smith before me and my brothers were all *Pyr* as well, or would have been."

"Were? Are they dead?"

Quinn nodded once, not dwelling on that detail. If he did, he'd start thinking hostile thoughts about Erik again, and this wasn't the time. "Legend holds that there can be only one female *Pyr* at any given point in time, that there really is only one female *Pyr*. When she dies, there is no female *Pyr* until she's reborn. She can be born to any family that carries the *Pyr* gene and her reappearance is never guaranteed. There can be long intervals of time without a Wyvern."

"So, she's pretty special."

"Doubly so, because the one female *Pyr* is reputed to have the power of prophecy. She's the one who can see the pending firestorms and she knows the names of our destined mates. In some eras, she's been seen as the guardian of our future." He paused, seeing that Sara was thinking furiously.

"So, if you were a *Slayer*, for example—"

"Don't even say that out loud," Quinn interrupted.

"Theoretically."

Quinn wouldn't even consider the concept. "Understand that I am of the true *Pyr*. That's nonnegotiable. Do not even mention *them* in the same sentence as me."

She put down her falafel to study him. "What's the difference? It must be important."

"Absolutely." Quinn took a deep breath, tried to think of a way to be succinct, and knew there wasn't one. "In the beginning, there was the fire. . . ."

"No, that's not how it goes." Sara interrupted. "Genesis says that in the beginning, there was the Word."

Quinn smiled. "That's your story. This is ours." She shook her head, but she was listening. He'd take what he could get. "In the beginning, there was the fire, and the fire burned hot because it was cradled by the earth. The fire burned bright because it was nurtured by the air. The fire burned lower only when it was quenched by the water. And these were the four elements of divine design, of which all would be built and with which all would be destroyed. And the elements were placed at the cornerstones of the material world and it was good."

He paused. "But the elements were alone and undefended, incapable of communicating with each other, snared within the matter that was theirs to control."

Quinn glanced at Sara, who was listening raptly. "And so, out of the endless void was created a race of guardians whose appointed task was to protect and defend the integrity of the four sacred elements. They were given powers, the better to fulfill their responsibilities; they were given strength and cunning and longevity to safeguard the treasures surrendered to their stewardship. To them alone would the elements respond. These guardians were—and are—the *Pyr*."

"So, your role is to protect the elements?" Sara asked.

"To protect the four elements, as represented by the earth. You've probably heard that dragons guard treasures, like piles of stolen gold, but that's propaganda. The treasure we guard is the earth."

"It's in pretty bad shape right now," Sara observed and Quinn had to agree.

"It's said that a time will come when the earth retaliates against the injustices done to it, and it's our responsibility to bring mankind through this great crisis."

"Why?"

"Mankind is an older species than ours and we are charged with the protection of your kind. Mankind is among the treasures of the earth we are charged to defend."

"But what about *Slayer*s? Aren't they *Pyr*? Wouldn't trying to kill me go against that mission?"

Quinn knew his expression turned grim. "The *Pyr* believe that mankind is part of the earth's bounty while the *Slayer*s believe that mankind is the parasite destroying the earth."

"So, they kill humans and *Pyr*, since the true *Pyr* protect humans."

Quinn nodded, feeling Sara's gaze upon him. She was making sense of what he had told her, and he gave her the time to do it.

He was busy trying to decide what to do about her vision.

She watched him for a moment. "Having access to the Wyvern would be pretty handy for a *Slayer* interested in stopping firestorms."

Quinn saw the direction of her thoughts. "You mean holding the Wyvern captive, torturing her to release that information, then targeting the *Pyr* and woman involved." The thought sickened Quinn; it was such an abomination of everything he'd been taught. But it explained how the *Slayer* the night before had found Sara so quickly.

They knew her name.

What else did they know about her?

Fear made his gut clench. He put his falafel aside and braced his elbows on his knees to think.

"Are you okay?"

"It's not the food," Quinn said quickly. "It's the idea of anyone injuring the Wyvern. It's forbidden. She should be revered and honored. To injure her would be wrong."

Sara shuddered. "It sounded wrong."

"Do you know where she was? Or who was holding her captive?"

Sara shook her head and her hair slipped free of her ponytail. "Sorry. I'm not very good at this stuff yet."

Quinn put his hand over hers and squeezed. "But you tried and you found out that you're better at it than you expected."

She forced a smile and turned her fingers to lock with his. That heat simmered between their palms and Quinn knew he wasn't the only one staring at their locked hands with fascination. The power of the firestorm was awesome and undeniable. It made him acutely aware of the woman sitting beside him, of the heat of her knee so close to his own, of the smoothness of her skin and the honey hue of her tan. . . .

Sara tugged her hand from his, as if she needed to pull her own thoughts together. "We need to help her, Quinn."

Quinn wasn't persuaded of that. If *Slayer*s held the Wyvern captive, the last thing he wanted to do was take Sara closer to their lair. There were too many unknowns to make a decision of such importance. "I'm not sure how."

"Shouldn't we tell Erik? Isn't he your leader?"

Quinn shrugged, restless and irritated again. "That's what he says. I don't recall being invited to the election."

"You don't like him."

"I don't know him well enough to know whether I like him or not. I don't trust him, though."

"Why not?"

Quinn leveled a look at Sara. "He killed my best friend."

Sara could see the fury simmering in Quinn's eyes and understood his animosity toward Erik.

Funny, but she wasn't very hungry anymore, either.

She had to ask. "Was it an accident? I mean, could it have been?"

"No. It was murder." Quinn spoke with resolve, biting off the words and allowing no argument. He stared across the Diag, as if he were casually having a light meal, but Sara wasn't fooled. She could feel the anger emanating from him and sensed his raw power.

"Did you see it?"

"Yes."

"What happened?"

Quinn shook his head and looked bitter. "He came out of the sky in dragon form and challenged my only friend and mentor. They fought until Ambrose was dead. I was young and inexperienced and couldn't help much."

Quinn blamed himself for his friend's death. Sara could see that in the taut line of his lips. "Did he attack you?"

Quinn shook his head with impatience. "Maybe he didn't think I was worth the trouble, then."

Sara's mouth went dry. That was why Quinn didn't like Erik showing up when he did. He was suspicious of the other *Pyr*'s motives and she was feeling suspicious herself.

"Do the *Pyr* usually have a leader?" she asked.

Quinn shook his head, looking determined and annoyed.

"We're solitary. It's easier that way." He gave her a bright glance. "The *Slayer*s, now, they've always fought together."

"You think Erik leads the *Slayer*s."

"I'm thinking he might not be surprised to learn that the Wyvern is being held captive." Quinn pushed to his feet and offered Sara his hand, his manner decisive. "Why don't we find out?"

She stood up and gathered the wrappings of their dinner, disposing of it in the trash can. She came back to Quinn and put her hand in his. It was comforting to feel the strength of his fingers closing over hers. He was strong, but gentle with her.

Protective.

Yet he answered her questions honestly.

Sara could get used to that combination. "Can you find him that easily?"

Quinn smiled. "I can find anyone once I know their scent. It takes time and concentration." He inhaled and even though his eyes narrowed, Sara saw them glitter. His smile broadened slightly, giving him a confident and rakish air. "Over there."

Quinn walked quickly, his steps quiet on the pavement. Sara couldn't help thinking of a predator on the hunt. They strolled up one street and down another, and Quinn said the trail had been muddied.

"Too many tourists," he complained.

Sara wondered whether the other *Pyr* had left a confused trail on purpose. She was pretty sure Quinn had thought of that, too.

It was falling dark when they turned down a quiet street, one where Sara knew a boutique hotel was located. Cars were parallel parked along the curb and there was an exotic black car parked right in front of the hotel.

Quinn strode directly to it, then past it. He made a little
sound of disgust as they walked past the car, which was a
gleaming black Lamborghini.

"Cocky," Quinn muttered.

Sara glanced back at the car, uncertain what he meant.
Then she saw that the car had Illinois custom plates.

PYROMAN.

Quinn was looking up, scanning the tops of the buildings,
seeking something. "What's that?" he asked, gesturing to a
tower.

"The Burton Memorial Bell Tower," Sara said. "They
play the bells there. . . ." She wasn't able to finish her description because Quinn moved immediately in that direction.

"Perfect," he said under his breath.

"But you can't go up there at night. It's locked."

Quinn smiled as they walked across the small park to the
entry to the tower. "Is it?" he mused and she had a feeling he
was going to pick the lock.

Great. Now she was breaking the law. Another thing she
would have thought impossible just twenty-four hours ago.

But Quinn didn't have to pick the lock. When they drew
alongside the tower, he bent, the shadows making them invisible to passersby, and whispered to it. Sara saw him exhale, saw a little puff of smoke curling into the keyhole. By
the time Quinn straightened, the tumblers were rolling. He
gave her a triumphant smile—one that made her wonder
who was cocky—then opened the door.

"How did you do that?" she whispered, when he ushered
her inside. They stood in the darkness, Quinn holding her
hands so that she couldn't reach for a switch. Sara couldn't
see anything but she felt the cold stone surrounding them.

"It's metal," Quinn murmured, as if it was obvious. "I
sang its song."

"But that's impossible."

"Not for the Smith."

She felt the weight of his glance, heard the amusement in his words. Even though she was impressed by his powers, she felt the need to tease him. "What if it had been a computerized lock?"

His chuckle echoed in the dark space, making Sara shiver in a pleasurable way. "Then we would have been out of luck. Silicon doesn't hear my songs. I sing for iron and steel and brass."

The metals closest to the earth. Sara was beginning to understand why Quinn seemed to have such a primal strength, why her desire for him was so strong. She was with a man in touch with ancient mysteries and possessed of old powers.

She should have been frightened, but she wanted to know more.

"What now?" she whispered. "It's too dark to see anything."

"Not for me," Quinn said.

"You have X-ray vision?"

"No. We're more sensitive to sensory data." He bent and whispered in her ear, the fan of his breath making her even more aware of his proximity. She wanted to touch him, or have him touch her. "You have goose bumps right now," he whispered, his voice low and rich again. "Dancing down your back and legs."

Sara swallowed because it was true. She could feel the heat emanating from his skin and the clean smell of his skin. She was thinking of chocolate again and not really wanting to stop.

"I can feel them rising," Quinn continued, his melodic words awakening a heat in Sara's belly. "I can smell your skin from twenty feet away, and I can tell the color of your eyes, even in this darkness."

"That's easy," Sara said, hating that she sounded breathless. "They're hazel."

"No, they change," he said with such complete certainty that she didn't doubt him. "They turn greener when you laugh and more brown when you're angry. And they turn gold when—" He stopped abruptly.

Sara swallowed the lump that had risen in her throat. "When?"

"First things first," Quinn said, his manner businesslike. "We have something to do." He caught her hand in his and she followed him across the dark foyer. "Ten stairs to the first landing, about six inches high each. All right?"

"All right," Sara said, amazed that she trusted him. She lifted her foot, following just behind Quinn, and found the first step exactly as he had said.

It became brighter as they climbed, the streetlights casting their light into the open arches that surrounded the bells. Quinn kept to the shadows and Sara remained at the top of the stairs while he chose a vantage point. He tucked himself into the darkness in one corner, then beckoned to her to join him.

Quinn pulled her in front of him. "Down there. You see his car?"

Sara could see the polished black of the sports car. She nodded, but before she could speak, Quinn folded her between himself and the stone pillar at the corner. "I told you I'm not that kind of woman," Sara teased, knowing that he was shielding her.

"Keep your eyes open," Quinn said, not sharing her humor. "Something might happen."

"What are you going to do?"

"Get someone's attention."

"How?"

"By starting a fire close to his heart, such as it is."

Quinn's eyes narrowed as Sara watched and his gaze fixed on the car far below. Sara felt his concentration and saw his eyes glitter again. His lips set in a thin line and she knew his attention was completely diverted. She twisted to peek around the edge of the pillar, but for a long time, there was nothing to see.

Suddenly flames leapt inside the black Lamborghini, orange dancing against the lines of the roof. She saw Erik running down the street toward the car in the same moment that she heard Quinn chuckle.

"Coffee cup left on the dash," Quinn muttered. "Fool."

"You started a fire in his car?"

"Just a little one. Here he comes."

Erik looked up, straight at the bell tower, and Sara was sure she could see the blaze of his eyes even at this distance. He jumped off the curb, shouting something. He changed shape in midair, becoming a pewter and onyx dragon right before her eyes. His dark wings beat hard to carry him skyward.

If Sara had been hallucinating when Quinn changed shape, her delusions were getting worse.

Much worse.

"Get down!" Quinn commanded but Sara didn't need the warning. She didn't have to be psychic to know that trouble was coming. She crouched on the stone floor and backed toward the center of the tower. At the same time, Quinn leapt off the half wall, shimmered, and shifted in midair. He reared back as he hovered, his leathery wings beating powerfully. The silver and blue of his scales glinted against the night. He looked like a large jeweled beast, made of metal and armored against assault. He snarled, ready to meet his opponent, and Sara was awed again by his strength and confidence.

Although she did wonder what had happened to his clothes. It was as if they had folded away in the blink of an eye and disappeared.

Sara peeked over the lip of stone and caught her breath in fear. An emerald and gold dragon was airborne behind Erik, smoke streaming from his nostrils as he ascended.

Two against one! No fair!

But Erik and his friend were the least of Quinn's troubles. Sara glanced around, wondering who else had noticed the strange doings in the sky. She couldn't believe what she saw. Five dragons were closing fast on the bell tower from the other side. They didn't look friendly.

Seven to one. Sara's heart pounded with fear. Quinn was outnumbered and there was nothing she could do to help him.

Quinn had been right: he did hear Sara decide to scream.

He felt her agitation and glanced away from Erik, who was climbing fast. He saw Erik's second cresting the buildings on State Street. That wasn't the source of Sara's fear, though. Quinn surveyed the night sky and found five more dragons, all flying furiously toward him.

It had been a long time since Quinn had seen so many of his kind in one place and he could have done without it at this particular point. He didn't think he knew any of them, although the golden one conjured memories of a golden dragon in his past.

There was no time for sentimentality. Quinn turned away from Erik, taking care of the most critical business first.

He had to protect Sara. Even if he was wounded, his territory mark would keep the others at bay for a while.

If he was killed, that was another problem, but he

wouldn't think about it. Quinn had no intention of dying just yet.

Quinn exhaled silvery smoke, cursing the slow speed at which it emanated. Marking territory was intended to be a leisurely pursuit. It required concentration and contemplation, precisely the opposite frame of mind as fighting to the death.

His desire to rip out Erik's throat slowed Quinn's smoke production, there was no doubt about it. He tried to push himself to produce more quickly and knew the line of smoke would break if he went too quickly.

He forced his breathing to slow as he curled the smoke around the interior of the bell tower, between the perimeter of the tower and the bells hanging in the middle. He struggled to encircle Sara completely as quickly as possible. He had to leave enough space that if she moved, she didn't leave his protection.

On the other hand, he didn't have a lot of time.

Erik bellowed and broke Quinn's concentration. The line of smoke snapped and he started another, anxious to close the circle. He'd have to go back and weave in the ends at the break to make Sara's protection complete.

He was attacked first.

"Curse the Smith!" roared a ruby red dragon in old-speak as he erupted around the corner of the tower. Quinn was startled by his appearance. The leader of the band of five had flown more quickly than Quinn had expected.

The ruby red dragon landed on the railing of the bell tower and flicked an appreciative glance at Sara. His scales seemed to be edged in brass, like garnets set in gold. He was impressive and clearly quite old, and Quinn was wary.

"Fresh meat tonight," he said in old-speak, grinning with anticipation. Sara couldn't hear him, Quinn knew, but she understood her peril. He could tell by the way she was nearly hyperventilating. "Princess? Virgin? Or just your routine damsel-in-distress?" His tongue flicked. "I do like the tang that adrenaline gives a fresh kill, don't you?"

Quinn's tail moved with lightning speed and caught his assailant across the side of the head. The ruby red dragon choked and took a step along the parapet to correct his balance so that he didn't fall into Quinn's smoke. Quinn roared dragonfire at his attacker, forcing him to step backward off the ledge.

The ruby red dragon swore in a language Quinn didn't know as he stumbled off the wall. He dropped a good ten feet before his bronze wings began to flap. Quinn lunged after him.

His attacker was old and wily, though, and made a miraculous recovery when Quinn was within range. He raged upward at Quinn, his eyes shining with triumph. The pair locked claws, thrashing their tails at each other as they tumbled toward the ground.

Quinn was vaguely aware that the ruby red dragon's fellows were locked in battle with Erik and his second, a fact that made him wonder whom he was fighting. If Erik was a *Slayer*, as he'd suspected, then who were these five?

He'd worry about that later.

Quinn felt the strength of his opponent and decided to save time by playing the same trick on him. He grunted as the ruby red dragon scored a strike with his tail, and pretended to be failing.

"You've spent too much time in your lair, Smith," the ruby red dragon chuckled, exuding smoke into Quinn's face.

Quinn coughed as if overwhelmed. "While you've spent too little time tending your teeth," he replied, letting his voice sound weak.

The ruby red dragon's eyes flashed. He swung his tail and Quinn went limp when he took the hit, as if it had been more fatal than it was. He groaned and stopped flapping his wings.

He thought he'd be left to fall, but his opponent snatched him out of the sky. Quinn stifled a smile as the ruby red dragon carried him upward. Quinn was all muscle: lifting him would exhaust his opponent and give Quinn an advantage in addition to surprise.

"You have been lazy, Smith," his attacker said, his voice strained even in old-speak. "Who would have imagined it would be so easy to eliminate you? I had hoped for a better fight."

Quinn listened while he played dead. The ruby red dragon must be a *Slayer*, because no true *Pyr* would have wanted to kill the Smith. If he was as old as that, Quinn should have known him, but his voice was unfamiliar. It had a Russian cadence and Quinn couldn't remember any *Pyr* from the East.

It wasn't as if he'd been paying attention to his fellow *Pyr* for the last centuries, though.

And really, it mattered less who this *Slayer* was than that he could be beaten. Quinn surveyed his opponent's chest through narrowed eyes and found what he was seeking. He let the ruby red dragon carry him over the bell tower and waited for him to gloat.

He poked Quinn with one of his bronze talons and chortled. "Come, all of you!" he cried to his fellows. "The Smith has fallen and our work here is done." He started to chortle again, but his laughter was cut short.

Quinn made a miraculous recovery. He twisted, lunged, and bit the ruby red dragon in the chest. He had seen that there was a scale missing and Quinn sank his teeth into the weak spot.

Quinn felt his victim's surprise, he tasted the darkness of his blood, and he knew for certain that this was an old and

irredeemable *Slayer*. He bit deeper and harder, locking his
claws around the ruby red dragon's chest and holding him in
a death grip as he tore open the flesh on his chest.

The ruby red dragon screamed and tried to fling Quinn
away from him. He thrashed and fought, to no avail. He bellowed in rage, then dug his talons into Quinn's back. Quinn
tossed him away, certain the wound he'd made would slow
the other dragon down.

"That enough fight for you?" Quinn taunted in old-speak,
expecting another round of locked claws and battle.

To his astonishment, the ruby red dragon smiled, hovered, then turned tail and flew away. Quinn would have
raged dragonfire to finish the fight, but two other dragons set
upon him from behind.

He understood now why the leader had retreated: he'd
left his minions to do his dirty work. Quinn swung in fury at
such cowardice and caught the malachite green and silver
dragon across the face with his tail. His powerful blow
tossed the more slender *Slayer*'s body against the bell tower
roof. That dragon hit his head and slid down the smooth
copper, leaving a trail of black blood that hissed as it cor-
roded the metal.

In the heartbeat he had, Quinn saw Erik's second battling
ferociously with a topaz yellow *Slayer*. The emerald and
gold *Pyr* was not doing well and Quinn was inclined to help.
In that moment, though, Quinn saw Erik emerge from behind the tower, presumably where the fifth *Slayer* had fallen,
and fly to his companion's aid.

Quinn took a quick inventory: the malachite green *Slayer*
knocked out, the ruby red dragon having left the fight, the
topaz yellow *Slayer* fighting with Erik's second, and another
Slayer down behind the tower made four. There had to be
another of the attackers left.

Quinn turned slowly, but saw nothing.

He heard nothing.

He knew better than to believe that he was alone. He braced himself for assault.

A garnet red *Slayer* suddenly came over the roof and leapt down on Quinn. Quinn spun to defend himself, and locked claws with his attacker. This one was strong, his eyes burning with bloodlust that obviously affected his thinking.

Because he breathed fire on Quinn. Dragonfire could kill or fatally injure all *Pyr*.

Quinn was the Smith, though, and the exception. The dragonfire singed Quinn's shoulder even as it sent new strength through him. The singe invigorated him, the fire giving him new strength, making him brighter and better and more powerful.

He tore his claws from those of the garnet red *Slayer* and in the heartbeat of his opponent's surprise, Quinn seized him by the throat with fearsome speed.

"You call that dragonfire?" Quinn asked in old-speak. His opponent's eyes widened in fear and he began to fight Quinn's grip with new vigor. Quinn held him captive easily. "I call *this* dragonfire." Quinn summoned his most impressive fire and loosed a torrent of it on the garnet red *Slayer*.

The *Slayer* bellowed in rage and pain. Quinn held fast as the red scales dulled and burned, as the scent of burning flesh rose. The *Slayer* fought Quinn's grip, but Quinn was older and more determined.

They had come to kill Quinn's mate.

This one wouldn't make the same mistake again.

The younger *Slayer*'s eyes filled with fear as his scales were incinerated. He must have seen something in Quinn's expression, because he had the wits not to beg for mercy. Quinn heard the *Slayer* scream, first in old-speak, then aloud, felt him writhe, yet summoned the last increment of fire from his own belly and loosed it on the attacker. He felt the life force of the *Slayer* join his own and welcomed the surge of power.

That was when Sara decided to scream again. Quinn felt her pulse leap with fear, even though she didn't utter a sound. She needed him, but didn't want to distract him.

Without another thought, Quinn released the limp and charred dragon and let him fall. He dove toward the bell tower.

He moved too quickly, and didn't see that the malachite green *Slayer* he'd cast against the roof had recovered. The other dragon had hidden behind the corner of the tower and emerged only when Quinn had flown past him.

Quinn felt a brush of wind, and glanced back in time to see a tail closing fast. The malachite green *Slayer* struck a ferocious blow across Quinn's head, one that took Quinn completely by surprise and sent him tumbling senselessly toward the earth.

Chapter 6

It was like something out of a fairy tale. Sara could hardly believe her eyes. The dragons fought with fury, their tails lashing and their claws tearing. They breathed fire and exhaled smoke, and their wings pounded against the night sky. When they locked claws to fight at close range and fell earthward, she was fascinated and fearful.

Sara had run to the edge of the tower when Quinn had fallen into the clutches of the ruby red dragon. Her heart pounded in terror that Quinn had been injured.

But it was a feint. He rallied and slashed back at the ruby red dragon and she wanted to cheer.

She did cheer when the ruby red dragon turned tail, a trail of black blood running from his chest as he flew away. Far below her, Erik and the emerald green dragon that had flown with him fought with a topaz yellow dragon who seemed particularly strong. She didn't think the emerald dragon was that experienced a fighter.

Sara was more interested in Quinn's fate, though. She couldn't stop staring at him, entranced as she was by his grace and power. He was magnificent, all silver and blue, gleaming in the night as if his scales were jewels. He fought with agility, practiced and aware of his capabilities.

"Potent," said a man, as if he heard her thoughts.

Sara pivoted to find a golden dragon perched on the lip of the railing around the bell tower. He looked old and wily, and there was a malice in his gaze that Sara didn't trust one bit. His scales changed color slightly in the light, reminding her of the light that often danced in tiger's eye stones.

She caught her breath and bit back the urge to scream. She hoped against hope that Quinn really could hear her decision to scream and that he'd arrive shortly.

She had to stall for time.

Her attacker smiled a chilly smile and continued. "Quinn was always a good fighter. Passionate. Powerful. Calculating." The smile broadened. "He learned that last bit from me."

Sara backed away, distrusting the gleam in this *Pyr*'s eyes.

He moved slowly, as if choosing a place to step down into the tower. There wasn't a lot of room for him, given how massive he was, and Sara thought that was his concern, but he seemed to be studying the floor. It was as if he was searching for something, but Sara couldn't see what he was looking at.

She knew when he found it, though. He sniffed, exhaling a puff of smoke, then smiled as he stepped very precisely onto the bell tower floor. He even lifted his tail with one claw, as if he were climbing a fence. There was no doubting his satisfaction.

"Those small neglected details can be so very critical," he said, fixing his gaze upon Sara.

She didn't have to understand what he meant to know that she was in major trouble. "You stay away from me."

He laughed at the very idea. "I can't seem to resist you, Sara Keegan. Maybe it's fate entwining our paths."

"I don't think so."

"We've met, of course, though we haven't been formally introduced."

"That was you last night," she guessed as she backed away. She touched her throat and he seemed to be amused.

"Sore today?"

"Of course not."

"Liar! Don't try to win me over with guile, Sara. You're my assignment, no matter how charming you might be."

"I don't understand."

"Of course not. You're only human, after all, a species that is remarkably feeble both physically and intellectually."

The trick was to keep him talking. "Maybe you should explain it to me."

He paused to survey her and she didn't think he would answer. "Let me simply say that my fate has been knotted to that of the Smith for a long, long time. We have history, Quinn and I, although it will soon pass into memory."

"You're going to kill Quinn."

"You seem to be a reasonably clever human, after all." His gaze turned, assessing. "Or maybe you cheated. Is it true that the Smith must mate with the Seer before our final battle?"

"That's what I've heard," Sara said.

"How convenient, then, that the Seer can so easily be eliminated. It's almost too easy, really." He turned to glance over the city and raised a claw to draw her attention to one side. "Oh, now things are getting interesting." Sara looked, knowing that she wouldn't like whatever she saw.

Quinn was flying directly toward her, his eyes blazing with protective fury; then a dragon of striped green appeared behind him. Just as Quinn, sensing his presence, glanced back, the dragon hit Quinn across the head with his tail. Quinn stumbled immediately, the fire dimming in his gaze as he fell toward the earth.

It could have been a feint. Sara hoped.

She couldn't watch him tumble. If Quinn recovered, she didn't want her attacker to be aware of it. She forced herself to look at the golden *Pyr*, even as she prayed for Quinn.

"Oops." Her attacker sighed with false regret. "It's so important to check one's mirrors, don't you think?"

"That's not funny." Sara backed away, knowing her own future was looking grim.

His eyes narrowed to hostile slits. "I don't think we have to worry about any interruptions now, although I must say that I'm disappointed. A good long battle is always more satisfactory to win." He winked. "But maybe Quinn should have taken the time to learn more from me than he did. Ah well. I hope you've said your prayers, Sara."

Before she could answer, he reared back and filled his chest.

This didn't look good.

The fire came like a wall of flames. There was nowhere to go to evade it. Sara was already backed into the corner. She cried out and fell against the stone, putting her arms across her face. The fire was vivid orange, so bright she squeezed her eyes shut, so hot that she smelled the hairs on her arms singe.

"I think not," interjected a familiar voice with a faintly British inflection. "It is inappropriate to fry the Seer."

Sara found herself scooped up and tossed over the lip of the railing. She'd gone from the frying pan to the fire, so to speak. She was falling toward the ground, her singed skirt ruffling around her knees.

Then she really did scream.

Sara's scream pulled Quinn from the lip of unconsciousness. His fear for her mustered his strength, made it possible for him to regain his flying rhythm. He awakened, changed course a dozen feet above the ground, and lunged skyward out of pure instinct.

He saw Sara's falling body and adjusted his course, snatching her out of the air in midflight.

She gasped but clutched at him instinctively. Her eyes were wide with fear and he felt her relief when she realized who had saved her from death.

"Quinn!" she breathed. "You're all right!"

Quinn didn't answer. He flew with all the power he could summon. It was good that he had turned dragonfire on that *Slayer*; he needed every increment of power he had, and more.

His urge to see Sara safe was primal and undeniable. He held her close, cradling her against his pounding heart with one claw as he spiraled skyward.

He wanted his mate away from the *Slayer*s, away from Erik, away from everyone and anyone inclined to injure her. He felt her tremble against him and only now could acknowledge the depth of his own fear.

He heard someone take a blow, heard the keening cry of a dying *Pyr*, but knew his priorities.

He should never have moved without ensuring that it was safe.

He should have learned years ago that traps were set and that fools sprang them.

He should have known better.

It was only when he reached a great height that Quinn paused to look back. The air was a bit cooler at this altitude and the stars seemed close enough to touch. A few clouds gathered in the distance. Ann Arbor spread beneath them and the fields beyond seemed to stretch to the horizon. There was no one else close to them and Quinn relaxed slightly.

Sara glanced down. Her fingers tightened on Quinn and her skirt fluttered against his scales. "Don't let go," she said, a thread of humor in her tone.

"Never," Quinn said softly, feeling her shiver when he tightened his grip upon her.

She looked down then and he admired her resilience once again. "It looks like a quilt," she said quietly and leaned her cheek against his chest with a sigh. "I thought you were dead."

"I had that feeling myself."

He felt the fight slip from her and felt her quiver again. Then he felt her thinking. He assumed she was reviewing what she had witnessed and in a way she was, but her words surprised him.

"They planned that, you know," she said against his chest, her tone surprisingly matter of fact.

"What do you mean?"

"They divided up, to distract you and Erik and Erik's friend while the other one attacked me. They had a plan. They worked as a team."

That might have been true, but Quinn didn't care. "Fortunately it didn't work. Were you hurt?"

"I think I'm going to have a bit of sunburn on my arms, but otherwise, no." She looked up, her gaze filled with concern. "You?"

"Scorches and bruises."

She smiled and touched the gash the malachite *Slayer* had left on his temple. Her gaze flicked over him and he guessed that he had several other wounds. "No big deal?"

Quinn was dismissive. "I've had worse."

"I'll bet." There was admiration in her eyes and her hands ran over his scaled flesh lightly. He had the sense that she was familiarizing herself with his dragon form and he was glad, even if her caress awakened a heat that was very distracting. "It's impressive to watch you fight."

"I've done a bit of it in my time."

They gazed at each other as the firestorm danced along

Quinn's veins. Sara's eyes changed color as she stared at him, turning to a molten gold that only fed Quinn's desire. He wondered how light and bright they would become when she was more aroused, or when she climaxed, and he wanted to find out.

Immediately.

She touched his scales in wonder, then rapped her knuckles on them. "I thought they'd be cold. They look like metal." Before Quinn could answer, she frowned and fingered a spot over his heart. Her touch made him flinch. "There's a damaged one here."

"Yes." Quinn was tense, disliking that she had found his vulnerability so easily.

"Why?"

"Shit happens," he said, trying to make a joke.

Sara didn't smile. She studied him, obviously aware that that wasn't the whole story, but Quinn wasn't inclined to enumerate his weaknesses.

Not now. Not when he'd been so close to losing.

Again.

"Look," he said, distracting her with the flurry of activity at the bell tower below.

The malachite green *Slayer* and the topaz yellow *Slayer* were hoisting the corpse of the garnet red *Slayer* between them. Quinn's eyes narrowed as a golden *Slayer* tumbled from the bell tower, his flight erratic. He flew down to the other pair, moving as if he were in pain, and helped them hoist the body of the emerald and gold *Pyr* who had fought with Erik.

An onyx and silver *Pyr* emerged from the bell tower as if he would intervene. The three *Slayer*s launched a torrent of dragonfire in his direction when he might have pursued them, and he fell back with obvious reluctance, but only after his third attempt. He watched as the *Slayer*s flew in pursuit of their departed leader, then began a quick ascent toward Quinn.

Erik was angry, there was no doubting that, even at a distance.

"We're going to have company," Sara said, but Quinn was watching the golden dragon retreat. He couldn't be sure at this distance but there was something familiar about the way the *Slayer* moved. And his coloring was distinctive, with that flicker of tiger eye. Could there be two with scales of that unusual hue?

Had Ambrose had a son, one who had turned to the *Slayer* side?

"It was Erik who saved me, you know," Sara said quietly. "I recognized his voice."

"That makes no sense," Quinn said impatiently.

"You might be wrong about him."

"Didn't he also toss you over the rail?"

"It worked out all right," Sara protested.

"He couldn't have anticipated that. He might have been trying to kill you himself."

"I don't know," Sara mused, but Quinn didn't listen. She didn't know the whole story and he didn't have the time— or the inclination—to share it all with her.

First things first.

Quinn held his position, letting Erik come to him, even if Erik was looking for trouble. He was impressed that the other *Pyr* flew quickly and wasn't out of breath when he reached them. His gaze flicked over Sara, then darted over the wound on Quinn's brow.

Quinn expected a challenge to a blood duel and had already decided to let the coin fall if it was tossed, but Erik was terse.

He also spoke aloud, presumably for Sara's benefit. "It's past time we talked," he said succinctly. "I'll send the others out to beguile; then we'll convene in my hotel suite in an hour."

"I don't need to talk to you," Quinn said.

Erik spared Quinn a cold look. "I've lost a good man on your account. We can duel or we can talk."

"Maybe a blood duel would be better."

"Maybe there aren't enough of us that we can afford to fight each other over every little thing." Erik's gaze sharpened, but Quinn wasn't easily intimidated. He glared right back. "It would be smarter not to make me regret choosing for the greater good."

Erik didn't wait for an answer, just dove toward the earth once more. He landed gracefully, shifting to human form right before he touched down. Four men emerged from the shadows to quickly join him. He seemed to give instructions and they departed in different directions. With a parting glance skyward, as if he would remind Quinn not to defy him, Erik strode away.

"I think you've been told," Sara said and Quinn snorted. "Are you going to go?"

Quinn was tempted to defy Erik, but he was aware of Sara's disapproval. "You'll be happier if I listen to what he has to say, won't you?"

"It never hurts to learn more."

"Then I'll go."

Sara fanned her hands across his chest, smoothing her fingertips across his scales. "I'd like to hear it, too, Quinn."

He gazed down at her, hiding nothing. He felt her catch her breath at the full blaze of protectiveness that he knew had to be in his eyes, but she needed to know that he would do his best. "I'm not letting you out of my sight again. You'll be there."

She smiled a little. "Am I a possession or a partner?"

He was riled up, not interested in nuance. "Does it matter? Both need protecting."

"But one has more of a say in her fate than the other."

He knew he spoke with force and he didn't care. "I will not
leave you alone and in danger, not until the *Slayer*s retreat."

Sara held his gaze without trepidation. "And maybe not
even then," she said wryly. Quinn was prepared to argue
with her, but she shook her head. "I'm not challenging you."
She glanced down at the ground, surveyed him, then met his
gaze. He liked the humor that danced in her eyes, which had
become sparkly green. "It's just been one hell of a day. I
think I've used up my ten impossible things before breakfast
for the next month."

Quinn chuckled. He couldn't help it. "Fair enough," he
agreed amiably, then turned earthward again. "So, we have
an hour. Any requests?"

"A shower and a change of clothes," Sara said firmly.

"Your house," Quinn guessed and at her nod, he descended to his truck. She was quiet and he assumed she was
trying to make sense of what she had seen.

He was both right and wrong about that.

Sara was glad to stay with Quinn. There was no mistaking his protective fury, and she liked it just fine. When there
were dragons to be fought, who better to do the dirty work
than a dragon of her own?

Sara was still trying to accept the fact that she'd witnessed a battle between dragons, right in Ann Arbor. She
was still shaking inside from her encounter with the golden
dragon, but the redness rising on her arms proved that she
hadn't imagined him. Within moments, she was seated in
Quinn's black truck and he was driving to her apartment,
just as if life was perfectly normal.

She realized as he parked at the curb in front of Magda's house that she hadn't given him directions.

"How did you know where I lived?"

Quinn, typically, didn't duck her question. Sara liked how direct he was. He spared her a glance as he turned off the engine. "I followed you home last night, to make sure that you got here."

"I didn't see you."

"You weren't supposed to."

She folded her arms across her chest but before she could argue with him, Quinn sighed and shoved a hand through his hair. He looked so frustrated that it was impossible to be angry with him. "I didn't want you to think you had a stalker."

"Another one, you mean. I saw that guy outside my window this morning. Watching."

Quinn nodded, unsurprised. "I figured as much."

Sara had to ask. "Did you hang around last night?"

"No. I didn't want to frighten you."

Sara sensed that there was something he wasn't telling her. "You just left me alone and undefended, even knowing what you knew?"

Quinn watched her as he smiled the slow smile that melted her resistance to him. "Who said you were undefended?" He got out of the truck then, and came around to open the door for her. His expression was grim as he looked up and down the street, wary for any sign that they had been pursued.

"Do you think they'll come after us again so soon?"

"No. But that might just mean that it's what they will do."

"So, how was I defended last night? Or is that a secret?"

"It's no secret. The question is whether or not you'll believe me when I tell you."

"Why wouldn't I?"

"You can't see what I do." Quinn dropped to one knee at

the base of the steps to Sara's apartment and moved his hand as if he could feel something. "Maybe you can feel it."

"Feel what?"

"My smoke. It's a territory mark."

Quinn guided Sara's hand and she felt a definite chill as he pushed her fingers through the air just above her ankles. She shivered and met his gaze, only to find him smiling at her again. "You *can* feel it."

"It's cold and almost slippery. You did that?"

Quinn nodded. "We protect our lairs by encircling them with our own smoke. It's something that takes time, because it's best to exhale the entire circle in one stream. It's almost meditative, but another *Pyr* cannot cross the line of smoke without the permission of the *Pyr* who created the mark."

Sara liked the idea of Quinn having put a protective barrier around her. Especially as it had worked. She looked around the house, peering at the foundation in an effort to see the smoke. She couldn't. "So, you marked my house as your territory last night?"

"It seemed the best choice, to protect you without spooking you."

Sara climbed the stairs, thinking. "And when you left my shop today?" She glanced over her shoulder in time to catch Quinn's smile. "You marked my shop as your territory, too?"

"What else could I do? And didn't it work?"

"Why don't you breathe smoke around me? It would take less . . ." Sara got no further before Quinn shook his head, dismissing the idea.

"I can't mark people, only physical territories." He met her gaze when she paused to fit her key into the lock, and his eyes were vibrantly blue. "Maybe that's the difference between partners and possessions."

Sara smiled, then thought of something else. "At the bell tower. You did it again."

Quinn was immediately disgusted with himself. "I didn't finish. There wasn't time. I hadn't explained to you about the smoke so I had to make the circle bigger, so that you couldn't inadvertently step through it."

"Humans can cross the boundary?"

"They're oblivious to it."

"And *Pyr* in human form?"

"*Pyr* is *Pyr*." Quinn spoke with resolve. "A *Pyr* who crossed a territory line would suffer physical injury."

Sara thought of the golden dragon easing along the parapet. "Was there a gap?"

Quinn nodded, obviously annoyed with himself.

"It's not your fault."

"Then whose fault is it?" he demanded, leaving himself no excuse. "It's my job to defend you and I failed. I don't have to be cheerful about it."

"That golden *Slayer* was stepping through the break," she said, understanding his behavior now. "He was looking for it."

"He probably sensed that the circle was incomplete," Quinn admitted. "The closed ring has a kind of resonance."

"You can hear it as well as see it?"

"*Pyr* have very keen senses."

"Because you're in tune with the four physical elements," Sara guessed. "What does it sound like?"

Quinn folded his arms across his chest and leaned back against her apartment door. They were in the foyer, the door locked behind them, and she watched him search for a description. She liked that he took her questions seriously, and never acted as if they were crazy.

"When I approach someone else's mark, I can hear it as well as see it and feel it. It has a silvery sound, like a crystal bell. A warning sound. When I examine my own mark, I can tell whether it's undisturbed by the temperature and the sound. And I can see it, of course, and check whether it's worn thin in any places."

"It fades?"

"It degenerates in time, like most material things. It has to be breathed again at regular intervals to maintain the defense of a specific area."

"There must come a time when it's easier to breach."

Quinn nodded. "That depends upon how powerful the *Pyr* intruder is. A really old and strong *Pyr* could break a single mark like this after a couple of days of inattention."

"Maybe you should reinforce it," Sara suggested and Quinn's smile flashed. He caught her hand in his and she watched the spark light at the point of contact.

He lifted her hand to his lips and Sara caught her breath at the heat surging through her veins. The admiration in his gaze made her feel both fascinating and beautiful.

In a tattered sundress, with a bruise on her neck and a burn coming up on her forearms. The man had some kind of power.

"Don't worry, princess," Quinn said with quiet force, his low voice making her think about chocolate, nakedness, and messy sheets. "I'll protect you with everything I've got."

Sara's mouth went dry as Quinn brushed his lips across her fingertips. It was hot in her apartment, hot and still. A bead of sweat meandered down her back and she could see a line of dampness on the front of Quinn's T-shirt. She thought of his muscled power in dragon form, eyed the breadth of his shoulders, and was tempted to peel off his shirt. She wanted to feel his skin beneath her hands and see the color of his tan.

His smile broadened as he watched her, as if he could guess her thoughts, and she wondered then whether he could. "How good is your hearing?" she whispered. "Can you hear what I'm thinking?"

"I can see what you're thinking," he said with confidence. "Your eyes have turned gold." Sara didn't have to ask what that meant: his satisfaction in that fact told her all she needed to know.

He turned her hand within his, cradling it within the strength of his fingers, and pressed a kiss to her palm. It sizzled, sending a pang of desire through Sara that nearly took her to her knees.

"I need to shower," she said, hardly recognizing her voice.

"I'll wait right here," Quinn said and Sara believed him. He released her hand with obvious reluctance, their fingers holding until she was several steps away.

She felt the loss of contact immediately, as if an electrical current had been broken. She retreated to the bathroom, aroused by the idea of his being in her apartment while she showered. She paused on the threshold of the bedroom to look back and saw from the line of his jeans that Quinn was aroused by the idea, too.

"I don't pounce, princess," he growled and she smiled, knowing that she could trust him. "But you can issue an invitation whenever you want."

"You have territory to mark," she reminded him and he smiled.

Then Quinn inhaled slowly and seemed to shine. Sara thought he was going to change shape but he didn't. She sensed that he turning inward and knew he was concentrating. He became brighter, as he stood with his arms folded across his chest in her foyer, and he seemed bigger.

More formidable.

More masculine.

He seemed to glitter, just as he had when he started the fire in Erik's car, just as he did right before he changed shape. Sara saw the vivid blue of his eyes before they narrowed to slits. He was almost motionless but she could feel the power of his will. He seemed to almost be in a trance state, his breathing so slow that Sara couldn't match its pace.

She watched, fascinated. When Quinn parted his lips and exhaled, Sara thought she could see the silvery tendrils of smoke drift toward the floor. If she squinted, she could almost see the line of wispy smoke emanating in a continuous stream, easing incrementally beneath the door.

Quinn was marking her apartment as his territory, which worked for Sara. She left him to it. She peeled off her clothes in the bedroom, and stepped into the adjacent bathroom. She could hear him breathing, slowly and steadily, and it was a comforting sound.

As if he slept while keeping vigil. But Sara knew that Quinn wasn't that complacent about protecting her. She hesitated before closing the bathroom door, then chose not to.

Sara knew that Quinn would wait for her invitation. It was the kind of man he was, and that suited her just fine.

If he saw the open door as an invitation, she was fine with that, too.

Sara smelled delicious. Quinn had a hard time focusing on breathing smoke. He heard her turn on the shower, heard the water falling against the tile and tub. He heard her clothes hit the floor, heard her slight sigh of irritation. He imagined that she was considering her reflection; she didn't like to look disheveled, although he found it distractingly sexy.

He heard her brush out her hair and could almost see it gleaming gold on her shoulders. He breathed deeply and focused on his task, trying to ignore the fact that he was raging and his mate was naked not a dozen steps away.

Steam drifted from the bathroom, carrying with it the scent of a shower gel. It smelled of vanilla, feminine but not floral. Perfectly Sara.

Utterly distracting. His concentration broke and he found

his rhythm with an effort, weaving together the ends of the smoke and continuing to breathe more.

Quinn was raging.

As was typical after a fight, he was ravenous and not just for food. Surviving a fight meant primal needs in full force. It traditionally meant a night of drinking, eating, and womanizing. Although Quinn's youth was far behind him, on this particular night, he felt the relentless surge of passion.

The firestorm seemed to enflame his normal reaction, and make it an order of magnitude stronger.

His mate had been attacked. He had fought for her defense and wanted to seal their union. He wanted to take her out for dinner—or better, abscond to his lair where he'd cook for her. They'd eat and drink, dance and talk, and end the night in bed.

They'd greet the dawn in his bed, still passionately entangled. It would be a perfect night.

But they'd been summoned by Erik instead.

Quinn thought that made for a lousy second choice. He wanted everything Sara had to offer, but was painfully aware that she might not be ready to offer all of that to him.

Quinn finished breathing smoke and wove in the ends. He glanced around Sara's apartment, painfully attuned to the presence of his scrumptious mate, and forced himself to think about what was going right.

Sara hadn't been killed yet, despite two attempts on her life.

She hadn't bolted at the sight of his changing shape, and didn't appear to find him revolting.

And she wasn't arguing his insistence on her remaining in his presence.

It wasn't bad for a first day, but Quinn didn't expect that last bit would continue forever. His mate was independent and accustomed to looking out for herself. She was a thinker and a problem solver, and a determined woman once she set her mind on something. He respected that, and he respected that she accepted his help when she knew she needed it. It was only a matter of time, though, before her self-reliance appeared again.

Quinn could only hope that the *Slayer*s hunting her were dead by then.

They would be, if he had anything to say about it. He cursed himself again for not showing more care and neglecting to notice the hidden green *Slayer*. If he didn't protect himself, they'd both be finished.

It was a reminder he didn't need of his vulnerability, just like the damaged scale Sara had fingered on his chest.

Quinn didn't much believe in prophecies or seers; he wasn't particularly convinced of the importance or the existence of the Wyvern and he was disinclined to help his fellow *Pyr* after everything that had been done to him in the past—especially seeing as they were led by the *Pyr* responsible for most of the losses in Quinn's past.

Quinn was solitary and self-reliant. He was a man in touch with the elements and with what he could hold in his hands.

He was experiencing a very earthy desire to feel more of Sara.

The fact was that Quinn would have noticed Sara Keegan anywhere, firestorm or not. He liked how she carried herself, how she walked tall, and how she sought solutions to problems. He liked her sense of humor, her intelligence, and her resilience. He respected that she had been wounded, but scars in Quinn's experience made a person stronger.

More intriguing.

The sound of the water changed, sluicing instead of dropping, and he knew with complete certainty that Sara was in the shower. Naked. Wet. Golden. She was smoothing the gel over herself with long, slow strokes. She was sleek and wet and gleaming. He dared to glance toward the bathroom for the first time.

The door was open. Was that an accident or a choice? He had a hard time believing that his Sara did anything by accident.

The open door was an invitation.

Quinn peeled off his T-shirt and kicked off his boots, heading for the bathroom before she could change her mind.

Sara felt Quinn's presence in the bathroom and her mouth went dry. The temperature rose in the small space and the air seemed more tropical than it had just moments before. She pulled back the curtain and found him in the doorway, his hands braced on the frame, his gaze smoldering.

He was wearing only his jeans. His chest was as broad and muscled as she'd imagined. He was tanned golden, as if he often worked without his shirt, and the hair on his chest was dark. His skin gleamed with a patina of perspiration and he seemed taut, as if he held himself back. He watched her, his eyes the most vivid blue she'd ever seen, and Sara simmered.

There was a question in his expression, one to which Sara knew the answer. She pulled back the curtain an increment more, letting him see her, then beckoned with one finger.

She didn't need to ask him twice.

Quinn chucked his jeans in one smooth move, cast his underwear after them, and crossed the bathroom in record time. He was huge and hard, even his presence making the bathroom seem smaller than it was. She felt tiny and delicate beside him, more feminine than she ever had. He paused outside the tub, maybe sensing her hesitation. He took her hand in his and the spark flashed between their fingers.

"Will the water extinguish it?" Sara asked, and he smiled that slow smile.

"Maybe we should find out," he murmured. Sara eased back as he stepped into the shower behind her. He was directly behind her, the space confined and shadowed. The water fell over them, the heat rose, and Sara couldn't catch her breath.

Quinn inhaled deeply, then spared her a hot glance. "Vanilla."

"Do you mind it? I might have something less girly. . . ." Sara would have stepped out of the shower to look, but Quinn tightened his grip on her hand.

"It's perfect," he murmured, shutting the curtain with his other hand. They were enclosed in the shadowed space, together under the onslaught of hot water. The shower felt intimate with the light filtered through the curtain.

Quinn lifted Sara's hand and kissed her fingertips. He let his tongue slide between her fingers as he watched her intently. Sara felt a sizzle and caught her breath.

She met Quinn's steady gaze and watched him deliberately mouth each of her fingertips. His lips were soft and firm, his touch persuasive. And hot. He was kindling the fire between them to an inferno, easily and slowly.

Sara could barely breathe. She laid her free hand on his chest, exploring him with her fingertips. His other hand landed on her waist. His fingers curved around her and his thumb eased across her flesh, as if he were memorizing her shape. His touch set her flesh afire.

Sara's blood began to simmer. She felt in charge of an unruly force, knowing with complete certainty that she could stop Quinn with a fingertip anytime she wanted.

But she didn't want to.

In fact, she wanted to add to Quinn's fire with some heat of her own. Sara stretched to her toes and leaned against

Quinn's chest. Her nipples beaded immediately and she rubbed them against his muscled strength. She heard Quinn inhale sharply, watched him incline his head toward her, but she pulled their entwined fingers to her lips instead.

Sparks danced between their hands, sizzling in the falling water, as she kissed his fingertips. She echoed his play but went one better. She slid her tongue between his fingers and dragged her teeth across his palm. She nipped at his skin and ran his fingers across her face. Quinn groaned and locked his hands around her waist, impatient for a kiss. He lifted her against him, pressing his erection against her belly, and claimed her lips.

Sara closed her eyes and surrendered to pleasure. She tangled her tongue with his, demanding as she had never been before. She'd never been so uninhibited, but it felt exactly right to be with Quinn.

She trusted him. For once in her life, she was going to go with that.

Quinn met her touch for touch, teasing her desire to burn brighter and hotter. Water rained down on the pair of them. It wet down their hair, left their bodies slick and smooth, simmered and steamed wherever their bodies were in contact.

Quinn's kiss drove everything else from Sara's universe—everything except the heat of the firestorm Quinn awakened. Sara could have lost herself in this blaze of passion, without regret. His hand swept over her breast, teasing her nipple to an even tighter peak. He cupped her breast in his palm, then broke their kiss. Sara made a sound of disappointment; then his mouth closed over her breast with surety. She arched back, gasping with pleasure at his demanding caress. With teeth and tongue, he teased her so that she was hotter than she had ever been.

Then his fingers were between her thighs. She gripped his shoulders, lost to his touch, and he held her fast with one arm. She moaned and writhed against him, murmuring incoherently until he kissed her again. His fingers were merciless in coaxing her pleasure, in tempting her higher and hotter in pursuit of her release.

Sara's skin seemed to shimmer; her blood boiled; her resistance melted. She closed one hand around Quinn's strength and was surprised by the size of him. Her caress made him growl and she felt power in her touch. He caught her closer and his fingers slipped inside her.

Sara cried out as the inferno of the firestorm claimed her and obliterated every coherent thought.

There was only Quinn.

He was all she needed.

She opened her eyes moments later to find him smiling down at her, a very male gleam of satisfaction in his eyes. "My mermaid," he murmured, then kissed her with such leisure that Sara had no complaints. He certainly had made her glow, just like the door knocker.

Except there was no threat to her with Quinn's presence.

When Quinn lifted his head, he sighed with such regret that Sara had a moment's fear. "Erik," he said with a grimace and reached for the shower gel.

Sara laughed at his rueful expression. "We can be late."

"Probably not a good idea," Quinn said, with such obvious disappointment that she couldn't doubt what he'd rather be doing.

"Let me do something first," she offered, and lathered up her hands. His eyes widened as she soaped down his chest and slipped her hands around his erection. "The least I can do is balance the books."

Chapter 7

They weren't too late in reaching Erik's hotel.

Although Quinn would have been happy to remain in Sara's shower all night.

Sara had knotted up her hair while it was wet and one lone tendril hung down the back of her neck, inviting Quinn's touch. She'd changed to a black-and-white halter sundress that looked retro and wore strappy sandals that would have been appropriate for a date. Long earrings dangled from her ears and brushed against her neck, making her look elegant and cool. He liked the way the heels showed off her legs and that the sundress left her back bare.

He also liked his sense that she had chosen to wear something special, maybe because she was going to spend the evening with him. She looked as if she wanted to tempt him; he wouldn't tell her yet how well she succeeded. Although she probably knew.

He'd come twice in the shower and was still so fired up that he could have gone another half dozen rounds.

The others were already gathered in Erik's room. Quinn could feel their collective presence as soon as he and Sara got off the elevator on the floor where Erik's suite was located.

"What's wrong?" she asked with concern. Quinn realized that she was becoming more observant in his presence.

"We're outnumbered." He smiled to reassure her. "It probably doesn't matter but I don't have to like it."

"Aren't Erik and his followers true *Pyr* like you?"

"I'm not sure. We'll find out soon enough." Quinn didn't think it was time to tell her that even true *Pyr* could destroy each other, if they believed it was for the greater good.

He hoped this exchange was short and sweet. Even bringing Sara into such company made him edgy. He lifted a hand to knock on the door, but Erik opened it before Quinn's knuckles made contact. Quinn noticed Sara's surprise. "He just heard us coming."

"All the way from Washtenaw Avenue," Erik confirmed.

"So you're not psychic, just extra-observant?"

Quinn nodded, noting Erik's smile. "That's the root of it, although many observations taken over a long time add up to a lot of experience. It becomes easier to anticipate what will happen."

"The benefit of experience," Erik agreed. "You begin to see the patterns of behavior and can better guess what choices any individual will make in any situation."

Sara seemed to think about this. "Did you know what would happen when you threw me from the tower?"

Erik nodded once and Quinn couldn't tell if he was lying or not. "Quinn has always been strongly attuned to others."

Quinn scoffed at that, but Sara ignored him.

"What others do you mean?" she asked Erik.

"Friends, family." Erik smiled. "Lovers. The pattern is apparent over time. He's rather like his father that way."

Erik had known Quinn's father? Quinn met the other *Pyr*'s gaze and wasn't sure what to think. He would have given a great deal to have had his father's assessment of Erik, but that was impossible.

Because Erik had made sure of it. Quinn knew his hostility showed, but he was surprised that Erik didn't respond in kind.

Sara gave Quinn a quizzical look. "Just how old are you?" she asked and he knew that wasn't the question she wanted to have answered.

Quinn spoke as much for Erik's benefit as for hers. "Old enough to know better," he said lightly and winked. He took her elbow as Erik coughed, then led her into Erik's temporary lair.

The perimeter of the suite was ringed with a territory mark, the smoke woven with dexterity as deep as Quinn's hips. Once again, he was impressed by Erik's abilities. He felt Sara shiver as she stepped through it and knew she felt the barrier she had crossed.

The way her gaze flicked over him, looking for injury, was evidence that she remembered what he had told her.

And maybe that she was concerned for his welfare.

Quinn would take encouragement wherever he could find it. He tightened his grip on her elbow, knowing that he didn't imagine the way she drew closer to him.

"Might as well be in a locker room," she murmured and Quinn stifled a smile. There was enough testosterone in Erik's suite to make even him take notice.

Four *Pyr* waited in the suite's living room. They were all fit and looked virile, handsome, and athletic, their poses showing various degrees of antagonism toward the new arrival.

Quinn hadn't expected anything different. He only recognized one of them and was surprised by that. What had happened to all the old *Pyr*? Several of Erik's fellows were

young—Quinn could tell by how lithe they were—and he
feared suddenly for the survival of his species.

Not that it was his concern. The focus of Quinn's attention was upon himself and Sara. The rest of the *Pyr* could
look out for themselves.

Quinn knew Donovan from times past and was glad, in a
way, to see that *Pyr* well. Donovan was tall and powerful,
auburn-haired, and quick to anger. He leaned against one
wall, arms folded across his broad chest, his tight T-shirt and
jeans showing his muscles to advantage. He had a gold stud
in his left ear, a tattoo of a dragon on his left bicep, and a
wicked smile that dropped women to their knees. Donovan
was a fighter whom it was best to have on one's own side.
Quinn inclined his head once in that *Pyr*'s direction but
Donovan didn't respond.

Erik introduced the others quickly. Niall was fair and
built more like a weight lifter, his eyes flashing with suspicion. He sat on a leather couch with Sloane, who was as dark
as Niall was fair. Sloane was the kind of wiry man whose
fighting prowess and strength were easily underestimated.
His expression was grim. They were both younger than
Quinn, maybe three or four hundred years old, and didn't
have the attitude and confidence of an old *Pyr*.

Rafferty was tall and older, and Quinn had heard his
name although they had never met. He waved a lazy fingertip in greeting, apparently conserving his strength for more
important encounters. Rafferty would also be underestimated, because of his laconic manner. Quinn wouldn't have
turned his back on Rafferty for a heartbeat, not when his
eyes gleamed as they did now.

Quinn felt them appraise his mate, Niall tilting back his
head to take Sara's scent in a very rude fashion. Quinn
wanted to deck him and maybe Erik perceived that because
he was quick to chastise the younger *Pyr*.

"Mind your manners, Niall," Erik snapped in old-speak. The *Pyr* in question settled back to simply look at Sara. "Quinn enters as a friend: he and his mate are under my protection."

"Maybe she doesn't want him," Donovan suggested in old-speak. An appreciative gleam lit his eye and his smile broadened ever so slightly.

Sara drew a little closer to Quinn, even though she couldn't hear what was being said. "What's going on?" she whispered. "It sounds like distant thunder."

"Keep out of my firestorm," Quinn said to Donovan, not bothering with old-speak. "If the lady wants your favors, she'll say so."

Sara caught her breath and gave Donovan a glare of her own. She put her hand deliberately into Quinn's and the firestorm sparked between them. Quinn noticed how Rafferty's expression changed to yearning as he watched the flickering sparks.

Donovan got to his feet, challenge in his stance. "The way you stay out of everything *Pyr*?" he demanded aloud. "Where have you been, Smith? Don't you think we could have used your services for the past centuries?" He glared at Sara. "You need to know the truth about this *Pyr*, if you're going to have his child. Why should his legacy continue, when he contributes so little to the rest of us?"

Sara blinked in surprise but said nothing. Quinn knew without looking at her that she'd have plenty of questions for him later and he liked that she didn't enter the fray now. She listened. That made things easier.

"I don't have to serve those who don't appreciate me," he told Donovan.

Donovan took a step closer and jabbed a finger through the air at Quinn's chest. "No one appreciates a craftsman who can't—or won't—do his destined job."

Quinn held his ground. "Why should I arm those who use their weapons against me?"

"No one attacked you," Erik contributed.

"No, not directly." Quinn eased Sara behind him. They were fighting with words, but that could change. The hostility in the room was rising steadily. "But I saw you kill Ambrose."

"Ambrose was a *Slayer*," Erik said.

"Ambrose was my friend," Quinn retorted.

"Then you place your trust poorly, Smith."

"Where were all of you when I had no one?" Quinn asked. He hadn't chosen to live in solitude and he knew that Erik knew it.

"Your past is your problem," Donovan snapped.

"Ambrose was the problem in your past," Erik insisted. "And I saw to it you were rid of him. You should thank me, not blame me."

"Because you say he was a *Slayer*." Quinn's eyes narrowed. "How convenient to make that charge when no one can challenge it."

Erik's eyes snapped. "You have my word upon it."

"Maybe that's not good enough," Quinn retorted.

"Maybe you should mind *your* manners, Smith," Niall interjected, getting to his feet as well.

"Maybe there is more to the truth than any of us guess," Rafferty drawled. His relaxed tone broke the tension and Quinn stepped back. He shoved a hand through his hair, certain that coming had been a bad idea. The others moved into a line as if creating a barrier before him. He was used to that.

"Ambrose was my mentor and my friend," Quinn said with quiet force. "He was my *only* mentor and my *only* friend. Where were the *Pyr* when I was alone, if my abilities were so important to you all?"

"Perhaps you did not see that we were there," Erik said.

"Perhaps you were not there at all," Quinn replied. "Why would I join forces with Ambrose's murderer?"

"Because he was a *Slayer*," hissed Niall. "Because his death was right."

"It didn't seem right to me." Quinn glared at Niall. "And what do you know about it? You're too young to remember Ambrose."

"I know what I've been taught."

"And anyone can be taught lies," Quinn concluded.

"That's precisely my point," Erik said crisply. "How do you know that what Ambrose taught you was the truth?"

"No one else offered lessons. Ambrose taught me to breathe smoke and he taught me to shift shape more quickly. He taught me to control my body's urges and to whisper to the fire. All that in less than two years. How much more could he have taught me if you hadn't cut him down?"

"How much indeed?" Erik asked softly. "*Pyr* are born but *Slayers* are made. Perhaps he would have taken the Smith to the other side."

"Don't insult me with such garbage," Quinn said, not hiding his disgust. The pair's gazes locked, anger simmering between them, until Quinn remembered Sara and stepped back. If a fight erupted, she alone would be undefended, and he was one against five.

"We're not here to talk about Ambrose," Erik said, his tone indicating that he also wanted to make peace. "The past is in the past. We need to think about the future and how to protect ourselves. The time of reckoning is upon us and we must fulfill our mission."

Donovan paced the room and looked unwilling to abandon the argument. "Even if our numbers were just diminished for nothing." He pointed at Quinn. "Delaney died for you today, because Erik abandoned him to defend your mate."

"That wasn't my choice," Quinn said. "I appreciate what he did, but your argument is with Erik."

"My intent was to serve the greater good," Erik said when Donovan turned upon him.

"You always say things like that, as if you can see the future," Donovan muttered. Quinn noticed again that Erik almost smiled. "Delaney is dead! And for what?" He faced Quinn in his frustration. "What have you ever done for the rest of us? What do you propose to do for us now?"

"They even took his body," grumbled Sloane. "We can't honor our fallen properly, or know that his body has been treated with respect. Why would they do that? What was the point?"

"They did it to demoralize us," Donovan said flatly.

"Looks like it's working," contributed Rafferty. He shrugged as the others glared at him. "But you're being distracted by details. Delaney was dead. You can't let the loss of his body affect your attitude, as unpleasant a fact as it is."

"I don't think that disrespect shown to the dead is just a detail," Donovan asserted and animosity rose between the two older *Pyr*. "And neither do I think that Delaney's death was irrelevant, or inevitable, or regrettable but unimportant." He threw himself into a chair and glared at the rest of them. "But maybe I'm biased about losing one of my kin for nothing."

Quinn could relate to that.

Before argument could continue, Sara cleared her throat. "Well, I appreciate everyone's assistance today. I have no doubt that the one dragon would have happily incinerated me." She turned to Donovan and her voice softened. "My parents died in an accident last winter, while they were on vacation, so I think I know how you feel. It's hard to lose someone so abruptly, without the chance to say good-bye."

" 'Tis," Donovan agreed grimly. Quinn felt the mood lighten slightly in the room.

To Quinn's surprise, Sara crossed the room and touched the other *Pyr*'s arm. "I wish Delaney hadn't died today," she said softly. "As glad as I am to be alive, I would never have asked anyone to pay such a price."

Donovan scowled at his boots and spoke gruffly. "Thanks."

"I wish they hadn't taken his body," Sloane grumbled. "It wouldn't have made any difference for them to do the decent thing."

"*Slayer*s don't do the decent thing," Erik said.

"Malicious bastards," Donovan muttered.

But Sara shook her head. "No. That's where you're wrong." She had the undivided attention of the *Pyr* then, including Quinn. She had a set to her chin that Quinn had already learned was a sign that she knew she was right.

"They took his body to make sure that he stayed dead," she said.

All six *Pyr* stared at her in astonishment, but Quinn felt pride seeping into his own expression. His warrior princess was turning the tables on his fellows and Quinn liked it.

He liked it a lot.

"What are you talking about?" Rafferty demanded after a heartbeat of silence. He roused himself, his eyes snapping with annoyance as he turned on Erik. "What nonsense is this that we're learning our own lore from a human?"

Erik looked embarrassed. "Much has been lost."

"Then it should be found!" Rafferty snarled.

Once again, Sara interjected and changed the tone of the conversation.

"It's better to learn it from me than not to know it at all," she said with her usual practicality. Quinn stifled a smile at Rafferty's obvious shock.

Sara rummaged in her purse, then triumphantly displayed

a leather-bound book. "You should have read it before you left it for me," she told Erik, much to Quinn's confusion and Erik's surprise. "Sigmund Guthrie explains in his book how to make sure a dead dragon stays dead. It's not a pleasant read, but apparently it's informative. And factual."

A ripple of mingled interest and alarm passed through the group. Quinn was surprised and intrigued himself.

Sara looked around for a seat. Donovan pulled one forward for her. The other *Pyr* sat attentively, waiting for whatever she had to say. Erik looked particularly grim and his gaze was fixed on the book Sara had.

She sat down and fanned the pages of the book. "I thought it was garbage when I read it," she said, nodding at Rafferty. "But now that Quinn has told me about your relationship with the four elements, it makes perfect sense. I think Guthrie was writing about *Pyr*, not mythical dragons, because he wrote that a dragon corpse has to be exposed to all four elements to remain dead."

Quinn straightened in surprise.

"Or?" prompted Erik.

Sara looked up at him. "Or the dragon can heal and return to fight again."

A murmur passed through the group. "That's why they took their own fallen back with them," muttered Niall. "They're going to heal them."

"Rouse them from the dead," agreed Sloane and shuddered.

The others agreed and noisy speculation launched about how that healing might be done. Everyone was talking at once, it seemed, leaning forward and fixing upon Sara.

"Does the book say how to do the healing?"

"What are the conditions?"

"How long does it take?"

"Are there any aftereffects?"

"Well, that part is a bit vague," Sara said, flipping through the book rapidly. "Let me see if I can find what it does say."

Quinn averted his gaze, ignoring the conversation for the moment. He was remembering. It hadn't rained on the night that Ambrose had died. That meant there had been fire, earth, and air, but no water. He thought about the golden dragon he'd seen slipping away from the tower on this very day, the one whose scales and rhythm of movement were so reminiscent of his old friend.

He found his gaze rising to meet Erik's and guessed that their thoughts were as one.

"What if Ambrose isn't dead?" Erik murmured in old-speak and Quinn could only shake his head.

It was incomprehensible. It had been more than seven centuries.

How long did this healing take?

It was crazy, and yet, it made a certain sense. He remembered the coin he'd picked up in the arcade the night before, the one he'd changed to his own mark to protect Sara's home.

It had been a gold florin. He'd thought that it had been a message from someone who knew that he was old, but Ambrose had introduced himself to Quinn with a gold florin, all those centuries ago.

Quinn saw the coin now as a message from an old friend.

Or an announcement.

Or a taunt.

Quinn thought again of the golden dragon trying to kill Sara earlier and had to wonder. He had trusted Ambrose implicitly. He'd believed everything Ambrose had told him. Had he been too young to detect an older *Pyr*'s guile? He glanced down and saw the redness rising on Sara's arm, a burn that was the result of the golden dragon's assault upon her.

Had that golden dragon been Ambrose?

But why would Ambrose try to kill Quinn's mate? The only logical reason was that Ambrose was a *Slayer*, that Erik had been right, and that Erik *was* true *Pyr*.

But what about the other deaths? What about the assassination of Quinn's parents and brothers? What about Elizabeth? Removing one crime from Erik's list didn't make that dragon innocent.

"Don't you know this lore?" Quinn asked Erik in oldspeak as the others talked aloud.

The other *Pyr* shook his head slowly, with more than an increment of regret. "It must have been lost to us."

But the *Slayer*s had the knowledge. The fact that they had taken the corpses with them was proof of that. They had advantage on their side in the old battle.

Quinn stared at the floor, feeling for the first time in centuries the burden of his responsibility to his kind. He knew that it was his obligation as the Smith to aid his fellows, but having been betrayed, he had focused on selfreliance instead.

It would have been easier to join the *Pyr* if Quinn hadn't had such mixed feelings about Erik Sorensson.

It would have been easier if he'd had only his own safety to consider. But there was Sara and she was vulnerable, and his first responsibility had to be to her.

"You saved my mate," Quinn said, continuing their conversation in old-speak.

"That puts you in my debt," Erik said and Quinn knew he didn't imagine the other *Pyr*'s smile of satisfaction.

Had Ambrose deceived Quinn in the past?

Or was Erik trying to deceive him now?

"Perhaps not, since you then cast her to what might have been her death."

Erik shrugged. "You needed a shock to return to the battle at hand. I chose one."

"You chose mercilessly."

"No. I had no doubt of the outcome."

"You sacrificed one of your own."

For the first time, Erik looked pained. "I had no choice. Your mate could not die, not if the Smith and the Seer are to unite right now."

"You can't believe that prophecy."

"You can't disbelieve it."

"I do. Prophecies are inaccurate nonsense."

"No." Erik shook his head. "They are infallible, once you understand them."

"And you claim that you do?"

"I do. The union of the Smith and the Seer is the key to our survival and to our victory. Without your mate, you cannot become what we need."

Quinn was dismissive of this attempt to draw him into a conflict he didn't want or need. "The *Pyr* do not need me, and I do not need the *Pyr.*"

Erik shook his head. "That is where you are wrong, Quinn Tyrrell."

"I say *you* are wrong. I take care of myself and my own, and the rest of you are welcome to do the same."

Erik shook his head again. "You can take care of your own only by embracing what you are destined to become."

"I don't believe it."

"And so we disagree." The pair surveyed each other for so long that it was Quinn who was obliged to blink first.

But that didn't mean that he was convinced. Quinn still believed Sara was at risk and that her protection was his primary task.

No one, not even the self-proclaimed leader of the *Pyr*, would convince him otherwise.

The rest of the meeting in Erik's hotel room passed in a jumble for Sara. She had the definite sense that there was more going on than she could hear. She sensed another level of communication, one in addition to the words she could hear and the body language she could see.

Maybe the *Pyr* practiced telepathy.

Maybe she needed to read more of the stock in The Scrying Glass. She'd never imagined that the day would come when she'd think such a thing, but here it was. She wondered whether Magda was laughing somewhere.

Quinn became very quiet after she revealed what she had read in Sigmund Guthrie's book. At first, she'd wondered whether her contribution had displeased him, but he seemed more introspective than annoyed. It was as if he were trying to solve a puzzle of some kind, and Sara wanted to know what it was.

She had a feeling that he wouldn't tell her about it until he was ready to do so.

Meanwhile, she tried to answer the questions of the *Pyr*. It wasn't really fair, to her thinking, as she had a lot more questions than they did. On the other hand, the stakes were higher in their battle than her satisfaction of her curiosity.

It sounded as if they were fighting for their survival.

She was sure she'd have a chance to ask questions of Quinn afterward, but he seemed tired and preoccupied. They ate a light dinner together and he drove her home. She knew she didn't imagine that he checked every intersection and shadow thoroughly.

"Are you going to tell me that you need to stay over, to protect me?" Sara meant to tease him, but her question didn't sound as light as she'd wanted it to.

The truth was that she didn't want to spend the night alone. She wanted to do more with Quinn.

But she'd known him only a day.

Sara decided that she was more nervous than she'd realized and that it was affecting her judgment. Almost being fried can do that to a person.

Quinn tapped his fingers on the steering wheel, which only drew her attention to the strength of his hands. It was all too easy to remember how he had touched her, and yearn for him to do it again. "You have to know that I'd prefer to be close, Sara."

Sara swallowed. "Will you sleep tonight?"

He smiled, as if the idea was ludicrous. "No. No matter where I am." He turned to meet her gaze, his own serious. "But the choice of where we go from here is all yours."

There was heat emanating from his skin and a promise in his eyes. Sara doubted she would regret anything she did with Quinn, on this night or any other.

His presence, his steady gaze, his surety all combined to mess with her mind.

Sara tore her gaze away from his and considered the darkened house. It looked lonely and she wondered how jumpy she'd be alone. "Did you make your territory mark?"

"Several times." Quinn said with a decisive nod. "And I'll add to it before I sleep."

"Is it enough?"

"Yes." He spoke with such confidence that she believed him. "It's freshly breathed, deep and well woven. I've been breathing smoke for a long time and this is as good as it gets. Once you get up the stairs and through the door, you'll be safe."

"And you'll watch until I do?"

"Of course."

Sara studied him, seeing the protectiveness that he tried

to hide. It was primal and powerful. Seductive. Quinn would kill for her without hesitation, but he was trying to give her the space she needed to trust him.

"You sound very sure," she said quietly.

His smile told her that he didn't have a shred of doubt.

She wanted to kiss that smile, but she knew that if she touched him at all, the decision would be made. Was that why he was keeping his distance in the cab? To let her make a logical choice?

Sara knew the truth when she thought it, but it only tempted her all the more.

"There isn't any old dragon magic that would allow a *Pyr* to cross the boundary mark of another *Pyr*?"

"There's no such thing as magic, Sara," Quinn chided. The way he arched one brow made him look mischievous and unpredictable, and Sara found her resistance to him crumbling even further. "I wouldn't think I'd have to tell you that."

Sara smiled. "Seriously."

"Seriously." Quinn sobered. "No *Pyr* can touch you when you're securely inside my smoke."

"Except you," Sara said, feeling obliged to clarify.

Quinn's eyes brightened as he held her gaze. "Except me," he ageed quietly, his low words doing something to her equilibrium that felt a whole lot like magic. "But even that, princess, is invitation-only."

He pulled a pad of paper from the glove box, his fingertips brushing her knees, his tough sending sparks over her flesh. He began writing in a decisive hand, then tore off the page. "Here's my cell phone number, and here's the hotel where I have a room. You can call me anytime."

"I thought you'd hear me decide to scream."

"I will." He fired a hot look across the cab. "But you might just want to talk."

Sara took the piece of paper and tucked it into her purse. Maybe she was too pragmatic, but having his cell phone number made her feel better. Quinn watched her, waiting for her to decide.

Sara had never been afraid of doing things on her own. Her family had been uprooted every two years and she'd made new friends every time. She'd traveled the world and walked into countless boardrooms and made a zillion presentations. She'd navigated cities with signs in languages she couldn't read; she'd tried local cuisine everywhere she'd traveled; she'd never backed down from a challenge. She wasn't afraid of counting on herself, and she wasn't afraid to let other people on her team do what they did best.

Protecting her was what Quinn did best. He'd messed up today and she knew he blamed himself more than she ever could. She was going to trust him to do his job.

And she was going to avoid temptation.

For now.

Which might be what she did best.

She wasn't going to think about that just yet.

"Thanks for your info. I think I'll be fine tonight." Sara stretched across the cab and brushed her lips across Quinn's cheek. She felt his surprise at her quick kiss and then his pleasure. "But do the smoke again," she urged in a whisper, her lips only a hairbreadth from his. "Lots of it."

"I'll do it twice, princess," Quinn said. He held her gaze and the heat kindled between them. Sara became aware that her breast was pressed against his arm, that her fingers were locked around his, that his mouth was only an inch away from hers.

Quinn leaned down so slowly that she thought she would die of anticipation. His mouth closed over hers with that blend of tenderness and conviction that could make her forget her own name. Sara closed her eyes and kissed him back.

She lost herself in the magic that Quinn awakened within her, and knew that she wouldn't hold out long in the battle against temptation.

She couldn't, in fact, remember why she wanted to try.

He broke the kiss and smiled at her, pushing a strand of hair behind her ear. That tantalizing taste of him had left her only yearning for more.

"You'd better leave now, Sara. Another kiss like that and we'll be shocking your neighbors."

She opened her mouth, unsure what she'd say, but Quinn laid a gentle fingertip across her lips.

"I'll see you tomorrow," he murmured. "Trust me."

And Sara did.

Sara climbed the stairs to her apartment under Quinn's vigilant gaze. She closed her eyes as she crossed the threshold, concentrating, and felt the cool brush of his smoke on her legs as she stepped through it. She glanced back, but Quinn was concentrating again.

Sara could see that he was staring at the pavement. His breathing was slow and he appeared to shimmer around the edges. Quinn was intense and focused, and she knew what he was doing.

He was keeping his promise.

He was protecting her.

And if he knew that was good enough, then so did she.

Sara entered her apartment and locked the door against more mundane intruders. She was restless despite being exhausted and doubted she would sleep at all. She opened the windows and turned on the fans, trying to get rid of some of the muggy air trapped in the apartment. She changed for the night and made a cup of herbal tea. She cleaned up the kitchen, although it didn't really need cleaning. She checked her phone messages and sorted her mail.

Each time she glanced out the window, Quinn was still

there, standing in the shadows of the quiet street and breathing smoke.

She went into the bedroom and sorted her laundry. She'd been in such a hurry to change that she'd just dropped it on the floor. In examining the damage to her favorite red dress, she felt something in one pocket.

It was the gold coin that had been outside the door of her shop earlier.

Sara turned it under the light. It looked old. There was a man on a horse on one side, a man who looked like a medieval knight. She couldn't make out the writing. She went to the window just in time to see Quinn getting into his truck and didn't want to call him back just for this. She watched the taillights of his truck disappear around the corner, and checked again that she had his phone numbers.

There had been a coin the night before, one thrown to distract her, one that had looked gold. There hadn't been one near the shop this morning, but then this one had appeared. Was it the same coin, or a similar one? There was no doubt in Sara's mind that its appearance had something to do with Quinn.

Gold coins, after all, didn't have a habit of dropping into her life. She didn't think she'd ever seen one before.

Maybe the coin was a message. Maybe it could tell her something about Quinn. Maybe she could summon a vision, the way she had earlier in the shop. Sara studied the coin, then closed her hand over it. She tried to relax, then tried to fall into the image on the coin, then tried to turn off her thoughts.

Nothing worked.

At last, she started to yawn. She put the coin on her nightstand and went to bed.

She was asleep in moments.

Chapter 8

The nightmare fell upon Sara like a thief jumping her from behind in a dark alley.

It's hot. It's sunny, the sun so bright that the young boy has to narrow his eyes against its glare. The air is dry, so hot and dry that the boy might be breathing dust.

Or desert.

He's playing hide-and-seek with his brothers, a favorite game that he has no idea he'll never play again. He's found the perfect hiding spot behind the millstone in the mill. The great stone is cool, cold even, and the shadow is dark behind it. There is no grain being ground on this day and the stone is still, so he is very quiet in his secret spot. The space is small, too small for his older brothers, and the boy is sure that he'll escape detection.

If he can keep from giggling to himself in triumph.

He has seen four summers, and is as tall for his age as his siblings. He shares their dark hair and good looks, as well as the vivid blue eyes of his mother. He is happy and well fed, a boy with a secure present and a bright future before him.

Or so it appears.

The villagers say the smith's wife is proud of her brood, and rightly so. Five boys, each one a survivor and a credit to his father. Such gossip must be true, for the youngest son of the smith overheard it in the bakery that very morning.

He also heard about the approaching army.

The villagers are certain that the walls will hold against military might and injustice. The boy yearns to see the horses, and his eldest brother, Jean, has promised to take him to the summit of the walls that evening to look upon the mustered force.

The boy bounces in anticipation. It would be best if he can hide successfully from Jean first—then they will laugh and his mother will smile at him with pride—so he strives to be still.

When the boy hears the first clash of steel on steel, he thinks his brothers are practicing their swordplay again. He assumes, actually, that they have forgotten him. It has happened before, with less interesting distractions than an army at the gates.

Perhaps they watch the army approach.

Perhaps he is missing something.

Or perhaps they are trying to trick him into revealing himself.

Ha! He squeezes farther back behind the millstone and barely dares to breathe.

When the boy hears the first man scream in pain, he thinks Michel is feigning injury again, to take advantage of the elder Jean. He smiles at Michel's cunning and knows he can be more cunning still. He folds himself even more tightly into his place.

It is the echo of hoofbeats that tempts the boy to peek out of his hiding place. There are hundreds of horses from the thunderous sound, a marvel he has never seen. He begins to move.

But the horses must be inside the city walls, which cannot be. He knows the gates will be barred, for he heard of that in the bakery as well. He stops for a moment that proves to be precious.

The miller shouts in such rage that it cannot be a feigned cry. There is a sound of battle very close at hand, but not the practice fighting of his brothers. The thump and groan of blades finding their mark is all too real, as is the gasp of pain of a man done injury.

The boy catches his breath as red splashes upon the wall above him. He cowers behind the millstone in fear.

Something is wrong.

He hears the miller fall and another man laugh. It is cruel laughter and it frightens him.

He hears the clash of mail as other men enter the mill and pushes himself so tightly into the shadow of the millstone that he knows he will be bruised. He doesn't care. He hears the gurgle of the miller's pain, of men kicking baskets of grain aside and the kernels spilling across the floor. He hears the miller's wife scream in the chamber behind the mill proper, then a rhythmic thump he has heard before but does not understand. The men laugh some more. He hears the miller's wife beg and plead and cry.

And then suddenly she is silent.

He hears the men leave, hears them speak to each other in a language he does not know. He covers his ears with his hands, but not so well that he does not hear his mother call his name.

She calls a dozen times before he dares to peek. He eases out of the shadow, his breath coming in anxious spurts.

The miller sees him. The man lies in a pool of blood, the

red glistening upon the stone floor and spreading quickly. He is injured, dreadfully injured.

The boy halts in shock at the violence done to his old friend.

The miller shakes his head once, with authority. The boy hesitates and the miller shakes his head again with vigor.

"Stay," he whispers. His voice is faint but that single word is heavy with the weight of command.

Footfalls resonate in the street. The miller's eyes widen in fear and the boy nods agreement. He slides back into his hiding spot and holds his breath.

When the men have passed, he peeks out again.

"Good boy," the miller murmurs, the words so faint that the boy reads the praise in the motion of his lips. He watches as the miller's eyes close slowly.

They do not open again, although the miller's blood continues to spread across the floor.

The boy crouches in his hiding place, terrified to disobey the miller even though that man moves no more. He watches the blood trickle down the stone wall behind him and knows that this is no jest of his brothers'. The church bells ring in summons, but the boy does not move. His mother has stopped calling his name and the street beyond the mill is quiet.

Too quiet.

It is not long before he smells the fire and hears the screams, although he is unable to make sense of what is happening. He smells another smell, the scent of burning flesh, and fears for the horses. When the soldiers ride past the mill again, laughing that cruel laughter, their horses cantering, the boy knows instinctively that the miller has given him good counsel.

He does not understand—not yet—that all he loves has been willfully destroyed.

Much less that it will happen again.

He smells the fire, sees the flames, hears the crackle of the fire consuming the cathedral. He stands outside its blackened walls as the fire finishes what it has begun. Smoke rises from the charred village and the streets are so silent that the boy knows he is alone.

That is the moment he sees the first dragon, circling in the twilight sky high overhead.

As if it's seeking something. It is ebony and pewter, a mythical magical beast, and one that strikes terror into the boy's heart.

That is the moment he runs.

Sara awakened immediately, her heart pounding. She felt helpless and heartbroken, so devastated that she wanted to cry.

The dream had been so vivid that she felt a bit sick. She didn't like the smell of roasting meat. It was part of the reason she was vegetarian. She sniffed her arms with their new burn, and wondered whether that was what had caused her dream.

But it had been as clear as a memory.

Quinn's memory. She instinctively knew it, even though it made no sense. Sara rubbed her forehead and tried to push the dream from her thoughts. She closed her eyes, hoping to doze, maybe snag a nicer dream.

It was going to be hot again. She was lying on her back in bed, a slight breeze wafting through the open window. She'd left the window open, because it was so small. Only a monkey could have scampered through it—not a dragon— and she would have suffocated without some air circulating. It was a hot breeze, the promise of a hotter day, but that wasn't why there was a sheen of perspiration over Sara's skin.

She couldn't stop thinking about that boy.

A woman screamed then, a scream of agony that set Sara's teeth on edge. She swung her legs out of the bed, meaning to help.

"It is forbidden—," the woman began to shout, her sentence ending in a shriek of pain. "Great Wyvern, help me," she whispered, her voice trembling in terror.

Then she screamed again.

It was the Wyvern, but this time Sara felt a knife cutting her own flesh. She arched in agony as pain sliced through the tendon at the back of her arm. She struggled but some dark force held her down and the knife bit deeper.

She was in a secluded place with no one to aid her. It was dark and damp and dungeonlike. Despair filled her heart. Blood was running from her shoulder; she could feel it spread onto the dirt floor. Her breath came in wrenching sobs as the pain spread down her arm.

Sara forced her eyes open and her breath caught. Her pulse was beating as if she'd run a race. Her shoulder throbbed.

She compelled herself to notice that she was in her own bedroom. Safe. She reached around to finger the wound and found her skin perfectly normal.

There was no cut.

There should be no pain.

The voice and the experience of the Wyvern was in her thoughts, not in her vicinity. Sara exhaled in relief, though she still trembled slightly.

The vision had been so real.

She got out of bed and went to the window. The curtain ruffled and the street was quiet below. A few birds chirped in the trees and the neighbor's cat stalked across the lawn. Everything was tranquil, even though Sara's hair was practically standing on end.

And there was a black pickup truck parked on the street in front of the house. Sara exhaled in relief as she recognized it.

The truck had a silver trailer and a dark-haired man in a T-shirt and shorts leaned against the passenger door. He wore a straw fedora that shaded his eyes but didn't disguise his identity one bit and had thrown a vivid Hawaiian shirt over his T-shirt. He held a cup of take-out coffee in one hand and sipped it as he watched the house. There was a second cup of coffee on the hood of the truck.

Sara smiled and her knees weakened slightly in relief. Quinn looked about as likely to move as the Rock of Gibraltar.

There was something sexy about a man who did what he thought was right, and who did what he said he was going to do. She took another long look. Quinn's arms were folded across his chest and he crossed his legs at the ankle. His legs were muscular and tanned; his shoulders stretched the T-shirt fabric taut.

There was a lot more that was sexy about Quinn Tyrrell than his sense of purpose. He lifted his gaze to the window she stood at; she was sure she could see the blue glint of his eyes, the intent in his expression. She watched him for a long moment, more reassured by his presence than she might have expected, then headed for the shower.

She felt lighter. Happier. More in charge of her universe.

Just because Quinn had brought her a coffee.

Had she dreamed of Quinn's past?

If so, when had that fire occurred?

What had happened to him after that? If it had been his memory, he had only been a little boy when everyone he knew had been killed. Sara's heart clenched in compassion. She was thirty years older than he had been, and she had been devastated by the loss of her parents, followed so quickly by Magda's death. How could a young boy have managed to survive?

He certainly would get used to taking care of himself.

Sara showered quickly, trying to scrub away the emotional wreckage of the nightmare with cold water and soap. She noticed the coin on her nightstand as she was dressing and, on instinct, she put it in her purse.

Quinn didn't move as she came down the steps, but smiled slowly when she waved at him. She stopped to pick up the newspaper on the walk, well aware of how intently he observed her every move.

Funny how she'd never felt sexy going to work in the morning before. She thought about what they'd done—what they hadn't yet done—and tingled right to her toes. Quinn smiled his languid smile and Sara knew that she could get used to having this man in her life.

In one way, she felt like they were from different worlds. In another way, she was the one who was hearing the Wyvern in distress. Maybe saving the Wyvern was something they could do together. Maybe it was a way that she and Quinn could merge their worlds.

Sara bit her lip as she remembered something. There was no denying that the dragon she had seen through his eyes, the one flying overhead as the church burned, had looked a lot like Erik.

Maybe Quinn's distrust of his fellows was deserved.

"Good morning," Sara said when she was crossing the street. She wore a crisp linen dress; this one was a tailored shirtdress in shades of turquoise. It made her tan look more golden and its clean lines suited her. She had her hair knotted up again and Quinn wished he'd met her when the weather was cooler, so he could see it spread over her shoulders.

Like spun gold.

"I thought you might like a coffee," he said, trying to read her expression. He wasn't sure whether she was glad to see him or not. It was entirely possible that he could cross the line from *protective* to *stalker* and Quinn was well aware of that danger. He handed Sara the coffee, and their fingers brushed in the transaction.

Sara smiled at the brief glimmer of light between their fingertips. She met his gaze, humor dancing in her own eyes, as she took a grateful sip. She closed her eyes, savoring the coffee as he'd expected she would, then smiled at him. "Just coffee? Not a ride to work?"

"That too, if you'd like." He opened the passenger door of the truck for her, holding her coffee while she climbed into the cab. When she reached to take it from him, he spoke quietly. "I don't want to spook you, Sara."

"But they're out there. I know." She held up her arm, which had a rosy glow like sunburn, and Quinn didn't need the reminder of his failure to protect her. "I'm glad to see you. Don't imagine otherwise."

"Fair enough." Quinn handed her the coffee, then shut her door. When he got into the driver's seat, Sara cleared her throat.

He suspected she wouldn't say anything he'd like and he was right.

"I heard the Wyvern again this morning."

Quinn stopped in the act of turning the key in the ignition. He didn't like these visions that Sara was having of the Wyvern, because he knew her well enough already to sense where this was going. "Are you sure?"

"Positive. They're hurting her." Sara shook her head and Quinn sensed her agitation. She took a deep breath. "I don't know why I'm the one who has to hear her. . . ."

Quinn pulled away from the curb. "Maybe you're psychic."

"I thought you didn't believe in that sort of thing."

"It's fine for other people. I'm not psychic and I'm not going to make decisions based on voices from nowhere." Quinn didn't want to argue with her but he had a feeling it was going to happen, anyway.

"I can't just listen and not do anything. We have to save her."

At least she had said *we*. Quinn shook his head all the same. "I don't think so."

"Excuse me?"

He kept his voice calm, hiding his impatience with the very idea. "Well, do you have any idea where she is?"

"No."

"There aren't any clues in what you hear?"

"No. I just hear her calling for help." Sara shrugged, then shuddered. "And begging someone to stop hurting her. It's awful. I can't listen to this forever."

"I'm sure it is. But that doesn't mean that we can save her."

Sara turned to face him and Quinn didn't have to look to feel her disapproval of what he'd said. "Don't you think it's important to try?"

"How are you going to try?" His fear for her safety flared into impatience. "You don't know where she is. You don't know who is holding her captive. You said yourself that you've never had visions before."

"Don't tell me that these dreams are just my imagination."

Quinn tried to quell his irritation and was pretty sure he failed. "Where would you go? What would you do? How would you start?"

Sara folded her arms across her chest. "Every problem has a solution. We just have to work it out." She fired a glance across the cab. "We just have to work together."

Quinn gritted his teeth. "So, let's walk through it. Who would be holding the Wyvern captive?"

"It must be *Slayers*."

"Exactly. And those would be the same *Slayers* who are determined to kill you." He looked at her, knowing he hadn't changed her mind. "I'm thinking that your going to them to try to free the Wyvern isn't a really great plan."

"Well, I can't just ignore her call for help."

"Then you tell someone else what you know and you let them solve it, if it's important enough to them. You take care of yourself first."

"I'm telling *you*. Why doesn't it seem as though you're going to do something about it?"

"I'm taking care of you first. If it makes you feel any better, I'll tell someone else about your visions."

"But you won't agree to try to save the Wyvern ourselves."

Quinn ground the gears in his frustration. "Sara, the most important thing to me right now is this firestorm. The only person I want to see safe is you. Understood?"

"But what about your responsibility to your kind?"

"My kind has not really done a great deal for me over the course of my life. I think they do all right without me."

"You don't trust Erik because you saw him when your parents were killed. You think he killed them, too."

Quinn stalled the truck and didn't care. He turned to stare at Sara, and saw conviction in her gaze. "How do you know that?"

"I dreamed last night about a four-year-old boy," she said so firmly that he couldn't doubt her. "He was hiding in a mill when an invading army came. They killed the miller and raped his wife before they killed her, then they burned the villagers in the church. The boy had four older brothers and I think he was the only one who survived."

Quinn swore. There was no way she could have known about his past. There was no record of his parents or their death or his brothers. He'd looked it up a thousand times and always found the assertion that everyone had been killed. He looked at Sara again. "That's impossible."

"Apparently not." Sara smiled slightly. "Maybe you're the one with ten impossible things to believe before breakfast today."

He started the truck roughly. "That's not funny, Sara."

"You were the one who told me I was the Seer."

"I told you about some prophecy. I didn't say I believed it."

"Maybe you should. Maybe *we* should."

Quinn was not persuaded. "It's impossible for you to have dreamed of what I've experienced. That's in the past. It's a memory. It's over."

"It's not over if you still feel passionate about it."

"It doesn't matter!" Quinn roared. "What matters is that you're my destined mate and it's my responsibility to protect you."

"Which you'll do, regardless of the cost to yourself."

"Pretty much." He glared at her but she didn't appear to be frightened.

They drove in silence until Sara sighed. "It's kind of weird, this effect you have on me."

Quinn had to agree with that. "Maybe it's Magda doing it to you, not me."

"Sure, blame somebody else," Sara said, but there was humor in her tone. Quinn glanced up to find that her eyes were green again, dancing with laughter. He loved how she used humor to deal with challenges and found himself smiling in response.

She arched a brow. "So what exactly would be my responsibility, as your destined mate?"

"To bear my child, of course. You heard that yesterday."

"Why am I thinking that delivering a dragon baby would hurt even more than delivering the usual kind?"

Quinn frowned. "The *Pyr* don't come into their abilities until puberty. Our young are indistinguishable from human young until then."

"Why do you want a child, Quinn?"

He chose to tell her half of the truth. "Because it's my responsibility to the *Pyr* to ensure that my legacy continues. Erik's right: we all have a duty to breed, and the firestorm means that my time has come."

"That sounds ominous."

"It doesn't have to be." He flicked a glance her way. "If my mate doesn't insist on entering the lairs of *Slayers*."

Sara's lips set. "Saving the Wyvern doesn't necessarily mean that I have to go into the lairs of *Slayers*."

"*Someone* is going to have to physically retrieve the Wyvern." Quinn turned down State Street. "The *Slayers* aren't going to hand her over just because you ask."

"Saving the Wyvern doesn't necessarily mean that I'll be in danger."

"Sara, you're already in danger." Quinn knew he was fighting a losing battle but he couldn't let it go. The idea of Sara going voluntarily to the *Slayers* who were determined to destroy her made his guts clench. What if *she* were the one being tortured? "I shouldn't have to tell you that. I don't think we should go looking for more trouble."

"Well, I don't think we have a choice. I can't listen to her screams every day for the rest of my life."

"Nothing says it will last that long," Quinn argued, irritated with the entire discussion.

"No, that's true. They might kill her."

He looked at Sara and saw the challenge in her gaze. She thought less of him, he could see that, but he couldn't see a way to save the Wyvern without putting Sara herself at risk.

And ensuring her safety was his primary concern.

He would protect her above all else.

"Every problem has a solution," Sara said flatly. "My father used to tell me that. He even had a system."

Quinn kept a grim silence. Sara could scheme and plan all she wanted—he couldn't stop her from doing that—but he would not allow her to go into a *Slayer*'s den, not for any price.

All he had to figure out was how to persuade her that he was right.

Even if that was looking like a long shot.

"I need to know more about what the Wyvern does," Sara said, looking at Quinn expectantly.

He was not going to encourage this. "I don't know."

"You just don't want to tell me."

Quinn hated that he was that transparent. "I'm not really sure. She's supposed to provide prophecies and advice, but it never makes a lot of sense."

"Give me an example."

"I remember only one."

Sara smiled. "Let me guess which one it is."

Quinn pulled into his assigned parking spot, backing the truck and trailer into the space beside his booth with practiced ease. He then turned to face Sara, and recited the old verse again.

> *When the Dragon's Tail demands its price,*
> *And the moon is devoured once, not twice,*
> *Seer and Smith will again unite.*
> *Water and air, with fire and earth*
> *This sacred union will give birth*
> *To the* Pyr*'s sole chance to save the Earth.*

"What does all of that mean?"

"I'm not sure. I'm not sure it matters, either."

Sara frowned. "Maybe it means that the Wyvern is your destined mate."

Quinn chuckled. "No."

"Why is that funny?"

"It takes a *Pyr* and a human to make more *Pyr*. I'm *Pyr*; she's *Pyr*: there's no mating potential there." He stretched one finger toward Sara, because there was one truth neither of them could avoid. She raised a finger herself and the spark lit between their fingertips.

"Sparks fly," she teased. "Signs don't get much clearer than that."

"The firestorm is the only sign that matters," Quinn murmured, feeling its increasingly familiar heat. The air in the cab seemed to crackle with electricity and he found himself noticing the ripe curve of Sara's lips.

But Sara frowned and pulled her hand away from his. She snatched her coffee from the cup holder and took a quick drink. "I think there's more to this than you'd like to believe. I need to know more about the Wyvern. Can you send Erik to me, and let him pass through your smoke into the bookstore?"

Quinn sat back, dissatisfied that she was so insistent about this. "I could."

"But you don't want to."

"I don't trust him."

"He saved me yesterday," Sara continued.

"Sort of. You're forgetting the bit about him tossing you out of the tower."

"I think you're too suspicious of him." Sara couldn't stop herself from challenging Quinn. "Is it because you saw him kill Ambrose, or because you saw him when your parents died?"

Quinn wasn't going to tell her that the third time was the charm. It was too close for comfort. "Does it matter?"

"I think it does. Erik said last night he killed Ambrose to protect you."

"There's no one to verify that," Quinn said grimly.

"But what if he did?" Sara demanded. "What if he's been looking out for you? They said Ambrose was a *Slayer*— what if Erik *was* protecting you?"

"Now, you're making stuff up." Quinn got out of the truck with impatience, but when he got to Sara's door, he saw that she wasn't ready to let it go.

"If Erik had wanted to kill me, he could have done it yesterday morning in my shop," she said when Quinn opened her door. "There was no one to stop him. Instead he gave me books to read. Does that sound like something a *Slayer* would do?"

"Just because he's sneaky doesn't mean I should trust him," Quinn insisted, even as he realized she was right.

"You'd just rather work alone," Sara accused as she slid out of the truck.

"It's worked pretty well so far."

"No. Working alone never works for the duration." Sara tapped a fingertip on Quinn's chest, sending little jolts of electricity over his skin. "You get better results working as a team. You should share information with Erik and strategize with him."

The very idea made everything in Quinn tighten with dread. He looked down at his coffee, knowing he wasn't getting anywhere fast.

"Will you try?" Sara asked. "Will you talk to him?"

He looked at her, letting her see the depths of his animosity for the other *Pyr*.

She didn't flinch. "Maybe he knows more than you do."

Quinn felt his eyes narrow. "Maybe I'm having a hard time letting the past go."

Sara studied him, then turned away. The street was

becoming busy but he knew she wasn't really looking at the pedestrians. He followed her gaze to the bell tower and could have done without the reminder of the night before. The last thing he wanted to do was set up his booth and try to be charming to potential customers, let alone leave Sara alone in her shop all day.

"How many *Pyr* friends have you had?" she asked quietly.

Quinn was startled. "One. Why?"

She turned to face him. "The *Slayer* who tried to kill me yesterday, the golden one, he acted as if he knew you."

Quinn's heart clenched, but Sara was going to tell him what she thought he needed to hear.

"He said he had taught you, that you had always been a good fighter but that you had learned to be calculating from him. He said you two had history."

Quinn looked away and his throat clenched.

It was true. Ambrose was alive and intent on killing Sara.

Quinn had been foolish and trusted the enemy once. There was no reason to make the same mistake twice—and Erik Sorensson was the last *Pyr* Quinn would let cross his smoke to be alone with Sara.

If he told her that, of course, she'd want to know why. Quinn was tired of meddling details. The most important thing was that his firestorm was here. He had to move fast, or risk being cheated again.

It was time to kindle the flame.

Sara knew she'd hit a nerve. She suspected that Quinn knew who her assailant was, but she didn't think he was going to tell her.

Yet.

"I'd prefer to walk you to your store," he said grimly.

Sara smiled to lighten the mood. "Lair to lair delivery?"

Quinn was obviously reassured that she wasn't going to argue with him. A wary twinkle lit in his eyes. "Something like that. Indulge me?"

"I think you're indulging me," she said. "Thanks for the ride and the coffee, too. I'm feeling quite spoiled this morning."

Quinn caught her hand in his. "Aren't princesses supposed to be spoiled?" he murmured, in that low voice she found so seductive.

She looked up as a sizzle danced over her skin, emanating from their interlaced fingers. Quinn studied her as if she were the most gorgeous woman in the world. His eyes darkened to indigo as his smile slowly faded. Sara could only stare back as her mouth went dry.

He touched her jaw with his other hand, a line of fire following the gentle caress of his fingertip. Sara's knees weakened as he cupped her chin in his hand. She knew what he was going to do, right in the middle of State Street, and couldn't decide whether she wanted him to hurry to the kiss or be leisurely about it.

He was watching her, seeking some hint that she didn't want him to kiss her. Sara held his gaze and smiled up at him. There was no one in her world but Quinn, nothing but the blaze of desire in his eyes. His thumb eased across her lips, a slow, steady caress that set her aflame. Sara felt hot and she couldn't quite catch her breath.

Quinn leaned closer, giving her time to evade him if she wanted, but Sara didn't move. She waited. He had the bluest eyes she'd ever seen. He had the longest and darkest lashes imaginable, but they made him look only more masculine. His lips were firm with a sensuous curve, one that curved an increment more as he studied her.

"I want you safe," he murmured. "First and foremost."

"Ditto," she whispered. Sara pushed back his straw

fedora with a playful fingertip and curved one hand around his face. She could feel the slight stubble of his whiskers even though he'd shaved, and could feel the determination in his jaw. His throat was muscled and tanned and she liked that he was both taller and stronger than she. "You make me feel safe," she admitted.

He turned his head and kissed the palm of her hand, sending fire through her veins with that fleeting touch.

"More," Sara whispered and he smiled.

It was the only encouragement he needed. He inclined his head and his lips brushed across hers once, tantalizing and teasing; then his mouth closed over hers with resolve.

Sara closed her eyes with satisfaction. His was a slow and powerful kiss, a leisurely kiss that explored and tempted and teased. Sara leaned against his chest and let her fingers tangle in his hair, closed her eyes, and surrendered to sensation. There were only Quinn and his fiery touch, only Quinn and his caress.

It was a kiss that melted the barriers between them. She tasted his fear and his desire, understood that his reluctance to seek the Wyvern was out of concern for her safety. She felt the mingling of strength and gentleness that she already appreciated in him; she savored the certainty that he was content to spend half a day on a single kiss.

If that was what it took to make it right. His kiss was by turns gentle and demanding. It was hot and sweet and powerful. It was a first kiss to eliminate all other kisses from Sara's thoughts. It was thorough and languorous and altogether fabulous.

She didn't want it to end, and neither, apparently, did Quinn.

Quinn's kiss was a more effective way to jump-start her system than a cup of strong coffee and a whole lot more pleasurable. Sara could have kissed Quinn all morning long.

She knew that she was being savored, and appreciated, and admired—just for being who she was.

If that wasn't seductive, she didn't know what was.

No one had ever made Sara forget where she was. No one had ever made her burn and yearn. No man had ever persuaded Sara with one kiss to slide her tongue between his teeth, much less to make her want to drag him home and have her way with him.

Immediately.

With chocolate sauce.

No one had ever kissed Sara the way Quinn did.

Someone honked impatiently and both Quinn and Sara jumped. The other driver wanted to park in the next spot, but couldn't because they were standing there, necking like teenagers. Sara eased away from Quinn with reluctance, her breath coming fast. He let her go, but not far. His eyes gleamed brightly when he joined her on the sidewalk.

"The firestorm," she whispered, unable to stop from touching her burning lips with her fingertips. Was the firestorm about more than physical attraction? Sara wanted to know but didn't know how to ask.

Quinn swallowed and nodded as they turned toward her shop. "The start of it, anyway."

Sara stared at him. "You mean it gets stronger?"

"From what I understand."

"You've never felt it before?"

He smiled that slow smile, the one that melted her bones and made her want to do things with him that weren't particularly sensible. "I've never met you before, Sara."

"No, I think I'd remember if we had."

Quinn chuckled, and she found herself laughing with him. He knotted their fingers together with purpose, the strength of his hand around hers making Sara feel sexy and safe.

She could feel his pulse, hammering against her own palm, and liked the evidence of his arousal. At least she wasn't the only one whose universe had been shaken by that kiss.

She wanted to do more than rattle Quinn, though, or at least she wanted to shake his world on an ongoing basis. She turned her morning newspaper as they walked into the arcade, halfway expecting to see headlines about Ann Arbor having been invaded by dragons. Instead, the front cover story was about the art fair. She eyeballed the index in confusion.

"What's the matter?" he asked.

"How can it be that no one saw that dragon fight last night? I thought it would be in the paper."

Quinn smiled. "They saw it but they don't remember."

"Why not?"

"Because they were beguiled."

Sara thought about that for a minute. "Erik said something like that. When he wanted us to come to his hotel room."

"Yes. They had to do the beguiling first."

Sara waited but Quinn didn't say anything more. "And?" she prompted when he didn't say more. For the first time, she sensed that he was evading one of her questions and she wondered why.

"And what?"

"What's beguiling?"

Quinn frowned. "It's a way of making humans believe things that aren't true."

"Like casting a spell?" Sara didn't like the sound of that, and it probably showed in her tone. Why didn't Quinn want to tell her about this power?

He wasn't using it on her, was he?

"More like hypnosis," Quinn said, his tone terse. "I don't

like it. I don't do it. That doesn't mean that other *Pyr* don't find it useful sometimes."

"Like with controlling crowds or public sightings."

"That's not what I do. I run a solo game."

"Wouldn't you have beguiled people last night?"

Quinn shook his head without hesitation. "I'd leave them to create their own explanations. People aren't prepared to believe that they've actually seen a dragon, let alone half a dozen of us. They'll come up with a rationalization quickly enough." His frown deepened. "I'd rather just be careful about showing myself publicly, and deal with any consequences when I do."

"It's more honest that way," Sara guessed. They reached the shop and she eyed the mermaid door knocker, relieved to see it cold and black.

"I am what I am, and *Pyr* is what I am." Quinn said with pride. "I'm not going to hide from the truth."

Sara understood what he didn't say. "You mean you're not really afraid of humans."

"Why should I be? The major threats to our survival are other *Pyr*." Quinn seemed to be checking his territory mark, then gave her a simmering glance that made her heart jump. He looked so intense that she was half-afraid of what he would say. His words surprised her all the same. "I'd appreciate it if you'd call me when you want to leave the shop."

Sara unlocked the shop door. "I can't bother you every time I go for a coffee."

"Yes, you can," Quinn insisted, his eyes blazing. "It's not safe for you to leave a protected area."

Sara took one look at him and surrendered the fight. She was never going to persuade him that she was safe alone, no matter how much she doubted the threat to her person in broad daylight.

Once he had seen her safely inside the store and gone

back to his booth, Sara looked around with dissatisfaction. She couldn't live her life, only able to move around in Quinn's presence. Every problem had a solution: she just had to find it.

She had a feeling it had something to do with Quinn's past.

And maybe something to do with the Wyvern.

Either way, she needed expert help. Sara surveyed the silent store, then took a chance. "Go ahead: help me, Magda," she invited.

"Please," she added when nothing happened.

Sara had two beats to feel silly, then the air conditioner whirred to life.

And a book fell to the floor in the back of the shop.

As she headed toward it, she had to admit that it was handy to have a ghost on her side.

Chapter 9

Quinn didn't believe that Sara was going to do what he asked, but short of parking outside of her shop for the day—and earning her animosity—he didn't know what to do. He set up his booth in poor humor, taking pride in lining up his wares in an orderly fashion. It was going to be another hot day and he was too short of sleep to be amiable.

He had just arranged the drawer pulls and door hardware to his satisfaction when a coin fell and rolled.

Quinn froze.

The silver coin rolled between his feet, spiraled, and fell heads-up right in front of him. He glanced over his shoulder, not really surprised to find Donovan leaning on one pole that supported the awning over Quinn's booth.

"Blood duel," Donovan murmured in old-speak.

Quinn snorted. He bent down and picked up the coin. It was a silver dollar, one of the old ones with a higher silver content.

"I save them for special occasions," Donovan said.

"Glad to know that I'm special," Quinn replied and put the coin down on his display table.

"Didn't you hear me?" Donovan demanded. "I challenged you to a blood duel. Or maybe you've been away from our kind so long that you've forgotten how things are done."

"I haven't forgotten anything."

"Then let's go."

Quinn slanted a glance at the other *Pyr*. "You really don't want to do this."

"Wrong, Smith. I really *do* want to do this."

Quinn picked up the silver dollar, his gaze locked with Donovan's, and closed his fist around the coin. He blew into his closed hand and willed the coin to change. He opened his hand a moment later and tossed the coin to Donovan, who caught it despite his surprise.

It had been transformed to show Quinn's hammer on one side and his mermaid on the other.

"So, you really are the Smith," Donovan said without admiration. "And you really do have a clue what you're doing." He looked Quinn up and down, his attitude unchanged. "That only makes it worse, in my opinion."

"Makes what worse?"

"Delaney was hit years ago and he never healed right. I used to look out for him; I thought Erik would look out for him."

"Your argument is with Erik. Call him out for your blood feud."

Donovan laughed. "My argument is with you, Smith, and we both know it. What's the matter? Afraid you'll lose before you've secured your legacy with your mate?"

Quinn met the other *Pyr*'s gaze steadily, giving him one last chance to let it go. "You don't know what you're getting into."

"Then let's find out." Donovan tossed the coin back and this time Quinn snatched it out of the air.

"You're on," he said, knowing there was only one way to solve this dispute. "But don't come whining to me when you get hurt."

Donovan laughed but Quinn had learned a lot since the last time they had seen each other fight. Sara was safe in her shop, with his territory mark around her.

The mermaid was stone cold.

And this wouldn't take long.

Sara glanced down the aisles and quickly spotted the fallen book. It was splayed open on the floor. Sara picked it up, fearing that one of the pages had been bent. *The Cathars.* Who were they? She hadn't reached this section in her reading yet and didn't have any idea what the book was about.

The book had opened to a double page spread entitled "The Massacre at Béziers." Sara might have thought she had the wrong book, at least until she noticed the photo at the bottom of the right page.

It was a photo of a coin, one that was identical to the one left in her purse. It was labeled as being the coinage of Raymond-Roger Trencavel, Viscount of Béziers and Carcassonne.

Sara took the book to the cash desk, sat down, and started to read. In half an hour, she knew that the house of Trencavel had controlled much of an area that had been associated with a heretical sect known as the Cathars. The Cathars had also been known as the Albigensians, a name taken from the Languedoc town of Albi where many of them had resided.

The Cathars didn't seem very shocking at eight centuries removal, but in those times, their presence and their teachings had been considered a threat to nearby Christians.

The Cathars had believed in a kind of reincarnation, by which a soul could be reborn in any life form. They did not consider plants or fish to have souls, so those foodstuffs

composed their diet. They were essentially vegetarians, in a
time during which most people relied heavily upon meat for
sustenance.

They read the Bible for themselves and discussed its lessons among themselves, instead of letting priests read and
interpret it for them. Again, after the Reformation and estab-
lishment of Christian denominations that promoted exactly
that teaching model, Sara couldn't find the practice very
awful.

Certainly not worth a death sentence.

Finally, and perhaps worst of all, the Cathars tithed to
their own priests instead of to the Roman Church. Sara
tapped her finger on the book. The language of money was
one that she spoke fluently and she suspected that this item
was the real root of the issue.

The house of Trencavel, it seemed, had been remarkably
tolerant in terms of religion. As long as the secular tithes
were paid, they didn't worry much about ecclesiastical tithes
being collected. Perhaps predictably, in time the Papacy
took exception to that policy.

In the early thirteenth century, the crusading fervor that
had gripped Europe turned from the Middle East to battle-
fields closer to home. It was expensive to travel—there was
the financial side of things again—and matters had turned
against the crusaders in Palestine. After the conquest of
Spain and Portugal from the Muslims, the crusaders looked
within Europe for new objectives. There were crusades in
the Baltics, in the Italian peninsula, and the Albigensian
Crusade in Languedoc.

The Cathars had to be exterminated, by thirteenth century
logic, for the good of the faith, the protection of orthodoxy,
and the uninterrupted flow of ecclesiastical tithes.

A town ruled by the tolerant Raymond-Roger, Béziers
had been targeted by the approaching army, despite Raymond-

Roger's attempts to negotiate at the last minute. It was believed that some two hundred Cathars were among Béziers's population of twenty thousand.

On July 22, 1209, the crusaders sacked the town. The residents fled to the churches for sanctuary, which should have saved their lives. In the cathedral, however, the priests conducted a mass for the dead.

Sara read with horror that it proved to be a mass for those who had taken refuge there. The crusaders sealed the doors from the outside and razed the church while it was fully occupied. The rest of the city's inhabitants were used for target practice or simply slaughtered.

The town was then burned to the ground.

By the end of the day, Arnaud Amaury, the Cistercian abbot-commander of the assault, sent triumphant word to the Papacy that twenty thousand people in Béziers had been killed, regardless of their age, rank, or gender. It was recorded that not so much as a single baby survived that day's massacre.

It was a horrific account of terrible events, made even more horrible by the fact that it had been recorded by ecclesiastics who crowed about their triumph in Béziers. Sara could think only of all those people who had been viciously killed, of a town that had been eliminated because 1 percent of its population was Bible-reading vegetarians.

The closing words of the summary were the ones that made Sara's blood run cold. At the launch of the assault, Arnaud Amaury had been asked how to tell Cathar from Catholic within the city walls. His reply resonated with the brutality of that day:

"Kill them all, for God will surely recognize his own."

Sara shut the book, shivered, and stared out the windows of her shop. Her instincts told her that this church fire might be the fire in which Quinn's mother had died. But that made no rational sense: Quinn would have been more than eight hundred years old, for that to be the case.

She thought of his joke that he was old enough to know better and wondered.

Maybe this was just another impossible thing to believe.

Maybe she had a couple of new questions for Quinn.

She thought of calling him for escort service and decided not to bother. After all, it was only midmorning, and the arcade was filled with tourists and shoppers. It couldn't be a hundred yards to his booth. He'd probably be busy at this hour. Maybe he'd be glad enough to see her that he'd forget to be annoyed.

Maybe she needed to prove to both of them that there were still some times she could be alone.

She turned the sign to read BACK IN FIVE MINUTES, took the coin and the book that Magda had chosen, and stepped out into the arcade. The mermaid was glowing faintly when Sara locked the door and she hesitated for a moment, then decided that the mermaid was simply resonating with Quinn's anxiety.

She hadn't taken more than a dozen steps toward State Street before she knew she'd called that wrong.

After Quinn asked a volunteer to mind his booth, he and Donovan moved quickly in search of a good spot. Donovan suggested a cluster of trees to the east of downtown that housed a business park. The density of the trees and the comparatively small number of businesses combined with the hour to mean that few humans would observe them.

"Stay low," he advised Donovan. "The less beguiling that needs to be done, the better."

Donovan grinned. "Maybe we'll just leave it be. It's about time that humans knew we walked among them, in my opinion."

"It's never been our way," Quinn said.

"It's honest," Donovan said with force and Quinn had to agree with him.

That same directness characterized Donovan's fighting. Once they were in the clearing they'd chosen, he turned on Quinn.

"This is for Delaney," he said and threw a punch at Quinn's face.

Quinn seized his fist and turned it behind him, forcing Donovan toward the ground. "We can end this now," he offered, but Donovan snarled.

He changed shape with impressive speed, shifting within Quinn's grip to a dragon too large and sinuous for Quinn to hold. Donovan was dark blue in dragon form, as if he were made of lapis lazuli set in gold, and moved with power. He wrestled free of Quinn's grip, pivoted, and slashed with his claws.

Quinn leapt backward, shifted shape, and met the attacking Donovan in midair. They locked claws in the traditional fighting pose and he felt the strength of his opponent. Upright, they were both beating their wings, which kept them a dozen feet off the ground.

Donovan was fighting to win. This was no play match: it was a blood duel in the old style. Quinn was more than ready for it.

"No room for mistakes," Donovan whispered in old-speak, with a mischievous glance at the ground. The pair grappled with each other, each trying to force the other to break his grip or to roll backward.

"It's better to win when the stakes are high," Quinn replied.

No sooner had he said as much than Donovan made his move: he swung his tail to strike at the same moment he bent Quinn's claws backward. Quinn snarled and retaliated in kind. They rolled in the air, tails locked and teeth bared, their powers evenly matched.

Quinn didn't really want to injure Donovan, but the other *Pyr* didn't share that perspective.

Donovan ripped his tail free of Quinn's grip, then swung it at Quinn with killing force. When Quinn ducked the blow, Donovan slapped him across the face from the other side with one leathery wing. They dropped in the air, but Quinn beat his wings higher, bearing the other *Pyr*'s weight upward.

Neither of them was breathing hard.

Donovan lunged upward at Quinn, baring his teeth to bite Quinn's scaled chest. Quinn slashed at the other *Pyr* with his legs and while Donovan evaded the full force of that blow, Quinn saw the flash of his sharp teeth. He breathed dragonfire to protect himself and Donovan loosed his grip.

Quinn let him fall.

Donovan caught himself just before impact. He glared at Quinn as he winced at the singe he'd taken.

"I won't be retaliating in kind," he muttered. "I've heard about the Smith and dragonfire."

"You can't believe every rumor you hear," Quinn said with a smile.

Donovan snorted. "You won't talk me into making you stronger that easily." He'd barely finished his old-speak when he dove at Quinn again.

Quinn realized he'd felt only a fraction of Donovan's power. This time, the other *Pyr* locked claws with Quinn with surprising vigor. Quinn couldn't tear his claws free. Donovan wrapped his tail around Quinn's as if he'd hold him captive.

"Now you can surrender," he taunted, but Quinn had other thoughts.

He wasn't going to waste all day satisfying Donovan's desire to fight. He wanted a fight: he'd get a fight.

And he'd get it now.

Quinn exhaled smoke in Donovan's face in the same moment that he thrashed Donovan with his tail, knowing he'd leave him bruised but not that injured. He dragged his teeth across the other *Pyr*'s shoulder, enough to draw blood, then flung him out of the sky with a heavy strike of his tail.

Donovan fell, pivoted right above the ground, and raged upward, fury in his eyes. He snatched at Quinn's wings, tearing one painfully with his claw, then slashed across Quinn's belly with his rear claw. Quinn glanced up in that moment.

It wasn't the sight of Donovan's tail, poised to strike, that surprised him.

A topaz yellow dragon came out of nowhere, slicing between them from above like a well-honed blade. Quinn had time to roar a warning but neither of them had a chance to respond. Donovan bellowed as his wing was nicked. Quinn took a swipe with his tail at the passing *Slayer* but only caught his back.

The yellow *Slayer* hovered not far from the pair and grinned. "What a pair of losers," he taunted in old-speak. "Looks like you've both gotten fat and lazy."

"Lucien," Donovan snarled.

"Donovan," Lucien purred, then made a mocking little bow. "How sweet it is to meet once more. Think I'll thump you again?"

Donovan exhaled a puff of smoke and Quinn could feel his anger. These two had battled before, and Donovan must have taken the worst of it. "He's sneaky," he muttered to Quinn. "He won before because he cheated. Make no assumptions."

"Fair enough." Quinn remembered Sara's observation

that the *Slayer*s fought as a team. He glanced around but couldn't see any other dragons in the vicinity. "We can take him together," he suggested and Donovan nodded.

"Yeah, well, don't blink," the other *Pyr* said. "You never know what the real game is with this one."

With that, the pair of *Pyr* dove at Lucien as one.

A man fell into step beside Sara. "Can you break a twenty?" he asked with quiet urgency, and Sara's city girl habits kicked in.

"No, I'm sorry," she said crisply, and hurried past him.

"Liar," he accused, and she glanced up in surprise. He was slightly older than she, trim and well dressed. There was something familiar about him, although Sara was sure she had never seen him before. He smiled and shook his head. "It's not nice to lie, Sara," he said.

She was shocked to hear him call her by name. She must know him, and there was something about him that caught at her memory. Maybe she'd met him at the Chamber of Commerce? Sara couldn't be sure. His eyes were a deep brown, with glints of gold and a faint glimmer of humor.

But it wasn't friendly humor. He was laughing at her and the malice in his gaze made Sara trust her instincts to get away from him. Fast.

"Excuse me, I have to go. I'm late."

"Yes, you are late," he agreed, surprising her again.

She paused to look at him. "Who are you?"

"Don't you know?" He smiled with deliberation and she guessed where they had met.

At the bell tower, the night before.

After all, there was only one other person who had called her a liar recently, only one who had made the accusation with such silky ease.

Not one other person precisely: one other dragon.

She pivoted to run and collided with another man, one who caught her shoulders in firm hands. "Easy, Sara," he said, his voice low and melodic. He was a large man, much taller than she, with fair hair and icy pale eyes.

"I don't know you. Excuse me."

"Of course you know me, Sara," he said with a smooth assurance that reminded her of a ruby red and brass dragon.

His smile broadened. "See? You do remember."

"You must be the ones holding the Wyvern captive," Sara said and saw his alarm.

"I beg your pardon? Did you hear that, Ambrose?"

Ambrose? Sara turned to look at the golden dragon, who simply smiled. "You're Ambrose?"

He held a finger to his lips, his smile unwavering.

"Look at me, Sara," whispered the other man. When Sara didn't turn, he snatched her chin and made her face him.

"Hey!" she began to protest, then forgot why.

Little flames danced in the depths of his pale eyes. They seemed to light the center of his irises but theirs was a cold flame.

Sara shivered, knew she was imagining things, and kept looking.

The fires in his eyes burned brighter and higher, whiter and colder, as the man's voice wound into her ears. He had a Russian accent and spoke with authority. That must have been why Sara wanted to agree with him so badly.

"I'm so glad we met you in time to give you a ride," he said smoothly. "Aren't you?"

It seemed very hard to Sara to remember what she had been doing, and even harder to disagree with the man with the flames in his eyes. "I don't think I need a ride," she managed to say; the two men laughed.

"But it's too hot to walk," the man said.

"But it's too hot to walk," Sara found herself echoing.

Some part of her brain struggled against his melodic voice and his force of will, but she could feel her resistance fading away.

What was happening to her?

"Miss?" asked a passerby. "Are these men bothering you?"

"Of course not: we're old friends," the Russian one insisted. The passerby looked skeptical but Sara couldn't tear her gaze away from those cold flames.

"We're old friends," she said.

"If you're sure," the passerby said with some hesitation.

Sara couldn't look away from the Russian, the old friend whom she wanted to please so much.

"Of course she's sure," said the Russian. "Our Sara is clever enough to know her own mind." He seemed to find this funny, but Sara knew it was true.

"I know my own mind," she said, barely recognizing her own voice. She sounded like a woman in a trance.

"Why don't we go this way?" suggested Ambrose. "The car is parked on the next street." Sara couldn't look at him, though, not with the Russian man staring at her so intently. She couldn't even watch the passerby walk away, she was so fixated upon watching those flames.

The Russian man was clearly amused by this.

It was quite beautiful how the flames burned in his eyes, though. Why hadn't she ever noticed anything similar before? She wanted to draw closer to him, to watch those flames forever.

And to agree with him.

"Why don't we go this way?" he suggested softly.

"Why don't we go this way?" Sara repeated.

"It'll be quicker in the car."

"It'll be quicker in the car."

"And you can have a nap in the car."

"I can have a nap."

"I know you're very tired, Sara. You must be so very tired."

Sara barely stifled a yawn. "Very tired," she agreed and he smiled.

He walked beside her, one hand on the small of her back, guiding her back toward Maynard Street. Sara couldn't look away from his mesmerizing gaze, even though her heart was pounding. It was good of him to guide her, because she would have tripped without his assistance.

He was such a good old friend.

"Soon we'll be among ourselves," he promised her.

"Soon we'll be among ourselves," Sara echoed and couldn't take a breath. Some part of her mind screamed in frustration, but she couldn't heed it, couldn't pay attention to it, couldn't do anything other than what the Russian man wanted her to do.

"Such a strange door knocker," Ambrose said as they passed Sara's shop. "How does anyone use it when it's burning hot?"

And then he laughed.

Lucien was slippery and sneaky, just as Donovan had predicted. He was fast and evasive: Donovan snatched him early and the *Slayer* wriggled free, as if he had no bones at all. He flew in erratic patterns, so that Quinn closed tight behind and just as he was about to strike, Lucien turned hard and escaped his grip.

Lucien's scales glittered and he was as hard to corner as a sunbeam. He stopped suddenly, then lunged forward unexpectedly, hammering once into Donovan in a collision that left the lapis lazuli *Pyr* gasping for breath. He attacked from behind and below and had no quibbles with taking advantage of a blind spot.

At least Donovan was getting the fight he wanted.

Quinn and Donovan became better at anticipating each other's moves with every passing minute. Quinn only hoped they learned to fight together quickly enough. Donovan surged after the willowy *Slayer* and slashed at his back with his claws, then breathed dragonfire. Lucien took his first hit and roared with pain.

Then he spun, his tail winding into a spiral below him. Quinn saw the hatred in Lucien's eyes before he slashed at Donovan. His talons were long and black and sharpened, and they sliced Donovan's belly like knives cutting in unison.

Donovan gasped, his pain too great for him to bellow, and began to fall to the earth. Quinn saw the blood running from the other *Pyr*'s belly and raged toward Lucien.

"One down, one to do," Lucien said with a chortle. The *Slayer* turned with slow confidence, bracing himself for Quinn's assault, and forgot about Donovan.

To his own detriment. Quinn focused on Lucien, knowing that Donovan would shortly come to his aid. He swung his tail and Lucien darted backward, taunting him.

"Oh, aren't we assertive," Lucien whispered in old-speak. "Afraid I might get the jump on you?"

He leapt at Quinn, and Quinn made to swat the *Slayer* out of the air with his tail. Lucien seized the end of Quinn's tail and rode Quinn's follow-through, laughing. Quinn spun and struck his tail hard against a large rock. Lucien took the brunt of the blow and sizzled with anger as he fell to the earth. He shook his head and came up fighting, fire emanating from his nostrils and his eyes blazing with anger.

He dove at Quinn, those black talons extended. Quinn backed toward a massive tree, letting Lucien draw closer and closer. At the last minute, Quinn darted behind the tree. He heard Lucien's talons drive into the wood.

The talons on both front claws had dug into the tree trunk, but Lucien immediately hauled one free. He was livid, almost glowing in his rage, and he turned to breathe dragonfire at Quinn.

Quinn hovered beside him, letting the dragonfire fill him with new power. He smiled at the *Slayer*'s obvious shock.

"Is that your best shot?" he asked mildly and Lucien belched smoke and fire again.

Quinn brushed a bit of ash off his shoulder, letting the *Slayer* see how his scales gleamed like forged steel.

"You really are the Smith," Lucien whispered.

"And you've given me the strength I need to finish the business at hand," Quinn said. Lucien's eyes widened and he struggled to free his one claw from the tree. The talons had sunk deep, though, with the force of impact, and he couldn't pull them out.

"I don't like these," Quinn said, seizing the *Slayer*'s free claw by the wrist. He examined the long talons, which looked to be made of metal. How could Lucien have metal talons? What technology was this? He glanced up to find the *Slayer* smiling.

"You have to come to the dark side to get a set, Smith."

"Maybe I'll just take these instead," Quinn said. "I like to collect souvenirs." He gave Lucien a moment to worry about it, before he slashed the joint with his claws. He tore the claw free and threw it to the ground, ignoring Lucien's furious screams.

The *Slayer* pulled himself free of the wood then, his eyes red with fury. Lucien came after Quinn but didn't manage to reach him before Donovan caught him by the throat. The other *Pyr* had quietly flown up behind the *Slayer* and now his claws were locked around Lucien's throat.

Lucien choked and squirmed. He scrabbled at Donovan's

grip with his other claw, drawing blood—at least until Quinn divested him of that claw as well.

"You will pay for this," Lucien muttered.

"I think you're the one paying," Quinn said.

Lucien smiled coldly. "That's where you're wrong, Smith."

Quinn was certain that this was just bravado. Donovan held Lucien's tail down with his own, then pinned out the *Slayer*'s two back claws with his own, holding an ankle on each side.

Donovan took great satisfaction in stretching out the injured *Slayer*, letting his victim feel that he was bigger and stronger. Donovan had lost a lot of blood, as Quinn could see from the red marks on the ground below, and that worried Quinn. Lucien was bleeding freely from his decapitated claws, the black blood sizzling when it hit the earth.

There was no doubt of the evil in his heart.

When Lucien was splayed out, his belly toward Quinn, the *Slayer* writhed in fear despite the defiant glint in his eyes. Donovan flapped his wings steadily, keeping the pair airborne despite Lucien's efforts to free himself.

"Cook him," Donovan said grimly to Quinn. "I like my traitors well done."

"You can't do this!" Lucien struggled wildly.

This time, it was Donovan who smiled. "Sure we can. Just watch."

"It's not fair!" Lucien protested. "Two against one. It's got to be against a rule. . . ."

"You're the one who attacked us," Quinn observed.

"I didn't think you guys played by the rules," Donovan said. "You didn't worry about playing fair with Delaney, did you?"

"Delaney? Was he the green one?"

"My cousin. I loved him like a brother. This daily special

is for him." He flicked a glance at Quinn, his own filled with resolve. "Supper time, Quinn."

Lucien screamed, but no one came to help him. Quinn drew on his deepest reserves and loosed the hottest and fiercest dragonfire that he could. He focused on the middle of the *Slayer*'s body, so that Donovan would be shielded by Lucien's body.

Lucien screamed and writhed, but he soon fell silent. The smell of burning flesh filled the clearing, sickening Quinn even though he knew they had had no other choice. Quinn watched the light yellow topaz of Lucien dull in color, turn to dark gold, then become brown and lifeless.

Then Donovan flung the *Slayer*'s corpse aside, hovering beside Quinn to watch. Lucien fell from the sky like a dead weight. He hit so hard against the earth that there would be a mark left in the soil.

"Thanks for helping with my tan," Donovan said, surveying the lightly singed scales on his forearms.

"I tried to focus the fire," Quinn said but before he could apologize further, Donovan brushed off his concern.

"It needed to be done, Quinn." He slanted a glance at Quinn and smiled. "That's pretty impressive how you can take the dragonfire. Is that hereditary, or can you teach me the trick?"

"I think it's wired right in."

"Doesn't that figure." Donovan surveyed himself ruefully, seeming to take inventory of his wounds.

"How's your stomach?" Quinn asked. The cuts looked bad, but Donovan was acting as if they looked worse than they were.

"Sore, but I'll heal with Sloane's help. He's got some powerful ointments in his apothecary."

"He can heal?"

"Surface cuts and bruises. He has herbal concoctions."

Donovan raised his eyebrows. "Secret recipes. Nobody else knows the handshake." Donovan poked one cut and winced at the pain. "I hope these are superficial enough that he can help me. Those talons of Lucien's were something else."

"They're tempered steel, made like knives," Quinn said. He flew down to the ground and picked up one of the claws to examine them. The talons glistened evilly, looking even more like retractable knives. But if they were implants, how would they work in human form? Quinn didn't know.

"So, that's why you wanted a closer look," Donovan said and Quinn realized that the other *Pyr* was close beside him.

"Maybe it's something that can be replicated."

"For yourself or for the rest of us?" Donovan demanded. "I could use a set of those, Smith, if you need ideas for Christmas."

Quinn didn't answer. The truth was that he was having his doubts about his ability to return to his old life. These *Slayer*s were merciless and evil, and he sensed that the *Pyr* needed every advantage they could get. Every pair of claws counted, especially if the competition didn't play fairly. Quinn had a feeling that he wasn't going to be able to forget their wickedness—much less sleep at night, knowing that they were out in the world, unchallenged.

He had a feeling that Sara wasn't going to go for that, either.

He looked at Lucien's broken body on the ground beneath them and wondered why the *Slayer* would have taken on two *Pyr* at once.

It made no sense.

"Remember what Sara said about the four elements," Quinn murmured to Donovan in old-speak.

Donovan snorted. "I wasn't going to forget. You take his

front legs. That way, if he's bluffing and blows dragonfire, you'll only get stronger instead of me getting roasted."

"Had enough tanning for one day?" Quinn teased and the other *Pyr* grinned.

"Even though I didn't finish you off, I think we can call it a settled dispute."

"Fair enough." Quinn grasped Lucien's front legs while Donovan took his back ones. Quinn also carried Lucien's claws so he could dispose of them the same way. Any worry that Lucien was bluffing was unfounded: the *Slayer* remained limp. His body was lighter than Quinn had expected.

The smell of roasted flesh reminded Quinn a little too vehemently of the death of his family. He even glanced upward, halfway expecting to see Erik circling overhead.

Then Quinn pushed useless memory from his thoughts. He and Donovan carried Lucien to the Washtenaw River and let his corpse drop into the water. Lucien hit the water with a splash, followed by his claws, then sank fast.

Without reviving.

The river boiled briefly where his body had disappeared and Quinn imagined he could see the dark shadow of the sinking dragon.

"For you, Delaney," Donovan whispered.

"That'll give the amateur divers something interesting to find," Quinn said.

Donovan nodded. "We worked pretty well together, Quinn."

But Quinn was scanning the sky, looking for other *Slayer*s. "But I can't help thinking it was too easy," he said. "Why would he come out of the blue to take us on alone?"

"*Slayer*s are nasty. They're not always logical."

"No," Quinn argued, remembering Sara's observations. "No. They're very logical. It's as though they plan it all out in advance. They work together. Like a team."

"How could they have known that I'd challenge you?" Donovan said, his tone skeptical.

Quinn sighed. "Sara thinks they're holding the Wyvern captive."

Donovan stared at him. "I didn't think there was a Wyvern anymore."

"Sara hears a woman in her dreams, screaming for help, telling her tormentor that it's forbidden to injure the Wyvern."

"Shit. They'd know everything if that were true." Donovan scowled. "We wouldn't have a chance."

Quinn didn't say anything. It was tempting to think that Sara was right, that they had to retrieve the Wyvern somehow. There just wasn't a way to do that without putting her at risk. Life had been much simpler when he'd had only himself to look out for—but he already couldn't wrap his mind around the idea of never seeing Sara again, for any reason.

Too bad he didn't trust Erik. Once burned, twice shy and all that. Quinn scanned the sky again, convinced that he was missing something.

Donovan stared at the spot where Lucien had sunk. "Do you think he was a distraction?"

It was possible. Quinn turned instinctively toward downtown, wanting to check on Sara, just to be sure. Let her think he was overprotective. He could live with that.

A pang shot through him then, like a red hot poker, and he knew his mermaid was calling to him. Someone had breached his smoke, or Sara had left the shop alone.

"It's Sara!" he bellowed and took off toward The Scrying Glass.

Donovan swore eloquently and to Quinn's surprise, the other *Pyr* flew right behind him. "It's time we fought together, too," Donovan said flatly. "Come on, Quinn. We can smoke the bastards if we play as a team."

"You're on," Quinn agreed and the pair streaked across the sky.

He just hoped that they got to Sara quickly enough.

Chapter 10

B oris Vassily was scheming.

He was always scheming on one level or another, although this piddling problem of how to execute the Smith's mate wasn't very compelling. It was always satisfactory to terminate a firestorm with the bloody execution of the human female, but over the centuries, that feat had lost its thrill.

Boris had killed humans in so many ways that the possibilities had all been explored. And really, they weren't that interesting in the end or that different. The human physiology was remarkably feeble—their survival could be attributed solely, in Boris's opinion, to their ability to breed with abandon.

Sara Keegan was proving to be more difficult to kill, which might be either the result of her being the Seer or a mark of Ambrose's ineptitude.

They headed out of Ann Arbor's core in the massive gold SUV that Boris favored, Ambrose driving. Sara slept in the backseat, dreamlessly and deeply. It hadn't been that hard to beguile her, which told Boris that she was skeptical of it or knew nothing about it.

He enjoyed that the Smith had left him such a nice loophole.

Boris lit another cigarette and with indifference watched the ember burn. Sara would die—it was only a matter of time—and as long as they took her out in the next nine months, there'd be no *Pyr* child, no matter what the Smith had already done.

It was all so predictable.

Boris yawned mightily. On the upside, it would be good to end a firestorm at the beginning of the much-foretold new age, just because the loss would particularly demoralize the *Pyr*. And he had to admit that there was a certain spice to the prospect of ensuring that the Smith didn't breed, that there was no inheritance of the Smith's talents and thus no chance of the old prediction coming true.

But still. It all seemed a bit flat to Boris. He wanted more. He wanted a big finish. He wanted to incinerate as many *Pyr* as possible. He wanted to *win*, and he wanted to win on the scale of a Hollywood blockbuster movie. He started to butt out his cigarette with impatience, half of it still intact, then had an idea.

It was so brilliant that he froze in midgesture.

But then, it was his idea. What could it have been *but* brilliant? Boris liked to think that he had a talent for seeing the big picture and this idea proved that to be true.

Thanks to Sara, the *Pyr* probably knew that the *Slayers* held the Wyvern captive. Boris knew enough about Erik—and the misguided noble impulses of the *Pyr*—to guess that they would want to save their prophetess. It would be a stupid and pointless exercise, since her prophecies were less than precise and far from useful, but Boris knew they would try.

All they needed was a hint as to her location.

He smiled and lit another cigarette, drawing on this one with real pleasure. It would be so easy to give the Smith's mate that clue and then *accidentally* allow her to escape. The *Pyr* would never suspect the trap that had been laid for them because they were almost as guileless as the humans they defended. They would attribute her escape to their own abilities, or to hers. They were ridiculous that way and Boris liked that he could use that trait to their disadvantage.

She would share the clue, and they would come to him.

Or more accurately, they would come to their own collective funeral.

Boris chuckled in satisfaction. This was exactly what he needed to bring back the old excitement of slaughter and destruction. As a bonus, he'd have no more opposition to obliterating the human population of the earth once this ploy was completed.

He could plan his big finish.

Boris had no doubt that the Smith's mate would try to escape, as that kind of survival instinct was part of her nature. He could facilitate her departure a bit without her knowledge.

It was almost too easy.

But not quite.

Boris chuckled happily to himself. "Take 23 south to 12 west," he instructed Ambrose who started in surprise.

"I thought we were going to leave her body in the forest at the Smith's place."

"I've changed my mind. We're going to Allen."

Ambrose frowned. "But it's my assignment. I want to leave her for the Smith to find."

"I don't care. Take the turn."

"But . . ."

"You've had your chance to do it your way." Boris

punched in a number on his cell phone, smiling when he recognized Everett's voice. "We're taking her to the cabin. When you get there, start making smoke." Not waiting for Everett's answer, he ended the connection and called Sigmund. "The cabin, now," he said when Sigmund answered. "Get there, tell the others, and make smoke immediately. I expect a solid territory mark by the time I arrive." He snapped the cell phone shut with satisfaction and took a long draw on his cigarette.

"You do know that the ley lines converge there, right under the cabin," Ambrose said, his tone snide.

Boris chose to forgive his attitude. "Yes."

"And if we all mingle our smoke, the territory mark will act like a beacon." Ambrose continued, as if he spoke to a fool. "It'll be easy for them to find us."

Boris smiled. "Exactly." He leaned across the front seat and flicked ash into the other *Slayer*'s lap. Ambrose jumped as Boris dropped his voice low. "Are you doubting me, Ambrose?"

"Of course not. I just don't understand."

"Because you're stupid. You're so stupid that you could be human."

"Hey!" Ambrose's eyes flashed but Boris watched him coldly.

He knew that his flat stare discomfited even the other *Slayer*s and Ambrose was no exception. He was old, so he would fight it longer, but he would succumb. "Go ahead," Boris whispered in old-speak. "Give me another reason to dispose of you."

Ambrose glared back. "You wouldn't dare."

"Oh, but I would." Boris exhaled, letting his dragonfire caress Ambrose's arm.

The other *Slayer* flinched. "You're crazy."

"But in charge all the same. Your fate lies in my hands and don't you forget it."

"You can be eliminated, too, Boris."

"Who will volunteer to take my job? Who could earn it?" Boris saw Ambrose's ambition and despised him for it. "Not you," he whispered. "You can't finish anything."

Their gazes held for a potent moment, the tension snapping between them. Then the SUV swerved, someone honked, and Ambrose looked back at the road. He was seething, but he had been the first to look away.

"Kick it up a notch," Boris snarled, savoring his cigarette. "An immortal shouldn't be afraid to break the speed limit. I want to get there today."

Ambrose put his foot to the floor, his mood obviously sour. Boris watched the countryside and knew he was already having the best time that he'd had in centuries.

And it was only going to get better.

Gone.

It was as if Sara had vanished into thin air. Neither Donovan nor Quinn could see her. They shifted back to human form in the Diag and Donovan did the beguiling while Quinn raced toward Sara's store.

The Scrying Glass was closed and Sara wasn't in Quinn's booth, either. She wasn't in the coffee shop she favored. The mermaid door knocker was already black again, the *Pyr* threat having moved away from her vicinity.

Along with Sara.

Quinn caught her scent in the arcade and followed it to the parking lot off Maynard Street. He lost it there and was pacing the upper floor of the lot when Donovan caught up to him.

Sara had moved far and fast.

Worse, Quinn knew that she hadn't moved alone.

"Well?" Donovan asked, even though he must have known.

"Gone. Completely gone." Quinn pushed a hand through his hair, unable to avoid the ugly truth that he'd failed someone yet again.

"You can't be everywhere," Donovan began to say, but Quinn interrupted him.

"I should have been here!" His voice rose to a shout and he couldn't stop it. "Sara's safety is my responsibility. I should have been here. I should have been with her. I should at least have been close!" He spun and put some distance between himself and the other *Pyr*, before he said something he might regret.

He could have incinerated everything in sight, but he knew it wouldn't make him feel any better.

"Blaming me?" Donovan demanded.

Quinn glanced back to find the other *Pyr* looking cocky and unrepentant. "I blame myself, for taking your challenge and forgetting my obligations."

"I wasn't going to let you decline my challenge."

"Even so." Quinn glared at the parking garage in frustration, wishing the concrete could talk to him the way that metal often did. He paced the perimeter again, anxiously seeking a hint of Sara's location, feeling the weight of Donovan's gaze.

"What if they knew?" Donovan asked quietly.

"What are you talking about?" Quinn was impatient.

"What if they knew what we were doing? You said that Sara was dreaming of the Wyvern being held captive—if they have the Wyvern, they could know anything. They could know that you and I went to fight. They could have sent Lucien to make sure we didn't finish too soon."

Quinn stared at Donovan. "They might even have known that we'd take him all the way to the river."

"It bought them time. I'm thinking that's not a coincidence."

"No. It was a plan. Sara said they worked as a team. They were just waiting for something to distract me, then worked to prolong the distraction."

"You were set up, Quinn," Donovan concluded. "Don't blame yourself."

Quinn gave the other *Pyr* a serious look. "Sara is missing. She's probably been kidnapped by the *Slayers* and she might already be dead. If she's so much as scratched, I'll blame myself for the rest of my life."

"Shit, that's a long time," Donovan said and grimaced. If he was making a joke, it fell flat. "We've got to talk to Erik."

"The last thing I need is his help. . . ."

Donovan interrupted Quinn before he could say more. "That's where you're wrong, Smith. This is too big. You need all of us and you need all of us right now."

Quinn would have loved to have had an alternative solution, but he didn't.

Out of the darkness creeps a dream. It sidles up beside Sara, infiltrates her senses, becomes her dream.

She knows it's not her dream. This is the seeing that is her gift. She is in the skin of another. She is in the skin of Quinn Tyrrell, long before he was named Quinn Tyrrell.

He was just Quinn. The young man who is Quinn leans on his shovel to rest. Before him are two mounds of freshly turned earth.

Two graves.

It is hot and he has shed his shirt. The sun beats down on the graves, the young man, the humble hut to one side.

Sara understands that Quinn has found—and now lost— a new family. He must be almost twenty now, and she guesses that the occupants of the two graves raised him from that frightened boy.

He wipes a tear from his face with impatience and looks back over his shoulder. His throat is tight with his loss and Sara feels his affection for the two that he has buried.

She can even see them in Quinn's mind's eye. Maria and Gaultier. Maria as plump as Gaultier is lean, both of them as wrinkled and baked and barren as the land they call home. He must have seemed God-given to them, an older and childless couple so wanting a son.

And he had needed them.

The land tumbles away from the hut, as jumbled as Quinn's recollection of sweet moments with this caring pair. The hillside falls roughly toward a town, a good distance below the hut.

Even from this distance, the town looks abandoned. No smoke curls from the homes within its walls and the walls themselves are so broken that they have begun to resemble the rough tumble of the stony hills around them. No horses or carts arrive or depart from the town. Black stains its center, and Quinn shudders in recollection of how long the church burned.

The smell is one he will never forget.

Although it has been many years since the town was assaulted, still it sits empty. The boy who had hidden behind the miller's stone is tall and strong, thanks to the elderly couple he has just buried. He returns the shovel to their hut, ensures that everything is as tidy as they would like, closes the door, and hoists a bag onto his shoulder. He pauses for a final farewell, then strides away.

Into the mountains.

Away from the past and into his future.

Whatever it is. His thoughts are filled with questions. His body has changed in many ways he does not understand. He *stares at his thumbnail as he walks and tries to find the elusive feeling that marks its change.*

The nail transforms to a gleaming talon before his very eyes. He panics and it returns to normal.

Without pain.

Without any lasting sign of what it had done.

What is he? Is he a demon as a neighbor once suggested? Or as blessed as Gaultier claimed? He doesn't know, but he means to find out. The answer is out in the world, somewhere.

Quinn will find it.

The days blend to weeks and months and years. His optimism and determination fade into something more primal. He walks far beyond the land he knows. He helps at farms when he can trade his labor for food and shelter. As time passes, though, fewer souls are inclined to invite him into their homes. He is tall and strong, his garments are tattered, and he is not as clean as he would prefer. There is a glint in his eyes, born of hunger and fed by desperation.

People bar their doors against him.

It is cold in the mountains and there is snow when he sees the village far below him. The church bells ring as he draws nearer, awakening an ache in his heart. Quinn is no better than an animal and he knows it, but he isn't sure how to turn the tide.

He does not know his age. He does not know how long he has wandered. He does not know how long it has been since Maria and Gaultier died.

All he knows is that his gut gnaws with hunger.

And where there are people, there is food. Dusting every surface with white, the snow falls out of the sky in fat flakes as he emerges from the woods. The gates are open and he guesses that it is market day.

He salivates in anticipation. With no clear plan, he ducks behind an oxcart, putting one hand to the cart and bowing his head as if he is part of their group as they pass through the town gates. As soon as they enter the village, he slips into the crowd.

So many people. So much sound. He is almost overwhelmed by his first contact in eons.

Then he smells the fresh bread. The warm scent winds into his nostrils and teases his hunger to a fever pitch. He finds the baker's window with ease, his nose leading him true. There are many gathered around the window, chattering as they buy their bread. His belly growls in demand.

He must eat, even though he has nothing to offer in exchange. He notes that the villagers are all shorter than he and more neatly dressed. On some level, he knows that he will not get away with it, but he is past such reasoning.

His body demands food. He is tall and strong. He is fast. He will take his chances.

He lunges through the crowd and seizes two loaves from the sill of the baker's window.

The baker shouts and Quinn runs.

A hue and cry arises. He flees through the square and into the alleys, shoving the warm bread into his mouth and swallowing as quickly as he can. He has a dim memory of a hound stealing a joint of meat from his father's kitchen and doing much the same, eating as much as possible before being caught.

Because being caught is inevitable.

He knows it even before they fall on him, even before they beat him and truss him and drag him to the square in the market. He is outnumbered and still weak from hunger.

And in a way, he only wants something in his life to change. He knows they are right. He knows he has done wrong and should be punished. Even death is preferable to

*how he has come to live. He has a vague sense that he could
loose that beast within him but he is afraid of it.*

*He cannot control that demon once it is released. He
doesn't understand it, much less trust it, and he will not turn
it on these villagers.*

*His hands are bound to the post in the square and his feet
are spread. He has no doubt of what is coming, even though
their language is unfamiliar to him. The townspeople gather
to watch, whispering as they do so. He feels dirty and un-
couth in their presence, and sees condemnation and fear
mingled in their gazes.*

*He is ashamed of what he has become. Can Maria see
him now? Can his mother? The magistrate makes a declara-
tion and the crowd cheers.*

Quinn bows his head and accepts his due.

*He grits his teeth as the first lash falls across his back
and tears what is left of his shirt. The second hurts less and
the third splits his skin open. The blood runs warmly across
his back, the cold snowflakes tingling in contrast. He knots
his fingers together and closes his eyes, bracing himself for
the next stroke.*

It never comes.

*A man calls something, something that halts the punish-
ment. The crowd turns, whispering. Quinn looks up without
comprehension.*

*Sara's heart stops as the man steps through the crowd.
He is dressed lavishly, and moves with the confidence of a
man accustomed to having his every desire. A massive jewel
hangs on his breast and the stone in its midst is a large
cabochon tiger-eye stone. His gaze is the same honey brown
hue and his smile is wide.*

Sara recognizes him all too well.

*He tosses a coin toward Quinn. The gold coin glints as it
spins through the air and the villagers gasp at the display of*

wealth. The coin bounces off Quinn's bound wrists and the magistrate is quick to claim it from the ground.

Quinn does not understand the exchange of words, but the rope is unknotted and the end handed to the wealthy benefactor.

Sara senses Quinn's astonishment as the other man unties his hands, lays a hand on his shoulder, and leads him to the stall where hot meat pastries are sold. Quinn is filled with gratitude as he eats and Sara feels his loyalty to the other man being forged.

But Sara knows that Quinn is wrong. This man, this supposed savior, is Ambrose. He is the golden dragon who has tried to kill Sara.

Twice.

He has bought Quinn's loyalty to gain his trust, only— Sara is certain—to betray it.

Quinn was impatient with the process of gathering the other *Pyr* and chafed at the delay as Niall tested the wind. In truth, they had come together remarkably quickly, and gathered on the roof of the parking garage. Donovan had summoned Erik in old-speak and Erik had somehow called the others. Quinn thought it was probably a refinement of old-speak that Erik used, but he didn't much care.

Every minute took Sara further away.

And deeper into peril.

Niall paced the lip of the parking garage roof, his eyes narrowed as he sniffed and murmured. Sloane instructed Donovan quietly on the application of some salve, and Donovan peeled up his T-shirt to smear it across the gashes on his torso. They looked like wicked wounds even after he had shifted shape, but Quinn could already see the unguent closing the cuts. Sloane seemed to be chanting as Donovan rubbed the salve into his own skin.

Under other circumstances, Quinn would have been fascinated by Sloane's ability to heal. In this moment, though,
he had other things on his mind.

Erik came to stand beside Quinn. "She's not dead," he
said softly.

"How do you know?"

"I know."

Quinn wasn't reassured. "That could change at any moment."

Erik nodded agreement as he watched Niall. "But every
moment that she lives increases the probability that they
have no intention of killing her."

"Or that they have a particular death in mind for her, one
that takes time to set up," Donovan said.

"Thanks for that," Quinn muttered. The *Slayer*s might
want to ensure that he had to watch Sara die.

They'd have a hard time holding him captive for that.

Or maybe they were waiting for Erik's arrival. Quinn still
didn't trust the older *Pyr*. This was all a bit too familiar for
that.

Donovan's smile flashed. "No worries. You can just wait
for her to incarnate again."

"A firestorm is worthy of more respect than that," Rafferty interjected with disapproval.

"I have nothing but respect for the fair sex," Donovan retorted. "But why wait for dessert when the buffet, so to
speak, is overloaded with goodies?"

"Some things are worth waiting for," Rafferty said, his
voice low and slow. Quinn exchanged a glance of understanding with him and the other *Pyr* nodded. "You're lucky."

"I've waited centuries," Quinn felt obliged to note.

"So have I." Rafferty looked rueful.

"Then you understand why I can't let these *Slayer*s steal
Sara away."

"I do."

The two *Pyr* eyed each other with an increment of new respect; then Quinn nodded. He gestured to Niall and spoke to Erik. "What is he doing?"

"Whispering to the wind," Erik said quietly. "We each have our affinities to different elements."

"The Smith can take dragonfire," Donovan said with admiration.

The others looked at Quinn in surprise but he said nothing.

Erik continued. "Niall can ask questions of the air, and he has a sharper sense of smell than any of us. He is a good tracker as a result."

Niall turned then and approached the others. His brow was furrowed in confusion. "They went southwest, following the old ley line. I had my doubts, but it's inescapable."

"How nice that they made it easy for us to follow them," Erik mused, his gaze flicking over the horizon.

"It's probably not an accident," Quinn said, but no one seemed to be listening to him.

"They may have made for the old convergence." Erik turned to issue instructions. "We fly in two groups to better evade detection. Niall will lead the first and I'll lead the second."

"I'm with Niall," Quinn said and Erik smiled.

"I wouldn't have dared to suggest otherwise," he said, seeming to take Quinn's distrust in stride. "You and Rafferty will fly with Niall. Take your cue from Niall and guard his flanks. The cost of intent focus is an inattentiveness to detail."

Quinn nodded. He knew that when he focused on the fire, he was oblivious to anything else. He'd never considered before that that made him vulnerable.

"I will lead the second group, with Donovan and Sloane. We'll hang back and defend your rear guard."

"I'll go with the first group," Donovan said. He was obviously eager to be in the thick of things, even with the wounds he had already sustained.

Erik shook his head curtly. "I need your power in case we're surprised. Their decision to follow the ley line might be a feint, or they might change direction suddenly."

"They might circle back on us," Donovan said. "And attack from behind. It would be the kind of sneaky thing they'd do."

"Exactly," Erik agreed. "Now, go! I'll take care of the beguiling." At his command, the six *Pyr* ran across the roof of the parking garage and leapt off the lip on the southwest side. They changed shape in seconds. Quinn was again impressed by how smoothly they shifted and how adroitly they folded their garments away. He felt clumsy in comparison, as if he'd missed a trick.

Good thing it wasn't a very important one.

Niall, gleaming amethyst and platinum, cut a speedy course toward the southwest, Rafferty—opal and gold—and Quinn fast behind him. Quinn glanced back to see Erik circling over the parking garage and heard the faint rumble of the *Pyr* leader's old-speak.

The wings of the lead three dragons pounded an insistent rhythm and they settled intuitively into a triangle formation in flight. Niall murmured constantly, holding his quiet conversation with the wind. The other two remained silent and vigilant, watching for treachery from either side or below, allowing Niall to focus.

Rafferty, Quinn noticed, was as large as he, if not quite as well muscled. Niall was smaller but virile. He was content that they'd make good fighting companions.

It wasn't long before the trio of *Pyr* swooped down toward an isolated cabin. Three *Slayer*s on the roof launched a volley of dragonfire toward them, without troubling to take flight. Quinn took the blast, protecting Rafferty and Niall from potential damage. They wheeled as one and ascended to a greater height.

Quinn could still feel his blood simmering from proximity to Sara. "She's in there," he said in old-speak.

"I can even feel your firestorm," Rafferty said with reverence.

"I have to go in," Quinn said, pivoting to dive back down to the cabin.

"The smoke is piled thick and high," Niall argued. "You'll never come out alive, Smith."

"You might not even get in alive," Rafferty said.

Quinn knew it was true, but he couldn't just wait. "I can't leave her there!"

"You'll accomplish nothing if you both die," Niall retorted. "She can be reborn, but you won't be. We can't afford to lose another *Pyr*."

"I can't surrender my mate to the *Slayer*s."

Rafferty interrupted, his tone thoughtful. "You don't have to. And you don't have to die."

"You can't be encouraging him," Niall said. "Attacking is certain death. There are three *Slayer*s on the roof. Who knows how many others are close by, and there's a serious territory mark. Even if the Smith can survive that much dragonfire, he'll never breach that smoke twice and live to tell about it."

"You don't know that," Quinn argued.

"Neither do you," Niall snapped. "Are you prepared to die to find out?"

Before Quinn could answer, Rafferty continued. "He doesn't have to, because there's another way." He fired a bright glance at Quinn and smiled. "I'll do this for your firestorm."

"Do what?"

"Trust me," Rafferty said and flew away from the cabin. Quinn exchanged a glance with Niall, then followed the other *Pyr* with reluctance.

Trusting other *Pyr* was a new concept for Quinn, after all.

In fact, if he'd been able to think of another solution, any other solution, he would have done it instead.

"Help me, please!"

The woman's moans awakened Sara once again.

This time, at least, the woman wasn't screaming.

It was hot and muggy, as if Sara had left the windows shut for the night. She was covered with a shimmer of perspiration and the air was thick and hard to breathe. Her back ached as if she'd slept on something hard.

Her dreams were getting worse. Sara opened her eyes, pretty much expecting to find herself home in bed.

Instead, she was in a rough log cabin. The windows had been boarded over and the door was solid wood. The only light came through the chinks between the logs. The sunlight seemed pale and thin, the way it did in the early morning. The floor was hard-packed dirt and that's what she'd been sleeping on. She was still wearing her clothes. Sara scrambled to stand up and realized that she wasn't alone.

A blond woman lay on her side on the other side of the cabin, her pale arms pillowing her head. There was dried blood on her arm and her ankles were shackled together. Her eyes were bright and of the most remarkable turquoise shade. They glinted as she watched Sara, and Sara guessed instantly who she was.

"You're the Wyvern," she whispered with awe.

The woman nodded weakly. "Or you can just call me Sophie."

"I hear you in my dreams."

"Yes, I know." The Wyvern smiled slightly. She seemed to be lethargic—or maybe she was hurt.

Sara eased closer, trying to see the dried blood better. "Are you all right?"

Sophie almost laughed. "Are you?" She sighed, not waiting for an answer. "I am sorry, Sara. They asked me for your name and I surrendered it to them. I was afraid, but I should never have told them."

"They were hurting you. What else could you have done?"

"You may not be so forgiving if they kill us both."

Sara crouched beside the other woman. She could see that the Wyvern's wrists were also shackled together and a heavy chain ran between her wrists and ankles. "They aren't taking any chances, are they?"

"Shape shifting is an unpredictable business," Sophie said and looked away. Sara sensed that she was hiding something.

"Can you become anything other than a dragon?" she whispered.

Sophie looked at her intently and shook her head. "Of course not," she said, but there was a current of steel beneath her words. "That's just mythology."

Sara understood that the Wyvern could take other shapes.

She also got the message that they were being watched.

Her gaze dropped to the dried blood on Sophie's shoulder. "Do you want me to look at that?"

Sophie's words were tinged with humor. "Are you a healer as well as the Seer?"

"No, but I was a Girl Scout. I can wash a cut as well as anybody."

Sophie smiled and rolled to her stomach. Her hair fell over her shoulders in a tangle, but it was the most beautiful and ethereal pale blond that Sara had ever seen. It might have been made of silver. Sara eased its silkiness aside and winced at the length of the gash across the Wyvern's shoulder. It had scabbed over, but even in this light, Sara could see that there was red puffiness at one end.

"I think it might be infected."

"How surprising, in such conditions," Sophie said, a thread of laughter in her tone. She sighed again and Sara wondered how much blood she had lost. If the wound had been left untended as it appeared to have been, it could have been quite a lot. Sophie certainly couldn't reach it herself, not with those shackles.

There was a bucket of water inside the door. "Is that for you? All the way over there?"

"They enjoy watching me slither on my belly," Sophie said, and again Sara heard that force of will in her voice.

"Is it clean?"

"Clean is a relative term." Sophie licked her lips. "If they wanted to poison me, there are more effective ways to do so than with polluted water."

Sara had enough rudimentary knowledge of emergency care to treat a basic wound. The water smelled as if it had been drawn from a river or pond, and using it to clean the wound might add to Sophie's troubles.

Sara's purse was dumped on the floor inside the door as well, its contents clearly having been rummaged through first. She habitually carried some sanitary wipes, for those scary moments in public restrooms, and they were still there.

She warned Sophie to expect the sting as she tore one open, and did her best to disinfect the wound. The scab lifted away easily, revealing a pocket of infection that Sara also cleaned away as well as she was able. It bled a bit, but the blood was clear and bright. Sophie quivered beneath Sara's ministrations, but didn't complain.

Sara tore a strip of fabric from the hem of her dress to make a makeshift bandage. "I meant to shorten it, anyway," she said when Sophie looked alarmed. Sara helped the Wyvern to sit up and used another wipe to clean her companion's face.

"That feels wonderful." Sophie sighed with pleasure and closed her eyes.

"Washing my face makes a huge difference in the middle of a long travel day." Sara grimaced. "Or a bad travel day. With these, I can do it anytime anywhere."

Sophie slanted a glance at Sara. "Funny. I did not think that you traveled much."

"I don't anymore."

"Since?"

"Since everything changed." Sara sighed. "I used to have a fistful of frequent flier cards and hotel guest cards."

"A glamorous life."

"An exhausting one. It paid well," Sara admitted. "But money isn't everything. I learned that this year."

"By losing what you had not realized you held so dear?"

"How did you know that?"

Sophie smiled enigmatically and said nothing.

"Anyway, I decided it was time to make a change and I did."

"You chose to pursue your desire for a home to call your own. A place to put down roots."

Sara felt self-conscious beneath that considering gaze. "Well, sure. I've always had this fantasy of planting a tree from seed and being there, in the same place, when it was big enough and tall enough for me to sit under it and read."

"An enchanting vision."

"Hasn't happened yet." Sara opened her purse instead of

thinking about her current predicament. "This was a recent decision, and I haven't cleaned out my purse yet. I'm still ready for scary bathrooms and twenty hour travel delays." She dug a brush and comb out of her purse. She waved them like the trophies they were and Sophie's eyes lit with anticipation. Sara set to making some order out of Sophie's hair.

"I can't begin to tell you how good that feels."

"I think I know," Sara said and the women exchanged a smile. When she was done, Sara dug through her purse some more. Her wallet was still there and the book on the Cathars was jammed in the side. Magda's tarot cards were safely nestled in their red velvet bag and her keys were at the bottom, just the way they always were. The Swiss Army knife was gone, but that would probably have been too much to hope for.

"Breath mint?" she asked Sophie, holding up two packages.

"That bad?" Sophie asked with a wince.

Sara smiled. "No, but it might be the best we can do in terms of nutrition. Spearmint or peppermint?"

"I like a balanced meal. How about one of each?" Sophie opened her mouth. Sara put the two mints on the Wyvern's tongue, then had a pair herself. She leaned back against the wall beside the other woman to consider their prison.

"I'll guess that the door is locked and that there's no other way out," she said finally.

"You are the Seer," Sophie teased.

"Are you really a prophetess?"

Sophie sighed. "Yes, but prophecy is a mysterious business."

"You mean in terms of how it works?"

"I mean in terms of what it means." Sophie shrugged. "My visions are not even as clear as dreams. And the verses that come to me are so enigmatic. It is hard to know what they mean."

"Like riddles."

Sophie nodded. "Sometimes they make sense only in hindsight." She shrugged. "Or perhaps I am not very good at my craft."

"Don't say that! Everyone needs time to learn."

"I did not anticipate these *Slayers* coming for me."

"Even if you had, it might not have made any difference. They're pretty brutal and you're just one Wyvern."

Sophie shuddered. "Brutal does not begin to describe them."

Sara looked around the cabin. "So, how are we going to get out of here?"

"We are not, not unless someone breaks in and releases us."

"I'm not waiting," Sara said and pushed to her feet.

"Is that so?"

Sara ignored the Wyvern. She prowled the perimeter of the cabin and peered through the cracks between the logs. All she could see was forest on all sides.

That didn't mean they were alone, though. Screaming might just annoy their captors, if they were around.

Where could they be?

On the roof?

Sara looked up at the trusses that held up the steel roof, then at the Wyvern. Sophie nodded once, so quickly that Sara almost thought she had imagined the gesture.

"You will tire yourself out for no good reason," Sophie warned, her tone despondent, but Sara saw the glint of determination in her eyes.

Sara tried the door, not really surprised to find it locked and barred from the other side. The boards over the windows must have been nailed down in two layers, judging by the pattern of light that came through the chinks. Without tools—and breath mints hardly counted—she couldn't break out.

Every puzzle has a solution.

Sara heard her father's voice echo in her thoughts, his familiar saying uttered with such conviction that she half thought the *Slayer*s would hear it.

Maybe Quinn would come for her. She pivoted to face Sophie, struck by a thought. The Wyvern's eyes glinted with watchfulness. "Is there smoke?" Sara mouthed the words, hoping the Wyvern knew she meant the *Pyr*'s territory mark.

Sophie nodded once, so emphatically that Sara couldn't misunderstand. "They breathed it together," she mouthed but Sara refused to accept defeat. "It is stronger that way."

Quinn couldn't come to her and neither could the other *Pyr*. Unless they were permitted to pass through the territory mark, which could only be an invitation to disaster.

There had to be a way to escape.

Sara just had to figure out what it was.

Soon.

Chapter 11

By morning, Quinn was restless and even more irritated than he had been before.

Which was saying something.

Rafferty had led the pair of *Pyr* to a copse of trees near the cabin but too far for Quinn to hear what was going on there. Niall had seemed to guess the other *Pyr*'s intent, even though Quinn hadn't known what to expect.

Rafferty had lain on the ground and shifted to human form. He had put his ear to the soil and closed his eyes, listening.

Quinn tried to ask a question, but Niall shushed him to silence.

And they sat, the three of them motionless. The sky, which had been pale blue and bright when they arrived, gradually darkened to indigo. The stars came out. The sounds of the forest around them changed to night whispers and still Rafferty hadn't moved.

Quinn had tried to push himself to his feet several times, but Niall had scowled at him and gestured him back to his seat. Erik and the others had come, and after a brief consultation, had returned to Ann Arbor to pack up Quinn's booth and secure his truck.

Quinn waited. The sky had begun to brighten in the east when Rafferty sat up. He took a deep breath, shifted to dragon form, and without opening his eyes, began to hum.

Quinn was fed up and might have left then, but a hole began to open in front of Rafferty, as if an invisible finger stirred the earth.

Sara settled back against the wall beside the Wyvern, impatient that there was so little she could do but wait.

Maybe she could find out something while they waited. The Wyvern should know pretty much everything, after all.

"I don't really understand all of this dragon stuff," she said lightly. "It's so very different from my real life."

"And seems so much less real," Sophie guessed. She tilted her head to study Sara, her slow perusal reminding Sara of the way Quinn looked at her.

As if he could watch her all day.

She yearned suddenly to be with him again, to feel his strength and heat beside her. She wished that she had had more than one kiss from him.

And maybe a little bit more. Her mother had told her that she should start living life instead of marking time—in fact, that had been the crux of their last discussion at JFK—and Sara was wondering whether she'd missed her chance.

"Are you frightened of the Smith?" Sophie asked.

Sara shook her head. "No. I'm not afraid of Quinn. I know he'd never hurt me." What she felt for Quinn was both simple and complicated. She wanted him more intensely than she'd ever wanted any man, but it wasn't just lust. She was fascinated by him, and she loved talking to him. He had a way of explaining things that made even the most bizarre notion make sense, and she liked how he challenged her to look at things from a different angle. She had a feeling that the way he smiled slowly would captivate her for the rest of her life.

Maybe he was happy to watch her: she was happy to watch his expression change from solemnity to humor.

And she loved the progress of that slow smile.

Sophie smiled. "But you are frightened of the firestorm?"

Sara summoned a smile of her own, feeling as if the discussion was a bit personal. "Well, it's not what we learned in Sex Ed, if you know what I mean."

"How so?"

"It's powerful."

"Yes."

Sara shrugged. "I'm used to being a little bit more in charge of my emotions."

The Wyvern considered that for a moment, then looked at Sara. "How interesting that your emotions are already engaged."

Sara was startled. "Isn't that the point? Isn't the firestorm about destined love?" She shrugged, feeling silly even saying the words. "I mean, assuming that you believe in that kind of thing."

Sophie smiled. "The firestorm is a mating sign."

"You mean it's about sex."

"Many *Pyr* believe as much."

Sara had the definite sense that the Wyvern wasn't telling her all of the truth. "What about Quinn?"

Sophie met her gaze steadily. "What about him?"

"Does he think the firestorm is about sex or love?"

"I have never met the Smith. How would I determine such a thing?"

"I thought you were the Wyvern."

Sophie smiled.

Sara leaned back against the wall with frustration. It was

obviously important that she ask the right question to get a useful answer, but unfortunately, she didn't know what that question was.

"I sense your resistance to Quinn's courtship," Sophie said, when they'd sat in silence for a long while. "Is it the prospect of mating with a dragon that troubles you?"

"Why?"

"I assure you that the shift is to a fighting pose: you need not worry about surprises in intimate moments, unless you are physically attacked in those moments."

"And then we'd have other problems," Sara mused.

Sophie chuckled. "Indeed. Are you worried then about the Smith's intentions, to use an old expression?"

Sara looked away, not particularly inclined to answer all of Sophie's questions when the Wyvern wasn't answering all of hers. As the silence stretched long again, she decided she had nothing to lose. "I don't think it's a crime to be a romantic, to hope for a long-term relationship based on love. The idea of being useful to a man who wants a son, like a brood mare, isn't appealing at all."

Sophie smiled, as if the notion amused her. "You believe in happily ever after," she teased, "regardless of how you express it."

"Well, it works. My parents were crazy in love with each other. It made them happy. It gave them a way to face obstacles and challenges. They worked together and gave each other strength; they balanced each other's strengths. When one was blue, the other lightened the mood." Sara stopped, her throat closing as she realized the weight of her loss.

Again.

Sophie didn't seem to notice. "And you do not believe you can have this with the Smith?"

"He seems very practical. And solitary."

"Those with the largest hearts often learn to hide them."

Sara studied her companion with interest. "Are you saying that Quinn was hurt?"

"I am saying that the greatest romantics are often idealists," Sophie mused. "Even if they hide that behind skepticism."

"Like Quinn?"

"You tell me."

Sara paused, needing to think about that. Quinn was practical and sensible, as far as she could see. He recycled materials so he appreciated the past and took the long view. He protected and defended her, even at his own expense. They were traits she admired, but she wasn't sure they made him idealistic, much less romantic. "He's purposeful. Focused on the end goal."

"Which is?"

"The firestorm, or its culmination."

"Is it?" Once again Sara found herself looking into the Wyvern's aquamarine eyes, so filled with mystery and humor. "Even the Seer is blind in a storm," she said quietly.

"Or a firestorm," Sara amended.

Sophie laughed lightly. "Fair enough," she said, speaking at so low a pitch that Sara knew she was mimicking Quinn.

Sara leaned against the wall, tired and impatient. The heat was making her irritable, and being hungry and thirsty didn't help. She thought about Quinn's experience with Ambrose and could see how he would have come to trust the *Slayer*—especially if the *Slayer* presented himself as a *Pyr* mentor. Quinn had no basis of comparison.

And he had been hungry for knowledge of his own powers.

Seeing Erik at the site of his parents' death, as well as witnessing Erik's killing of Ambrose, could explain Quinn's distrust of the leader of the *Pyr*. All the same, her sense that Quinn had it backward was even stronger than it had been before. She wondered if there was more to the story than either she or Quinn knew. She reviewed her dream, feeling as if she was missing something. There had been something that had struck her as odd.

It was the look in Ambrose's eyes as he threw the coin.

As if the gesture should mean something. His expression of benign friendliness had changed for an instant, as if a mask had slipped, to reveal a brutal determination.

What was it with gold coins? There had been a coin on the threshold of her shop the day before. Sara rummaged in her purse and dug it out of the bottom. It shone in the dim light and she had a feeling that it held a secret she needed to know.

There had been a coin in the arcade before she had been attacked, as well. Had it been the same kind? She wished in a way that she'd seen it.

"There is a pretty challenge," Sophie said from beside her.

"What do you mean?"

"Was that tossed at the Smith?"

Sara was getting used to Sophie answering questions indirectly, if at all. She frowned at the coin. "It was left at the door of my shop yesterday. Why?"

"How strange," Sophie mused. She lifted her hands and Sara gave her the coin. She peered at it for a minute, arched a brow, then handed it back to Sara. "It speaks of the Smith's origins. A pretty challenge from someone who knows who he is and where to find him. You say it was outside your shop?"

"My bookstore, yes."

"And no one entered it?"

"No. I had locked the door at Quinn's request, and he had made a territory mark around the shop. . . ."

"Ah!" said the Wyvern as if that explained everything. "So the challenge could not be delivered."

"Why do you keep calling it a challenge?"

"Because that is what the *Pyr* do. They challenge each other to blood duels, when they perceive that justice must be served. The *Slayer*s do it just to provoke a fight to the death, because no *Pyr* of honor will decline a challenge to his integrity."

"Challenge how?" Sara asked, her scalp prickling.

"The challenger tosses a coin at the one with whom he would fight. If the coin is caught, the battle is accepted, and they will fight to the death."

Sara remembered Ambrose tossing the coin at Quinn in that village, the gold coin bouncing off Quinn's bound hands. "Why a coin?"

"It is tradition. I suppose it is derived from the winner claiming the hoard of the loser as spoils of the blood duel. Once upon a time, our assets were almost purely gold." She shrugged. "It must be somewhat more complicated to claim the stock holdings of a losing *Pyr*."

So, Ambrose had declared his intention, to fight Quinn to the death, on that first meeting. But Quinn hadn't understood and maybe over the years, he had forgotten that detail.

She hoped she had a chance to tell him. It might make the difference in his trusting Erik.

She pushed herself to her feet and paced, trying the bolted door again. She paced the cabin once again, feeling silence and inactivity weigh heavily upon her.

The Wyvern simply watched.

Sara wasn't even sure she was breathing.

Sophie spoke softly, as if for Sara's ears alone. "Tell me, Sara, where is it writ that what you and the Smith create together must be a child?"

Sara pivoted to find Sophie's gaze solemn and steady. There was something a bit creepy about how seldom she blinked, how she seemed to see Sara's most secret thoughts.

"The prophecy," Sara began, but Sophie shook her head.
"That is not what it says."

Sara sat back on her heels, trying to remember Quinn's verse. Sophie filled in the gaps that she couldn't recall, until they recited it together.

> *When the Dragon's Tail demands its price,*
> *And the moon is devoured once, not twice,*
> *Seer and Smith will again unite.*
> *Water and air, with fire and earth*
> *This sacred union will give birth*
> *To the* Pyr's *sole chance to save the Earth.*

The Wyvern was right. It didn't specify what would result from the union. "I'd assumed," she began but Sophie shook her head.

"You know what they say about assumptions. I think sometimes that prophecies exist to make us all look like fools." That wry amusement lit Sophie's eyes again. "And that the Great Wyvern greatly enjoys a joke at our expense."

Sara folded her arms across her chest and leaned back against the wall. She'd have to think about that.

It looked as if she would have the time.

Sara knew she wasn't imagining that it was getting hotter by the minute in the cabin. The Wyvern had gone to sleep and Sara sat beside her, restless and uncomfortable.

Hours had passed. It might as well have been weeks. The air was stagnant with the cabin sealed so tightly and Sara was sure that she could feel heat emanating from the metal roof above. She guessed it was approaching noon, which meant that she'd slept through at least one night.

Maybe more.

What had happened to Quinn?

The pail of water was warm and its swampy smell got stronger with every passing minute. One fly buzzed around the interior. Sara couldn't see it but she could hear it, especially when it flew against the cracks of the boarded-up windows in frustration.

A fly couldn't even get out. How would they?

The Wyvern slept deeply. She almost seemed to glow in the darkness, she was so pale, but she didn't look strong. Sara again had the impression that Sophie was more wounded than she appeared to be. How much blood had she lost? How much hope had she lost? She seemed so fragile, as if she were half-faded from the world already.

As if she didn't care whether she lived or not.

But then, Sara had heard the determination in Sophie's voice more than once. Was she disguising her true strength? Or was she stubborn despite being down?

Sara wished she could have known.

The fly slammed itself into a crack of daylight and fell heavily to the soil. Sara could hear it buzzing, probably spinning in circles from the sound of it. On the one hand, its noise was so irritating that she wanted to get up and squish it under her shoe.

On the other, she respected its determination to live. She leaned her head back against the logs and closed her eyes, letting the sound of the fly fill her senses. She was hungry. She was tired. She didn't know what to do, and that made her feel more tired.

The sound of the fly grew louder. Sara licked her dry lips and wondered how long it would take her to become thirsty enough to drink swamp water.

She wasn't there yet.

The buzz of the fly became *much* louder.

It sounded, in fact, more like a rumble. Sara opened her eyes and looked around. She heard the fly thwack itself against the other boarded-up window, again without success. But the rumbling continued. It was getting louder, as though a truck was driving closer.

Or a train.

Sara spread her hands flat on the dirt floor and her eyes widened as she felt the vibration beneath her palms. It got stronger.

An earthquake? There was an earthquake when she was trapped in a small cabin?

What kind of rotten luck was that?

The whole cabin began to shake and Sara got to her feet. She shook Sophie awake.

"What's the matter?"

"There's an earthquake. You have to get up. We might have to run."

"I can't run anywhere," Sophie said, then yawned.

"Well, you can't just lie there and wait!"

"Why not?" Sophie smiled serenely. "The planet knows who keeps her safe. I am in Gaia's good care."

Sara, however, didn't feel quite so certain of that. She crossed the shaking cabin and tried the door, without any success. She pounded on it.

"Hey! Let us out!" There was no answer. Sara banged on the door some more. "Let us out!" The cabin rocked and Sara hoped for a moment that it might tip right over.

Instead, a hole opened in the middle of the floor, between her and Sophie.

And the shaking stopped.

It wasn't the kind of hole that an earthquake makes, a long crack that threatens to close again without warning. It was a round hole, like the end of a tunnel, about four feet across.

The Wyvern began to smile. "I feel the earth move," she sang lightly, just as Quinn's head appeared in the tunnel.

Sara gasped.

He looked around, narrowed his eyes, and she knew the moment he saw her. He braced his hands on the sides of the hole to pull himself up to the cabin floor.

Sara sputtered for a moment before she managed to make a coherent sound. The Wyvern continued to sing, just a little bit off-key, and the cabin became markedly hotter. "Quinn! But how did you do this?"

"We'll talk about it later, princess." He caught her hand in his, pulled her close to his side, then looked down into her eyes. He felt strong and warm and solid. Sara was very glad to see him and she didn't care if he knew it. There was a glint of satisfaction in his eyes that warmed her to her toes.

Or was that the firestorm?

"Are you all right?" he asked, not for the first time in their acquaintance.

"Thirsty, hot, but otherwise uninjured."

"Good. Let's go." He pivoted and tugged her toward the hole.

"We have to help the Wyvern," Sara said, digging in her heels.

Sophie waved her fingertips at Quinn from the far side of the cabin. Sara felt Quinn jump in surprise. Sophie's move showed that her hands were shackled together, a fact that couldn't be missed when the chain jingled. "Hello, Smith."

He paused for only a beat before stepping toward her. "Go, Sara. Jump!"

"I'll help you."

"It'll be faster if you just go, Sara."

"But . . ."

"Now!" Quinn roared. Sara turned to the dark hole just as the door to the cabin was opened. Sunlight flooded into the dark cabin, and she could see three men silhouetted in the doorway.

"Quinn," she whispered. He took one look and shoved her toward the hole. Sara took the hint. Quinn leapt toward the Wyvern, obviously intending to pick her up and carry her. Sara wondered why the three *Slayer*s didn't even come over the threshold.

Were they afraid of Quinn?

Or of the Wyvern?

Then she saw that they were shimmering around their edges and all were exhaling in unison.

"Even the Seer is blind in a fog," whispered the Wyvern.

Quinn glanced back and swore. Sara watched him, knowing he could see the smoke that the *Slayer*s were exhaling. She understood from his grim expression and the direction of his glance that they were sending it toward the hole.

They were trying to block his escape.

And the smoke moved fast.

Quinn couldn't believe how quickly the *Slayer*s were breathing smoke. They created an incredible volume, breathing in unison, and it moved swiftly toward the hole that Rafferty had created for him. In the blink of an eye, he knew that he couldn't reach the hole before the smoke if he took the extra steps to fetch the Wyvern.

But he couldn't leave her.

"Go, Smith," she whispered in old-speak. "You are the prey they seek." He was still torn, but she dispatched her last command with force. "Breed for all of us."

Put that way, Quinn had no choice. He leapt across the cabin, landing beside the hole just as the smoke edged to its rim. Sara had jumped down into it and he could see only her head. She pulled him over the lip and into the hole, pushing him in front of her.

The smoke tumbled over the lip of the hole in pursuit.

When the tunnel became horizontal, it was as tall as

Quinn, by Rafferty's design. He could stand upright, without a lot of extra space to walk.

"I want you in front of me," Quinn argued but Sara poked at him from behind.

"It can't hurt me the way it can hurt you. Run!"

Not for the first time, Quinn was glad that she was so sensible. He reached back and seized her hand, then ran. She stumbled behind him, tired and weak, and he squatted in front of her. "On my back."

"We'll be slowed down."

"We're already too slow. Move it."

Sara put her hands around his neck and Quinn started to run. She swung up her legs and he caught her knees around his waist. She wasn't that heavy and he felt better knowing precisely where she was.

The tunnel that Rafferty had opened was reasonably level, so even in the darkness Quinn didn't slip. He had his sharp *Pyr* vision to guide him, as well. The smoke, however, was similarly unobstructed and it seemed to gain speed once it was swirling to fill the tunnel.

Or maybe the *Slayer*s exhaled even faster.

Either way, Quinn quickly realized it would outrun him before he got to the other end. There was no going back to the cabin, either. He sent a thought to Niall in old-speak, hoping that they had made enough of a connection that the younger *Pyr* would hear him.

"They're sending smoke into the tunnel behind me," he murmured and felt the jolt of the other *Pyr*'s surprise.

Quinn didn't know what would happen when the smoke reached the end of the tunnel. If it spilled out, would it injure the other two *Pyr*? Could it surround them and leave them trapped until the *Slayer*s came to finish them off? Quinn realized that he didn't know nearly enough about using smoke as a weapon.

Probably because he'd never thought of doing so before.

He was faintly aware of a change in the pitch of Rafferty's song then. The other *Pyr* had sung to the earth to coax it into creating a fissure, then had chanted a low chorus that had persuaded the hole to broaden and become more round. Quinn had descended into the opening and followed its course as Rafferty compelled the earth to do his will.

It was much as Quinn sang to fire and metal, but the song had a different rhythm, one that sounded sufficiently alien to him that he couldn't anticipate it.

He knew when it changed though and some deep old part of him seemed to recognize it.

Clumps of soil began to fall from the roof of the tunnel when Rafferty's song changed. Quinn glanced back to see the tunnel closing behind him. It wasn't tumbling in on itself: it was simply and seamlessly closing, as if it had never been there.

He was afraid then that Rafferty would close the tunnel, securing the safety of himself and Niall but condemning Quinn and Sara.

Sara swore. Quinn bolted.

Even if Rafferty intended to help him, how did the other *Pyr* know exactly where they were? Quinn ran even faster.

Sara's fingers dug into his shoulders. "Quinn?"

"Rafferty's closing the hole to seal off the smoke," Quinn said between heaving breaths. He spoke as if he'd expected this, as there was no reason for her to be frightened.

More frightened.

He felt her glance back. "Can you run fast enough?"

"I have to." Quinn pushed himself then, his feet pounding. He could see the light that marked his destination. A beam of sunlight fell through the opening, painting a golden circle on the floor of the tunnel.

Quinn had never been a runner. He was built too solid to

be fast and he feared that he would let Sara down in the last minute.

He could hear the tunnel closing behind him. He looked back to find a persistent waft of smoke hard on his heels.

"A hundred steps," Sara whispered into his ear. "You can do it. It's not that far."

Quinn ran faster. The sweat was running down his temples and streaming down his back. His grip on Sara's knees was slippery and he had a moment's fear that he would drop her.

She tightened her knees around him. "I'm not that easy to lose," she murmured, knotting her fingers beneath his chin. "Fifty more steps, Quinn. Make them big ones. Fast ones. You can do it. One more. One more." Her encouragement gave him strength and seemed to lend speed to his steps.

Then the smoke touched his heel and sent a vicious pain through his entire body. Quinn stumbled, came up gasping, and kept running.

"Twenty steps," Sara urged. "Just eighteen more."

They were nearing the closing point of the tunnel since his stumble and the dirt rained down upon them.

Quinn kept his focus on his goal.

The circle of light became bigger and brighter. He could see the green leaves and blue sky overhead. Niall's head appeared as he looked; then he leaned over the edge and reached for Sara. Quinn swung her around and flung her into the other *Pyr*'s arms. He reached for the lip of the hole and the smoke that had been fast behind him caught him across the shin.

It was like a brand, searing his flesh, sucking the life out of him. Quinn shouted in pain and lost his grip. His fingers scrabbled for a hold on the lip of the earthen hole, but he was shaking from exertion.

"Quinn!" Sara shouted in fear. She snatched at his wrist.

Niall grabbed Quinn's other wrist, giving him a hearty tug. Quinn heard Rafferty's song cease and knew what that meant. He scrambled to get his legs out of the hole. The smoke teased at his foot, a burning torment that made him want to scream. His left leg was numb from the knee down and felt useless.

Then the earth snapped shut, trapping Quinn's wounded shin within its grip. Quinn couldn't tug it free. He collapsed on the earth in exhaustion, fearing he was done.

He would be the lame Smith, after all.

Rafferty opened his eyes, leaned over, and whispered to the soil. He grabbed Quinn's knee and pulled his leg free of the soil's grip effortlessly.

Quinn just wanted to lie back and catch his breath, but Niall nudged him. "We've got to go. They're coming after us."

"How do you know?" Sara demanded, but Quinn knew better than to question the other *Pyr*'s counsel.

"He heard it in the wind," Rafferty said with a smile, then caught Quinn under the elbow to help him get to his feet. "Can you carry your mate?"

"No one else will, so long as I have anything to say about it," Quinn muttered and the other *Pyr* smiled.

"I had a feeling he'd say that," he said to Sara, whose smile was more tentative. "He doesn't need that leg to fly, at least."

"Are you all right?" she whispered when Quinn caught her against his chest.

"Close enough, princess," he said and shifted shape. She didn't need to know that his leg was killing him, and that he was wondering whether he'd be able to walk or not.

They could work that out later.

The three *Pyr* took flight in unison. They exploded out of the leafy canopy of the copse of trees Rafferty had chosen.

The sun was hot on Quinn's back, sapping his strength a bit more. They were so close to victory: he couldn't fail now.

Black-bellied thunderhead clouds were gathering on the horizon and there was a rumble of distant thunder. Three *Slayers* ascended in the distance, their silhouettes dark and menacing against the sky.

"There they are," Niall said.

"They see us already," Rafferty said as the *Slayers* changed direction.

Quinn was only aware of how far it was to Ann Arbor. He was glad that Sara was light. He drew on his reserves and his determination and flew steadily toward Ann Arbor. Sara spoke to him, but he couldn't spare the energy to answer her.

She watched him with concern, her gaze trailing to his deadened foot, and he was afraid she'd ask one of her perceptive questions.

Later.

She could ask him *anything* later.

What she said surprised him completely.

"Can one of you breathe fire on Quinn?" she called to the others. "He needs it."

The other two *Pyr* appeared to be shocked by the idea. "I don't think so," Niall argued, obviously insulted at the notion of injuring a fellow *Pyr*.

Quinn knew otherwise. Sara's idea was brilliant.

"No, she's right," he interjected. "Dragonfire strengthens me."

"Because you're the Smith," Rafferty mused.

The two exchanged a glance, Rafferty's gaze falling on Quinn's injured leg. He must have been holding it awkwardly but didn't have the strength to do more than let it dangle.

"Lift your mate high," Rafferty counseled in old-speak and Quinn swung Sara's knees up into his arms. Rafferty and Niall exchanged a nod, then the pair of them breathed dragonfire on Quinn's left side.

It was a jolt of adrenaline, sending power through Quinn's veins.

"More!" Quinn demanded.

"Please," Sara added.

Both *Pyr* let loose another stream of fire. Quinn arched his back with pleasure as new power swept through him. He could feel his toes. He could flex his foot again. The other two were awed. Quinn laughed at how invigorated he felt and caught Sara closer as he soared high. His mate had known what he needed.

The three *Pyr* set a killing pace for Ann Arbor and soon left their *Slayer* pursuers far behind.

"Wimps," Niall said with disdain.

Rafferty simply watched their diminishing shapes, his eyes narrowed. The thunder rumbled as the storm rolled closer. The humidity had increased to the level that it was difficult to breathe, but Quinn felt several centuries younger.

"That was brilliant," he breathed for Sara's ears alone and she smiled in her relief.

"It was the logical choice," she said and he wanted to laugh again. They understood each other. They were both practical and could fill the gap when one was overwhelmed. Theirs was a partnership, Quinn felt, that would be beneficial to both of them and make both of them stronger.

"Where to, princess?"

She tipped back her head and met his gaze, her own fearless and steady. "Home," she said with resolve. "With you." She stretched up to whisper to him. "I understand there's a firestorm that needs tending."

The prospect sent a heat wave through Quinn and he knew exactly how he wanted to spend this night. In bed, with his mate, coaxing and sampling the firestorm. He was raging with desire, but for Sara alone, and he knew theirs would be a mating to remember.

One glance at the golden hue of her eyes and he knew their thoughts were as one. If that wasn't enough to encourage him to fly faster, he didn't know what was.

Chapter 12

The Wyvern closed her eyes. The *Slayer*s had hurt her again, and in so doing, had inadvertently revealed their plans to her. She understood that she was the bait in the trap set for the *Pyr*.

Sophie understood that she might not survive the conflict, but she was at ease with that possibility now. All had changed on this day. The Wyvern would always be reborn and reappear on earth for the *Pyr*. She was important to them as a beacon of hope, but in this moment, others were more critical to their success.

Specifically, the *Pyr* needed the Smith and the Seer.

They needed this Smith and this Seer.

And encountering that destined pair had given Sophie her own source of hope. She had met the Seer and been impressed by Sara's strength. She had seen the Smith come in defense of his mate and felt the power of his devotion. She knew that the foretold union could be forged between those two, if only they overcame the obstacles they themselves had set. She liked to think that her comments to the Seer would help with that.

She let herself doze, let herself slide into the dreaming place. The Smith commanded earth and fire, whether he knew it or not, bringing the persistent power of earth and the passion of fire to all he touched. The Seer held the reins of water and air, again whether she knew it or not, bringing the intuitive understanding of water and the cold reason of air to every puzzle she encountered. The four elements would join with their union and create a greater fusion of their abilities.

A child would be a bonus.

The Wyvern breathed slowly as the thunder rumbled high above the cabin. She let her thoughts float above the dark clouds, into the night sky, up to the stars. She caught a beam of starlight and focused her will upon it.

Now that she had met the Seer, Sophie had Sara's scent. She could send the other woman the dream she needed to have. There was something about Quinn Tyrrell that Sara Keegan needed to know. It would allow her to give him the chance he didn't even know he wanted.

Yet.

At Quinn's direction, the *Pyr* landed in a small park near Sara's home. Storm clouds were gathering in the west and rolling steadily closer. The air was thick with humidity and a distant crackle of electricity.

Quinn was impressed again by how smoothly Niall and Rafferty shifted shape, so adept that there was no glimpse of their nudity. One minute, there were three dragons descending out of the sky; a heartbeat later, three fit men in jeans and T-shirts stood chatting with Sara in the shade of the trees.

"How do you conjure your clothes so smoothly?" Quinn asked.

"It's all in the wrist," Niall said with a smile.

"How do you do it at all?" Sara asked.

"It's a mental trick," Quinn explained. "You fold away

your clothes as you shift, folding them smaller and smaller, then tuck them somewhere on your person."

"Why?" she asked.

Quinn smiled. "Because you'll probably need them again."

"Where do you hide them?" she asked but Rafferty shook his head.

"Don't share all your secrets, Smith."

"Even with my mate?" Quinn protested but Rafferty was stern.

"Who taught you to hide your clothes?"

"Ambrose, but I could obviously use more practice."

"It's not practice you need but instruction. The way you were taught to do it leaves you vulnerable."

Quinn stared at the other *Pyr*. "How so?"

Rafferty smiled. "He neglected to tell you that you have to hide them not only on your person, but that where you store them should remain secret. Anyone can be tortured into revealing the secrets of another. It's better to keep such matters to oneself. Safer."

Ambrose had taught Quinn only half the truth. His old friend was seeming less and less like an ally with everything Quinn learned.

"Why?" Sara asked Rafferty.

"There is an old story that a *Pyr* who loses track of his clothing while in dragon form will not be able to shift back to human form."

"So, the location of the clothes needs to be a secret," Sara concluded. "That way, you can't be betrayed."

"Or it needs to change constantly," Niall amended.

"Is the story true?" Sara asked.

Rafferty smiled. "No one, including me, particularly wants to find out."

"Thank you," Quinn said to Rafferty. "Thank you for setting me straight, and also for helping me today."

"It was our responsibility to one of our kind," Niall said, his words making it clear to Quinn that others expected him to show the same responsibility.

"It was our obligation to aid the firestorm," Rafferty said quietly. Quinn took Sara's hand in his and noticed again how hungrily the other *Pyr* watched the spark dance between them. The thunder rumbled as the storm came closer. A flash of lightning was illuminated against the slate clouds, although the sound of its impact was distant.

With Sara's hand held fast in his, he was aware of a different storm rising. She stood closely beside him, and there was dirt on her hands and her knees. Her hair was loose and her left bra strap had slipped to her upper arm. She was disheveled and probably didn't like it, but he knew he'd never found a woman so alluring.

It was the sweet hot smile she cast his way when she felt the weight of his gaze that clinched it. His heart contracted tightly with relief that she was safe.

For the moment. Quinn was aware that the situation probably wouldn't last. "How'd they take you?" he asked and she frowned.

"I don't know. I went with them. I had no choice."

"Beguiled," Niall said and spat at the ground. "It's not right."

"They had flames in their eyes," Sara mused.

"That's beguiling," Quinn confirmed. "It's like hypnosis."

Sara got her stubborn look. "You have to teach me how to defend myself against it." Quinn wasn't sure what to say.

"It can be done, Smith. I have heard the song and would teach your mate." Rafferty sighed, then forced a smile.

"There are many things we could teach each other, mysteries neither of us understood could be unraveled."

"What could I teach you?"

"How to not only take dragonfire but draw strength from it." Rafferty spared Quinn a sharp glance. "How's your leg?"

"Fine, thanks to both of you." Quinn pulled up the cuff of his jeans, showing his leg healed.

"What would it have looked like otherwise?" Sara asked.

Niall grimaced. "Burned."

"No, more shriveled and lifeless," Rafferty said, then shuddered. "Smoke is nasty stuff. It sucks the life from any part of a *Pyr* it touches, leaving only a hollow, twisted shell."

Sara shivered.

Rafferty looked at Quinn's leg again, his wonder obvious. "That's a trick that I wish you could teach us, Smith."

Quinn frowned. "I think that would be similar to your explaining how you made the earth part, or Niall telling us how to listen to the wind." The other *Pyr* nodded, accepting the impossibility of that.

"We each have our gifts," Niall agreed.

"But wait," Sara interjected. "Aren't you *Pyr* supposed to command all of the elements? What if each of you has a tendency in one direction or another, but you can all learn to command *all* of the elements?"

There was a beat of silence as the three *Pyr* considered each other and her suggestion.

"That would be incredible," Niall said slowly.

"But it makes a lot of sense." Quinn was excited by the possibility.

"I don't see why it wouldn't work," Rafferty mused.

"We'd be invincible," Niall said wistfully.

"We'd have to work together," Quinn agreed, seeing the benefit of the exchange. They would all be stronger.

"If we could learn each other's skills in time," Rafferty

sighed. "It's too bad we didn't think of this earlier. The final battle has obviously begun, just as Erik anticipated. I've seen more *Slayer*s and battles in the past two days than in two centuries."

"It would be good to have the Smith with us in this war," Niall said, glancing at Quinn.

Quinn felt the burden of their expectation, yet at the same time, he couldn't trust Erik. It was more than the death of Ambrose—or the supposed death of Ambrose—Erik had been present a little too often at crises in Quinn's life for Quinn to accept the other *Pyr*'s interest as benign.

He felt the presence of Elizabeth's ghost and feared for his mate. He felt Sara watching him and was aware that she had a few expectations of her own.

"You've forgotten something," she said and Quinn was startled even though she spoke softly. Her eyes were wide and clear. "You thought Ambrose was your friend, but that's only because you forgot how you met."

"I remember how we met," Quinn replied. "He bought me . . ."

"No, he challenged you, but you didn't understand it." Sara was so sure of herself that she had the undivided attention of the other two *Pyr*. "Didn't he throw the coin directly at you? It bounced off your hands and the magistrate took it as payment, but Ambrose threw the coin *at* you."

"A challenge to a blood duel," Niall breathed.

Quinn blinked and looked away, astonished to realize that she was right. "How do you know this?"

"I dreamed it." Sara shrugged. "I dreamed of your past, probably because of the coin." She wrinkled her nose as she looked up at him. "Are you *really* eight hundred years old?"

"Yes, but that's unimportant." Quinn frowned even as Sara blinked. He was thinking about what she had said.

"I thought you would deny it, or sugarcoat it."

"Not the Smith," Niall joked. "He serves it straight."

Rafferty chuckled lightly at Sara's surprise. "He's too young for you," he teased. "I'm twelve hundred years old, which is just getting respectable."

"Go on," Sara said, but she didn't sound as shocked.

"He's just a kid, though," Rafferty said of Niall.

That *Pyr* grinned at Sara's enquiring glance. "Three-fifty and change. Young and energetic. These old guys lose their, um, power." He winked and Sara's cheeks turned pink.

"I don't think so," Rafferty retorted, but didn't get any further.

Quinn spoke quickly to Sara. "But you never saw the coin in the arcade Tuesday night."

"Was that a coin?" Sara asked, then nodded. She was fitting together puzzle pieces with a dexterity that impressed him. It was amazing to watch her make the connections. "I wondered. So, he was challenging you to a blood duel again, but you didn't catch the coin that time, either. That means it doesn't count, right?"

"But the intent is there," Niall said darkly.

"Two challenges." Rafferty whistled through his teeth. "No wonder he's trying to kill your mate as well. Ambrose has it in for you in a big way."

Quinn was more interested in the other detail Sara had revealed. "But what coin gave you the dreams?"

Sara rummaged in her purse and produced a gold coin. "This one." She handed it to Quinn and his heart leapt at its familiarity. He'd never thought to see the currency of Raymond-Roger Trencaval again and yet here it was, in his own hand.

He turned the coin over in awe, the sight of it taking him back to cheerful childhood memories. Hide-and-seek with his brothers. His parents laughing. His father hammering.

Then Quinn recalled his last day in Béziers and closed his

hand over the coin as if making it disappear could change the past. He averted his gaze, the pain of an old loss tightening his throat with fearsome force.

"It made me dream of Béziers," Sara said. "And of the fire there." She squeezed his fingers and her voice softened. "Your parents died, didn't they? And you saw Erik afterward, so you thought he was responsible, but I'm not so sure."

Quinn glanced at the others to find Rafferty looking amused and Niall astonished.

"She really is the Seer," Niall whispered. "She dreams of your past and sees its import for the future."

"No. I'm just an accountant," Sara corrected with a smile.

"You can't know what happened to me . . . ," Quinn began to argue, but Sara interrupted him flatly.

"I don't think you know, either." She held his gaze with certainty in her own. "Erik could have killed you in Béziers, if that had been his plan. He could have killed you when he killed Ambrose, if that had been his plan. Did you confront him when Ambrose died?"

"No. I hid while he searched for me. Then I ran. I was sure he meant to kill me, too."

"But he didn't throw a coin at you in challenge," Niall observed. Quinn had to agree.

Rafferty shook his head. "He would have been able to sniff you out at such close proximity. Erik is very perceptive, even for a *Pyr*."

Quinn hadn't thought of that before.

Sara tapped his arm with a fingertip. "You have to at least consider that his intentions are good."

"Ambrose taught you half of the truth," Rafferty contributed. "He left out the important bits."

"How long did you travel with him?" Niall asked.

"Two years, at most. He was generous and taught me a lot."

"But not enough," Rafferty concluded.

"But in two years, he could have killed the Smith a number of times, as well," Niall argued.

"I wonder whether he didn't think you were a worthy opponent," Sara said. "Maybe he was teaching you enough, maybe playing with you a bit, to have a more satisfactory fight in the end."

"But Erik killed him instead," Quinn mused. "It would make a certain sense for Ambrose to teach me part of the truth."

"How so?" Rafferty asked.

"Ambrose made his living by gambling, in those days. He would bet any man on the result of anything, and he always won."

"Because of his keen *Pyr* senses," Rafferty said with disgust. "It's cheating."

"It's comparatively easy to read humans by their reactions," Niall told Sara and she nodded understanding. Quinn saw that she wasn't surprised.

"But he would walk away from a wager he thought was too easy to win," Quinn said. "He thought it was beneath his dignity to bet on something obvious, or to win a wager with a man who wouldn't regret the loss. He liked to take someone's last coin. He always said he liked a win with impact."

"So, he *was* fattening you up for the kill," Rafferty concluded. "Nice."

Sara leaned against Quinn, the curve of her breast nestling against his arm. "I think it's time you had the whole story from Erik." She smiled, as if sensing his resistance. "It's the only way anyone can make a good decision."

Quinn wasn't at all convinced of that, but he didn't want to argue with Sara. Not now.

He wanted something else.

The golden hue of her eyes was the invitation he wanted to answer. He smiled down at her and felt sparks fly between them.

The dark clouds had continued to roll closer as they talked and now black clouds boiled directly overhead. The next flash of lightning struck close enough to make them all jump at the sound of its strike.

"We're going to get wet," Rafferty said.

"It's not that far to my house," Sara said, but Niall shook his head.

"We have to report back to Erik. He needs to know about the Wyvern."

Quinn cleared his throat, knowing it was possible that he had missed some detail. He was skeptical, but he knew what Sara wanted him to do. "Will you ask Erik to come to me?" he asked Rafferty and felt Sara's pleasure. "I need to remain with Sara tonight, but I want to hear his version of events."

"Fair enough, Smith," the older *Pyr* said, his smile indicating his approval. The storm grumbled overhead as the leaves on the trees were tossed and turned. The other two *Pyr* turned to stride downtown, while Quinn and Sara ran hand in hand for Magda's house.

To Quinn's relief, the smoke he had breathed around it was intact.

Their haven was safe.

Sara stood in her shower, eyes closed as the cool water washed over her. She felt a thousand times better as she scrubbed away the muck of that filthy cabin. It wasn't all bad that Quinn was sitting in her living room breathing smoke to protect her.

She only wished they'd managed to bring the Wyvern. Quinn couldn't have carried both of them, though, and in hindsight, she could see his point in getting the two of them to safety first. He, of course, saw his primary (and maybe even his sole) responsibility to be Sara, and there was something more than a little bit seductive about that.

In fact, there was a lot that was seductive about Quinn. Sara thought of the way he looked so intently at her. He put everything on the line to ensure her safety, without a second thought. It was true that he didn't talk about love and marriage, but hadn't she learned enough from Tom about empty promises?

Quinn's *Pyr* nature made planning for the long term somewhat tenuous, after all. Sara could see that he was being drawn back into the world of the *Pyr* and that his days of quiet isolation were likely coming to an end.

She thought the *Pyr* would do better with Quinn in their ranks, but maybe she had a biased opinion.

She got out of the shower and tried to dry herself off. The humidity had increased to the point that the towel didn't even seem to be absorbent anymore. The air could have been cut with a knife.

Thunder rumbled overhead and Sara remembered her mother's admonitions not to be in the bathroom during a thunderstorm. She combed out her wet hair and knotted it up. She reached for the clean shorts and T-shirt she'd brought into the bathroom, then changed her mind.

She stood and listened to Quinn breathing slowly. The sound made her feel safe and protected. It also aroused her. She was very aware that she wasn't alone in her little apartment.

In fact, her apartment seemed a lot smaller when Quinn was in it.

It was a good feeling. She thought about how Quinn made her feel, about his integrity and his determination, and wondered why she was resisting temptation so hard. Maybe it would be good for her to be seduced.

Maybe she was rationalizing what she wanted to do.

Maybe she didn't care.

No, there was no maybe about it: she was rationalizing and she *didn't* care. She wanted Quinn. He wanted her. It was simple. In the blink of an eye, Sara's decision was made.

She wrapped a fresh towel around herself and stepped out of the bathroom. Quinn hadn't moved from the chair he had chosen, and still sat with his arms folded across his chest. Once again, he seemed to glimmer around the edges and his eyes glowed like brilliant sapphires. He surveyed her with appreciation, then smiled that slow smile.

"I didn't want to interrupt you," she said. A bead of sweat trailed down her back. Sara remembered Quinn caressing the mermaid door knocker with one strong finger. She could still see him sliding the weight of that finger down the length of the mermaid, and remembered him touching her with the same deliberate, attentive caress.

Her mouth went dry.

"All done," he murmured and got to his feet. Lightning flashed outside the window and a crack close by made Sara jump. The lights went out a second later. The fans in the windows slowly stopped spinning and the streetlights winked into darkness.

She could see Quinn's silhouette in front of her, and thought she could still see the gleam of his eyes. She remembered the sight of him without his shirt, the water from the shower beaded in his dark hair.

He was waiting for her move and Sara knew it. The air between them crackled with desire and she knew that he wanted her. Quinn would make love slowly and thoroughly. It could take all night.

It would be a night to remember forever.

"That white towel almost glows, princess," he said quietly. "Are you trying to tempt me?"

"I'm no temptress," Sara said with a laugh.

Quinn didn't laugh. He came toward her, the firestorm making the air crackle with heat between them. "Wrong." Quinn spoke with a conviction that surprised her. "You look like my mermaid, her hair all wild and her eyes filled with promises."

He reached and took the clip out of her hair as Sara held her breath. Sara shook her head when he put the clip aside, letting her wet hair fall over her shoulders.

"Fresh from the sea," he whispered. He bent and brushed his lips across her cheek, his quick caress leaving Sara breathless. His thumb moved against her skin and she was tempted to drop the towel.

"Promises I mean to keep or not?"

Quinn smiled slowly and his fingers slipped around to her nape. "You tell me. It's tough to tell what a seductress has in mind."

"I'm not a seductress. I'm an acc—"

Quinn placed his other thumb over her lips, silencing her. Sara liked the weight of his thumb against her skin and rubbed her lips against his hand. "Whatever you call yourself, Sara Keegan, you're welcome to seduce me." His eyes gleamed in the darkness, lit by a blue heat that made Sara's mouth go dry.

"I thought you were seducing me," she whispered.

Quinn smiled and Sara thought that her yearning would take her to her knees. "Maybe it's destiny doing the seducing." Sara stared up at him, snared by the heat of the firestorm, and watched as he bent his head.

Quinn captured Sara's lips beneath his own, and sparks

danced along her veins. She rose to her toes to kiss him back, sliding her arms around his neck.

The towel fell to the floor.

Quinn kissed Sara deeply, as if he had all the time in the world, as if he were memorizing the shape of her lips. Sara felt his strong fingers in her hair as he cupped the back of her neck. She knew the moment he realized that the towel was gone. He paused in his kiss and drew back ever so slightly, just so she could see the vivid blue of his eyes.

And his smile. His left hand swept down her back, the side of his thumb launching a line of sizzling flames beneath her skin. Sara shuddered and gasped, and whispered his name.

This time she reached for his kiss and he was quick to claim what she offered. His kiss was hotter than it had been, potent enough to make Sara dizzy. She closed her eyes and hung on. Quinn lifted her against him and she rubbed her bare breasts against the cotton of his T-shirt. His other hand fell to the back of her waist, drawing her more tightly against him, and she thought he made a low growl of desire. She felt his erection against her belly, the denim of his jeans stretched taut.

"You have too many clothes on," she complained. He stepped back, peeled off his T-shirt, and cast it aside. He undressed with quick efficiency, the same way he did everything else. He was direct and honest and straightforward. What Sara saw was what she would get.

What she saw stole her breath away. He watched her, his gaze simmering, as he cast away his underwear, then stood nude and proud before her. This time, she had a good look and she knew her eyes widened at the size of him.

"Don't worry, princess," he murmured as he caught her fingers in his. His admiration made her feel sexy, special, treasured. The heat between their palms made her give some credence to the idea of destiny. Either way, being with Quinn was right. "We'll take it slow."

"How slow?" she whispered as the first raindrops slashed against the window.

"Very slow," he assured her. Quinn laced his fingers into hers and drew her closer as if they were going to dance. Sara stepped into the circle of his arms, as impressed by his strength as by how carefully he controlled his power. He held so much in check, so that he wouldn't hurt her.

"Not more than once?"

"That too," he assured her. "Over and over again, until we get it perfect."

"Just perfect," she agreed and he smiled. Sara ran her hands over Quinn's shoulders and felt his muscles flex beneath her caress. She was aware of him watching her, of the glimmer of his eyes, of his bemused smile. His fingers splayed across the back of her waist, holding her captive before him and lifting her to her toes. Sara felt the heat of him beneath her hands and the sizzle that was awakened by the sweep of her fingertips across his flesh.

She let her hands trail to frame his neck, savoring the smooth texture of his skin. She wanted to touch him all over and she leaned her stomach more fully against him. He caught his breath when his erection pressed against her belly but Sara liked the feel of him.

She held her hands at his throat, feeling his pulse beat beneath her hands, certain it matched the pace of her own. Her fingertips trailed upward, over his jaw, across the prickle of stubble on his cheeks. Then she pushed her fingers into his hair, losing sight of them in the dark waves, and pulled his head down.

Quinn bent his head and kissed her. This kiss was more potent than the last, tinged with an urgency that made Sara's heart skip. Quinn lifted her to the tips of her toes and kissed her thoroughly. She opened her mouth to him, loving how their tongues dueled and danced. Her nipples beaded tightly and she rubbed them against his chest. The wind rattled the windowpanes and the thunder boomed. Lightning struck close at hand. Sara wasn't sure whether that was why the hair rose on her neck, or whether it was Quinn.

She didn't care. He broke their kiss and nuzzled her ear, his kisses making a river of fire across her skin. Quinn's hand rose to cup Sara's breast and he slid his thumb across her nipple in a deliberate caress. Sara caught her breath and arched her back. Quinn lifted her fully against him with one hand cupped around her buttock, then bent to flick his tongue across her taut nipple.

Sara gasped and writhed against him. She wanted more of him. She wanted all of him. She wanted to taste the firestorm fully.

Now.

Quinn seemed to guess her thoughts. He swung her into his arms and headed for the bedroom with purpose. Rain slashed against the windows, leaving rivers of water running down the glass. Trees were thrashing in the wind, but Sara had eyes only for Quinn. He laid her across the mattress, then stretched out beside her.

Mischief gleamed in his eyes as his fingers slid into the slick heat between her thighs. He touched her with surety. Sara gasped and then she moaned. Quinn found precisely the right spot and toyed with it mercilessly. He held her fast against his side, his one arm wrapped beneath her and around her, as his other hand stoked her passion.

He teased her, his fingertips moving slowly and purpose-fully. He took her to the brink of release time and again, with relentless ease. Sara was gasping and twisting. She was consumed with desire. She was. on fire.

And only Quinn could sate the flames. She whispered his name and pulled him over her. "Now."

"You first," he insisted.

"No. Together."

"That's a myth, princess."

She almost laughed at the wry humor in his tone, but he moved his thumb and shook her universe instead. "Quinn! I want you inside me."

She didn't have to make the argument twice.

He loomed over her and she cried out with pleasure when he eased himself inside her. He paused when he was buried in her, but she kissed his shoulder to reassure him. "It feels perfect," she managed to whisper.

And he agreed before he kissed her again.

Sara closed her eyes as he moved inside her, each caress stoking the firestorm to an inferno. There was only Quinn; Quinn and his pounding heart, his undeniable passion, his talent for awakening all that had been asleep within her.

It was more, far more, than enough.

Hours later, Quinn, with reluctance, left Sara sleeping. He got out of bed only because he was afraid he would awaken her.

Or that Erik would, whenever he arrived. He was anxious about the interview ahead, hoping it would give him another increment of truth.

Hoping he'd be able to tell the difference between truth and guile.

Sara's hair was strewn across the pillows, a glorious golden shimmer in the darkness. It had dried and looked like honey in sunshine. Her lips were parted, her lashes splayed across her cheeks. He could hear the faint whisper of her breath despite the steady drum of rain on the window.

What was the perfume she wore? Or was it the scent of

her soap? Either way, it was the perfect scent for her, touched with vanilla, both sexy and sweet. Quinn knew that just the faintest waft of it would drive him wild for the rest of his life. He wondered then whether mortals had their own power to beguile. Certainly, Sara Keegan had wound her way into his heart and soul, making it impossible for Quinn to imagine being without her.

They'd made love three times and he was ready for more.

He had a feeling that he was never going to get enough of her.

Surprisingly, that didn't bother Quinn, even though he'd spent the vast majority of his life ensuring that he had no reliance on anyone.

Maybe Sara would be the exception to his own rule. He wanted to make love to her in the grassy fields at his home, in the forest, in his own bed, on the thick rug on the floor of his cabin. He wanted to hear her make that little gasp of pleasure when the sun was shining, when spring rain fell around them, when the snow swirled out of the sky and the fire on the hearth crackled.

The fury of the thunderstorm had moved east and rain fell steadily, beating a rhythm against the roof. He opened the window slightly and a cool breeze smelling of plants and soil and flowers, wafted into the room. It reminded him of his cabin and acreage. He was less comfortable in cities and towns than in the country and he yearned to show Sara what he had built.

The street looked slick and black, and the shadows seemed particularly dark with the power still out. Quinn inhaled deeply, missing his land.

He couldn't think about the future, not yet. He was still tingling with the aftermath of the firestorm and he wanted to savor it. Sara stirred in her sleep as he stood at the window and rolled to her back, sighing contentment.

A smile played over her lips and Quinn wondered whether it came from memory or from her dreams. He tugged the sheet over her legs so the draft wouldn't chill her. He wanted fiercely to be the one responsible for making her smile.

Forever.

Quinn could have watched her sleep all night long. The gentle rise and fall of her breasts mesmerized him, as did the insistent beat of her heart, echoing in his ears. His own heart sped up slightly, matching its pace to hers, and it seemed to him that when they beat in unison, he felt a new power.

She nestled her cheek into the palm of one hand, looking small and vulnerable. Her other hand lay curled against the white sheets, looking as fragile as the rest of her.

But she was strong, stronger than she even guessed herself. If Sara was a princess, she was from a warrior clan.

Or maybe she was a mermaid, after all, an undine as slender as a reed and as forceful as the tides.

He smiled at the uncharacteristic whimsy of his thoughts and headed for the bathroom. He was restless, impatient, ready to do whatever was necessary to protect Sara.

The problem was that Quinn wasn't certain what that was.

Confident in the power of his own smoke—thrice breathed—he took a shower himself. There was a package of disposable razors in the medicine cabinet, so he helped himself to one and shaved. Quinn always took great pleasure in shaving: for some reason, having his jaw smooth made him more aware that he was human.

Not a beast.

Much less a monster.

He peered in the mirror, checking that he hadn't missed a spot, and what he saw shocked him completely.

There was a gray hair on his temple. It winked at him,

one strand of silver that had never been there before. It was unmistakable. It hadn't been there that morning. He knew it. But it was there now, and it was attached.

It hurt when he pulled it out.

He was aging, and worse, he knew why. Quinn studied his reflection but there was no other sign of change. He cleaned out the sink, frowning at his own realization. It had happened already. So quickly. He had created an heir, after being only one night with Sara. Her body probably didn't even know as much as yet, but his did.

Quinn had often been accused of being purposeful and goal oriented, but on this night, he had a profound sense of having been cheated.

He wasn't ready to be without Sara Keegan.

He wasn't ready for his firestorm to be over.

And he wasn't ready to be alone again.

He wondered whether he ever would be.

Then he glared at the silver hair he had pulled out and flushed the traitor down the toilet.

It was gone.

Quinn wondered whether three more would grow in its place, just to make sure he got the message. He dressed with impatient haste, unable to quell his annoyance.

When Erik quietly announced his presence, Quinn's response was blunt and grim, even for old-speak.

Chapter 13

Quinn opened the door but there was no one there. He moved to the top of the stairs that led to Sara's apartment and saw Erik standing on the path from the sidewalk.

"You'd better give me permission to cross your smoke before this woman calls the police," Erik said in old-speak.

Quinn belatedly remembered that Sara had a tenant in the main part of the house. Even so, he wasn't ready to invite Erik into his temporary lair, not with Sara there. Her purse was on the floor where she had dropped it, and her keys were on the top.

He took her keys, locked the door behind himself, and descended the stairs instead. "Let's go for a walk," he suggested tersely.

Erik gave him a wry smile. "Still don't trust me?"

"There's no reason for us to awaken Sara."

Erik snorted in disbelief but Quinn didn't care. Erik's leather jacket was wet, but the rain had slowed to almost nothing. The clouds were moving quickly across the sky. Quinn didn't mind a few sprinkles on his shoulders.

"You have a question for me," Erik prompted.

"I have many. Let's begin with the big one. Why were you in Béziers when my family died?"

"They didn't die, Quinn. They were killed. Don't imagine that it was anything other than murder."

"Everyone is murdered in a way, if you want to think about it that way."

"No. There's always a war that can be used in the service of the greater war. An artful member of our kind can always infiltrate human society, can always bend the target of an individual battle to his will."

"You're joking."

"I am not. The cohesive element of human history is that the humans who recorded it seldom knew what was truly at stake."

Quinn was still skeptical. "The entire town was slaughtered so that my father could be killed?"

Erik pursed his lips. "Recognize that your father was the Smith of his time, although he had not had the years to perfect his skills as you have done. He was powerful and he was feared by *Slayer*s in his day. I doubt that many would have believed they could have eliminated him in a fair battle."

"So they chose to fight unfairly."

"It is the *Slayer* way."

"But my mother?"

"She could have been carrying his seed." Erik arched a brow. "And you can guess why your elder brothers were killed. You were all supposed to die, Quinn, but the Great Wyvern held *you* in the palm of her hand."

"If only to drop me into the fire later."

"Who can say what each of us must experience to become what we are destined to be? Your experience made you what you are: there is no denying that you are the most powerful Smith in all my lifetime."

Quinn averted his gaze. He still needed to hear Erik's answer before he could pledge to serve with the *Pyr*.

The two walked in silence for a long time, up one sleepy street and down another. Quinn cast his thoughts back and heard the steady rhythm of Sara's sleeping, pinged his smoke and heard it ring true.

"I had a friend, a long time ago," Erik finally said. "A friend who taught me a great deal. His name was Thierry de Béziers."

"You said before that you knew my father."

~ "But not that I loved him as dearly as a brother."

"Why should I believe you?" Quinn asked.

"I will tell you." Erik waited for a few moments before he said more and when he did speak, his words surprised Quinn. "There is an old conviction among our kind that love is a whimsy of mortals, that to love a woman is to lose something of what makes one *Pyr*. To link oneself to a mortal woman is to create a binding tie with one place and time, to rip asunder our connection to infinity. According to such thinking, women serve their purpose in bearing our young and have no merit beyond that. We may protect them and we may honor them by force of that debt, but it is inadvisable for us to surrender any of our affection to them. I have known many who have lived to that code."

Quinn said nothing.

Erik pursed his lips and shoved his hands into the pockets of his jacket. "There is power in that choice and for a long time, I respected it as the truth."

Quinn was intrigued by the implication. "But?"

"But your father argued otherwise. Your father bound himself to your mother, in every possible way, and did so against much protest from the others."

"What do you mean?"

Erik held Quinn's gaze. "I mean that he loved her, and he was unafraid as to who knew as much."

Quinn looked at the sidewalk, remembering. There certainly had been affection between his parents and he knew that his father must have been *Pyr*. He hadn't ever seen his father in dragon form, but he remembered the tricks his father would play with flames. It had been as if the fire listened to him, but as a child, Quinn had believed his father could do anything.

Erik continued his story. "Your father insisted that he gained more by his surrender to love than he lost."

"Was he right?"

Erik looked Quinn in the eye. "He died young, too young, and it is hard for me to accept that he believed his choice to have been a worthy one at the end. He died because he had a weak spot."

"Us?" Quinn guessed.

Erik shook his head and didn't answer the question. "You ask why I was there. I was there because I smelled the fire, though I was not close at hand. I did not arrive in time to make a difference to your father's fate."

"He was dead."

"Not quite. He could not speak aloud, he could not see me and if he had been mortal, the barrier between us would have been insurmountable. But he sensed my arrival and he recognized me with keener senses than sight." Erik swallowed. "We had old-speak between us that one last time."

Erik fell silent and Quinn glanced up at the other *Pyr*. He was surprised to see that Erik looked older and more drawn.

"Thierry had taught me so much," he said, his words thick. "The debt between us was long and the bonds between us numerous, even though we had argued over his choice with regard to Margaux. I was honored to have old-speak between us that last time, to hear his rumble in my own thoughts. He was my mentor in many ways and it was not easy to see him in such pain."

Quinn was remembering a thousand details. He remembered that there had always been a fire in the grate in his parents' home, despite the weather. He remembered sparks flying between his brothers' swords as they fought. He remembered stories that his father could always start a blaze, no matter how wet the wood or cold the hearth. He remembered his mother saying that his father "warmed her heart," then smiling a mysterious little smile.

"Your father bade me find his other sons," Erik said hoarsely. "We both knew that he had fallen in defense of Jean, for Jean's body was near him."

"My brother."

"Your father took a blow intended for Jean. He was wounded severely, but the *Slayer* let him live long enough to see his eldest son slaughtered before his eyes. Thierry had been teaching Jean his craft and was proud at what promise the boy showed." Erik shook his head. "The only thing that saved him from madness at the end was the hope that one of you, one of the other four, had lived."

Quinn knew that his brothers had not.

"I promised him that I would find all of his sons. I promised that I would raise them as my own, and I did not share my doubts that any of you had survived. Thierry had not seen the destruction of the town and I did not tell him how horrific it was. I could not bear the sight of it, myself. He would have been devastated to know that his friends and neighbors had suffered so much because he had been targeted."

Yes. Quinn knew that was true.

Erik cleared his throat. "While Thierry's strength faded, I went into that town. I went through its every alley and passageway. I looked at every corpse. In dragon form, I could even examine the ones that were still smoking. It was not an easy task, but I did it for my friend." Erik's voice tightened. "I did it because he asked it of me and it was the only thing left that I could do for him."

"And?" Quinn prompted when the other *Pyr* fell silent.

Erik fired a hot glance his way. "I found three more of Thierry's sons."

"Dead," Quinn said quietly, no question in his tone.

"Dead," Erik confirmed and Quinn hung his head. They walked in silence for a moment. "I could not find the fifth, the youngest. I could not find you, and that gave me hope. It gave me a mission and it gave me a deadline."

"My mother was in the church when it burned. I heard her call to me."

"I wondered what had happened to Margaux," Erik said softly. "The church, well, it was the hardest place of all. I confess that I looked for young boys first and tried to ignore the rest. Bless the Great Wyvern that you did not heed her."

Quinn sighed.

Erik nodded. "For a long time, I hoped that you and she were together somewhere, that you had managed to flee in her care."

"No." Quinn shook his head.

Erik swallowed. "It is a blessing that Thierry never knew that it was fire that destroyed her. He had two loves: the fire that defines us and the woman who gave meaning to his existence. It would have broken him to have known that truth."

Quinn bit his tongue. A similar truth had nearly broken him. Was he tougher than his father? Or less compassionate? Or had his commitment to Elizabeth been less than the love his father had felt for his mother? Quinn didn't really want to know.

The other *Pyr*'s grief was tangible. Erik shoved a hand

through his hair and frowned. "I went back to him. It was the hardest thing I have ever done, but at least there was that chance that you and Margaux had escaped."

"And he died?"

"And he died, clutching that last fragile hope, along with my promise to do my all to find you." He knotted his hands together, searching for the words. "It rained that night, you know, great torrents of rain."

"I'd forgotten."

"Until this week, I had no idea how important that was." Erik sighed, then looked at Quinn. "Tell me. Did you hide in the mill?"

Quinn was shocked. "Why do you ask?"

"Because there was a glimmer of a scent there, one that I tried to follow. It was so faint that it wasn't trustworthy, but it was the only one I found."

Quinn nodded. "I was there."

"And afterward?"

"After I saw the church burning and I saw you, I ran."

"I wish I had seen you then." Erik's voice was tinged with such regret that Quinn was tempted to believe him. "You were too young to have come into your inherited powers, so you left little hint of your passage. I was determined to find you by the time you reached puberty and came into your own."

"You never did," Quinn felt compelled to observe.

"No. I never did, but it wasn't for lack of trying."

"What about Ambrose?"

"What about Ambrose?" Erik's gaze was steady.

Quinn frowned in his turn. "I guess he wasn't the friend I thought him to be."

"Worse, Quinn. It is worse than that."

"What do you mean?"

"Who do you think was the *Slayer* who killed your father

and your brothers?" Erik held Quinn's gaze, his own bright with conviction. "Who do you think was assigned the task of eliminating the Smith's line, and is still driven to finish his task?"

Quinn walked more quickly in his agitation. It would have been nice to deny Erik's claim, but it made too much sense, especially given recent events.

If that were true, then Sara would never be safe until Ambrose was dead. If that were true, he should be the one challenging Ambrose to a blood duel. But Quinn had been deceived once before and he had learned something from it.

Belief wasn't good enough. Persuasiveness wasn't good enough.

He needed proof.

"Why should I believe you?" he demanded of Erik.

"I have defended your mate and helped to save her."

"You could be trying to win my confidence, like Ambrose did."

Erik nodded agreement. "That's true." He pulled his hand from the pocket of his jacket and something glinted gold on his palm. "I think you will recognize this."

Quinn did. It was the Roman coin that his father had always rolled between his knuckles, making it disappear and reappear when the family sat by the fire in the evening. Quinn had been entranced by that coin as a child, though his father had never let him touch it.

Thierry had never let any of his sons or his wife touch the coin and now Quinn knew why. It was the coin he used to challenge other *Pyr* to a blood duel.

Erik offered it to Quinn. "He gave it to me, at the end, as his legacy to his son. He assumed that I would find you and that you would survive."

"You could have taken it from him, if you were his killer."

"Then I would challenge you with it." Erik shrugged. "Instead, I give it to you."

Quinn took the coin, still unconvinced. There was too much at stake to take anything on faith.

Erik frowned, then indicated that he'd take the next turn back to his hotel. "By the way, Thierry told me to say that the Smith can make any coin his own. I don't know what that means, but maybe you do." He held Quinn's gaze for a moment, then turned to walk down the street that led back downtown.

"You're right, Erik," Quinn called after him. "I do."

Erik paused and glanced back. As the other *Pyr* watched, Quinn closed his hand over the coin. He breathed into his fist three times. He murmured to the gold of its own song and felt it transform within his grasp. Then he opened his palm for Erik to see how the coin had changed. "It means that you're telling the truth."

Erik had to walk back to him to see what he had done. When he did, he looked between the coin and Quinn, but he looked more resigned than astonished. "But you still don't fully trust me."

There was no question in his voice and Quinn didn't answer him. He didn't have to: they both knew it was true.

He was closer to trusting the older *Pyr* though, and he could prove it.

"Sun's coming up," he said. "You want a cup of coffee?"

Erik nodded at a donut shop. "Over there?"

"No. I'm going to make some for Sara." Quinn held Erik's gaze steadily. "In her apartment." He saw the moment that Erik realized he was being invited to cross Quinn's smoke. The depth of the other *Pyr*'s relief persuaded Quinn that he had made the right choice.

Sara had been right about finding out the truth.

The trick would be proving Erik innocent of the third

crime against Quinn and his loved ones. There were no witnesses of Elizabeth's death, and Quinn saw no point in asking Erik about his role.

A lie would be indistinguishable from the truth.

There is fire.

There is so much fire.

*Sara tosses and turns, aware that she dreams but know-
ing she can't evade this dream's truth.*

It is about Quinn.

*Everything around her is burning bright, orange with
hungry, licking flames. They crackle and hiss and leap so
high that she can't see the walls of the kitchen, much less
guess where to find the door. She feels a woman's panic as
she tries to escape the inferno. She cannot feel Quinn, but
this woman's thoughts are full of him.*

*There's a gold band on the woman's left hand. Sara lets
herself slide into the thoughts of Quinn's wife, knowing this
is why she is having this dream. The force of Elizabeth's love
for Quinn is staggering.*

*She is praying for him, even as she herself is condemned
to burn alive. Elizabeth pounds on the walls and shouts for
help, help that she knows will not come.*

*No one will help her. Elizabeth has been shunned by her
family and her friends, she has moved with Quinn into the
wilderness to establish a farm away from those who would
condemn them both, and she knows that the others will take
satisfaction in her death when they learn of it.*

They will say she reaped what she had sown.

Because they are fools.

*Quinn is the only one who would help her. But Quinn is
traveling, doing his regular route of repairing the shoes of
plough horses. Elizabeth knows he will be at the most dis-*

tant point by now, close to Boston, and also knows that it is no accident the golden dragon chose this day for his attack.

By the time Quinn returns to their farm, only smoking ash will remain. Elizabeth prays, even as she beats at the burning walls with her bare hands, desperate to escape. The stones of the chimney that Quinn built are hot, the thatch on the roof is burning, the kitchen is filled with blinding orange light.

Her father said that she deserved to burn for giving her hand and her heart to a demon. Her father said she would burn forever for her defiance of him, for her choice to marry a man who could take dragon form.

She never expected him to be proven right, not so soon.

Her heart had stopped when she opened the kitchen door, intending to milk the cow. A golden dragon landed in the space between house and barn, scattering the chickens and stirring the dust. When he smiled, she knew she would not see midday.

His beauty was deceptive yet fascinating. He might have been a jewel from a king's treasury, made of glittering gold and the gleam of the stone she knew as tiger eye.

Her father would have said that the wrath of God had come upon her. Elizabeth knew it was the wrath of the Slayers.

Of one particular Slayer. She knew from Quinn that his name must be Erik, but when she called him such, he laughed. He loosed a torrent of fire on the house, on her precious house that Quinn had built with his own hands, and Elizabeth dropped her bucket. She snatched a broom and tried to beat out the flames, only to find that the dragon continued his fiery assault.

She felt the heat and turned to find a wall of flames at her back. Her only escape was back into her kitchen and she didn't expect she'd leave it alive.

She didn't beg. She didn't plead. She lifted her chin and picked up her bucket and her broom. "You are evil," she told the Slayer, *whose smile only broadened. "And justice will be visited upon you. I only regret that I shall not live to see that day."*

He blew fire at her and Elizabeth retreated into the kitchen. She thought to bar the door against him but heard him moving something across the farmyard.

It was Quinn's anvil. He moved it with ease to block the door and smiled at her through the window.

"I hope you have said your prayers, Elizabeth," he taunted, then loosed the flames.

Sara shivers in her sleep, remembering Ambrose taunting her with the same words. She knows the moment Elizabeth realizes she is doomed, the instant that the last spark of hope is extinguished. It is when the hungry flames catch the hem of Elizabeth's skirt. She beats at her clothing as the flames surround her, lick at her, devour her. Her golden ring flashes in the light, a mark of her vows, a reminder of the reason she is paying this price.

But Elizabeth has no regrets. She would love Quinn again, without hesitation. Her only disappointment is that she never bore Quinn's son. It was the only desire she ever had that Quinn didn't fulfill.

She fears then that he will blame himself for her death, and she wishes there was some way she could tell him not to do so. She chose to love Quinn, or chose not to deny the love she felt for him.

And that, Elizabeth knows in her heart, made their short life together worth every breath. The fire takes her clothing, her hair, her skin, and the pain seems more than she can possibly bear. The ring burns on her finger but she will not remove it.

Elizabeth does not scream and she does not beg for

mercy. She has loved with all her heart and soul, and she has been loved in return.

And that, for her, is eulogy enough.

Sara awakened in the darkness, her breath coming in quick pants. Her dream had been so vivid that she got up to check the room for stray sparks. She sniffed for smoke and smelled only freshly brewed coffee. There was no fire, just the light waft of a cool breeze coming through the open window. She could feel Quinn's presence in the living room.

He hadn't left yet. For the moment, that was enough.

Before she spoke to him, Sara had to think about her dream. She lay back down and pulled a sheet over herself. If Quinn had been gone to Boston, then he and Elizabeth had lived near there. Sara reviewed the glimpses she'd had through Elizabeth's eyes of Elizabeth's dress and the simplicity of her kitchen.

Quinn had lived with Elizabeth in colonial America.

She recalled the golden ring and her heart clenched. No, Quinn had been *married* to Elizabeth in colonial America. But they had had no child. Did that mean that there had been no firestorm between them?

Sara curled up beneath the sheet, feeling again the power of Elizabeth's feelings for Quinn. She could understand that woman's love pretty easily.

Elizabeth had loved Quinn. She had known what he was and had accepted him, despite the censure of her father, despite the condemnation of everyone she knew.

And Ambrose had murdered her. It couldn't have been a coincidence that Quinn had been too far away to save Elizabeth.

Sara didn't doubt that Quinn blamed himself for failing her.

She rolled to her back, thinking furiously. Was this why Quinn insisted on being alone? Did he still love Elizabeth? Was he afraid of putting anyone he cared about in danger? Sara could imagine as much, given how protective he was.

Her stomach grumbled and she couldn't remember when she'd last eaten. She got out of bed and had grabbed a robe before she thought of something.

Quinn had a damaged scale on his chest when he was in dragon form. She had seen it when he had saved her from falling from the bell tower. His skin was exposed there and it was obviously a vulnerable spot.

It was also obviously something he didn't want to talk about, given how he'd avoided Sara's question when she'd first seen it.

How did the *Pyr* lose scales? Sara had a whimsical idea of what might have damaged that scale, one that she'd seen in the children's book that Erik had chosen for her. She'd flipped through the story before putting the book away, enchanted by the illustrations.

The dragon next door had a problem, in that he had loved someone he had lost and he had lost a scale from his chest as a result. That made him vulnerable when the other dragons fought, but the child in the story had proven so helpful that the dragon had loved again. And his love for the child next door had healed his wound.

It made a kind of sense. After all, Ambrose's chest showed no such vulnerability. She could imagine that the *Slayer* had never loved anyone, other than maybe himself.

Was Quinn vulnerable because he had loved Elizabeth?

If she could find out for certain what had damaged that scale of Quinn's, she might be able to figure out how to repair it.

Another woman might have been daunted by the revelation

that he had loved and lost before, but Sara had loved and lost before and she was still standing. She thought it gave them something else in common. The feelings she was starting to have for Quinn proved that the heart could take a hit and recover. She interpreted her dream as evidence that Quinn could love again.

Besides, Sara Keegan wasn't afraid to work for what she wanted.

She knotted the belt of her teal silk kimono and headed for the living room. There was only one way to get an answer to her question, although she wasn't at all sure that Quinn would be eager to enumerate his weak spots.

It wouldn't stop her from solving the puzzle, either way.

Quinn wasn't surprised when the smell of fresh coffee drew Sara from the bedroom. She wore a robe in greenish blue that made her look fresh from the sea. The fabric was smooth and silky and flowed over her curves like water over a beach. Her feet were bare and he could see the tan lines from her sandals, as well as the shell pink polish she had used on her toenails. He thought of her wrapped around him, all softness and strength, and was ready for another round.

He smiled that she had left her hair loose, although he didn't know whether she'd left it that way because he liked it or because she'd forgotten to knot it up.

She did look preoccupied.

Come to think of it, she looked determined. Quinn knew enough about Sara to brace himself for trouble.

"Good morning," Erik said, saluting Sara with his coffee cup.

"Hi," she said, smiling for him. If she was surprised to find that they had company, she hid it well. "I'm glad you're here," she said, looking serious again. "We've got to talk about saving the Wyvern."

"I agree," Erik said, sparing a pointed glance at Quinn.

Quinn ignored them both. He got a mug out of the cupboard and poured Sara a cup of coffee, placing it on the end of the counter near the fridge and sugar bowl, then returned to the juicer.

"You're making yourself at home," she teased as she got out the cream and he smiled at her.

He fed another carrot into the juicer. "A guy's got to keep up his strength," he teased in return, liking how she flushed.

"Wheat germ?" she asked, holding up a jar from the fridge. "It's really good in carrot juice."

"I'll take all the vitamins I can get," Quinn agreed easily. He took the jar from her and their fingers brushed in the transfer. There was no spark, no kindling of heat. Sara didn't seem to notice but Quinn was shocked to see evidence of what he already suspected.

Erik nodded once slowly, looking wise as he sipped his coffee. Sara meanwhile was stirring raw sugar into her coffee, blissfully unaware of what was lacking.

That wouldn't last. The woman was almost observant enough to be *Pyr*. Obviously, she was feeling a lack of caffeine.

Quinn returned to making his breakfast. He'd known the connection with Sara would be fleeting, but still. He supposed that the firestorm had to burn hot, so it couldn't last long. All the same, it seemed unfair to wait so long for something that endured only a couple of days.

He should have taken longer to court her.

On the other hand, the urgency of the firestorm was undeniable. Maybe it would have been over by this morning, anyway.

The next carrot had a rougher time going into the juicer.

"So, when do we save the Wyvern?" Sara asked brightly.

"Ask Quinn," Erik demurred.

Quinn gave them both a dark look, disliking how readily they looked like coconspirators. "The Wyvern told me to leave her behind."

"Time was of the essence," Sara agreed. "Now we have to go back."

"I don't think so," Quinn said with force. "She said it was more important to ensure your safety, and I'm inclined to agree."

"She can't have meant that she wanted to stay there." Sara was dismissive. "How long do you think it will take to assemble the other *Pyr*?" she asked Erik.

Before he could answer, Quinn interjected. "This isn't going to happen, Sara. *We* aren't going to save the Wyvern."

She looked between him and Erik. "Are you?"

"Possibly," Quinn said. Erik said nothing.

Sara's lips set. "I think you need me there."

"I think it would be smart for you to stay safe."

"I think you're forgetting that she's surrounded by *Slayer* smoke. Who else can cross it but me?"

Quinn glared at Sara because he couldn't think of a reply.

"She's right," Erik said mildly when the silence had stretched long.

Quinn shoveled wheat germ into his juice with undisguised irritation. "No, Sara's *not* right. She's not going anywhere near the Wyvern, seeing as the Wyvern is guarded by a team of *Slayers* determined to kill Sara." He glared at the two, and threw back a swallow of juice.

"You could all work together the way you did before," Sara began but Quinn interrupted her.

"No. There will be no working together. Erik has his team of *Pyr*: they have their agenda and I have mine. Our goals intersected and while I'm grateful for the help of the *Pyr*, it's not a long-term alliance. Understood?"

"Perfectly," Erik said tightly.

Sara pushed to her feet and came to face Quinn over the counter. "You still blame Erik for Elizabeth's death, but he didn't kill her. It was Ambrose. I saw him laugh when Elizabeth called him Erik."

Quinn nearly dropped his glass of juice.

Chapter 14

He stared at Sara but saw complete conviction in her eyes. "You've been dreaming again."

She nodded. "I saw it. I was there. It was awful and I can't imagine how you felt when you came back to the farm you had shared with her and found it in ashes."

Quinn looked away, his throat working in silence.

"But it was Ambrose who killed her," Sara whispered urgently.

Quinn studied Erik, who was listening avidly but didn't seem to know what Sara was talking about. Quinn couldn't sense any guile in him at all.

Was it true? He turned to Sara, who watched him with sympathy in her eyes. "Her last thought was that she would make the choice to love you again," she whispered, tears shimmering in her eyes. "Her only regret was that she hadn't bore your child."

Quinn had to turn away. He paced the length of Sara's small kitchen, his chest tight with emotion that he'd long pushed away.

"You had a firestorm already?" Erik asked with obvious

surprise. "I should have felt it. I should have been able to find you."

Quinn shook his head. "There was no firestorm," he said gruffly and stared out the window. "She wanted a child so badly. I couldn't tell her that it was impossible."

Erik sighed, as if sympathetic with that view. When Quinn glanced his way, the other *Pyr* was sipping coffee and looking out that window, lost in his own thoughts.

Quinn turned to face Sara across the kitchen, liking how she stood straight and proud. She was so fearless, and he thought it was because she didn't understand. "I can't do it, Sara. I can't take you toward the *Slayers*."

She grimaced and put down her mug of coffee, looking as if she was choosing her words. "You think I don't understand how awful it is to lose somebody," she said, her words thick.

"Not like that."

"Wrong." She impaled him with a glance. "My parents were burned to death. Their rental car went off the road, and turned end over end until it exploded. The military sent dental records to the consulate for their bodies to be identified. The final identification came from this."

She crossed the kitchen and opened a drawer near Quinn. There was only a padded mailing envelope in it, one that had already been opened. Sara opened it again, dumped two rings into her palm, then showed them to Quinn. They were blackened and bent, and her hand shook as she held them out.

The breath was stolen right out of him, not just by the power of her anguish but by the parallel with his own.

Not to mention the similarity of the mementos they had.

"My father's West Point graduation ring and my mother's plain sterling wedding band, although you can hardly tell now," Sara said. "It was all they could afford when they got married and she would never let him buy a fancier one." Her tears fell then, splashing on her hand as her words caught. "She said it would be like saying the original model wasn't good enough anymore."

"I'm sorry, Sara."

"Yes. So am I." She spoke quickly but there was no sting in her voice. He wanted to touch her but wasn't sure that he should. Her grip on her composure seemed tenuous and he knew it was important to her to appear strong.

If Erik hadn't been there, he would have worried about it less.

Sara meanwhile touched her lips to the rings, then put them back into the envelope. She placed the envelope back in the drawer, which she then closed, her hands remaining across the front for a moment. "I don't know what to do with them," she admitted softly, her hands moving in a helpless gesture. "But I have to keep them."

"Of course you do," Quinn said. "But it's your memories that are more important." Her breath caught at the truth in that, and then Quinn knew what to do. He slipped an arm around her shoulders and drew her closer. She turned into his embrace easily, intuitively, and laid her cheek on his chest as she quietly cried. Quinn held her close, feeling her arms steal around his waist. He wished more than he'd ever wished for anything that he could erase the ache of her loss.

Erik cleared his throat. "Your parents were killed, with fire?"

"It was a car accident," Sara said, glancing up but not moving out of Quinn's embrace. "The consul said those roads near Machu Picchu are dangerous."

"And they're isolated." Erik drained his cup, frowning. "There are seldom witnesses to what happens in the mountains. When did this happen, if you don't mind me asking?"

"In March. Just this past winter."

"After the seventh?"

Sara seemed confused. She looked at Quinn before turning to Erik. "It was later in the month. My mother wanted to see Machu Picchu on the equinox."

"After the eclipse that signaled your firestorm then," Erik said without surprise.

"What are you saying?" Sara asked.

"When the moon is devoured once not twice," Erik quoted quietly. "There was a lunar eclipse on March 7, the first one after the moon's node changed. The second one will be in August, and I knew that there would be a firestorm between the two eclipses."

"But what about the bit about the Dragon's Tail?"

"The moon's node changed in June 2006. It moves backward through the signs and moved from Aries into Pisces then, which has long been considered a time of reckoning and karmic balance. The ascending node is called the Dragon's Head and the descending node the Dragon's Tail."

Sara was fascinated. "So, an astrologer could date that prediction pretty accurately." Erik nodded as if this wasn't any big deal.

Quinn supposed that it wasn't. He was still horrified by Erik's earlier implication. "Sara's parents had their accident right after the eclipse that marked our firestorm," he said and Erik nodded. "She was supposed to be with them." The other *Pyr*'s gaze brightened.

"I was," she agreed easily. "But we had a potential deal come up and I changed my mind on the day of departure. I met them at JFK to tell them and my mother wasn't happy . . . oh!" She lifted a hand to her lips as she followed the direction of Quinn's thoughts, and she looked between the two of them. "You don't think that they meant to kill me?"

"They hold the Wyvern captive," Erik said curtly. "They could know your name."

Sara turned pale. "She apologized to me for telling them my name."

Quinn swore and held Sara more tightly. Erik looked grim. "You must know what this means, Quinn. You are your father's son."

Quinn's gaze flicked to the coin still on Sara's counter. He knew what it meant. Sara would never be safe as long as Ambrose was alive, and for once, he knew exactly where to find the *Slayer* that had killed so many people and *Pyr* dear to him. Ambrose wasn't going to survive to do that again.

He had to avenge the past to ensure the future. Sara had given him this gift of a fresh perspective, by compelling him to reexamine what he believed to be true. Resolving the past was the only way to move forward, to begin anew.

Later, he'd tease her about auditing and balancing his books. First, there was work to do.

"It means we have to save the Wyvern," Quinn said with determination. "And we need to do it today."

"You're not going without me," Sara said, lifting her chin in that stubborn way she had. As much as Quinn wanted to protect her, he knew he could do that only if she stayed with him.

And that meant that she was right, again.

Saturday was the first morning that Sara hadn't heard the Wyvern cry for help and that made her nervous.

It troubled the other *Pyr* when she told them about it.

The *Pyr* discussion to which they were all summoned that morning had been short but not sweet. They all recognized that they might not return from this attempt to save the Wyvern. They all knew that they had no choice. The Wyvern needed their aid, and hers was a call no decent *Pyr* could ignore.

The bulk of their argument had been persuading Quinn that Sara had to be the one to go through the smoke to get the Wyvern. Quinn wanted to go himself, but there was consensus that passing through a thick wall of smoke wasn't the same as being touched on the shin with it. Quinn hadn't been able to persuade the others that even dragonfire could heal him of that, and Sara had seen that he wasn't sure himself. The others likely sensed his doubts.

It made no sense to Sara to risk Quinn and his skills, when she could walk right through the smoke. Seeing that Quinn hadn't had another alternative to present, and that the *Pyr* similarly valued him, Sara's view had taken the vote.

When the vote was in, Quinn had become even more grim and silent. He had closed the meeting by insisting that Rafferty teach Sara about blocking any attempt to beguile her. That was the last thing he'd said to her, and she certainly hadn't seen him smile since.

It was more than their being separated by their tasks. There was a rift between herself and Quinn, although Sara hoped it was just because he had lost his argument in their council that morning. She knew he would have preferred to have left her secure elsewhere, but the ugly truth was that there was no such place.

The other *Pyr* spent the day strategizing, perfecting Quinn's skills at folding away his garments, working out signals between each other. They'd speculated on the nature of Lucien's claws and how they could be replicated. Quinn hadn't set up his booth, even though it was the last day of the show.

Sara knew that Quinn's time in Ann Arbor was pretty much at an end. What next? Would he go back to his land near Traverse City? She had a keen sense that Quinn was slipping into the world of the *Pyr*. He was taking up the responsibility that was his, but at the same time, he was less a part of the world she knew. She still felt him watching her, but she had a sense that something had ended.

Or changed.

Maybe it hadn't been such a great idea to remind him of his lost wife. Maybe Sara had reminded him of his love for Elizabeth and that had put an end to their relationship before it really started.

She wished there was a way to know for sure. Part of what she admired about Quinn was his code of honor, but she would have liked to have remained on the right side of it.

Sara remembered the Wyvern's words and wondered. Was the transformation in Quinn the product of their relationship that would save the *Pyr*? It was undeniable that the *Pyr* were stronger with his abilities, and that he was stronger with their tutelage. That would only increase with time.

In the middle of the afternoon, Sara watched Erik brace himself for a hit of dragonfire and heard the others cheer as he managed to deflect some of its force. The *Pyr* huddled closer to review what had happened and listen to Quinn, who spoke to them with authority. In one way, she yearned to be a part of their group and hear what he was saying. In another, she knew such knowledge wasn't hers to have. She wanted Quinn to be all that he could be and to embrace what he was.

Rafferty had to summon her attention back to his lessons repeatedly. When she made excuses, there was sympathy in his gaze and patience in his tone. Sara could have asked him about the firestorm, but instead she turned to a voice she could trust.

At her request and with Quinn's approval, Rafferty escorted Sara back to The Scrying Glass. The sight of the mermaid door knocker, all black and cold, made Sara a bit sad, as if the mermaid spoke of something past. She felt a bit funny talking to Magda in Rafferty's presence. "I have to talk to the ghost," she said to him. "It's my aunt Magda."

Rafferty smiled and leaned against the cash desk. "Little surprises me after so many centuries, Sara."

"Then you believe in ghosts?"

"There is little that I disbelieve. What is more important is what you believe."

He had a way of answering questions that left Sara with more questions, much like the Wyvern, but Sara didn't say as much. It was an annoying trait, and one she was glad that Quinn didn't share.

"All right, Magda," she said to the empty store. "Give me a clue."

She waited for a book to fall.

Instead, the air conditioner, which had been silent, whirred into action and ran efficiently. Rafferty looked up at the ceiling. Meanwhile, something seemed to be fidgeting in Sara's purse. She opened it, beneath Rafferty's bemused gaze, and found the red velvet bag of Magda's tarot cards at the very top. She'd been sure that they'd sunk to the bottom, along with the breath mints. She pulled them out and went to the cash desk, putting her bag down there while she shuffled.

"I think Magda likes to play games," she told Rafferty.

"Most ghosts do."

Sara considered the cards, then thought she had a better source of information. She was a bit worried about what the cards might say, a bit concerned that her instincts would be supported.

"Is the firestorm only about mating, Rafferty?"

He frowned slightly. "I would be lying if I told you that it is more than that for all *Pyr*. Many regard it simply as a chance to breed."

"And others?"

He nodded. "There is a view among some *Pyr* that the

union of a firestorm is greater than that of biology. There is a persistent idea that *Pyr* and mate can be more together than apart." Rafferty smiled. "But for the first group, of course, that's just a persistent myth."

"Do you know what Quinn believes?"

Rafferty shook his head. "I don't know him well enough and haven't known him long enough to have discussed such things. You have to realize that the firestorm is very intimate, that many *Pyr* will never discuss it with anyone."

Sara refrained from saying anything about men refusing to discuss their emotions. Instead, she shuffled the cards, focusing her mind on her questions. She pulled one from the deck and placed it on the counter.

It was the "Falling Tower," which seemed unlikely to be a good omen. The card was right side up and showed a stone tower being struck by lightning.

She fanned through the book of interpretations, hoping for the best. She didn't find it under the meanings for this card. *"Sudden changes are afoot. The walls are tumbling and nothing will ever be the same again. Get ready to be shocked—or struck by lightning."*

Rafferty chuckled. "Magda doesn't pull any punches, does she?"

"It sounds really bad."

"Change always sounds bad," Rafferty said with a reassuring smile. "I think we make it worse by resisting it. Sometimes the only thing worth pursuing is change. How else would we learn anything?"

"So maybe I asked the wrong question. Change is ahead, but what are the stakes?"

"An apt question," Rafferty said with approval.

Sara drew a card. It was the "Magician," and it was inverted.

"How interesting that you draw only the higher arcana

cards," Rafferty mused. "You must be keenly attuned to this deck."

Sara was too busy looking up the card. The "Magician" spoke of a skilled craftsperson, or someone focused on solving a specific problem or achieving a goal. Sara knew someone like that. But when the card was inverted, it meant that person wasn't working at his full potential, or that he might fail.

"What kind of a man makes promises that he can't know he can fulfill?" Rafferty whispered. "Not an honest one."

"Not Quinn," Sara said. "But nothing will go wrong. . . ."

"Much can go wrong, Sara. And if you do not return quickly with the Wyvern, who do you think will go after you?"

Sara met the *Pyr*'s steady gaze. "It's too risky for Quinn to cross the smoke. It could kill him."

"We already have seen that he will sacrifice for the greater good. He is that kind of *Pyr*."

"Then you have to stop him."

"Not all arguments are persuasive to all men, Sara."

Sara frowned and put the cards away. "Then we have to win," she said with determination. "There's no other acceptable answer."

She was well aware that Rafferty didn't agree with her.

It was a bruised but determined crew that met on the roof of Erik's hotel that evening. Sara was tired from her day under Rafferty's instruction, but she felt better able to defend herself against beguiling.

She was going to need all the help she could get.

When the *Pyr* met on the roof of Erik's hotel, they were as ready as they could be in just a day. Donovan's stomach was still wounded, although the cuts had closed, and he had a nick out of the top of his wings. Sara still wouldn't have wanted to face him in a dark alley, not with his eyes flashing fire the way they did now. Quinn had a similarly closed wound on his temple and Sara had a vivid purple bruise around her neck. Niall, Rafferty, and Erik had no physical injuries, but their expressions were grim.

The sun was setting on a day that had been sunny and clear, and the first stars were emerging. It could have been a romantic moment to be on a roof, but Sara was filled with determination and dread. Quinn offered his hand to her and she put her hand in his, noting that he didn't smile. No spark danced between them. She frowned, wondering when that had slipped away, and met his gaze.

He shook his head and frowned, his gaze turning skyward.

"It's over then?" she asked, her throat tight.

"I didn't know it would be so fleeting," Quinn murmured, as if in apology.

But what did that mean? Was that the change indicated by the cards? Or was there more?

Sara had no chance to ask. Erik gave the signal and the six of them leapt from the roof, shifting shape in unison. There was something glorious about the sight of them, the last of the sunlight winking off their scales. They were magnificent creatures, almost pure power. The only one Sara hadn't seen in dragon form before was Sloane and he was eye-catching—his scales shaded in all the hues of tourmaline, easing from green to purple through gold and back again.

Sara heard a rumble like thunder and as she watched, she knew that the *Pyr* had to be aware of each other's intentions. It wasn't the first time she'd sensed that there was more going on than she could perceive. It wasn't telepathy, maybe just speech on a sound wave that she couldn't hear well.

It made her feel alone, isolated. Maybe just useful.

But Sara had volunteered to help. She was the one who heard the Wyvern and the call must have come to her for a reason. She wanted to help the *Pyr* and wanted to save the earth.

Mostly, she wanted to help Quinn. Sara felt Quinn's tension as he carried her aloft and wondered at its source.

Had he volunteered to save the Wyvern because their firestorm was over and his legacy had been passed along? Did he see his life as ended because of the firestorm?

Was she pregnant?

How exactly were things supposed to work from this point onward? Well, she knew how the pregnancy would progress, given that Quinn had said it would be exactly like a human pregnancy, but what about her relationship with Quinn?

Or did they even have a relationship?

It seemed a bit late for her to have so many questions, especially as they were good ones. The wind stirred her hair and Sara acknowledged just how much she wanted to have a future with Quinn.

Of course, that didn't always change anything—she'd thought she'd wanted a relationship with Tom, but that hadn't stopped him from packing and moving out.

Quinn was different. Sara was sure of it.

As Rafferty had said, change was important. Change was how everyone learned. Some change was necessary, given the state of the world. Sara had to believe that if she and Quinn survived this challenge, they could make a future together.

She chose to believe it.

The cabin looked precisely the same. Quinn still didn't like it. Only one *Slayer* perched on the roof and Quinn knew he wasn't the only one who sniffed intently for the presence of others.

"One to the south," Niall murmured in old-speak. "About a mile away. Sleeping. The others are not close."

"That leaves three unaccounted for, assuming they haven't replaced Lucien," Erik said. "Any idea who is where?"

"That's Everett on the roof," Donovan said. "I recognize his turquoise scales and his size."

"You've met?" Quinn asked.

Donovan nodded. "Mean bastard, and strong."

"It's Xavier who is sleeping nearby," Rafferty contributed. "The earth sings to me of his healing wounds."

"He's the one you almost killed the other night," Erik said to Quinn. "The garnet red one. I'm surprised he's alive at all."

"We probably don't have to worry about him much then." Sloane was convinced that the *Slayer* couldn't have healed that quickly, but Erik remained skeptical.

"I don't think we should make such assumptions," he said. "We don't know what secrets they've learned, and you've said yourself that much healing lore is lost."

Sloane looked grim. "Why do the evil ones have to have all the advantages?" he muttered.

"Because they plan it that way," Donovan said.

Erik surveyed the cabin far below. "I dislike that the oldest *Slayer*s are the ones that seem absent."

"What do you mean?" Niall demanded. "I can't smell them, so they aren't here."

"Not necessarily. There are old ways of disguising one's presence. Be prepared for surprise," Erik spoke curtly. "When something looks too easy, it often is."

"It's the *Slayer* way," Rafferty agreed easily.

"Quinn and I will take the Seer down," Erik said. "That's

what they'll expect. The rest of you turn back as if you're leaving us to it, as if we've taken this situation at face value. Remain high and hidden until I call." At his nod, the others turned their course back to Ann Arbor and Quinn turned into a dive beside Erik.

The two *Pyrs'* wings whistled in the wind as they fell upon Everett with fearsome speed. They split at the last minute, and attacked Everett from two sides. The *Slayer* roared and took flight. He was large, just as Donovan had said, and there was a hatred in his eyes that would give him extra strength.

"Back claw," Quinn murmured to Sara, deftly changing his grip upon her. He needed his front claws free to fight and he was glad that she gripped his talon herself. She'd be less likely to fall.

She kept quiet but he was aware of the terrified pounding of her heart. He couldn't imagine being the partner of a woman inclined to hysterics. Sara's outward calm let him concentrate on doing his part.

It ensured that they worked better as a team.

Quinn turned a stream of dragonfire on Everett, and the *Slayer* fell back. Erik struck him across the head from behind.

The blow, which would have felled a smaller *Pyr*, had no discernible effect upon Everett. He spied Sara and leapt toward Quinn, claws extended.

"How thoughtful of you to bring me a snack," he hissed in old-speak. Quinn locked front claws with him and felt his power. They grappled for dominance, tumbling out of the sky as they wrestled each other's grip. Sara had a death grip on Quinn's talon and he could feel her biting back her scream, especially when Everett tried to snatch her away with his own back claw.

Quinn struck Everett hard with his tail, using all of his

might, then sank his teeth into the *Slayer*'s neck. Everett tore his neck free, his dark blood running over his scales. Quinn held Sara away from the volatile blood, knowing it would injure her if it splashed on her. Everett's eyes glinted; then he loosed dragonfire in Sara's direction.

Quinn twisted to take the flames on his back and lifted Sara in front of his chest to protect her. Everett latched on to Quinn's wings from behind. His talons sank deep and Quinn had a hard time staying aloft with the *Slayer* on his back. To his relief, Sara was breathing quickly, but uninjured. She had that set to her chin that meant she was ready to fight.

Erik fell on Everett from behind, ripping into the *Slayer*'s leathery wings. Everett bellowed in pain, released Quinn, and turned on Erik. He breathed dragonfire with such force that Erik fell back. The *Slayer* followed the leader of the *Pyr*, evidently thinking that he could finish the kill.

"Now," Sara whispered. She was right: this was their chance.

Quinn set Sara down quickly in front of the cabin. The door was still nailed shut and he couldn't cross the smoke to open it for her. Instead he breathed his fire, being careful not to incinerate much more than the door. His stores of dragonfire were running low, and he had to save some for their escape.

"Good," Sara said. She glanced up. "Behind you!" she cried, then darted into the cabin.

Quinn spun to find the malachite green dragon closing fast on him. The others were close by! Somehow they had hidden themselves from perception.

But then, Boris and Ambrose were very old, old enough to have learned such tricks. Quinn didn't know this *Slayer*, but he'd kill him just the same. He left Sara to the Wyvern's wisdom for the moment. He lunged skyward, and struck the green *Slayer* out of the air with a mighty crack of his tail.

Unlike last time, though, Quinn knew better than to trust this *Slayer* to stay down.

"Time to render the balance due," Quinn said as the green dragon came up with his front claws extended to fight.

"Suits me, Smith," he agreed, and they locked claws in battle.

"We have to hurry!" Sara said to the Wyvern. The cabin was filled with smoke. Sara couldn't see it but she could feel its chill on her skin.

Rafferty was right: Quinn would follow her if she took too long and Sara knew this much smoke would kill him.

The Wyvern, though, wasn't looking too healthy. She was even more pale than before and didn't seem to have the strength to even lift her head.

"You have to help me," Sara insisted, trying to pick up the shackled woman. Sophie was heavy, despite her slenderness, and Sara quickly realized she couldn't carry her.

"My task is fulfilled," Sophie murmured. "You should not have come."

"You said yourself that you can't always understand your own prophecies. We're here and you're coming with us."

"I have not the strength."

"You can do something to save yourself."

Sophie looked up at Sara and smiled. "Perhaps what I already did was enough to save the world."

Sara exhaled with impatience. "The world isn't going to be saved if Quinn dies trying to get me out of this cabin. Losing the Smith would be pointless and stupid. The *Pyr* need him, just like they need you."

Sophie frowned slightly and moved her shackles. The blast of dragonfire sounded overhead, along with the grunts of battle. Something landed so heavily on the roof that Sara thought it might come right through. The roof bent beneath the weight and she would see daylight around its perimeter.

"I couldn't be so lucky as to see him dead," Sophie muttered with that determination Sara had glimpsed before. She glanced upward as the roof groaned and the weight was removed.

"We have to get out of here, now," Sara insisted.

Sophie opened one bright eye. "How?"

It was as if she were asking a riddle. Or testing Sara. Sara knew then that her answer was important. She heard a familiar laugh from outside the cabin, then the whisper that she knew would haunt her nightmares.

"Said your prayers, Sara?" The words came hissing through the cracks of the wood, the sound of that voice making Sara shiver.

It was Ambrose and she knew what he was going to do a heartbeat before he did it. She heard the flames kindling and felt the heat. Then dragonfire licked the wood of the cabin, flicking between the logs like hungry orange tongues. Ambrose was moving around the perimeter of the cabin, setting the back alight to drive Sara to the door.

She didn't need Magda's cards to know that there was a special surprise waiting for her there. This *Slayer* had a system for killing those important to Quinn, and Sara could see the pattern.

She had to break it somehow.

She felt Sophie's expectant gaze on her and knew then what she was supposed to remember. "You can change to other shapes," she said, excitement making her whisper rise. "Become small, so you can slip out of the shackles. I'll do the rest."

Sophie smiled; then she closed her eyes. Sara thought for a minute that the Wyvern might not have the strength to shift, but then the edges of her body began to shimmer.

While Quinn seemed to take on a golden glimmer, Sophie had a pearlescent glow that was even harder to look at directly.

Sara blinked, and when she looked again, a silver salamander with bright clear eyes looked back at her from the midst of the empty shackles. Fortunately Sara had never been afraid of crawly things. She bent down and lifted the salamander, then tucked the creature that was the Wyvern into the pocket of her shorts.

"You could have done that before and saved everyone a lot of trouble," Sara felt the need to say.

She heard the Wyvern chuckle from inside her pocket. "And what would have happened to the union of the Smith and the Seer, had you not had a mission to accomplish together?"

Sara had to admit that there was truth in that, although it still astounded her. "But you could have been killed."

"True, but sometimes, Sara, only self-sacrifice will serve the greater good."

Sara was awed that her union with Quinn was considered to be so critical. "Well, it's not going to help anyone if Quinn or I don't survive this."

She heard Sophie's knowing chuckle, but didn't have time to think about what it might mean. The wooden walls were all burning, encasing them in a box of flame. Sara remembered how Elizabeth had died, how Quinn's mother had died, and knew she wasn't going to be the next one on that ill-fated list.

She caught a glimpse of Ambrose through the burned doorway, gave him time to gloat over her lack of choices, then decided to scream.

Chapter 15

The green dragon had divided Erik and Quinn, providing relief to Everett. Quinn had thought they still had a chance when he saw the ruby red dragon silently crest the canopy of trees, right near the cabin, Ambrose fast behind him.

"Boris," Erik breathed in recognition. He ascended to meet the leader of the *Slayers*, his claws ready for battle. The green Slayer moved to follow Erik, but Quinn saw he wouldn't get far.

There were four *Pyr* streaking across the sky toward them, and not a moment too soon.

Quinn confronted Everett, who was so busy laughing at Quinn that he was oblivious to the arriving *Pyr*. "Four to two, Smith. Want to change to the winning side?"

"I'm *on* the winning side," Quinn said. He moved as if he'd lock claws with the *Slayer*, but struck him hard against the head instead. At the same time, he grasped one of Everett's back claws, then hit him again so that he turned. One more strike and Everett was spinning from Quinn's claw. Quinn flung him at the cabin's metal roof, using the *Slayer*'s weight against him.

Everett hit the metal with a loud bang, shook his head, and took flight again. The roof had bent from the impact and the smoke inside began to filter through the gap at the eaves.

The malachite *Slayer* jumped Quinn from behind, but Quinn had been ready for him. He spun and exhaled dragon-fire at the smaller dragon, who yelped and flew toward his leader. The other *Pyr* swooped down on the battle then. Erik flung off Boris's grip, the two snarling at each other as they returned to their respective team mates. The five hovered together, considering their foes.

"Five to four, Everett," Quinn taunted. "But we don't want you to change sides."

Everett looked down at the cabin and smiled coldly. "Maybe I'll just wait for supper to be sautéed to perfection."

The walls of the cabin blazed with fire. Quinn knew that Sara was trapped inside. He lunged toward the ground, glancing to either side before he did so. Rafferty was slightly behind him and to his right, Donovan slightly behind and to his left.

The *Slayer*s obviously understood the *Pyr* intentions, because they sprang into action, as well. Boris and Everett intercepted the *Pyr* before they could reach the cabin door. Quinn could hear Ambrose laughing as Everett moved to block their path and Boris retreated.

"Leaving the others to do the dirty work, as usual," Rafferty muttered. "No wonder Boris has lived so long." Boris snarled but didn't hover out of reach. Quinn heard Erik battling behind them.

"Oh, look out," Donovan said in old-speak. "It's Fat Everett. Or should I say Dumb Everett? I never could decide which was your defining trait."

Everett snarled, a puff of smoke rising from his nostril as

his gaze flicked between the three of them. "I can take all of you. That's my defining trait."

"Might doesn't always make right, kiddo," Donovan taunted. "Haven't you learned that yet?"

"Don't make him angry," Rafferty advised and Quinn knew that the *Pyr* were working together.

Donovan laughed. "Why not? What's he going to do? Breathe fire?" He laughed harder. "We all know that Everett failed Fire 101."

"I did not!" Everett roared. He belched an enormous stream of dragonfire. Quinn leapt forward to take the brunt of it. While Everett concentrated on showing off his prowess, the other two *Pyr* circled behind him.

Then they breathed fire on his back.

Everett screamed and his fire stopped. He pivoted to face Donovan and Rafferty, and Quinn seized the moment. He locked his claws around Everett's neck, heard the *Slayer*'s gasp of surprise, then used the extra strength from the drag-onfire to squeeze the breath out of Everett.

When Everett began to lose consciousness and sag against him, Rafferty and Donovan seized the *Slayer*'s legs.

"You're heavier than ever," Rafferty told the stunned *Slayer*.

"Maybe you should lay off consuming entire villages for a while," Donovan advised. "Cut back on the size of the herds you devour in one go, you know?"

"Just until you're fighting trim again," Rafferty added, as if to console him.

The breath left Everett in a long slow hiss as Quinn squeezed. Everett's eyes closed and he went limp. Quinn hit him on the side of the head with his tail, just to be sure. Then Rafferty and Donovan lifted the *Slayer* high, swinging his weight between them.

"One," they shouted in unison. "Two!" Quinn added his

voice as they swung Everett's considerable bulk even higher. "Three!" And they flung the *Slayer* through the sky, over the forest to the far fields. The ground shuddered when he fell and a boom echoed through the air.

"Some farmer is going to be really confused tomorrow morning," Donovan mused, then winked at Quinn.

Quinn had more immediate concerns. It had been a long time since Sara had gone into the cabin, to his thinking. What could be taking so long? Had she been overwhelmed by the flames?

Sloane looked at the ground and frowned. "There's new smoke gathering. Someone's breathing more."

Rafferty narrowed his eyes as if listening. "The one who sleeps not far from here. He's awake enough to breathe smoke."

"It must be Xavier," Sloane said.

"But he was fried with dragonfire the other night," Niall protested.

"Then they've learned some new healing secrets," Sloane said darkly, then nodded to Niall. "Come on!"

The pair flew off together, leaving the four *Pyr* to face the three remaining *Slayer*s. Erik was locked in combat with the malachite green *Slayer* and Boris eyed the three *Pyr* with amusement. He was murmuring something, chanting an old song that prompted a reverberation in Quinn's bones.

"Why doesn't he get to it?" Donovan muttered, eager as always to fight.

Rafferty followed Boris's gaze and looked west. "He's conjuring a storm instead." He was right: thunderclouds were gathering on the horizon with astonishing speed. They were dark and ominous and moving quickly toward the dragon battle. They weren't just coming from the west, but from all sides, looking as if they'd converge over the dragon battle.

"Anyone who falls won't fight again," Quinn said and the other two *Pyr* agreed grimly. It was a fight to the death, then.

That was the moment Quinn realized that he'd lost track of Ambrose.

"Sara!" he whispered, knowing that she must be inside the cabin. He would have descended, but Donovan snagged his tail.

"The cabin's full of smoke," Donovan said, sparing Quinn a glare. "Don't even think about going in there, Quinn."

"We need you," Rafferty asserted.

"I need Sara."

Rafferty nodded and considered the dent Everett's body had made in the steel roof. "Did you two have your Wheaties this morning?"

"What does that mean?" Donovan demanded.

"It means I have an idea. Let's move, while Boris is busy." Rafferty dove toward the cabin, Quinn and Donovan right beside him.

Erik pummeled the green *Slayer* that was keeping him from engaging Boris. It was typical of Boris to let his minions do the dirty work, but Erik sensed that they were playing a game with him.

He didn't much care. They had to get the Seer and the Wyvern out of this cabin soon.

He struck the smaller *Slayer* hard and the green dragon lost his flying rhythm. He hovered just out of range of Erik's fire and smiled.

There was something familiar about him.

"What's your name?" Erik demanded.

"Is that just a formality before you kill me?" the *Slayer* asked, evidently having no fear of dying soon. "How quaint to insist on introductions."

Erik scanned the sky around himself quickly but there were no other *Slayer*s in range.

Why was this one so confident? He was smaller, he was younger, he was bleeding. He would die. There was no doubt about it.

Except that Erik couldn't foresee the *Slayer*'s death, the way he foresaw most things moments before they happened. What was he missing?

"I'm a little offended that you don't recognize me," the *Slayer* said. "Because I recognize you, Erik Sorensson." He paused for a moment, just long enough to let Erik see the clear blue of his eyes. "Father."

"Sigmund," Erik breathed, shocked to his core to find his only son alive. But then he'd learned a bit in recent days about ensuring that dragons stayed dead.

"Sigmund Guthrie, now," the younger dragon sneered. "I shed your name when I shed your alliances."

"Sigmund Guthrie was human."

"No. Sigmund Guthrie has always been me."

Erik stared at his son in shock. "You wrote that book, the one that makes us vulnerable."

"How better to exterminate the *Pyr*? Once the *Pyr* are gone, it will be easy to eliminate humans. Then we can have the entire planet to ourselves."

It sickened Erik that this was the result of his own firestorm.

It would have sickened Louisa to see their child now.

Erik couldn't say that it would have broken her heart, because he had done that himself.

"So, how exactly does the leader of the *Pyr* rationalize the murder of his own blood?" Sigmund bobbed in the air, tempting Erik to take that last hit. "Especially when he believes his kind should breed, whenever possible."

"How could you become a *Slayer*?" Erik demanded. "I

taught you everything I knew. Your mother raised you with such love and care. You knew right from wrong."

"I knew that the only way to get what I wanted was to take it," Sigmund replied. "And I learned from my father that everything has to be sacrificed to ambition. You taught me that nothing else matters."

"No!" Erik roared and lunged after his son. They locked claws and grappled.

"I notice that you didn't lose a scale over Mother," Sigmund growled. "But then, why would that surprise me? You abandoned her."

"I did not," Erik argued, but he knew the charge held truth.

"Was I the only one who really loved her?" Sigmund hissed, then displayed the torn scale on his own breast with pride. There was knowingness in his eyes. "You are so much stronger than I am, Father. Go ahead, take advantage of my vulnerability."

He was daring Erik to make the kill.

But Erik looked into Sigmund's blue eyes and saw Louisa, the woman he had wronged. He couldn't kill Sigmund, couldn't kill the child she had borne him, no matter what his son had done. He flung Sigmund away from him, not caring where the *Slayer* fell, and rocketed toward Boris.

Erik knew who had led his son astray. His argument was with Boris.

Erik knew that Boris's whispers wouldn't have found fertile soil if he had taught his son right.

Louisa had expected better of him.

Erik didn't want to know how badly his blow had injured his son, so he didn't listen to his own voice of foresight. That was why he never anticipated that Sigmund would recover in midair, change course, and come after him. He was so focused on Boris—who smiled at his approach—that he didn't hear the *Slayer*'s pursuit.

After Sigmund struck him hard from behind, Erik had a moment to realize why Boris had been amused.

Then Sigmund hit him twice more, Boris breathed fire on him, and Erik lost consciousness as he fell toward the earth.

Ambrose stepped into the cabin when Sara didn't take his dare. "It's getting hot out there," he said with a smile that seemed hungry. He eased farther into the cabin, ensuring that his tail didn't touch the flames, then glanced around. He seemed to glow in the firelight. "Don't tell me that the Wyvern left without you?"

Sara wasn't inclined to give him more information than she had to. The Wyvern shivered in her pocket. "What if she did?"

Ambrose laughed, taking Sara's words at face value. "It would serve you right for risking your life for nothing. Not that it bothers me."

He breathed fire, almost idly enclosing Sara in a circle of flames. Sara jumped and tried to escape the closing circle, but Ambrose moved too fast and the flames were too high to jump. The circle was about ten feet in diameter and the flames burned against the hardpack of the dirt floor. Sara was sure they'd extinguish themselves for lack of fuel, but they continued to burn, the tips of the flames as high as her shoulders.

It was impossible, but it was happening all the same.

She turned in place, looking for an escape, as the heat made her perspire.

"No exit clause," Ambrose said idly. "Sorry."

"You're not sorry at all."

"No. I'm not." He sauntered closer, sending a stream of flame to make Sara's space smaller. The circle was only six feet in diameter when he was done and the flames just seemed to burn higher with every passing moment.

Sara was trying not to panic. The Wyvern had gone completely still.

"Dragonfire doesn't need fuel," Ambrose informed her, then examined his talons with indifference. "Life is power enough."

"There's no life in dirt."

"There's life in anything. Too bad you're not sensitive enough to recognize it." He granted her a cold smile. "Such an ignorant species."

A tongue of fire licked at Sara's leg and she smacked at it with her hand.

"If fuel for the fire . . ." Ambrose mused. Sara understood then that the fire would exhaust her before it consumed her.

Ambrose cut the circle in half with an exhalation of flame. Sara danced to one side and the flames caught the hem of her shorts. She beat out the fire with her hands on one side, only to find the hem on the other side burning. When she had the flames out and was breathing quickly in fear, she glanced up to find Ambrose smiling.

"You've been a more worthy opponent than most," he acknowledged, "but then, as Boris says, the ending is always the same. How dull." He yawned magnificently and Sara saw the flame gathering in his throat. She couldn't jump up. She couldn't burrow down. She couldn't move from the spot he'd chosen for her.

And sadly, she couldn't take dragonfire the way Quinn could.

Ambrose's eyes glinted with satisfaction. Sara glared at him, refusing to surrender to the inevitable, at least in spirit. He took a deep breath and she braced herself for the inferno he'd unleash.

It was a crappy way to die, but at least it would be quick.

Instead of Ambrose's torrent of flame, there was the sound of destruction from above. A cool breeze caressed Sara's skin as the sky became visible overhead.

Ambrose swore as the roof was torn from the cabin and tossed aside. Three *Pyr* had taken the corners of the roof and wrenched it from the building. Sara wanted to cheer when she saw Quinn, looking grim and powerful, his steel blue scales glinting. She felt something slippery passing her and knew that the *Slayer* smoke was dispersing into the sky.

She also guessed that it was stinging the *Pyr*. Rafferty, Donovan, and Quinn recoiled immediately. Sara understood that they couldn't retrieve her from below. She saw Quinn's determination and knew he would try.

And that the smoke would kill him.

"No fair!" Ambrose roared and leapt skyward after the *Pyr*, abandoning Sara to the flames.

Sara saw her chance. She lunged skyward and seized the tip of his tail, holding tight as he carried her out of the smoke and flames. He twisted in midflight in rage; then his eyes gleamed when he saw her. Before Sara could gasp, Ambrose swung his tail up and opened his mouth beneath her.

Being burned to death was looking like the better option.

Ambrose's teeth were long and sharp and yellowed. His throat gaped large and dark, a dark abyss with nothing good at the other end. The scales on his tail were slippery, and Sara felt like she was trying to hold on to a large fish. Sara clutched at a pair of scales, but her palms were sweaty and Ambrose writhed so that she swung in the wind.

"Sara!"

She turned at the sound of Quinn's bellow and saw him closing fast. She also saw Boris move a lazy finger as if guiding something upward. She couldn't see the smoke in the cabin rise to follow his bidding, but she knew the moment that Quinn hit its wall.

He recoiled with a bellow of pain, steam rising from him from the *Slayer* smoke's vile touch. He writhed and beat at his chest with his claws, as if trying to turn something back. He breathed fire on himself even and Sara was afraid for him. Rafferty and Donovan closed ranks around Quinn, fighting to defend the Smith as Boris moved toward them. Sara knew that Quinn was badly hurt.

She could tell by the way Boris laughed.

She saw the blackened hole in Quinn's chest and remembered that was where his damaged scale was located. The smoke must have targeted the weak spot, the vulnerability created by his loving Elizabeth.

Who else could help?

Erik was down and motionless, Sara saw then. Niall and Sloane were nowhere in sight. The green *Slayer* ascended from Erik's fallen form to attack the three *Pyr* while Boris glanced skyward with pleasure. Sara saw him murmur, as if he were talking to the sky.

Or casting a spell. Was that possible? Dark clouds collided overhead with a crack of thunder and the wind swirled in unpredictable patterns. The sky had a greenish tinge and the wind was restless, a combination that Sara knew meant big trouble.

Where had the bad weather come from? The sky had been clear when she went into the cabin. And how had the clouds gathered from every direction? Boris must have been summoning a storm.

Because rain would ensure that fallen *Pyr* became dead *Pyr*.

"Seen enough?" Ambrose whispered beneath her and Sara realized he'd been watching her. "I love when everyone appreciates the stakes, although it did take you a while." He wiggled his tail, forcing Sara to snatch at his scales in panic. The first heavy drops of rain fell, making her grip even more tenuous. "Don't miss the big finish, Quinn," Ambrose shouted.

Quinn raged dragonfire, but it couldn't permeate the smoke. He was failing, Sara knew it, and there was nothing she could do.

Ambrose loved it. He was the focus of attention and worked the moment for all it was worth. He undulated with ease, chuckling as Sara's one hand slipped free.

"Oops!" he whispered, then wriggled again.

Sara gasped and snatched. She got a grip with one hand, her legs waving in the wind as she struggled. Ambrose ran his tongue across his teeth, gave his tail a flick, and Sara lost her grasp on him completely. She fell, right toward his open mouth.

This time, Sara did say her prayers.

To her astonishment, they were answered.

Quinn saw Sara dangling from the end of Ambrose's tail. He wanted to shred the *Slayer* who had taken so much from him and would have tried, if Donovan and Rafferty hadn't held him back.

He saw Ambrose wiggle his tail.

He saw Sara struggle for a grip. "I have to help her!"

"The smoke will kill you," Donovan said.

"She'll be reborn," Rafferty agreed sadly.

"That's not good enough!"

"Look at it this way," Rafferty said. "You won't be the only one waiting for a firestorm."

"We need you, Quinn," Donovan said. "We need you *now*."

"There's nothing you can do," Rafferty concluded, but he was wrong.

"There's one thing I can do," Quinn said. He whistled at

Ambrose, then shouted, "Catch!" Quinn flipped his father's coin in Ambrose's direction.

The Roman coin glinted as it spun toward the *Slayer*. Ambrose's eyes lit at the sight of it. He abandoned Sara and lunged toward the coin, so anxious was he to catch it.

Quinn had been right: Ambrose's real argument was with him.

The coin began to tumble toward the earth, but Ambrose swooped in fast pursuit. He plunged through the *Slayer* smoke, and snatched it out of the air just before it hit the ground.

"You're on, Smith!" he roared in triumph, holding the coin aloft.

But Sara was still falling. Quinn fought against the two *Pyr*, wanting to help her no matter the price.

"Look!" whispered Rafferty.

A cloud of white emanated from Sara's pocket as she fell. It spread with astonishing speed, changing from a shapeless mass into a dragon unlike any *Pyr* Quinn had ever seen. The slender white dragon caught Sara in her claws and flew skyward, moving with effortless ease. She passed through the *Slayer* smoke like a wind slipping between the raindrops and seemed to feel no ill effects.

"It's the Wyvern," Donovan whispered with awe.

He had to be right, because this dragon was unmistakably female. She was more sleek than any of the *Pyr* and so pale that she might have been made of spun glass. Her wings seemed embellished with feathers, more like those of an exotic bird than a bat, and were so translucent that they might have been made of sheer silk. They fluttered rather than flapped, as if she floated in agreement with the wind instead of flying with her own effort.

"Few see this sight," Rafferty whispered with reverence.

"Something to tell the kids," Donovan teased, earning a dark look from Rafferty.

"There's nothing wrong with wanting offspring," he said, his gaze returning to the Wyvern.

She moved with a languid grace that made her look spectral and unreal. She carried Sara with tremendous care—something that worked for Quinn—then spread her wings over Erik's fallen form.

She lost altitude slowly as the rain began to fall with force, sheltering Erik from the water like a massive umbrella. She settled over him much as a swan shelters her cygnets beneath her wings.

"She's protecting him from the last element," Rafferty said and the others could only nod agreement. Why Erik? Why did the Wyvern protect him? Quinn could only guess that it wasn't time for Erik Sorensson to die, that the Great Wyvern had another expectation of that *Pyr*.

Quinn had a glimpse of Sara disappearing beneath the Wyvern and didn't doubt that she was trying to help Erik herself.

Then he looked up and found Ambrose closing fast, his father's coin glinting in the *Slayer*'s grip. "Protect the Wyvern," he said to Rafferty and Donovan.

"But you're too injured to fight," Donovan protested. "You need us."

"The challenge is mine to fight," Quinn replied. "I gave it and he accepted it."

"But . . . ," Rafferty began to argue.

Quinn interrupted him. "Sara carries the new Smith."

Donovan gave a low whistle. "Quick work, Quinn."

Quinn agreed. The firestorm had come and gone too fast. He wanted years with Sara, not moments, but the choice wasn't his. If his dying deed was the killing of Ambrose, it would be the best possible gift to Sara and their barely conceived child. The *Pyr* would ensure that the boy was taught what he needed to know and Sara would help him understand what he had inherited.

He brushed off the concern of his companions and braced himself for Ambrose's assault. "You have to protect the future, not the past."

Rafferty was the first to go, the wisdom in his gaze showing that he understood Quinn's choice. Donovan had a harder time with it. "I'll kill him for you."

"You can't," Quinn said. "The challenge was mine so the battle's mine."

Even Donovan couldn't argue with that. Quinn still sensed that Donovan was torn, but the way Boris and Sigmund turned toward the Wyvern made up his mind. He flew to Rafferty's aid, leaving Quinn to face his oldest adversary.

The battle could have happened at a better time. Quinn's chest ached where the scale was damaged and the smoke had slid beneath it. He was determined, though, to resolve his old feud, whatever the price.

To Quinn's surprise, Donovan pivoted as he departed and spewed dragonfire on Quinn from behind. It was the gift of a friend and ally. Quinn smiled as the surge rolled through him, invigorating him and making him feel radiant once more.

He felt the power of fighting as a team, of covering each other's flanks, and knew that if he survived this fight, he could never go back to his solitary ways. Opening himself to trust others was something Sara had taught him. He wanted to learn all she had to share. He wanted to see their child. He wanted to make her eyes turn gold a thousand times.

Quinn wanted—and needed—to win.

Sara could hear the Wyvern chanting something low and deep, something Sara couldn't quite hear, but even she could feel Erik respond to the song. He was unconscious and his breathing was shallow. The wounds he had sustained cut deep and he was burned on one side.

"There is something greater broken within him, Seer," the Wyvern murmured. "The spirit must heal before the body can be repaired."

That made sense to Sara in general, even if she didn't understand the specifics. Sophie continued her chant, though, effectively ignoring Sara as she concentrated on Erik.

To Sara's dismay, Rafferty and Donovan left Quinn to battle alone with Ambrose. The pair flew toward her just as Niall and Sloane came back over the forest. The amethyst and tourmaline dragons carried the charred body of the garnet red *Slayer* that had been Xavier. They tossed his carcass into the burning remains of the cabin, glanced toward Quinn, then also flew toward Sara.

"Sneaky," Niall said with disgust.

"They all are," Donovan agreed, his eyes narrowing as Boris and the green *Slayer* streaked toward the *Pyr*. "Here they come."

Niall murmured something low, his brow furrowing. "Heads up," Sloane warned, watching the churning sky overhead as well as the other *Pyr*. "This is unpredictable stuff."

Even as he spoke, a funnel cloud emanated from one dark cloud, then retreated. Niall continued to murmur, then another larger one spun toward the earth with fearsome speed.

It fell upon Boris and the green *Slayer*. They never saw it coming and Sara heard the roar of Boris's shock as the two disappeared into the churning air.

"Easy, Niall," Sloane said when the burgeoning tornado veered closer.

The *Pyr*'s eyes narrowed as he fought to turn the unruly clouds to his will.

They all breathed a sigh of relief when the funnel cloud pulled back into the dark clouds above and the dark thundercloud seemed to boil while it was incorporated.

"Can you control storms?" Sara asked and an exhausted Niall shook his head.

"They're unpredictable, especially violent ones, and often have intent of their own. I'd never invite one like this, because you just don't know what it will choose to do." He exhaled mightily, spent from his efforts, and the other *Pyr* quietly congratulated him.

Sara was trying to wrap her mind about the idea of a storm having an intention.

Meanwhile, Quinn and Ambrose fought vigorously.

The *Pyr*, to Sara's surprise, landed in a circle around Erik. "Why don't you help Quinn?" she demanded.

Rafferty bowed his head. "Because he asked us to protect you instead."

"But that's not right! That's not fair," Sara argued. "I thought you needed the Smith to save the earth. . . ."

"They need the product of the union between the Smith and the Seer," the Wyvern interjected calmly.

Sara turned to meet her steady gaze as she understood. She put her hand on her belly. "You said it wouldn't be a child."

"I said it wasn't necessarily going to be a child. The possibility was always present." Sophie smiled serenely at Sara's shock, then returned to her healing song. She beckoned to Sloane who knelt beside her to learn her chant.

"But I'm not ready to trade Quinn for his child," Sara said, even though no one was listening.

Rafferty settled beside her, his manner calm and thoughtful. "It is our way, Sara. The blood duel is a challenge to fight to the death. Once it is accepted, no other *Pyr* or *Slayer* can intervene."

"So you just watch?"

"There've been times when dragon fighting has been a spectator sport," Donovan said, his gaze fixed on the battle.

"Right. I'll bet the *Slayer*s play by those rules all the time," Sara said bitterly. "Couldn't you at least keep tabs on Boris and Sigmund? It would be like them to double back." She turned to Niall. "I mean, if you aren't sure about controlling storms, maybe it was Boris who made it look like you controlled it."

She again had the sense that the *Pyr* consulted each other. Niall took flight, his expression that of someone who listened intently, albeit to something Sara couldn't hear. The storm was passing; the rain had settled into a more steady downpour. The clouds were still dark, but that uncertain energy was dissipating. "They've turned south," he murmured, peering into the distance.

"I'll go with you and intercept them," Donovan said. "Sara's right that the *Slayer*s don't play by the rules."

Some other comment was passed between them; Sara felt it more than heard it. Then Rafferty eased closer to her. He was her guardian; she understood as much without words.

But there was another guardian she would have preferred. She watched Quinn battle Ambrose, wishing there was something she could do to help.

"You can stay out of it," Rafferty said. "The conviction that you are safe is his bedrock."

"How did you know what I was thinking?"

Rafferty smiled. "Humans are enchantingly transparent." He sighed and pulled his tail around, then patted it in invitation. Sara sighed in her turn and sat down on the opalescent scales, telling herself to be patient.

It wasn't her best trick.

Especially when it became apparent that Quinn was losing.

"I don't like spectator sports," she grumbled, unable to keep herself from watching.

"Neither do I," Rafferty agreed. "Blood sports are worse."

Sara couldn't argue with that.

Chapter 16

Quinn knew that he had to use Ambrose's pride against him to triumph. It was the only weak spot the *Slayer* had. The hole in Quinn's chest ached as he ascended to meet Ambrose over the woods that encircled the burning cabin. Rain beat down, turning their scales slick, and the wind swirled around the pair as they locked claws.

They thrashed their tails at each other, clawed, bit, and parted when Quinn exhaled dragonfire on the *Slayer*.

"I won't be breathing fire on you," Ambrose muttered. "No matter how much you tempt me."

"An old dragon like you should be easy to beat, anyway."

"Age gives experience!"

"Age gives weakness and infirmity. Look at you, for example."

"I'm stronger than ever!" Ambrose raged.

"I don't think so. Erik sent you from the tower with your tail between your legs the other night," Quinn taunted, knowing that Ambrose didn't like reminders of failure. "Maybe you're getting old, Ambrose, too old to fight."

The other *Pyr* launched himself at Quinn with fearsome

fury. Quinn was startled by how quickly he moved. They grappled with each other, claws locked, and fell from the sky as they fought for advantage. Quinn could see the hatred in his opponent's eyes and feel the heat of his breath as he snapped at Quinn's chest.

Quinn thought they would crash into the trees, but he wasn't going to be the one to let go first. He lashed at Ambrose with his back claws, but the *Slayer* struck Quinn with his tail first.

Quinn tumbled toward the treetops, stunned by the force of the blow.

"I let Erik defeat me that night," Ambrose bellowed, loosing a stream of fire. He ensured that it didn't come near Quinn. "I *chose* to leave."

Ambrose was furious and Quinn decided to prod him more. He pretended to be more injured than he was, taking his time recovering his balance and flying upward to engage again. "What about the night before in the arcade? You ran like a little boy who didn't know how to shift shape."

"Like the one you used to be?" Ambrose sneered. "I chose to leave your mate that first night and let you think it was a mugging."

"I wasn't fooled," Quinn scoffed. "You left the coin."

Ambrose smiled, his teeth gleaming yellow. "A nice touch, wasn't it? A little reminder of our past."

"And evidence of who threatened my mate." Quinn said. "Not very clever, Ambrose. I would have been at a greater disadvantage if I still believed you were dead. The element of surprise is powerful."

Ambrose flew straight for Quinn, four sets of claws extended. "I don't need another advantage to finish what I started in Béziers," he snarled.

"It's taken you long enough to get around to it."

"I waited!"

"You *hid*. You're nothing but a big coward."

Ambrose breathed fire all over the treetops in his frustration, setting most of their branches alight. "Look at your mate. My marks are all over her. She might as well be mine."

"But she's not yours and never will be." The *Slayer* hissed and Quinn knew he'd found a sore point. The pair locked claws and tumbled above the burning trees, their tails pummeling each other. The flames hissed as the rain fell on them, but the forest continued to burn as the fire spread down from the crown.

Ambrose tried to bite Quinn's chest. Quinn shoved him into a deadened tree bough and knocked the wind from him for a moment.

"Is that the problem, Ambrose? Are you lonely? Afraid no woman will ever love you?" Quinn saw the flash of anger in the *Slayer*'s eyes and pushed him further. "Maybe that you'll never have your own firestorm? What a loss that would be, to see your strain erased from the world." Quinn flipped Ambrose and tossed him toward the burning trees.

Ambrose spun and came up fighting. "It *would* be a loss! I should have had a firestorm!"

"I have to trust the wisdom of the Great Wyvern on this one."

"Audacity!" He swung his tail at Quinn, who ducked. They gained altitude together, slashing at each other and circling. "You never used to be so impertinent."

"Live and learn."

"I had hope for you."

"I wouldn't call it hope."

Ambrose feinted and dove at Quinn. He caught the end of Quinn's tail in his grasp, his talons digging deeply. Quinn turned and spouted fire at Ambrose's belly, then slashed his claws across the other *Pyr*'s back. Ambrose swung his tail with force.

Quinn saw the blow coming, though. He snatched at Ambrose's tail, breathed fire to make Ambrose release his grip, then flung the *Slayer* across the sky. Ambrose came raging back, his fury tangible. He fell on Quinn in a torrent of claws and snapping jaws. Quinn pretended to falter beneath Ambrose's blows and let himself lose altitude.

He had an idea.

Ambrose snorted as Quinn's wings beat out of rhythm. "Your skills are nonexistent," he sneered.

They locked claws again, Ambrose's tail knotting around Quinn's to hold it down. His eyes gleamed and he exhaled smoke toward Quinn's chest. The smoke burned and Quinn fought to release himself from the *Slayer*'s grip.

Ambrose held tighter and exhaled more smoke. "You have your mother's eyes," he hissed. "It will make it so much more pleasurable to kill you."

Quinn was surprised. "You knew my mother?"

"I knew Margaux *first*," Ambrose insisted, his eyes flashing. "She was ripe and luscious, a virgin well worth stealing and claiming. I took her for my own. I took her to be my mate."

Quinn was beginning to understand what the *Slayer* had against his family. "She must not have liked you," he said. "Or you would have been my father."

"The Smith saved her—or that was what he told everyone," Ambrose spoke with bitterness, but it kept him from breathing more smoke. Quinn wondered whether he could provoke the *Slayer* into forgetting himself and breathing dragonfire. He let himself go slack and moaned as if he was almost finished. "The truth is that Thierry stole Margaux from me. He took what should have been mine and made it his own."

"Was she a partner or a possession?" Quinn pretended to

be breathing hard, pretended to be having difficulty in flying as high as Ambrose.

He lunged at the other *Pyr* as if making his last effort and Ambrose locked claws with him again. They struggled against each other, Quinn being careful to hide his full strength from his opponent.

"Does it matter?" Ambrose laughed. "He bred with her, bred as abundantly as a human. He had the sons with her who should have been mine. He filled her head with the lie of the firestorm. . . ."

"It's not a lie!"

Ambrose spat into the trees and the flames hissed. "Margaux loved the notion of being a destined lover more than she could possibly have loved Thierry. She loved *me*, but he took her. I vowed that he would pay."

Quinn let his voice fade, left it to Ambrose to keep the weight of both of them airborne. "You waited, until he had a lot to lose."

Ambrose smiled even as he gritted his teeth at the burden of Quinn. "He had everything. I gave him time to gather it. Material success. The respect of friends and neighbors. Prowess in his craft. Five sons from that faithless bitch's womb, all *Pyr*."

"Who knew you had such patience?"

"I waited many years for my due, and the prize was all the sweeter for having ripened. I let Thierry think he was safe and secure. He was cocky then: he didn't think he needed any other *Pyr* to protect what was his own." Ambrose chuckled. "I enjoyed teaching him just how wrong he was."

"And the people who died along with him?"

"Vermin." Ambrose snorted. "Collateral damage, as they say these days. They will all be exterminated sooner or later."

"But you missed me," Quinn taunted. "Maybe you're not as powerful as you think you are."

"I let you go!" Ambrose bellowed and the dragonfire slipped from his mouth. Quinn gave no sign of how it invigorated him; he just hoped for more. "I let you run and I tracked you. I waited until you were reduced to nothing more than a dog, and then I tempted you."

Quinn was shocked. "You meant to make me a *Slayer*."

"*Pyr* are born: *Slayer*s are made. You would have made a good one, if you'd had the heart for it. I even slaughtered your mate, thinking that would turn you against the world."

"You couldn't make me evil. Ever."

"Why not? What do you get from these *Pyr*? They argue that they're noble, that they're true *Pyr*, that they fight for the greater good." Ambrose sneered. "But here you are, the Smith they've waited centuries to find, and they abandon you to me. You're dragon fodder, Quinn Tyrrell, while they cluster around your mate. What does that tell you about your valiant friends?"

Quinn had no chance to concoct a reply before Ambrose caught his breath.

"They're protecting your mate instead of you," Ambrose said slowly as understanding clearly dawned. "Your seed has taken fruit and she will bear the new Smith. Your days are numbered, Smith, and they know it."

"No, no, that's not it," Quinn argued in desperation.

Ambrose laughed then, taking a deep breath to finish Quinn with his smoke. "I'll claim your mate as the spoils of this challenge," he hissed, the first tendrils of smoke emanating from his nostrils. "I'll take your Smith son and turn him to my purposes. The fruit that can save the world can surely be used to condemn it. That will be true justice against Thierry the Smith!"

The prospect so horrified Quinn that he didn't need drag-onfire for more strength.

This was the moment he'd waited for.

Quinn cried out as if dying.

Ambrose laughed and let him fall.

Quinn crashed into the crown canopy of the forest, pray-ing the trees would hold his weight. They did, although he broke a number of branches on impact. He lay as if stunned, a dozen feet down from the summit of the forest. He kept one eye open a slit to watch for Ambrose, and moaned.

Quinn was certain that Ambrose wouldn't be able to deny himself a killing blow. And he was right. The other *Pyr* de-scended in a glorious swoop of gold and yellow, completely confident.

Ambrose raged against Quinn, thrashing the younger *Pyr* with his tail and breathing smoke. He walloped Quinn on one side and Quinn let himself fall through the branches even farther. Ambrose incinerated trees to make way for himself, and Quinn stifled a smile as he felt the surge of dragonfire.

The trees were burning with dragonfire. The source of the flame was the same, whether it directly landed on Quinn or was passed via the burning trees. The flames touched him, caressed him, built the strength within him to a fever pitch.

And Ambrose thrashed with his tail. Quinn let himself be assaulted as his strength built. He moaned and pretended to crumble beneath the *Slayer's* blows.

"You fooled me before," Ambrose declared, his breathing labored. "I'll be sure you're dead this time, Smith."

Ambrose breathed smoke with vigor, letting its tendrils wind around Quinn. It would have weakened Quinn further, if not for the presence of the dragonfire, but Quinn played along.

"So close to dead. Let's see it done." Ambrose gave a

laugh and lunged for Quinn, his claws bared. Quinn realized that Ambrose was aiming for the missing scale on Quinn's chest. Quinn waited, feigning unconsciousness, letting his assailant come close.

This was for his mother, and his father, and his brothers.

This was for Elizabeth.

This was for the future; the future he and Sara would share.

Ambrose's talons touched Quinn's chest. The tips just barely tore into Quinn's flesh and Ambrose chuckled in anticipation.

Then Ambrose had the last surprise of his life.

Sara saw Quinn fall into the burning forest and feared for his survival. She bounced to her feet.

"You're not going anywhere," Rafferty said with authority, putting one heavy claw on Sara's shoulder.

"You could go breathe fire on Quinn," she charged but Rafferty shook his head.

"You need me. You have no other defender now," he said, drawing himself taller. She could feel him gathering his strength and knew things were turning bad. "We must keep our gaze fixed on the prize."

Sara didn't like the idea of being a prize. She didn't have time to argue with Rafferty, though, because Quinn emerged from the forest in a blaze of power, Ambrose trapped in his grip. The *Slayer* struggled, to no avail.

Quinn twisted Ambrose's wings, then tore open his chest. He spouted dragonfire until Ambrose screamed. He slashed at the *Slayer* with steady strokes of his tail, clawing at him at irregular intervals. He shredded Ambrose's wings and ripped the claws from his body. All the while, Quinn's dragonfire blazed and flared, sizzling Ambrose in midair.

Ambrose didn't have a chance. He struggled to defend himself and remain aloft, but was losing badly.

Sara was on her feet, jumping and cheering, when Ambrose fell out of the sky. Quinn followed his opponent's descent with a stream of brilliant fire. He began to glimmer and Sara guessed that he was breathing an ever-tightening circle of smoke around the *Slayer*. She saw the truth in how Ambrose recoiled and twitched.

She heard him moan and then he writhed.

Quinn breathed steadily. Ambrose tried to rouse himself to fight, then obviously realized that breathing dragonfire on his assailant would only make matters worse. He shifted rapidly from human to dragon and back, over and over again, as if caught in a cycle he couldn't break.

Sara saw all of this through the haze of orange dragonfire. She smelled roasting flesh and heard the sizzle of rain on embers. A smoke rose from the *Slayer*'s body as she watched, but she knew it couldn't be dragon smoke. It was simply the smoke from a fire, because Quinn kept up his assault.

The rain settled into a steady torrent, beating a rhythm on the ground. Within moments, a wind came up and brushed the clouds away, clearing the sky as surely as if the storm had never been.

The cabin was a blackened shell, the flames that had destroyed it extinguished by the rain. The forest that had been set ablaze had burned branches sticking toward the sky. There was a distant sound of approaching sirens as the Wyvern stretched her wings. Her movement revealed Erik, unconscious but in human form. He looked to be asleep.

"You mended his spirit," Sloane said with awe and Sophie smiled.

"There are a few things I've learned," she said, then stretched her wings again. She surveyed the sky, then studied the *Pyr* and Sara each in turn. "You have no need of me now," she said, then gracefully took flight. Her white wings were bright against the blue sky, and Sara knew that the *Pyr* watched her fly west until they couldn't see her anymore.

Sara, though, was watching Quinn. She was nervous about his plan, his thoughts, his idea of the future.

She had a very firm idea of what she wanted to happen.

Sara watched Quinn exhaust his supply of dragonfire, then kick the ashes of what had been Ambrose. He scattered the ashes with purpose, then heaved a sigh of relief. He tipped his head back and glowed brightly as he shifted to human form.

Then he looked directly at Sara with the intensity that she had associated with the firestorm.

Sara realized it was just Quinn and his effect upon her. He was a man of honor, one who kept his word, one whose company she would be honored to share. His lips tugged into that slow smile she loved so much and he began to walk toward her.

"Now you can go," Rafferty rumbled, but Sara was already running toward Quinn.

Quinn had never felt such relief. The dread that had haunted him for centuries was finally gone. Sara ran to him and he knew she was safe from his past forevermore. She leapt into his arms and he swung her around, fiercely glad to have the chance to hold her close again. He buried his fingers in her hair and felt her strength pressed against his chest, then pulled back to study her.

"You're all right?"

Sara smiled. "I want to ask you that. What happened in the woods?"

"I thumped him. Don't tell me I have to do it again, just for you to be able to see."

Sara laughed. "No. But I thought you were fading."

"I pretended to be."

"That smoke went right for your damaged scale."

Quinn inhaled as she put her hand over his heart. He could feel her pulse through her palm and listened as his own heart matched the pace of hers. There was no firestorm, but maybe there didn't need to be.

They seemed to be good at building a heat of their own.

"It's too bad the elements can only injure you in unison," she said with a frown. "Instead of healing you."

Quinn blinked, struck by the elegance of her suggestion. He wondered whether it was possible, and knew he'd think more about it later.

"The forest was lit with dragonfire," he said, watching delight shine in her eyes. "I thought I could use it."

"So the dragonfire made you stronger at least."

Quinn nodded, content to hold Sara close and stare into her eyes. They were hazel but it seemed to him that the flicks of gold were getting brighter.

"*Are* you all right?" she asked with concern. "Let me see your chest."

"Right here, in front of everyone?" he teased and she blushed. "Maybe we should save that for later."

She pulled back to study him, her eyes changing hue as he watched. He caught his breath at their golden glimmer and felt his body respond.

"The firestorm's over," she said quietly. "What does that mean?"

Quinn shrugged. "Maybe that we need to make our own sparks."

Her smile was fleeting. "I thought it would mean that you were leaving."

He liked how much that prospect troubled her and was encouraged. "Not unless you want me to."

Sara shook her head. "I'm thinking Magda wouldn't want me to let you get away that easily."

"So you only want me around for my effect on your air conditioner."

"No! More than that." Sara looked up at him again and his chest clenched at the bright promise in her eyes.

"Far more than that," he murmured. There was electricity between them of a different kind, maybe a more enduring kind, and Quinn liked it a lot.

He bent and kissed Sara, slowly and sweetly, savoring the way she made his pulse leap. When he lifted his head, she looked tousled and happy. He tucked a tendril of hair behind her ear with a gentle fingertip, feeling luckier than he ever had. "I'm wondering, though, how I'm supposed to follow all this."

"What do you mean?"

"Well, traditionally, winning a challenge meant celebration."

"What kind of celebration?"

"Earthly pleasures, pretty much," Quinn admitted, leading her toward the other *Pyr*. "Eating, drinking and, um, making merry," Quinn said, sparing Sara a look that told her what kind of merrymaking he meant. She smiled at him, which had to be a good sign. "But an invitation to dinner seems a bit flat in comparison to a dragon attack."

Sara slanted a mischievous glance his way. "Not if it includes dessert."

Quinn was mystified. "I didn't think you had that much of a sweet tooth."

"Oh, I do," she said in a way that made him think he was missing something. Something important, from the way

Sara seemed to be on the verge of laughter. She glanced up, her eyes dancing. "I really like chocolate sauce, in fact."

Quinn still didn't understand why she found this so amusing. "Really?"

"Really. And you know, I've been thinking that there's one particular way I'd like to try it," Sara said.

When he held her gaze, mystified, she stretched to her toes and whispered. "It involves you and me naked and no spoons."

Quinn was both surprised and intrigued. He'd never been much for chocolate sauce, but he had a feeling that was going to change.

Sara laughed at his response, then put her arms around his neck. "And you know, since life is so uncertain, maybe we should have dessert first."

Quinn could only agree with that.

Chapter 17

It was the end of August when Sara drove toward Traverse City in her rented hybrid car. As always, she felt a tingle of anticipation when heading toward Quinn and his studio. His home was like a haven to her.

They'd been seeing each other regularly since the art show, commuting back and forth. Sara had been doing some research in the shop, with Magda's help, and Quinn had been experimenting at the forge between commissions. She sensed that they were on the cusp of a revelation about using the elements to heal the *Pyr*.

They were on the cusp of another adventure, as well. Sara had had a blood test in the past few days that had confirmed what she and Quinn had suspected for a while. She was going to have his child. Something about having a medical report made it seem all the more real to Sara. Something about having Quinn become a fixture in her life made everything seem worthwhile to her.

She took her time, enjoying the drive. She had the window open and the stereo on, and was singing along with the oldies station. There would be changes to make with the baby coming, but Magda had gotten right to the point: she'd left the Yellow Pages open to the ad for a real estate agent in Traverse City, one who specialized in retail property. Sara had an appointment the next day to look at potential locations.

She had a feeling Quinn would go with her. He'd look at the foundation, the furnace, the bones of the building. She'd look at the traffic, the sunlight, and take the vibe of the location. It was funny how they had intuitively realized their areas of specialty, how they contributed information and worked together. It was so easy.

It was perfect.

She was excited as well about the eclipse they were going to see later this day. Quinn had invited her to go with him and the *Pyr*, to see the forecast of the firestorm to come. He'd been enigmatic about the location where they'd view it, and Sara wondered whether he knew or whether he was being protective of *Pyr* secrets. She was curious to know more about Quinn's world, and honored to have been invited.

Seeing a full lunar eclipse would be exciting, too.

A motorcycle roared behind her and Sara slowed down, content to let the biker zoom past her. The rider must have been serious as he was wearing black biker leathers even under the summer sun.

Instead of passing, he slowed down to drive alongside her and raised his visor.

She recognized his cocky grin right away. "Donovan! It's not safe to drive like that!"

He laughed. "Safe is for accountants," he teased.

"Safe is for those who want to live."

"Being immortal has its perks."

"You just like to show off."

He laughed. "See you up there," he shouted, then gunned the bike and roared ahead.

Moments later, Sara turned into the drive that led to Quinn's shop. She loved his parcel of land because it seemed to be away from everything else. The hills rose behind his studio and were crested with a pine forest. There was a hardwood forest to the east of that and cedars where the land was lower. A sparkling stream cut through the property and Sara had awakened on more than one night to find deer outside Quinn's bedroom window.

There were more stars than she'd ever imagined seeing at one time. The sky here was thick with them.

Quinn's cabin was simple and he'd told her it was temporary. His intention was to build a larger house with his partner, and he'd taken her one day to see the spot. Sara had been enchanted by the wind in the trees that surrounded the site, the view of the countryside, and the sheer tranquility. They'd made love in the grass there and she'd hoped with all her heart that they'd be making love there for the rest of her life.

She had fallen hard and fast for Quinn Tyrrell and Sara had a pretty good idea that the feeling was mutual.

Even though their firestorm was over.

A curl of smoke rose from the chimney of the workshop when she parked the car beside Donovan's gleaming bike. Sara could hear Quinn's hammer. She didn't doubt that Donovan was commenting on everything Quinn did. She left her bag in the cabin and went to the workshop. She loved to see him work.

The shop was dark, as always, and warm. The forge glowed red hot, and the clang of Quinn's hammer echoed through the building. He was before the fire in his leather apron and heavy boots, leather gloves up to his elbows, and a guard over his eyes. He looked as if he was concentrating and Sara moved closer to see what he was working on.

It was a small flat item, almost shield-shaped, glowing red. He held it with tongs and hammered it thinner on the anvil, then shoved it into the fire of the forge one last time.

He spared her a glance and smiled a welcome that heated Sara to her toes. He held up a warning finger and she knew to approach no closer without safety gear. She waited and watched. Donovan cast her a grin and she felt his anticipation.

Quinn pulled the piece from the fire one last time and held it up in the tongs to examine it. He frowned, gave it a couple more blows, then tapped the edges with a smaller mallet. He returned it to the fire and wiped the sweat from his brow.

The next time he pulled the piece from the fire, he nodded with satisfaction and left it to cool. He turned the forge off and stepped toward Sara, shedding his gloves and gear as he came.

"You're earlier than I expected," he said with obvious pleasure. "Did you drive too fast?"

"Not me. I'm just an accountant, taking it safe."

Donovan laughed at that.

Quinn's kiss was welcoming and warm, and it left Sara breathing quickly.

"Keep it clean, people," Donovan complained.

"I left work earlier than I'd planned," Sara admitted, very aware of Donovan's presence.

"Slow day?" Quinn asked, his gaze searching hers.

She shook her head quickly. "Different reason."

"Oh, lover talk," Donovan complained amiably. "Should I go ahead without you?"

"Don't leave before you get what you came for," Quinn said.

"Presents?" Donovan asked with obvious excitement. "There are presents involved? Is this a new *Pyr* tradition?"

"Let's just say that Christmas came early." Quinn retrieved a box from the far side of the shop and offered it to Donovan. "I guess you were good this year. Who would have believed it?"

"Oh, I'm very good. Ask any of the ladies." Donovan grinned. "I knew you asked me here first for a reason." He ripped open the box and pulled out what looked like a pair of gloves. They were made of very fine leather but odd-looking.

"Do they have nails?" Sara asked as Donovan pulled them on.

There was no mistaking the *Pyr*'s glee. He flicked his hand open abruptly and knives opened on each of his fingertips. He danced around the shop, pretending he was fighting with someone. He looked menacing in his biker leathers with those knives on his fingertips, and Sara kept her distance.

"I'm loving it," he said to Quinn. "But what about when I shift?"

"Fold the gloves away with your clothes. It takes some practice, but if I can do it . . ."

Donovan snorted. "Then I'm all over it."

"Maybe you should retract the knives the first time you try," Quinn suggested, arching a brow.

Donovan laughed and folded each blade away with care. He granted Sara a wicked glance. "It's the same old story. Give the kids new toys so the lovers can play their own games in privacy."

"So shouldn't you go play already?" Sara teased and Donovan took the hint.

"I'll let you know how it works out," he told Quinn.

"I've got 911 on speed dial. If you get into trouble, just try to be human when the paramedics come."

"Picky, picky, picky," Donovan complained. He gave them a jaunty wave from the door to the studio, then left. Sara saw him striding toward the forest.

"Don't worry. He'll conquer it in one," Quinn said. "Besides, it's better he not see this just yet." He held Sara close against his side and as always, the gleam in his eyes made her very aware of her femininity. "The *Pyr* can't be witness to all my secrets. Smithing is an ancient and magical craft, after all."

"Smithing isn't what's ancient and magical about you."

"It's not what's magical about you, either," he said, kissing her soundly. "Want to see?"

He was so proud of what he'd done that Sara guessed it was something to do with the *Pyr*. "What are you making?"

"I had this idea, but I can't finish the process alone. I suppose that's fitting." Quinn took her hand in his and led her to the anvil, where his work was cooling.

"It's already black," Sara said.

"Wrought iron," Quinn spoke with satisfaction. He picked up the piece and turned it in his hands, nodding at its slightly curved shape. "It came out exactly as I wanted it to."

Sara thought of the mermaid door knocker and Quinn's story of how she had come to be so perfect. "As if it shaped itself?"

He smiled that slow smile. "Pretty much."

He handed it to Sara and she studied it, mystified. It was a puzzle of some kind, one that he was challenging her to solve.

"Is it a commissioned piece?"

"No. It's for us."

Sara blinked. "Is it part of a larger project?"

Quinn grinned. "You could say that."

"You're being evasive again," she said, putting a hand on her hip. "I need another clue to figure this out."

Quinn folded his arms across his chest and leaned back against the anvil, enjoying himself a little too much to be entirely trustworthy. His eyes sparkled as if they were filled with starlight. "What if I tell you that I've been thinking about your question, the one you asked about the elements being able to destroy the *Pyr* but not heal us?"

"I still wouldn't get it."

"And that I asked Erik for his thoughts."

Sara caught her breath and looked at the piece of wrought iron in her hands. It was the shape of a *Pyr* scale.

"And Erik, being Erik, said he had to ask the Wyvern."

"And the Wyvern, being the Wyvern, said something incomprehensible and possibly irrelevant," Sara guessed and Quinn laughed.

"*Smith, heal thyself,* was what she said." He sobered as he looked at her. "Maybe it's not that incomprehensible, or irrelevant."

Sara looked up at him, liking the glint in his eyes. She knew exactly what he intended to heal and she agreed. "Will it work?"

"Let's find out." Quinn took a deep breath and flexed his muscles. When Sara heard his breathing slow, she knew to take a step back. She watched again, fascinated as always by his transformation to *Pyr* form.

It was so quick. No matter how intently she watched, she was always surprised by the speed of his transformation. It wasn't her imagination that he was getting faster at it, either.

Donovan was a bad influence that way.

Quinn's scales glittered like jewels in the light cast by the forge, as if he were a hidden treasure discovered by Sara. He reared up immediately and revealed his chest to her.

Sara looked immediately for the damaged scale, the one

that was evidence of his love for Elizabeth. To her astonishment, it was growing back all by itself.

But a little farther down and to the left, an entire scale was missing. The lost scale was directly over his heart, and a large section of flesh was left unprotected. Sara caught her breath and met the knowingness in Quinn's gaze, not daring to believe the implication of what she saw.

He had lost the scale because he had lost his heart.

He was vulnerable because he loved her.

Sara was both frightened and happy about this revelation. She wanted Quinn to be strong and invincible. She wanted his love, but she didn't want to ever be the reason he lost a battle. She stepped closer and reached up to the tender spot. Quinn bent down so that she could reach. She ran her fingers over it gently, feeling how he shivered at her touch. The skin was sensitive, having been shielded for so very long.

What had she done by falling in love with him?

Sara was afraid; then she understood what he had made. He was trying to restore his armor, so that he could better defend them both. She tested the fit of the wrought-iron scale, not surprised to find that it was perfectly sized and shaped to fit the space.

It was made of iron, which came from the earth.

It had been shaped in the fire.

There were two elements to go.

"But how will we attach it?" she asked. "I can't breathe dragonfire. I don't want to make you vulnerable, Quinn."

"My father believed that his love for my mother made him stronger," Quinn said. "Or maybe it was her love for him that was the charm."

"But how can that be? If you're vulnerable like this . . ." Sara choked on her words and looked down at the scale, feeling powerless and not knowing what to do. The pregnancy hormones took over, making her eyes fill with tears.

"I'm stronger, because of you."

She looked up and the first tear fell. To her surprise, Quinn touched her cheek with infinite tenderness. That first tear fell on his talon. He transferred the glistening bead to the scale she held.

It sizzled and Sara saw the edge of the iron waver and glow, exactly the way that Quinn glowed before he transformed from man to dragon.

Was it instinct or intuition or plain old logic that told her what to do next? Sara would never really be sure, but she reached up and put that makeshift scale in place. She heard the sizzle of her tear against Quinn's skin and saw him draw up, as if he felt a pang.

The scale looked black and wrong, even though it was attached.

But they had only allowed for three elements.

Air was left.

Sara reached up and kissed the scale, letting her love for Quinn flow through her touch. Then she whispered the words, fanning the scale with her breath. "I love you, Quinn Tyrrell," she said, then said it again. She touched her lips to the scale once more.

The scale shimmered as she lifted her head, as if it were lit by an inner fire or as if it had just come from the forge. Its light became brighter and brighter, until Sara had to close her eyes.

When she looked again, that one scale might have been made of polished sterling. It shone brilliantly, like a badge of honor upon Quinn's chest.

Four elements, present and accounted for.

Four elements, healing a *Pyr* as readily as they could destroy him. By working together, she and Quinn had done it!

Quinn threw back his head and bellowed, a sound of jubilation and pride that made Sara's heart sing and the floor of the shop vibrate.

She laughed as he shifted back to human form before her eyes. Then he caught her in his arms and swung her around, as happy as she had ever seen him. She pushed away his shirt and examined his chest. He had a freckle there that he hadn't had before, but when Sara looked closely at it, it had a silvery gleam.

Sara pressed her lips to it as Quinn held her close. "I love you," he said and she smiled up at him.

"I know. And I'm pregnant."

Joy lit his eyes, turning them an even more brilliant hue of sapphire. Quinn bent to kiss her but just before his lips touched hers, Donovan knocked loudly on the door of the shop.

"These are fine pieces of equipment," he announced, waving the gloves at Quinn. "You're going to be busy, Quinn: once everyone sees these babies at the eclipse, they're going to want their own set." Donovan pulled on the gloves and shadow-fought in the shop. "I'll be showing them how it's done."

"Maybe you'll be busy with your own firestorm," Quinn said and Donovan snorted.

"Be serious. I'm never going to have a firestorm and that's just fine by me. It should be Rafferty. He's been waiting long enough."

But Sara met Quinn's gaze. She had a feeling that Donovan was wrong, and she was the Seer. Quinn obviously read her thoughts because he smiled that languorous smile, the one that was far more powerful than a firestorm.

"No secret jokes," Donovan complained. "Let's go: we're going to be late for the big moon show."

"One more thing," Quinn said quietly. "There's another present to share."

"For me?" Donovan asked.

"No." Quinn's tone was dismissive. "Wait for us outside."

"More lovers' secrets," Donovan groused, but he did what he was told.

Sara was more interested in the gleam in Quinn's eyes. He got another box from the shelf and handed it to her. "So in the course of these discussions with the Wyvern, I asked her a question," he said, his voice so low that it gave Sara shivers. "And she sent me a dream."

Sara opened the box and caught her breath. There was an acorn inside, all by itself. She remembered what she had told the Wyvern about her own dreams, and met the conviction in Quinn's gaze.

"Want to plant it here?"

"I know just the spot," Sara said, and Quinn laughed.

"Of course you do," he teased. "It's your job as the Seer to know things like that."

But what Sara saw when Quinn kissed her was a future together, years that were never dull, given the comings and goings of the *Pyr*. She saw appliances that seemed to start themselves and a ghost that shared her opinions and books on impossible things that proved to be possible in the end. She saw Quinn, with silver in his hair, and a son, tall and strong, with dark hair and very blue eyes.

It was a vision of her own future that was a perfect fit.

Just perfect.

Read on for a sneak preview of the second
book in Deborah Cooke's Dragonfire series

KISS OF FURY

On sale in August 2008

*For millennia, the shape-shifting dragon warriors known as
the* Pyr *have lived peacefully as commanders of the four
elements and guardians of the earth's treasures. But now
the final reckoning between the* Pyr, *who count humans
among these treasures, and the* Slayers, *who would
eradicate both humans and the* Pyr *who protect
them, has begun. . . .*

Scientist Alexandra Madison was on the verge of unveiling
an invention that would change the world—then her partner
was murdered, their lab burned, and their prototype
destroyed. And when recurring dragon-haunted nightmares
land her in the hospital, Alex knows she has to escape to
rebuild her prototype in time. But first she must
return to her ruined lab.

Handsome, daring, and impulsive, Donovan Shea knows the
Madison project is of great importance to the ongoing
Pyr/Slayer war, but he still resents being assigned to watch a
lab. While performing surveillance, he's surprised by Alex.
She's been followed by a *Slayer*, and in an instant of fire
he reacts to defend her, never imagining that she's his
destined mate. As *Slayers* close in on their prey, Donovan
knows he'll surrender his life to protect Alex—and
lose his heart to possess her.

Minneapolis
The following October

*H*ell had erupted all around her.
And there was nothing she could do about it.

The flames raged from every side, their orange tongues greedily devouring files. She kept a damp cloth over her mouth and crouched under her desk, fearing discovery.

She heard the intruders fling open file drawers, heard the flames crackle as fuel was added to the fire. She heard computers crash and screens shatter. She heard the fire alarm dinging as the smoke got thicker.

Worse, she heard them laughing as they destroyed everything.

The laughter infuriated her. She had worked years on this project and was within reach of solving its last riddle. She had forfeited everything; Mark had mortgaged everything; they had begged and borrowed and the project was within a hair of paying off.

But someone was trying to destroy that dream.

She heard Mark scream.

She bounded from her hiding place, and the first breath

she took burned her lungs. The carpet in the corridor was in flames. The file room had become an inferno. None of it stopped her.

Because Mark screamed again.

They were partners. She wasn't going to abandon him now, no matter what was happening.

But what she saw in his office was worse than any vision of hell she could have expected.

Alex awakened in a cold sweat. She was in a cold and un-familiar room. She was lying in an elevated bed and the lighting was low. Darkness pressed against the large win-dow. The walls of the room were pale mint green and the furniture was stainless steel.

There were no flames.

She looked again, then exhaled shakily.

An IV hung at her side, the needle buried in the back of her hand. There were bandages on her arms and she could feel her skin sticking to the gauze. She was sore, as if she had been bashed and bruised all over.

But she was safe. Alex forced herself to breathe slowly. Her heart was still galloping and there was a trickle of sweat running down her back. She closed her eyes and tried to slow her body's response.

She was safe.

There was no fire.

She opened her eyes and looked around the unfamiliar room. It looked institutional, like a hospital or an asylum. Somehow she knew that no one would answer her questions here. How long had she been here? There was a band on her right wrist with her name and the name of a doctor she didn't know.

Mark was dead. Alex knew that with complete certainty, although she didn't want to think about why or how she knew. And Gilchrist Enterprises, the focus of her life for the past five years, had been destroyed by fire. Alex knew that, too. The fire hadn't been an accident. No. Someone had de-liberately tried to destroy her project before its completion.

That made her mad.

She might be down, but she wasn't yet out.

She peeked under the gauze at her healing wounds. Apparently she had burns to show for having been in the wrong place at the wrong time. Mark . . . well, she wasn't going to think about Mark. She'd focus on the practical.

What was the date? It couldn't be too late.

Could it?

Alex heard voices approaching and did what she had always done when there was trouble: she closed her eyes and pretended to be asleep. It was the next best thing to hiding.

"She's had a quiet night tonight, at least," a woman said, compassion in her tone. "Although it's almost three. That seems to be when she has the nightmares."

"Every night?" a man asked.

"Every night," the woman replied. "Sometimes two or three of them in a row." Alex felt a stroke on the back of her hand. "It's wearing her out, poor thing."

"I was hoping to witness one tonight."

The woman snorted. "Looks like you didn't luck out."

"It says here that she talks about dragons," the man said, and Alex's breath caught at the word.

Dragons. There were dragons in the fire, even though that was impossible. Her breath hitched and she struggled to remain impassive.

"She does," the woman said softly. "She screams and fights, and she shouts out for Mark. Then she cries. It's terrible to watch."

"Well, she needs sleep to heal," the man said crisply. "We're going to kick up the dosage on the sedative. Put it in her drip tonight and see if we can avoid tonight's nightmare." Alex heard him scribbling. "And I'm going to have the people from Psych stop by in the morning to consider a transfer."

"You're not going to transfer her to the psych ward, are you? I think she's just traumatized, and who wouldn't be—"

"When I want your opinion, Nurse, I'll ask for it," the man interrupted. "It's been two weeks without any change, and we need the bed. Nobody can argue with that." A piece of paper tore and Alex heard footsteps as the man walked away. "Who's next?"

The woman lingered for a moment, then her fingertips brushed across Alex's hand once more. Alex felt the nurse lean closer and feared she knew that Alex was faking.

But no. "Poor thing. I would have given you another couple days." She gave Alex's hand one last pat. Then she strode after the doctor, the soles of her shoes squeaking on the linoleum floor.

Alex had seen enough movies to not be thrilled about a move to the psychiatric ward. She wasn't going to be able to do any thinking when she was drugged up and tied down, and she sure wasn't going to be able to get her backup prototype running in time. The best way to avoid the transfer was to leave, and to leave when her move was least expected.

The nurse was getting a sedative to put in her drip. Right now looked like a really good time to blow out of here.

But not in this backless gown.

Donovan's vigil finally paid off.

He'd spent two weeks watching the offices of Gilchrist Enterprises—under orders from Erik and under protest. Surveillance was a thankless job, and one for which Donovan didn't believe he had the credentials.

He hated staying in one place for hours at a time.

He especially hated that Erik had forbidden him to trawl around the office park on his beloved Ducati Monster motorcycle. Erik said the bike made too much noise. Donovan said that was the point. They had agreed to disagree.

Donovan spent his long nights of surveillance composing lists of the better things he could be doing. There were a surprising number of activities more interesting than lounging in the shadows of a deserted industrial park, watching the burned wreckage of an office, many of which involved the joys of riding a noisy bike fast.

Most of the others featured beautiful women.

Donovan's current count of women—beautiful or otherwise—in the Rolling Hills Industrial Park was zip. He was trying to figure out a good way to evade another night in his shadow of choice when he heard the car engine.

Donovan straightened in the shadows, but the car parked at the far end of the lot. A man got out of the car and Donovan settled back into his spot with dissatisfaction.

The man, though, walked quickly through the darkness. He was large and heavyset, and his footfalls were far from silent. He walked all the way along the building to Gilchrist Enterprises.

Why park so far away?

Obviously because he didn't want anyone to know that he was inside Gilchrist Enterprises. Donovan straightened again. This had to be Alex Madison, the brilliant inventor who had survived the fire, the person Donovan was supposed to find. Donovan sniffed, seeking the distinctive scent of the inventor, then recoiled in shock.

He was *Pyr.*

Donovan kept silent, trusting his instincts, and watched.

The other *Pyr* was trying to override the security system to the research lab. It made no sense that a brilliant scientist was having so much trouble with a security system he should have known well.

It was possible that Alex Madison was an absentminded genius.

It was a lot more likely that this *Pyr* wasn't Alex Madison at all.

Was he a *Slayer*? That would explain why Donovan didn't know his scent and didn't recognize him. *Slayer*s had trashed this lab; Erik had said so. Donovan felt himself on the cusp of change as the other *Pyr* muttered a curse. He fiddled a bit more aggressively with the card-key lock, and the alarm was triggered.

"Shit!" The *Pyr* looked up at the light that began to flash over the door and Donovan saw his face.

He was a complete stranger. How interesting. Where were the *Slayer*s finding new recruits? The *Pyr* glanced over his shoulder. Donovan heard it, too.

A car was driving closer.

Quickly.

The other *Pyr* bolted, disappearing into the darkness between the buildings. Donovan might have followed him, but a taupe Buick sedan came rocketing around the corner. Its headlights sliced through the night and its tires squealed. The driver braked too hard and the car slid sideways to a stop in front of the door with the blinking alarm.

Gilchrist Enterprises was a busy place.

A woman flung herself out of the car; she'd had her door open before the car had come completely to a halt. She left the door open and the engine running as she ran to Gilchrist Enterprises. For all Donovan knew, she'd left the car in gear.

She certainly was in a hurry.

She was wearing pale green surgical scrubs and it looked as if she was barefoot. Donovan glimpsed bandages on her hands and watched, fascinated.

It wasn't because of the way she was dressed.

It was because a beautiful woman had finally appeared in the Rolling Hills Industrial Park. Her hair was dark and cut short, and she was both slender and tall. He liked long, lean women—women with athletic builds and strong cheekbones, and here was one. He might have been dreaming, so he pinched himself to be sure.

She was real.

Things were looking up.

Donovan wondered what color her eyes were and leaned out of the shadows. He caught a whiff of fear and hospital antiseptic. In the red blink of the alarm light, she appeared to be thirty or so. She spared a glance to the flashing light, then swore with an earthiness that charmed him completely.

She'd definitely been worth waiting for.

Who was she and what was she doing here? Donovan wanted to know, although he told himself his interest was purely professional.

He heard the *Pyr*'s car start from the far end of the building but knew he could pick up the other *Pyr*'s scent whenever he chose to do so.

This woman was far more intriguing.

She punched some numbers into the keypad. The steel door opened soundlessly. She got the security code right the first time. The light continued to flash as she ran into the darkened building.

As if she knew what she would find inside.

Or she didn't care. She left the door swinging open behind her, a sure sign of her disregard for the building's security and lack of fear that she would be followed.

Donovan liked women with confidence.

He decided to introduce himself to this one. After all, she might know something about the business of Gilchrist Enterprises. He knew that was an excuse but didn't care. It wasn't his fault that he was heterosexual. Donovan separated himself from the shadows and silently slipped into the backseat of the Buick to wait.

He leaned forward and looked at the tag hanging from the key in the ignition. It proclaimed that Archibald Forrester was a WWII vet.

She looked a bit young to have such a service record.

Donovan grinned. He'd never met a woman who stole cars, and he was looking forward to meeting this one.

He didn't think he'd have to wait long.

About the Author

Deborah Cooke has always been fascinated by dragons, although she has never understood why they have to be the bad guys. She has an honors degree in history with a focus on medieval studies and is an avid reader of medieval vernacular literature, fairy tales, and fantasy novels. Since 1992, Deborah has written more than thirty romance novels under the names Claire Cross and Claire Delacroix.

Deborah makes her home in Canada with her husband. When she isn't writing, she can be found knitting, sewing, or hunting for vintage patterns. To learn more about the Dragonfire series and Deborah, please visit her Web site, www.deborahcooke.com; to access her blog, Alive & Knitting, go to www.delacroix.net/blog.

Also Available

THE SECOND NOVEL IN THE DRAGONFIRE TRILOGY

KISS OF FURY
A Dragonfire Novel

by DEBORAH COOKE

Scientist Alexandra Madison was on the verge of releasing her invention which could save the world—until her partner was murdered, their lab burned and their prototype destroyed. When Alex learns that her recurring nightmares of dragons have led to a transfer to a psychiatric hospital, she knows she has to escape to rebuild her prototype in time. The problem is that she has to return to the wreckage of the lab for one last thing...

Handsome, daring, impulsive Donovan Shea knows the Madison project is of dire importance to the ongoing Pyr/Slayer war, but resents being assigned to surveillance of the lab. He's surprised by the arrival of a beautiful woman there in the middle of the night—not that she's being followed by a Slayer, not that she won't admit her name, but that she's his destined mate. As the sparks of the firestorm ignite and the Slayers close in on their prey, Donovan knows he'll surrender his life to protect Alex—even lose his heart, if that's what it takes...

Available wherever books are sold or at penguin.com